Cash

Saint and Sinners

Ruby Vincent

Published by Ruby Vincent, 2021.

Prologue

"Everything?"

"Everything."

Wind beat at us. It howled its victory for reaching us where we left the world behind. Whipping through our clothes, pulling our hair, shoving our backs. Its final aim to drag us into its arms, and let go.

I clung tighter to him, burying my face in his neck.

"Don't be scared, brown eyes," he said. "Daddy's got you."

And with those words, I wasn't.

I raised my head, peering down the thirty-story drop to the concrete below. All the wind would have to do is succeed in its battle to push us off the ledge. But it wouldn't.

Daddy never lost.

"The whole city?" I asked.

"The whole city."

I curled my tiny fist in his hair.

I loved his hair. Loved the soft kinks and coils. Loved the springy curls that crushed between my fingers and didn't lose their shape. I asked him once why his hair was different from mine and he said, "Because I'm Black."

I asked him if I was Black too, and he said, "You are everything that Daddy is. Strong. Brave. Destined for greatness."

I didn't know what he meant at the time. I was four. All I knew was I was the only one allowed to touch his hair. Kiss his cheek. Walk down the street holding his hand.

Only me because I was his princess.

"Cinco will be your kingdom," he said, sweeping his hand over the loud, grimy city pulsing beneath our feet. "You, its queen.

"That's my gift to you, brown eyes. All of Cinco City," he repeated. "Nothing less for my girl."

"When will it be mine?" I stretched to touch a bird flying high above my fingertips.

"When you take it."

Chapter One

I blinked awake.

The remains of the dream seeped out of my consciousness.

Too bad.

It was a good one. The best kind—a memory. Better than that—a happy memory.

I always seemed to wake up in the middle of those. My nightmares hung around to stay, and they never let me go.

A figure moved in the dark.

You're who woke me up.

They hovered over the bed. My vision cleared on the pillow clutched in their hands.

"I know you're awake," said a dry voice. "Move over."

"Other side," I said. "I'm all sliced up on this one."

"Talk about an exit strategy." Gianna moved around the bed and climbed in next to me. She plopped her pillow down, then snuggled on mine. "How are you, babe?"

"Fine. Naturally, I didn't do too much damage. How'd you get in?"

She scoffed. "Like I can't sneak into a hospital. How did you get here is the question. I'm surprised they brought you here."

North Quay General Hospital to be exact. Sinjin rushed me in sans mask and knit cap. The trail of blood I left from the puddle in his truck to the front desk was enough to alarm anyone. It certainly freaked out the people we blew by.

It looked bad, but a few stitches and one night in the hospital fixed me up. I'd be out in the morning.

"They had to," I said. "They took out the guys in the station. All of them. There was no one left to tell us if Angelo spread their location to every King, and if more were on their way. The guys left me in the tender care of the North Quay General doctors, so they could strip, scrub, and wipe every trace of our presence from the place."

"Then it's just you and me." She kissed my cheek. "I'll stay until your knights in shining armor come for you."

We laughed. It hurt my side, so I stopped.

"Thanks for the assist, by the way." My smile stretched in the dark. "Got a bit dicey there in the middle."

I felt her shake her head. "I'm so fired. I literally ran out in the middle of my shift. Left the Hendersons gaping at my smoke outline in the middle of checking them in. But if my girl needs a sniper, she needs a sniper."

"Thankfully, I've got the best one in Cinco City on speed dial."

"Don't know if I'm the best," she breezed. "Top five for sure."

We laughed again and I cut myself off, wincing. "Seriously, G. Thank you. I thought they were dead."

Gianna sobered too. "And that would have bothered you," she said softly.

"Yes."

She was quiet for a moment. "I said you were getting too close."

"As close as it gets. You should've seen me packing up my car to leave. I was a fucking wreck. Completely embarrassing."

"You love Sinjin."

"He has no idea how meant for each other we really are."

"What about the others?"

"They're all mine now, G. Whether they know it or not."

"Does this change the plan?"

"Only slightly. I've taken out the part where I kill them, seize control of the Merchants, and set them on hunting down Kieran and the ledger." The words dropped from my lips without a twinge of conscience. "The boys will find Kieran for me, and then I'll help myself to the ledger. There might be a bit of an argument about it, but in the end, people always see things my way."

"Especially when their cocks are wrapped around your finger."

"That does make it easier. Yes."

I bit back the laugh on that one. It contracted my stomach all the same, reminding me of Brutal's fingers skating the edges of my bandage. Light, warm, perfect, and tightening my skin.

Yes. I got too close.

"I even told Brutal about Mom," I whispered. "Everything. I don't know why."

"I do." Gianna pressed us cheek to cheek. "All that stuff with Corbin and the kids. It was too much for you, Addy. To walk into something like that after everything you've been through... I'm sorry I wasn't there. We should have done this together."

I squeezed her hand. "You couldn't be there, G. You're a better actor than I am, but even through rescuing the kids I had to play like I was this wide-eyed, innocent creature being swept along. Seeing both of us kick ass would've made them question."

"I don't care," she said. "It's been weeks of phone calls where we hide what we're really talking about, while you were left to do it all by yourself. The Kings got you, Addy. They assaulted and tried to take you. It wouldn't have gotten that far if I'd been there. I could've acted sooner."

I picked up the remote and raised the head of the bed. The lights followed. My white, clinical space lit up.

There wasn't much to see in the room besides the bed, rollaway tray, television, and the sink next to the bathroom door. Its biggest draw was that it was private. We could speak freely.

"Things had to play out a certain way, G. What matters is they trust me, and we've dealt the first serious blow to the Kings in decades. There's a power vacuum. They'll be rushing—and fighting—over Angelo's replacement. The cops are hunting them down as child traffickers. They watched a good chunk of their hideaways burn to the ground. While they're scrambling, it's time to strike blow number two."

Gianna gave me a look. "I like how you avoided the conversation by steering back to the Kings."

"I like how you noticed," I mumbled.

"Addy, are you okay? I get you need to keep your *cover* but a few days away from this won't hurt. It might do some good, actually. Stay with me," she said, popping a kiss on my cheek. "Just for a while to get your head on straight. We need to rework the plan anyway. It went way off track since you got trapped in that bathroom."

That much was true.

Yes. I was interested in the Merchants.

Yes. I wanted a gang to lend its power, knowledge, and firepower in the search for Kieran.

Yes. I wasn't willing to start off at the bottom—playing everybody's bitch until I worked my way up to right hand.

All of those things were true. But still I never could've planned for Sinjin, Brutal, Mercer, and Cash.

"I am okay, G." I said it, and meant it. "You're right, I was blindsided. I walked into that auction thinking it was a simple job and ended up in my personal nightmare. I ended up in many children's nightmares. But we saved them, Gianna, and we got the Kings out of the trafficking business for good. I'm all right now.

"I can breathe."

"You're still staying with me."

"I—"

"Keep that no on your tongue. If you don't care about alleviating my worries, then at least do something about my uncertainty. I'm done with this calling-when-you-can, speaking-in-code thing. We need to properly plan our next move now that the Kings have taken that hit. You said it yourself."

"I do care about your worries," I said. "What about Raul?"

"He's got friends. They've got couches."

"I doubt Sinjin will be cool with it."

"Sinjin doesn't have a fortified fire station to trap you inside anymore. While he's rectifying that, you need somewhere to recover. Are you out of excuses now?"

I cracked a smile. "Yes, I am."

CASH

"We'll set up in Leighbridge."

Twentysomething. Shouting. Hands waving.

"The Leighbridge place has one bedroom and one way in and out," Mercer said.

Driving ten to eleven miles over the speed limit.

"We can't stay there long-term," Mercer said. "We weren't meant to."

Smacks dash. Eyes mirror. Right rearview light—

I hit the brakes, sliding out of the way as a blubbering Gen Xer dove into our lane without checking her blind spot. She continued her fight in earnest, arms flailing clear through the window—unaware her day would've gotten ten times worse if she succeeded in sideswiping my car.

"We're not," I said, changing lanes for the express to the hospital. "I started negotiations on a new place in Waterford when we took up this fight against the Kings. I assumed they'd locate the fire station sooner or later."

"Waterford? The Seventh Street gang and Bowery Boys claimed Waterford."

"Now the Merchants have too."

"What's this place like?" Sinjin asked. He stretched out long in the passenger seat, absentmindedly fingering his knife hilt. "How soon can we get in?"

"End of this week or next. It's three floors. Six bedrooms. A basement with two exits. The bottom floor was a sandwich shop. We'll buy the building."

"Can we afford an entire building in Waterford?" Mercer added. "It's been a while since we've done a job."

"I moved a few things around," I said simply. "Sold some assets. But yes, we're low. Between renovations on the new place, Redgrave's hospital stay, and the eight thousand a month Sinjin agreed to pay her, we'll be hard up sooner rather than later."

"Bunny offers a valuable service," Sinjin said, grinning.

"Riding your dick?"

"Now, now. She's long past proven her worth. Bunny keeps Brutal happy. We eat like kings instead of refugees now. She planned the attack on the Castian, and do I have to remind you, the person who actually took out our most dangerous enemy, was her."

"No." My grip tightened on the wheel recalling the scene we walked into. Adeline on the floor clutching her bleeding stomach. Angelo slumped against the cage with a knife in his neck. The look of surprise on his face. "You don't."

"She'll have the salary we agreed to," Sinjin went on. "It's not much less than the cut we take for ourselves, and she's one of us."

"It's more than our cut," I said. "We're running on less than nothing until we refill the bank, Sinjin."

"Why are we buying a place we have to renovate?" Mercer asked. "We'd save ourselves money right there if we found ourselves another fixed-up station and stayed in North Quay."

I shook my head. "We have to assume our address went wide. Once the Kings find out Angelo is dead, they'll comb North Quay hunting us down. That borough is burned. As for the place, one of those basement exits is a tunnel that opens out to the storage room in the grocery store across the street. It's not on any plans. If something like this happens again, we won't be trapped."

"If it's not on any plans, how did you find out about it?"

"I have my sources."

"Sources that won't crack?" Sinjin asked.

I nodded.

"Good enough for me. What do we need to do to this place?"

"Gut the downstairs. It's all windows. Those will need to be covered up."

"The windows in our last place saved our asses," Mercer said. "We going to talk about that at any point? Someone took out Angelo and held his men back. Who?"

I looked to Sinjin, and he was looking at me. "Wasn't me," I confirmed. "My contingencies did not include Corbin breaking his own thumb, getting free, and bringing Angelo down on us while his only bargaining chip was alone in the house. There was no time for me to set one of the guys on the opposite roof. I don't know who that was."

"Who could it have been?" Sinjin mused, mostly to himself. "I didn't call in the reinforcements either. The only people who knew we were there were the Kings. It's possible one of them took their shot. If Angelo is killed in the middle of taking us out, the Merchants are blamed and his successor rises to the top promising vengeance. It's genius."

"Only one flaw in that logic," Mercer said. "Why didn't this turncoat King wait until we were dead to take Angelo out of play? The Kings' enemies and the man in his way in one fell swoop. He would've had it if he waited ten seconds."

We fell silent. As silent as Brutal still and calm in the back seat, not offering a word of his thoughts.

"Taking us out may not be the endgame," Sinjin said. "Angelo wanted us in the Kings. Angelo 2.0 could want the same. Speaking of, who is next in line?"

Names, dates, faces, and rap sheets filed through my mind one after the other.

"Angelo had no children nor did he groom anyone in particular," I said. "He likely feared filling some bloodthirsty junior's head with visions of power would result in a knife in his back when they got impatient. Without a named successor, we're down to four guys with enough clout in the gang to get the men to follow them. They are also the ones who want it enough to kill the other three.

"Jace Parker. Xavier Jameson. Thiago Pais. Lorenzo 'Enzo' Bianchi."

"What do we got on them?"

"Parker was Angelo's man on the fights. He coordinated them, found the men, took the bets, and personally visited those who didn't pay up. Former fighter himself," I said. "He doesn't farm out his beatings."

Sinjin inclined his head. "I respect that. Tell me about Jameson."

"Jameson is the smart pick, but like I said, this won't be a democracy. He's cool. Levelheaded. Intelligent. Rich parents were able to afford his ride to the academic top. He has a JSD from Cinco Law School, and a legit business front as an attorney. His only clients are the Kings."

"Rich boy lawyer who can walk away from the life at any time. Probably has a penthouse in Leighbridge with a perfect wife and two point five kids that he'll choose above the gang if shit goes sour." Sinjin shook his head. "No, it won't be him. Or at least, it won't just be him. If Jameson takes over, he'll farm the everyday dealings to the second-in-command who'll ultimately take the fall if things go wrong."

I nodded, accepting his reasoning. I knew the numbers, stats, data, and probability. Sinjin knew the depths of a despicable mind.

"Thiago," he prompted.

"Thiago runs the escorts," I continued. "Mercer probably knows more about him than I do."

"I don't doubt your research," Mercer said, "but in this case, I have personal knowledge on the guy."

"Client?"

"Colleague. Thiago used to be an escort. He saved up enough to buy a strip club, then started his own business in Harlow. He got away with it because he worked out a deal with Angelo. Eventually he took over the Kings' hand in that enterprise," Mercer said. "He's respected for the most part. He was in the business, so he knows what we deal with. He used to run the auction, and he made sure everyone who signed up was clean, willing, and discreet. The seventy-thirty split in favor of the escorts was his idea. Then Corbin took over that part of the business."

The statement hung in the air for a beat.

"Do we believe he didn't know what Corbin was up to?" Sinjin asked. "Pais put a lot of effort into building up the auction. Would he have washed his hands and let Corbin disappear his work into a grotty basement?"

"I want to say yes," Mercer said carefully. "Seventy percent for the escorts made the auction the least profitable of the businesses. If he was taking on too much, I can see him passing it on to Corbin without a fight. As for if he knew, I told you I have personal experience with the guy. We crossed paths at more than a few parties. Talked. Traded stories. Thiago's disgust when he spoke about pimps turning out girls as young as sixteen was real. I don't think he knew."

"Or he did know and he walked himself and his escorts away because he wanted no part in it," Sinjin shot back. "Bunny said it's a different crowd catering to the deceased Corbin's new clients. It's just as possible he was disapproving, but happy to look the other way."

"It's possible," Mercer agreed.

"The guy is no Boy Scout, or he wouldn't be willing to kill his own brothers to elbow into Angelo's spot. What else do I need to know?"

"Because he is *generous* with his escorts, he takes it as a personal affront when they let him down," Mercer said. "Coming up short. Taking jobs on the side. Trying to get out of the life. If they're caught, Thiago makes examples of them."

I caught Sinjin's frown out of the corner of my eye. "Is he the guy who—?"

"Yes."

No more needed to be said. I said it anyway. "He disfigures people who crosses him. Slices up their faces and dumps them on the docks. If they stumble their way to a hospital in time, they're one of the lucky ones."

Sinjin whistled. "I could see a cold bastard like that making a play for number one. Lorenzo Bianchi, I've met. We've stood across the craps table once or twice. Cagey player. Doesn't bet too much. Doesn't lose too much. Doesn't give much away. He's a man who knows when to walk away from the table. I've always hated guys like that."

"He's the Kings' Cash," Mercer said.

"That explains it."

"He's the money guy," I corrected. "He handles what comes in and what goes out. Enzo structured the business to operate through so many shell companies and offshore accounts, I can't track all the money down. If a new player enters the scene looking to make a deal with the Kings, Enzo negotiates the terms."

"They're all strong contenders, but it will be Enzo," I said. "Sixty-nine percent probability."

"Why?"

I turned into the hospital parking lot. "Because the others have the clout, fear, power, and respect. Enzo has the money. He'll pay off their right hands to sink a knife in their backs while they're in the middle of getting dressed for Angelo's funeral."

"I assume you're thinking of a plan to take each one of them out as we speak," Sinjin said.

"I am."

"Is that where we're going with this?" Mercer asked. "Killing all four before one assumes the mantle? I can easily get to Thiago."

We climbed out, falling in step and cutting a path through sneaking glances.

"No," I said. "Too many variables unaccounted for. Corbin ran loose through our fucking house for hours, calling whoever he wanted. We don't know who else he talked to or what he told them about us. You could set a trap for Thiago that turns into a trap for you."

"So we lie low?"

"We change the plan," I said. "Wait until we know as much, and then more than they do. I will say we're not letting an opportunity pass. I wouldn't have suggested killing the four. It won't do any good. The Kings have dozens of guys ready and willing to take their place."

"There are three steps to taking down an empire," Sinjin said. "Drain their funds, shake their followers' loyalty, and cut off the head. We've cut off the head and kicked off a surge of infighting that will hold their attention. On to the next."

We strode past the nurses' desk, ignoring the woman who called out to us.

"But, first." Sinjin jabbed the button for the elevator. "My bunny."

His bunny was not alone.

Gianna Soren Cross. Born August 15th. Works the front desk of Harmony Hotel. Grew up in Waterford. Currently lives in Rockchapel with boyfriend, Raul Perez.

Redgrave's best, and only, friend strode around the room cleaning up and setting out a change of clothes. Comparing the tight, thigh-length leopard dress she wore with the skin-clinging cutout dress she laid on the bed, I assumed she was dressing Redgrave in her own clothes.

Adeline Redgrave. Daughter of Oscar Redgrave. Born January 5th. Twenty-three years old. Hospitality management major. On-the-job-trained chef. Younger than the average sous chef. Dedicated. Determined. Single-minded. Likely history of abuse. Two known weaknesses: Gianna Cross and Oscar Redgrave.

"Hi, boys." She gave us a wane smile. "I'm so glad to see you. You brought me here without a phone. I've been worried sick—"

Pulling off her sheet, I drew Adeline's hospital gown over her waist.

"That's one way to say hi."

I peeled away the bandage, examining the cut and neat row of stitches above her hip. Her doctor did good work. This would heal with the faintest scar.

But then, it wasn't very deep.

I met those big, blinking brown eyes. "Tell me again how this happened."

"What? What do you mean?"

I waited her out.

"Angelo was hiding in the basement," she said. "He pulled a knife. We struggled and he slashed me. I got it away from him and..."

"You struggled?"

"More like he threw me against the cage and jumped on me." She shuddered. "It was horrible. He was saying these awful things, and all I could think was the room was soundproof. I could scream and you wouldn't come."

I hovered over the line of her cut, calculating the slash angle. This woman jumped off a two-story balcony into a bramble bush. She ran away torn up and bleeding from a band of armed thugs shooting to kill, and she didn't cry.

Not when she ran to me. Not in the drive to the pizzeria. Not when I treated her wounds—though her eyes shone with unshed tears.

She didn't cry, but the day before she burst into tears over a single cut that will barely scar. In a room that showed no sign of struggle. Next to a man who died with shock in his unseeing eyes.

Adeline Redgrave.

Liar.

"Forced to kill him in that way. Up close and personal," I said. "Must have been hard for you."

"It was," she whispered. "I didn't think, I reacted. I think both of us couldn't believe what I'd done." Redgrave took a deep breath. "But I had no choice. Angelo Castillo was a beast. He broke in and ordered his men to assault me. He was going to kill all of you. It was kill or be killed. I did what I had to do."

She slid her fingers through mine, smiling. "It's uncharacteristically nice of you to worry about me, Cash. I'll be okay."

I narrowed on our linked hands. The frequency of her touching had increased with no reason she should have started in the first place.

The first touch was odd. The second time she sought comfort. The other times were unexplainable.

She settled into the blankets, still smiling—content to hang on to me.

Redgrave is clearly convinced I have feelings for her that I'm hiding under twelve layers of brooding ice man. All she has to do is keep drilling until she finds what she's gotten out of Saint, Brutal, and soon, Mercer.

How she hooked all three of them was as confusing as her constant desire to touch me. Her beauty couldn't be denied. Neither could her strength. But introducing a wild card into a carefully crafted play is suicide that nearly delivered exactly what she promised. Our deaths.

I would've died to save you, I thought, *and I have no fucking idea why.*

I let go of her hand—suddenly annoyed.

"No."

Sinjin and the best friend were facing off.

"Yes," she said. "Adeline is staying with me. It's just for a few days."

"Doesn't matter if it's for a few minutes. Bunny's coming with us."

"Does Bunny get a say in this?" Adeline spoke up.

"Let me remind you four that I know who you really are. You're dangerous gangbanging killers and it finally caught up to you."

Our fingers twitched for our weapons out of reflex.

"A reason to celebrate," the best friend went on. "If it wasn't for Adeline getting caught in the crosshairs. Big, scary men are hunting you down and you no longer have a place to live. While you sort that out, Adeline will be with me where she's safe."

"No."

"We're not asking your permission," she cried, hands flying to her hips.

"You won't ask for forgiveness either."

"Okay, guys. Let's take it down," Adeline cut in. "Gianna is right. A few days with me out of the way so you can assess the damage is a good move. We don't know if your identities are still protected, or how much Angelo told the Kings. We also don't know how much time we've got until one of them figures out Angelo and the friends he brought with him are all dead."

I nodded along unthinkingly. Like her cooking, lack of brains was not one of her faults.

"You're not in our way," Mercer said. "You're one of us."

"She's injured." I backed Sinjin down. "The cut's not bad, but it needs time to heal."

"She can do that in Leighbridge."

"We can't play nursemaid right now. Cross can."

She started at being addressed directly. "What he said. I'll look after my best friend while you guys take care of whatever mess you got her into. Get back to us when it's settled."

"End of the week," I broke into whatever Sinjin was going to say in response. "We'll have the new place by then. I'll make it happen."

"Where is it?" Adeline asked. "Are we still in North Quay?"

Mercer stretched out next to her, throwing his arm around her shoulder. "Nah. Cash hooked us up with a place in Waterford. It comes with a sandwich shop for you. You can convert it into your own little eatery."

"Really?" Her eyes lit up. "You're doing that for me? Thank you, Cash."

"No." My annoyance ratcheted up tenfold. "It's not for you. Cut the shit, Mercer. We don't have money for that."

"When we have the money, it's all yours," Mercer told her. "Least we can do for getting you into our mess."

Redgrave kissed his cheek, beaming from ear to ear. Sinjin and I brought Mercer Santos on for the precise reason he could put a smile like that on anyone's face. If he had gone to the meeting with Angelo, they'd have come out best friends and drove straight to a parlor for matching "thug buddies" tattoos.

I knew all of this. Brought up his contributions to Sinjin when the mercurial bastard threatened to kill him, and yet right then I was wondering why the fuck we kept him around.

"Do you want that first-floor sandwich shop?" I asked. "Or for us to get you at the end of the week? I seem to recall moving a car filled with your suitcases."

Redgrave's smile disappeared. "Things are different now."

"How?"

Sinjin was going to let her go. Back to her shitty apartment and her thirty-hour-a-week job running around a steamy kitchen. She was free and clear to return to her old life less than twenty-four hours ago. Why should she choose the men who kidnapped her and kicked off the events that made her a target of the most dangerous gang in the city?

Probability of an average twenty-three-year-old woman making the same choice?

Zero.

"I wasn't leaving because I wanted to." She pulled Mercer closer. I wonder if she noticed. "I thought I was just the cook and maid to you four. To be gotten rid of when I'm no longer useful. Now I know that you guys..."

Sinjin landed on the bed and dropped his head on her lap. "Now she knows she belongs to us. Bunny will spend the rest of our lives feeding me and catering to my sexual needs. I should've gotten on board with this girlfriend thing years ago."

Redgrave rolled her eyes, but she didn't correct his use of the word girlfriend.

"I see." I made for the door. "If she's leaving with Cross, we're going. We have something in our basement to take care of."

Sinjin got a kiss off her. He leaned in to whisper something that made her duck her head and say "I love you" back. Brutal was next to kiss her, though he saved the whispered message. Finally Mercer kissed her knuckles and promised we'd have everything arranged for her soon.

I let the guys file past me, jaw tightening as I spared a last look through the closing door. For the man who sees everything, I somehow missed this girl becoming so entrenched in our lives they—we—would do anything to protect her.

Probability we'd regret her not getting into that car and making it out of the parking lot?

One hundred percent.

Chapter Two

A*deline*
"Raul didn't kick up a fuss at being thrown out?"

Gianna shoved open her door and helped me over the threshold. I was perfectly capable of walking on my own, but I let her fuss if it made her feel better.

"Course he did," she said, kicking aside strewn clothes. "I told him you'd make that five-alarm chili, collard greens, and buttermilk biscuits and leave leftovers for him. He packed pretty sharpish after that."

"Ahh. The truth comes out." Gianna eased me onto her pillows. "You wanted me to stay to get your hands on my cooking again."

She laughed. "Those boys have been keeping it all to themselves for the last month and a half. A girl does what she has to do."

I relaxed on her bed—the only place I spent as much time in as my own. If Raul hadn't moved in, this room would take top spot.

A huge, old-timey armoire sat next to the matching white vanity with gold around the mirror. There was a classic diva vibe about the whole place. How she got her hands on an upholstered platform bed with a headboard shaped like a crown, I'd never know, but it was clearly the only bed for her.

Gianna Cross seemed a chaotic personality from the unsure life of a budding actress, the flings, and Raul. But the untidiness in the room was laid at the boyfriend's feet. The clothes on the floor were his. The person who didn't return items to their labeled spots was Raul. The crumbs ground into the carpet. The bongs scattered all over the apartment. The dishes that didn't make it into the dishwasher.

Raul.

Raul.

Raul.

He granted the chaos people expected of her. Which left Gianna free to be... unexpected.

Kind of like the crappy apartment and the demanding chef job for the struggling hospitality major. No one looked further.

Still, I loved this picture she painted for herself because, at its heart, it was real.

This room was cozy in a way the spaces I lived in never were. Covering each wall were dozens of pictures of our childhood. Little Adeline and Gianna on their first day of middle school. The day my father took us both to the animal sanctuary. Us cheesing over matching acceptances to Cinco University.

I had the same photos to display. They filled me with the same happy nostalgia.

For a moment.

Then I'd think of the woman missing from every single shot. I'd remember I had to be ripped from the arms of my own mother to stop her callous, relentless destruction of my soul. I'd remember why the backdrop of a nice, charming neighborhood morphed into a run-down apartment with cracks in the plaster.

I'd remember, and close the photos in their box.

Gianna drew my head onto her shoulder. "You okay?"

"Fine," I said. "Just thinking about the past."

"Never a good idea."

"You're right. I should be thinking about the promise I made to Angelo Castillo to wipe his gang from the face of the earth. It'd be wrong to betray a vow to a dying man."

"My thoughts exactly."

I picked my head up, reaching for the laptop on the bedside table, and ignoring the twinge in my side. "Who is next in line now that Angelo is gone?"

"We know the four obvious choices based on their command structure." Just like that, we were all business.

Gianna opened the file labeled "Speech Exercises" and our amassed information on the Kings flooded the screen.

"Jace Parker. Xavier Jameson. Thiago Pais. Lorenzo 'Enzo' Bianchi," she read. "Though we can't exclude the dark horse that kills all of them and takes top spot."

I hummed, squinting at the screen. "True. Even so, my money is on the money. Lorenzo Bianchi."

"You've had more contact with the Kings recently. Learn anything that should be in the file?"

"I have. The Castian Hotel and the vile setup Corbin and those monsters utilized."

She held my hand. "What about it?"

"I highly doubt a fool like that thought it up on his own. He wasn't smart enough to write the auction *guest book* in code. Corbin wrote 'website' plain next to a dozen names. He had the book in an unlocked drawer in a room we broke into in twenty minutes. Let me not even get into all the stuff he blabbed to Candy.

"For years no one knew what was truly going on in that hotel. Someone as lax with security as Corbin couldn't have been the mastermind behind it, even if he was the manager. They'd have been found out in a week."

"So, the others did know."

I shook my head. "Angelo wasn't in a position to lie to me when he said he had nothing to do with the child sex ring. Corbin stole the idea, and then he put it to his own use."

"Stole from who?"

"Do you know the Imperial Majesty Hotel?"

She whistled. "Yeah. Swanky hotel in Leighbridge. One night there is my rent for two months."

"Bryan Acker took me there on our ill-fated date. I got a strange feeling when I was walking through that place, G," I said. "The way the cameras were positioned. The placement of the plants. Employees hanging back instead of running up to greet you. It's the perfect place for an affair."

Gianna pulled up the internet and searched Imperial Majesty Hotel. "There are four Imperial Majesties in the country. Another five abroad. Are you saying these board of directors built a hotel chain for cheaters and sleazes, and no one knows about it?"

"I'm saying Cash told me that day the Kings run their sex rooms out of hotels ever since The Pleasure Center was busted. He just didn't know which ones. I'm guessing we found one. I'm also guessing—although I'm sure I'm right—that they operate under the same security. A website that doesn't let you book without a code. Employees clocking everyone who goes in and out."

"The Cinco sex trade has gotten way more sophisticated than we thought," she said. "Taking it over without a weapon like the ledger will be... difficult."

"We can't sit around until we find Kieran. Corbin adopted the idea into his house of horrors. Others could be doing the same. We still don't know who the miserable shit is that cuts up escorts and leaves their bodies on the docks. We have our targets among the Kings. Time to become real players in this game."

"Knowing who we're after doesn't make it easier to get to them. Lorenzo Bianchi especially. The Kings will get more cautious after they discover Angelo and all of his men are dead. No more standing in front of windows or busting into unfamiliar territory. No trusting outsiders either. It'll be harder to get close to a King like you did with the Merchants."

"Getting close to Sinjin and the boys worked so well *because* I didn't try to get close to them. Raiden Spencer was divine timing. They tracked me down. They forced me to work for them. You don't expect a person is spying on you when you invite them in.

"It's the same plan we had, Gianna. I was working my way to becoming the next Ryan Sinclair. Caterer to the rich and disreputable of Leighbridge society. The Kings' preferred clients. They'd invite us into their homes—their lives—and I'd find out what I needed to break them from the Kings and bind them to me. At least until we found the ledger."

I leaned back, trailing my eyes up to the ceiling. "I was willing to be patient. So very patient. But a certain blue-haired devil blew that plan to pieces," I muttered. "Now, we improvise."

"The Merchants will want to capitalize on this too. They'll come up with their own plan, and they'll have the men and weapons to carry it out. Are we better hanging back and going along until we find an opening?"

"An opening."

I dropped my head, falling on the folder peeking out behind the window. *Scripts.*

Otherwise known as our file on Kieran. I didn't need to open that one.

It was empty.

"Depends," I said. "The boys have to realize the best move from this point isn't bloodshed. We have to be smart. Further weaken a crumbling foundation."

She nodded. "Wiping out the Kings is one goal, but it doesn't get us to the endgame in and of itself. If Kieran was or is one of them, we need the leverage to pull him out of hiding. We need money, babe," she said bluntly. "Money to hire out hits, so I don't lose my job every time an Angelo is begging to be shot. Money to buy out places like the Imperial Majesty, or offer the escorts working for thugs like the Slasher a better alternative. Money to pay off informants that will get us closer to Kieran. If we had cash like that, this bed frame would be made out of gold."

"Gianna, you know I only come to you with solutions." Winking, I pointed over her shoulder. "Pass me a pen and paper, please."

Slowly, she did—giving me a funny look the whole way. She propped her chin on me as I wrote.

"Ava Graham. Jake Leon. Who are these people?"

"These are the clients of the auction," I replied. "Corbin was nice enough to write their full name, preferences, and how much they drop every two weeks to get their particular needs met. The details are burned in my mind. They won't go until I do something about them and now we will.

"Blackmail everyone on this list. Ava Graham was happy to drop a total of one hundred thousand dollars to sleep with a string of fifteen- and sixteen-year-old boys, she'll have no problem paying that much to prevent her society friends from finding out. Some will pay. Some won't. But in the end, we'll be flush with plenty of seed money, and all of them will see their faces on the news."

"We're exposing them either way?" she asked.

"Yes." My voice was little more than a hiss. "They sat in that disgusting room and watched those children be trotted on and off the auction block. All of them weren't there for the kids, but every single one let it happen."

"I'll take care of it." Gianna took the list, typing in the first name. "Drop-offs in crowded locations. I'll get randoms to pick up the money and take it somewhere else. It'll never be traced back to us." She gave me a look. "Unless word gets out and your boyfriends put two and two together."

I waved a hand. "They'll be too busy with the Kings. And yes, as long as the boys keep cool heads and plan their next move, I'll play along without a fuss. If not, we'll work to achieve our own ends behind their backs."

"This won't be a conflict of interest for you?" Her teasing lilt let me know she was joking.

The creature unfurled her wings. Stepping into the light as the Adeline Redgrave the world knew and loved was swallowed by shadows.

"When will it be mine?"

"When you take it."

"I can't feel guilt for taking what belongs to me."

FOUR DAYS.

Four days of lying in Gianna's bed plotting, planning, and watching reruns in between earning my keep cooking her meals.

Four days of recovering. Now it was time to work.

I climbed off the bus, breathing in the air wafting from the Cuban restaurant on the corner. Raised voices poured out of the eatery. A lively mix of conversation, laughter, and singing along to the music.

A woman posted against the bus sign tossed a cigarette at my feet and raced to the front—unknowing or uncaring of my standing there. I barely noticed in the midst of dodging flyaway papers from the knocked-over newspaper stand.

Back home to Rockchapel.

I walked a familiar path to my old apartment, wishing hard for my car.

It's not that one of the guys wouldn't have driven it over to me. I'm certain they would have. Just as I was certain they weren't above putting a tracker in the car. I was safer taking the bus—even if my side was sore from the elderly woman dropping her grocery bag on me.

This neighborhood does not change.

The sights, sounds, and smells were the same. The men in red bandanas idling on the corner were right where I left them. The graffiti decorating my former building was yet to be painted over.

"Addy! Where you going, girl?"

And of course, this man would never be more than fifty feet from that couch.

"I'm going your way, Captain," I said as he fell in step with me. "Came to check on you."

"Finally taking me up on that ride on my couch."

Captain looked in better shape than when I'd last seen him. The clothes falling apart on his frame were new. New to me at least.

The cut healing badly above his eye a month and a half ago was a clean, jagged scar. He was fuller, as though getting semi-regular meals, and he had an overall pleased sense about him. Whether it was from following through on my help or Sinjin's treat, I couldn't tell. Maybe both.

"'Fraid not," I said. "I'm taking you out to lunch. Hope that will do."

He grinned. "Afterward, we'll—"

"Don't make me go for the pepper spray instead."

Captain mumbled something that suspiciously sounded like cocktease.

The two of us looped around my building and made for a restaurant two blocks down, *From Scratch*.

Josephine glanced up from laying out menus. "Addy, long time no see, babe. Where have you been?"

"You didn't hear?" I accepted her warm hug. "I moved out. I live in North Quay now."

Or I did.

"North Quay? Wow," she crowed. "The lady's moving up and forgetting about us little people."

"Like I could. First chance I got, I hopped on a bus for more of your Italian wedding soup. I'll have a bowl of that and whatever Captain wants."

"Scottish chowder," he said.

She smacked my butt with a menu. "Coming right up."

Captain and I opted for outdoor seating, pulling up chairs under the bright green awning.

I loved From Scratch. Josephine was one of the few cooks that rivaled me in the kitchen. Her whole theme was soup. All kinds of soups from around the world, paired with their traditional sides. The best part was she made everything from the stock to the bread from scratch.

Dedication like that usually came with a high price, but hers didn't stray far above the mom-and-pop eateries in our neighborhood. I'd be suspicious of this if I hadn't long suspected she had other creative, *criminal* ways of making her money. Probably why I liked her so much.

Josephine was a sturdy pillar of warmth, frizzy hair, and muscle. If she was getting up to something in the kitchens of From Scratch, she wasn't letting anyone get past her to find out.

But I will find out eventually. The knowledge may come in handy.

"How you been, C?" I reclined in my chair, crossing my leg over the other.

"Good, good." Captain swept his gaze over a busy street. "Went to that shelter you told me about."

"I'm glad. You look good."

"Whaddya got for me?" he asked point-blank. "Usual price?"

"More," I said, keeping the same weathered eye on our surroundings. "Triple."

"Triple? Triple the price?" Captain tried to sound cool. He failed. "Why?"

"You saved my life. You got Sinjin's thanks. Now you'll receive mine."

Captain shot forward, nearly toppling the table. "Neighborhood's been mostly quiet. Blood Brothers, Flaming Hogs MC, Kravets family. No wars brewing."

"The Blood Brothers that attacked us didn't make it back to tell the rest. Am I in the clear?"

He nodded. "You took out their leader and his brother. A new guy, Silas, put out the word that info on whoever did it would reward a grand. Ivan killed him and took over less than a day later. He dropped the reward. Went around telling everyone he'd kill the bastards who messed with the Brothers. With no money involved, no one was interested in helping him find out who."

"Glad to hear I can put that particular issue to rest," I said. "Tell me about this Ivan guy. Sounds like a hothead."

"He is. The BBs have gotten bolder since he stepped up. They're jacking cars left and right. Been a lot of burglaries too. Five just last week. The couple was home for one of them, and they were both killed. The Blood Brothers haven't taken credit, but everyone knows it's them."

I clicked my tongue. "That won't do. The people in Rockchapel have it hard enough. Most of them work three jobs just to make enough to be broke. The little they have goes to running those clunky cars and keeping a roof over their children's heads. This isn't jacking a bunch of university kids who come here trolling for drugs and a good time. A gang looks out for their neighborhood. They don't drain it dry.

"No," I repeated. "Ivan's not going to make the cut. He'll have to go, and the rest of the BBs with him if they don't get the message."

"Do you... uh—" Captain leaned in closer, dropping his voice. "Need someone to take care of him? I know a couple of guys."

I smiled. "No, C. I prefer to take care of these things myself. It's free that way."

"Here we are." Josephine emerged from the café carrying a tray. She placed a vibrant, steamy broth filled with meatballs and greens in front of me. My meal was topped off with fresh bread and a Caesar salad. Captain descended on his bowl before she put it down.

"Anything else I can get you?" she asked.

"No, thank you."

Captain and I broke off the conversation to eat.

I ate at a slower pace, thinking of the boys and what they were doing at that moment. Mercer said they got us a new place in Waterford.

And they say you can never go back home.

My fist balled on my lap. It was right that I should end up back there. It had been my mission since the first domino fell that kicked off the destruction of my life.

Waterford was where I belonged. It should be where I took my stand.

"What about outside the neighborhood?" I asked. Captain's soup was consumed and the bowl was in the process of being licked clean. "Heard anything?"

"Uh…" Captain paused to rip off a bit of bread. "One thing," he said around the mouthful.

"Angelo Castillo's gone missing. The official word is he's on vacation out of the city, but I'm not buying it. Him not turning up after the stuff with the Castian, and then half of the Kings' properties burning down? I say someone finally set fire to the right building."

You're not far off, my friend.

"They like anyone for it?"

"The Merchants."

My sip of water held on my tongue. Captain claimed my salad, chowing down unaware of my gaze sharpening on him.

I swallowed. "Is there word out about them? Names? Descriptions?"

"No idea what any of them look like, but there is one name going around," he replied. "Sinjin."

Of course. Sinjin called Angelo personally and announced himself. Apparently, he spread the name around. Likely while he was trying to dig up information on him.

"Just the name? Nothing else?" I pressed.

"Nothing."

Taking a breath, I forced my fingers to unclench. Captain was everywhere no one wanted him, and anywhere I needed him. He was one of my best informants. Too good for me to give up, even though he came with a steady stream of sexual harassment. If he knew one name, then that's all anyone else knew. Angelo didn't get a chance to tell the Kings about the black-jack-loving Sinjin Bellisario and his companion, Adeline Redgrave.

So no one else would know that he found me. Not until he decided what to do with me.

At least the paranoid old gangster did one thing in my favor.

"That's good, C. Exactly what I needed to know," I said. "While I'm here, you can help me update my files. Fill me in on the others. The Flaming Hogs MC. The Kravets. Any deaths or new members?"

"Sure thing, but why do you need to know this stuff?"

"I told you." I retrieved a pen and notepad from my purse. "One day, I'm going to clean this city up. I have to know exactly who'll be in my way."

He shrugged. Captain didn't give a rat's ass. I was the only one to look out for him since his son died twenty years ago. He'd give me all the information I asked for.

"Marko Kravet died a few days after you took off," he began. "Heart attack. The Flaming Hogs..."

CASH

"Another beer, my man?"

"No, Coke this time." I held up a bill without looking away. "Keep the change."

"Thanks." He plucked the fifty before I could change my mind. "Be right back with that Coke."

"Hey, Tuck," a customer called. "Where's our food? We ordered forty-five minutes ago."

The service in this place wasn't the best for those not flashing fifties, but it did grant a perfect view of From Scratch.

Captain. Real name unknown. Lived on the streets for an indeterminant amount of time. Friend of Redgrave?

They seemed to be friends. Sitting there eating their soup and deep in conversation. Adeline lived in this neighborhood since she left university.

That she should want to visit was likely.

That she would take her friends out to lunch was reasonable.

That an old man hardened by years on the street would clock everyone passing by, clamming up as they did also fell squarely within the odds. On the face, nothing about this was out of the ordinary.

I narrowed on the notepad. *Except that. What's this guy have to tell her that's so important?*

Four days since Redgrave left the hospital with her buxom friend, and for four days, I'd been tailing her.

Angelo's body was disposed of off the docks along with his men. Final negotiations had gone through for our backroom sale of the new hideout, and the next strike against the Kings would be leveled in the time it took for me to plan it out. There was only one problem left.

Adeline.

Redgrave rose from the table. She put her notepad away and handed him a pouch from her purse. The question of whether I'd have to rob an old man was answered when he opened and pulled out the contents. Toothpaste, razor, toothbrush, and the like. It was easy to tell from across the street.

Adeline waved goodbye and set off.

I walked out as Tuck returned with my drink, paying no mind to his call. *Where to next, Redgrave?*

ADELINE

"Addy!" Natalya hugged the stuffing out of me. "I missed you. How are you doing? I heard about the accident."

"I'm much better now. All healed up."

"And you couldn't resist coming back to the old place." She glanced behind her. "You might regret that. Ryan's here."

"That's good. I wanted to see him."

"Addy, if that man gets his hands on you, you'll wake up chained to the stove."

I laughed.

"I hope it flatters you to hear you're irreplaceable."

"It does." I popped a kiss on her cheek. "Time to venture into the belly of the beast."

I walked into the kitchen with a smile. Ryan wiped it off in six seconds flat.

"Think you can strut in here like nothing happened?"

"No, Chef."

"Weeks. Weeks!" His cleaver split the chicken in two on the first strike. The second made his point. The third drove it home. "Weeks, Adeline. Do you know how long that is in culinary years?"

"Decades, Chef."

"Decades!" he carried on. "I couldn't wait for you while you lay around in bed. I've moved on. Hired a new sous chef that's *worthless*!"

Ryan whipped around on a hapless man carrying a bowl of ingredients.

"Useless," Ryan flung. "A disgrace."

"Yes, Chef," the man agreed.

"He isn't worth half of you." Sinclair strode into the walk-in, expecting me to follow. "Refuses to stay past eleven at night. Constantly brings me sub-par ingredients. When are you coming back?"

I blinked. "Do you want me back?"

"Didn't I just say I can't work with that idiot? You have to come back." Ryan grabbed a head of broccoli and gave it to me. "You'll claim your previous position. Salvatore will agree to a pay raise of five dollars an hour."

"That's really generous, Chef."

Two zucchinis and three carrots were placed on my pile. Ryan topped me off with cauliflower and walked out again.

"But I didn't come to get my job back," I called, staying on his heels. "My doctor says I have to take it easy for the next few months."

He frowned. "Then why are you here?"

"I hate the way I left you hanging. Before my accident, we talked about me working with you on private catering jobs."

He set my load on his station, still giving me a strange look.

"I learned so much from working with you, Chef. I'd like to continue doing so. If another wedding or charity event comes up, I'll make myself available."

"Hmpf. Well, you are the only chef I've trained myself. The one person I could rely on until two months ago."

I weathered the sting.

A part of me burst to say I was held captive by four sinfully hot gang-bangers, but that wouldn't have helped matters. Pleading coma barely did.

My love and devotion to this job were real. I couldn't endure the hell Ryan Sinclair put me through if it wasn't. Like I told Sinjin, this is how I do good. In a sea of deliciously dark deeds, there was a little island home to a young girl who used to bake treats to take on her outings with her dad. As long as that island remained, the Adeline Redgrave I used to be wasn't completely washed away.

"Alright," he said. "As long as you've kept your skills sharp, I'll let you work the Rothchild-Lysandro wedding coming up. We'll see how you do today."

"Today?"

"Get a move on, Adeline. There's a spare coat and pants in my office."

"I—"

"Or do you have better things to do?"

"No, Chef. I'll be ready in five minutes."

"Three," he barked. "Start chopping these for the cauliflower Bolognese. Two orders. Then, slice radishes for..."

My day veered off track and remained in the kitchen till after the dinner rush.

My side ached something fierce. I didn't let it show. Ryan was hunting for a sniff of weakness. Any sign of it and my future as his protégé was over.

I sent the last order out and ducked into the fridge. Frigid air cooled my heated cheeks, bringing me down from the rush of excitement that was the kitchen. My feet killed. My back hurt. My hair was a mess, and I desperately wanted to curl into a hot bath with Sinjin and have him rub me all over. But damn if I hadn't put some grudging respect on Ryan's face.

He won't be the only man forced to acknowledge my skill tonight.

"Addy?" Stevie stuck her head in the fridge. "Are you staying for family dinner?"

"Can't. I'm supposed to meet a friend. Hey, what was that club you warned me about a while ago? Optimum?"

"Opium," she said. "That's not where you're meeting your friend, are you? Addy, you can't. It's dangerous."

"Bangers?"

"It's their favorite place." Closing the door, she dropped her voice though it was just us. "We're both out of Rockchapel now. You, me, and our families. Far as I see, there's no reason either one of us should ever go back. It's only gotten worse since we left."

"You're right. I'll tell my friend we'll meet somewhere else."

"Good," she replied, relaxing. "I know you have to go, but stay and have something with us really quick. We haven't seen you for weeks."

I gave in, joining my old crew to eat and trade stories about what we missed. At nine, I headed out pleading I had to catch my bus.

"We'll talk about the wedding, Adeline," Ryan said. "Good job today."

"Thank you, Chef."

I raced out, darting to the bus stop.

CASH

Redgrave slipped inside the car.

I restarted the engine, easing into traffic. I was no closer to understanding what she was doing. First the meeting with the old man. Then the hour I sat outside her restaurant before finally going inside and spotting her rushing around the kitchen in a chef's uniform.

Why would she take up her old job? She was sitting on thousands in cash. Four days of not cooking and cleaning for us and she was already tapped out? What the hell did she spend it on?

My confusion further compounded by her returning to the best friend's place and walking out forty-five minutes later in a tight black dress and heels. Cross's boyfriend arrived while she was inside. She drove off in his car, leaving me to follow.

What the hell are you up to, Redgrave?

ADELINE

"When will you be back?" Raul's mouth was stuffed with my homemade ravioli. "I need the hmm huh uh."

"What?"

Raul was, in a word, a mess. In another word, he was gorgeous. We weren't talking the regular kind of gorgeous that ended up a girl's boy-next-door crush. I meant the only-seen-in-magazines gorgeous.

Tousled black curls skimmed the lashes framing his moss-green eyes. He had a long face, strong jaw, trim beard, and these full, silky lips that put the "ooh" in your "ooh-la-la" whenever he smiled.

The man looked like a model, so it was fitting that he was one. Too bad he was even more of a diva than Gianna, almost no one wanted to work with him, and he rarely booked jobs.

"I need it back by eleven or I'm sleeping in my own fucking bed," he stated.

Gianna shoved his shoulder. "Stop it, Raul. She's made us enough food to feed us for three weeks. You can let her use your car for one night."

He grunted something, curling a hand around her waist. Raul buried his face in her chest. "Haven't you missed me, baby?"

She nipped his nose. "Give me a reason to miss you."

"I'll give that pussy a reason."

"Still in the room," I deadpanned. "Standing right here."

Gianna giggled. "Why are you dipping out in the middle of the night anyway? You were wrecked when you came in here. Clutching your side, though I bet you didn't think I noticed."

"Ryan made me work the dinner shift."

"How are you that man's bitch again?"

"Sous chef," I corrected. "Remarkably close to bitch, but not quite."

"Seriously, Adeline. Go to bed."

Raul winked. "After we're done with it."

"I can't. The Blood Brothers have been acting up since my love forced a change in leadership. I can't help but feel partially responsible. I'm dropping in on Ivan for a chat."

He dropped his smirk. "You need him taken out? I can handle that, Addy. Been too long if I'm honest."

It's amazing how the right people find each other. I found the Merchants. Gianna found Cinco's top drug dealer for the model, actor, and society elite. Raul could afford to bail on every job he got since his extra-curricular activities kept him flush—in between pissing it away on crap he didn't need.

"Thanks, but this one is going to require some finesse. I'll be back as soon as he's dead. Bye."

"Bye."

They were making out before the door closed.

I hopped in Raul's outrageously expensive car and made the ride deep into Rockchapel. If I didn't find Ivan in the club, the Lambo would draw him and his band of car thieves out like bees to honey.

My drive was short. Gianna's apartment sat square on the Rockchapel-Waterford border. I once asked her if she didn't move farther away because she wanted to stick close to me. She kissed my forehead and said not to let that big head sink me. That was Gianna-speak for yes.

The girl always has my back. Support that would be invaluable tonight.

But this mess is mine. It's my job to clean it up.

I pulled up to the curb across from Opium.

Rockchapel nightclubs weren't so much clubs as they were dive bars that played their music too loud. You could dance between the pool tables and rickety furniture, but mostly you were there to get drunk.

Opium bucked the stereotype. A line to rival the best of Harlow's club street stretched to the beauty parlor four doors down. Two bouncers posted up at the entrance. Flashing lights and club music poured out with each scantily clad twentysomething they let in.

I was fairly certain Opium did not look like this when Stevie warned me off years ago. Someone with money came in and gave the place an upgrade.

They upgraded a known banger hideout and did nothing about the fact they kept coming back? Curious.

Angling the mirror, I gazed into those infamous brown eyes as I tied my hair into a bun and perched fake glasses on my nose. Final touch, smearing on pale purple lipstick. A simple disguise that did the trick better than assumed.

Hair up, glasses on, and covered in makeup, Adeline Redgrave became her bookish fraternal twin.

I climbed out, bypassed the line, and flashed a smile at the bouncers. Gianna's black lattice dress cut all the right lines around my figure.

"Go right in, darling." The flashing lights welcomed me. "Have fun."

"Oh, I will."

CASH

Redgrave emerged from the car.

"What the fuck?"

Adeline didn't wear glasses. Twenty-twenty vision let her cook and watch the living room television, switching off the news saying I wasn't paying attention to it if I was on my computer. She also hated wearing her hair up. Why do so when she could slip over the back of my chair, cloaking us both in a jasmine-scented rain of strangely reddish locks? Her heat soaking into me as she asked what I was working on.

Disguise, my mind supplied in the split second of seeing her. *But why?*

I shoved out, striding across the street. She was in before I reached the bouncers.

"Hold up, mate." They fell in shoulder to shoulder—blocking the door. "Back of the line."

"I'm with the nineteen-year-old girl you just let in without carding. Older brother." The matching menacing looks slipped. "Move aside and I'll get her out of here without a fuss. If not, the cops get a tip the owner of Opium likes to get teenage girls drunk in the back room and film them taking their clothes off."

"Alright, mate," Bouncer One cried. "Easy. We didn't know the girl was nineteen. Go on."

They stood aside. I pressed in the crush of bodies, searching for the sneaking bunny.

ADELINE

Long hair. Thick beard. Wears a big gold watch. Bandana hanging from his hip.

Captain's description was spot on. Lounging in the VIP area with two women under his arm was Ivan Stallard. The gold watch glinted between the woman's breasts. His full, impressive beard fell prey to the other woman's stroking. I couldn't see what hung from his hip, but the bandanas sported by the guys talking, loitering, or dancing around him gave me a hint.

I could still see the ghost of dive bars past. The bar top was a long, wooden thing lined with leather stools. The floors were checkered tile and the back wall boasted exposed brick. The biggest transformation was the blue leather couches lining the walls, and the tables loaded down with alcohol and a candle atop. It all left room for the dance floor—complete with wriggling, grinding bodies.

I leaned against the bar, sipping my ginger ale. Sweeping lights lit me green, orange, purple, and yellow in a dizzying array. Everyone on the floor seemed to be dancing with each other at the same time, and bumping into me while doing it.

It was loud, messy, packed, and perfect. I'd be in and out, and Ivan would be dead. No one would suspect a thing.

Just have to wait for his groupies to—

The women stood up. Wining and grinding, they tried tugging him along. He broke free of their grip, shooing them away. The two scuttled off to dance, cueing my signal to go.

Ivan didn't clock my approach until I grabbed the velvet rope. Boldly, I lifted it and stepped onto the platform.

"Hey."

Furrows formed around his eyes. Up close, I observed his flat, smooshed nose and protruding brow ridge. He spread out on the couch like he owned it. An entire booth with more than enough room for the men posted around him like decoration. A king determined to stand out among the serfs.

Ivan looked me up and down—equal parts attraction and suspicion played on his face. "What can I do for you? I don't dance, but you're welcome to give me a show."

I shrugged. "I just wanted a look at the guy they say can't hold his liquor."

"What?"

"Two shots and you're on the floor."

He jumped up. "Who the fuck said that?"

"Doesn't matter," I said, grin curling into my cheeks. "Because you're about to prove them wrong. Let's see you drink this girl under the table."

I shoved him on the lounge, stretching next to him. The smirk was back on his face.

"I took a guy for five hundred the other night," I said. "But this time we can wager your pride."

"My pride's not on the line, baby." He slinked an arm around my hip. "But I'll bet your"—Ivan squeezed my ass—"pride."

"Fine by me." I shifted to knock his hand off. "The real stuff. Vodka. Whoever's still standing goes home with their prize?"

Ivan pulled a guy down by the collar. "Sixteen shots of vodka. Go."

The Blood Brother scurried off to comply.

I stroked my purse, grinning as he returned with a tray. *This is almost too—*

A flash of golden hair peeked through the crowd. Brow crumpling, I rose up, searching the person in the chaos.

Was that...?

"Looking for your boyfriend?" Ivan tugged me down. "He'll have to get in line."

He picked up two shots, passing one to me. "Cheers."

"Cheers."

We clinked.

CASH

The hilt dug grooves in my palm. I grabbed the gun hidden inside my coat when the oily, smashed-faced shit touched her ass, and the urge to use it grew with every laugh, shot, and accidental brush.

The air bent around them—hazy through the heat of my rage. I wanted to know what Redgrave was hiding, and I got my answer.

So this was what the disguise was for. Redgrave hit up her old neighborhood to get with some guy, thinking it'd never get back to us?

He dropped his head on her chest, howling. I popped the strap.

Name unknown. Approximately six feet and two hundred pounds. Gang affiliation: Blood Brothers. Weapons: Likely.

Death: Certainty.

ADELINE

"Too much for you?" I slurred.

Ivan thrust a shot at me, spilling half the contents on my lap. "I'm just getting started. Don't know where the hell they got this vodka. Might as well be water." He said that, though he blinked one eyelid at a time—swaying slightly in his seat. "Another."

We picked up our glasses. Throwing my head back, I tipped the whole thing down the side of my mouth, spilling down my neck. My entire back was soaked by this point.

"Whoo," I cried. "Water for sure. Let's get another tray."

"Damn, girl. You're hardcore." Ivan grabbed my knee. "I like that in a woman."

I crossed my legs, knocking him off. "But it's all about what I like in a man." I skated my fingers down his arm. "I like 'em dark. Dangerous. A bad boy in every sense of the word. A man who takes what's his through pain and blood."

I licked my purple lips. "Know any men like that?"

"You're looking at a man like that. I run this borough from Annie's Grocers on the high street to the Waterford tunnel. It's all Blood Brother territory."

Do the Kravets, Flaming Hogs, and Locos know that?

"They're my gang, and this is my city."

"The Blood Brothers?" I shouted over the noise, drawing back. "Maybe you didn't hear me. I said I want a real man. A brutal, ruthless son of a bitch that would make an example of a bastard in this very club with everyone watching. The Blood Brothers are small time. All they do is jack a few worthless cars."

"That's what we used to do," he growled. "Ronin was weak. He held us back. The one thing he did right was get his fucking throat slit." He thumped his chest, shot and all, spilling it on his shirt. "I'm in charge now. The Blood Brothers will become the most feared name in this city."

"More feared than the Merchants?"

He barked a laugh. "Those pussies? Fuck, yeah. They're terrified of a little blood. Never killed on a job. Not me." Ivan's smile was nasty. "I've got no problem cutting down someone in my way."

"You killed?" I leaned back, slipping my hand between my legs. His pants tented for what he thought I was doing. "Who?"

"Just last week I wasted some old couple and made off with the family jewels. You should've heard that leathery bitch screaming when I shot her husband. Now that would've gotten you off."

I smiled. "That's all I needed to know."

I made him take another shot. Then another.

"I'm going to the bathroom," I announced. "If you're my real man, you'll know what to do next."

Ivan smacked my ass on the way down. I'd need a long, hot, scouring shower after this. It was just as well I was killing him tonight. If Saint found out, he'd cut off his fingers and feed them to him.

Pushing through the dancers, I followed the shining sign directing me down a darkened hallway. The women's bathroom was at the very end.

It was a tiny space with two stalls and two sinks beneath a dirty, cracked mirror. I checked under the doors for feet.

No one.

The mirror told me I was a mess. All that flailing around and throwing my head back knocked my bun askew. One shot made it into my mouth. The rest soaked my back like rivers of sweat. No one said ruling Cinco City would be easy or pretty, but my law is the law. Judgment had been handed down.

The door flew open. Ivan stumbled in, his momentum careening him into the stall.

"Ass up, bitch."

Such a charmer.

I hopped on the counter and opened my arms. Ivan fell on me, sucking and slurping on my neck. His erection ground insistently into my thigh.

My fingertips drew my bag closer to me. Holding his head firm, I slipped the note from my purse and tucked it into his pocket. Then I closed over the needle. There was no time for anything fancy. A syringe full of Gianna's eye drops, and a slow death by tetrahydrozoline would get the job done. The wannabe king would stumble home drunk, believing his symptoms needed to be slept off. By the time his body, and the note, were found, my point would be made.

Ivan found my zipper and ripped it down. I responded in kind.

Lifting his shirt up, I exposed his back. The tip pressed to his skin.

Bang!

A golden-haired menace of cold-blooded savagery filled the doorway. The light graced the tips of his hair, bends of his cheekbones, and snarl on his lips.

My eyes bugged. "Cash?"

"Fuck off!" Ivan shouted.

Roaring, Cash ripped him off me. The needle flew from my hand.

"Cash, wait!"

He punched Ivan, doubling him over. The banger responded with in-grained instincts. He shot forward and rammed Cash into the stall. They went down fists flying.

What the hell is happening? What's Cash even doing here?!

The syringe lay next to the garbage can. I kicked it behind. "Cash, please, stop."

Ivan came flying out of the stall. Cash emerged—whole and fero-cious—gold melting in the fire of his glare. Ivan caught himself on the door handle. Straightening, he charged Cash.

Cash ripped the gun from his holster.

He fired once. Twice. Three times.

Ivan collapsed at his feet, blood pooling on the grimy tiled floor.

I stared at him wide-eyed. "You killed him."

"You fucked him."

"I—" Cash advanced on me. "Wait. It's not what you think."

"Not what I think!?"

The shout blew me back. I'd never heard Cash shout. Bark orders? Yes. Snap off biting, asshole comments? Absolutely. But lose his temper? No.

"What the fuck are you doing here, Redgrave?! Dressed like this." He snatched the glasses off and flung them across the room. "Letting that guy put his hands on you!"

"It's not like that. Nothing was going to happen."

"Plenty happened." Cash's fist dented the paper dispenser. "This is what you were hiding! You're fucking around on us?!"

I blinked. *Us?*

"No," I said. "This is a misunderstanding. I came here to— to blow off steam. Dance. Drink. Have fun. He followed me into the bathroom. You busted in before I had a chance to push him off—"

Cash hauled me around. Spit and teeth marks shone clear on my neck.

"You think you got us tamed, don't you, Redgrave?"

There was nothing tame about Killian Hunt at that moment. Gripping my chin, he pulled me back onto him, face pressing against mine. "That we bend and scrape at your knee?"

"No," I whispered. "Cash, I swear nothing was going to happen."

"You chose us. The Merchants. Twisted, vicious, and depraved is what you wanted. It's what you wanted from me." His breath rolled hot over my cheek. "You kept pushing, Adeline. Digging and digging until you brought this man out. You want to know where the line between Cash and Killian is?"

I couldn't speak even if I had the power. I was trapped in his hold. Heart thumping on his arm. Throat pulsing in his grip.

"You found it."

Spinning me to face him, Cash ripped my panties down in one move. The stalls blurred.

Cash lifted me onto the counter and spread my legs like they'd been for Ivan. The sound of his zipper yanking down was the preparation I got.

I choked on a cry. Cash filled me to the hilt, stretching a pussy only recently reawakened to steady sex. He started pumping—a punishing, relentless pace that smashed me into the mirror.

"Cash!"

If you'd asked me how I thought my night would go, Cash balls deep inside me wouldn't even have made my list of impossible events. I was still confused by his presence. Rattled by the obvious conclusion he followed me. Thrown by his—there was no other phrase for it—raging jealousy.

He struck that spot dead center, ripping a moan/scream from me. I kicked the dispenser clean off the wall.

Cash grabbed my ankles, holding them above our heads, and using the leverage to plow deeper still.

My eyes rolled up in my head—mouth open in a silent cry. Colliding bolts of electricity zinged through my veins. It was like finding the pleasure button and rapidly striking it until you left yourself a drooling heap twitching and giggling on the floor.

Cash was a beast unleashed. Cold, refined, and hard, the man towering over me didn't know the meaning of those words. Heat stained his cheeks with color. Golden locks stuck to his forehead. His grunts were maddened and satisfied. It was hard to explain how I sensed they were both.

But they were.

He thrust deeper, banging his thighs on the countertop, and I came so hard I cracked my back arching off the sink. Loud and violent, the orgasm tore my sanity to shreds. I flopped on the faucet in a daze. Unable to comprehend what just happened.

Cash tightened on my ankles. His body tensed up, head thrown back. I reached a shaky hand. My fingers brushed his lips as he emptied inside me.

For the barest second, I felt the pressure of his kiss.

Cash released my legs.

I tipped off the sink, dropping on the floor to Ivan's unseeing eye level. Cash tucked himself in and swept out of the bathroom.

My fogged mind took a minute to catch up.

"Wait," I croaked.

Snatching up the syringe, I shot up, and nearly fell on Ivan. My left heel had snapped off. Probably when I took out the dispenser.

Cursing, I yanked off my heels, grabbed my bag, and chased after Cash.

His head bobbed through breaks in the crowd. He was moving fast, making for the exit and out into the street where I'd lose him. Lose all of them if he told Brutal, Mercer, and Saint I cheated.

After everything I've done. Everything we've been through. I'm not losing my boys over a piece of shit like Ivan.

I dropped the syringe on the packed floor. It was crushed underfoot almost immediately. Evidence gone.

I burst out of the club. "Cash!"

Running to the edge of the sidewalk, I scanned the street for that brilliant crown and sweeping coat. Headlights flashed two cars behind Raul's. I charged after him.

"Cash, listen to me." I slammed his door shut. "What is wrong with you?! What do you have to be mad at me about? How long have you been following me?"

"How long have you been fucking other guys behind our back?"

"I haven't," I gritted.

"This what you do on your weekends?" It was like he hadn't heard me. "Pick up other bangers. The Merchants aren't enough of a thrill."

"I wasn't picking him up! I told you I was—"

Cash punched the car window, showering his seat with glass. "Fucking lie to me again and we go with plan B. Find a use for you, or kill you."

My jaw clenched. "You won't kill me."

He leaned in, forcing my back to the car. "I won't care if I did either way because we'll be done with you. You won't see us again. Not even on the security tape of us running around in our masks."

Our heated gaze burned the other through for a long spell. A watching crowd lingered behind us.

"I came here to find Ivan," I said quietly. "I heard this is his favorite club. Last week, an elderly couple in Rockchapel were killed in their apartment during a B and E. Mr. and Mrs. Maldonado."

"What's that got to do with you being here?"

"The Blood Brothers did it. Everyone in the borough knew, but they didn't have proof. So, I came to get it."

His forehead crumpled in a frown. "Why?"

"I knew the Maldonados." I didn't but Cash couldn't say otherwise. "They were good people. Never hurt a soul. When Saint killed Ronin and his brother, he cleared the path for that Ivan bastard to take over. Ronin was no choir boy, but he had respect for his neighborhood. He knew where the line was.

"Since Ivan took over, the Blood Brothers have terrorized Rockchapel and he told me himself this was just the beginning. It was indirectly, but all this setting off was our fault."

"And what did you think you were going to do about it?"

"I did it," I replied. "I got Ivan drunk and goaded him into admitting he murdered the Maldonados. In the bathroom, I wrote a note saying I knew what he'd done, and he'd regret it if the Blood Brothers didn't go back to jacking rich pricks and stay out of innocent people's homes. I slipped it into his pocket while he was slobbering all over me."

I gave Cash a hard look. "Check if you don't believe me. And you better hurry. Any minute now some girl is going to run screaming out the door yelling murder."

Cash didn't move. He scanned the lines of my face searching for a lie.

I held my breath, locking steady on his gaze. Every good lie has a kernel of truth at the root. He'd pick up on that even if he made it past the righteous anger poising the creature to strike. Or the smoldering attraction Cash had lit into an inferno less than twenty minutes ago.

I felt him throbbing inside me. The pressure in my core. His iron grip on my ankles. Cash had found the line between Adeline and my other half. And neither one knew what to do next.

He turned his back on me, stalking into the club. Cash didn't believe me. But he would.

Consider this your official warning.

The Blood Brothers are out of the burglary business. The Maldonados are the last innocent couple you kill. The Burgesses are the last poor family to wake up and find their car gone.

You no longer live by Ronin's or Ivan's rules. You live by mine.

-Bunny

Slumping against the car, I thanked every deity of fortune that I didn't reference Ivan's death. My point was to be made by his men finding the note on his body with no idea of where it came from or who got to him and when. I anticipated having to make my point a few more times. Gangbangers were hardheaded. But the note would let them know they were being watched.

Cash came out of the club, gripping a slip of paper in his hand.

Or it would've.

"Cute." Cash tossed the crumpled paper in his car. "You've got a thing for notes, Redgrave. Let's see what else you've written today."

"Wha— Hey!"

Cash snatched my bag and took out the notepad. He tore through the pages.

"What is wrong with you?!" I cried. "Is this a breakdown?"

"What did that homeless man have to say that needed to be written down word for word? Tips for bathing in a puddle?"

My mouth fell open. "You followed me to the restaurant too?"

How in the bloody fuck did I not see him? What did he see? I thought, frantically running through the past few days.

"Where is it?"

"It's here!" Ripping it from him, I flipped to the notes I wrote from Captain and shoved it in his face. "Are you happy? There's my big secret, Cash. I get recipes from a homeless man."

In dark blue ink, "Turkey Bolognese" was written on top of the page. Beneath it, I wrote out various ingredients and quantities. Two tablespoons of olive oil. Five cups of marinara sauce. Seven carrots.

"This is it?"

"Yes," I said.

"No. That's not what you wrote."

It was actually. All the information Captain gave me on the gangs of Rockchapel, written in my carefully devised code.

Turkey Bolognese for the Flaming Hogs. Five cups of marinara for the five new members. Two tablespoons of olive oil for their losses. Seven carrots for the seventy kilos of cocaine they were hiding in the back room of their bar.

I wasn't an idiot. Even my school notes were written in code. If anyone actually tried to cook these, they'd end up with a bowl of the most disgusting mush. Otherwise, there was nothing out of place about a chef with a book full of recipes.

"If you were watching, you know this is the same notepad," I said. "Captain didn't always live on the streets. He once had a home. A family. He gives me recipes and I cook for him when I can."

A muscle ticced in his jaw. Rippling veins went down the hand crunching my notepad, stark along his arm. For some reason, he was only getting angrier. "Got an explanation for everything, don't you, Redgrave?"

"Yes, because there is an explanation." I shoved him. "How about you give me one? Why are you following me?"

"Why? Because there's something not right about you," he hissed. "You're not what you should be, Adeline Redgrave."

Stiffening, a cold sweat dripped down my spine.

"The day Sinjin was stabbed, you drove him back to the station instead of dumping him at a hospital and taking off in his car. You do shit like roll into a banger club by yourself to trap and threaten a gang leader.

"You killed Angelo, and you cried." His nose brushed mine. "I don't trust you. I never have. I never will."

I swallowed hard. Three things were very clear to me. Cash would have time to stop me if I dove for the shards of glass on his seat. There were too many witnesses on the street. And I gravely underestimated this man. The whole time, it was Cash, not Saint I needed to hide from, and he's seen me the whole time.

"If you wanted to know something," I began, choosing my words carefully. "You should've asked. I didn't run that day because I couldn't—wouldn't—leave my dad and Gianna behind. I came after Ivan by myself because if I involved you guys, you'd kill him. Turns out I was right.

"And I cried after I killed Angelo? What's that supposed to mean, Cash? Why wouldn't I cry?"

"You didn't after beating Felix, taking out Acker, jumping off a balcony, or attacking the Castian. But down in the basement with no signs of a struggle, you weep and wail over the body of that surprised bastard. I think you killed him," he said, "because Angelo knew something about you that I need to know. It's why he tried to trade you off Sinjin. Why don't you tell me what that something is, Redgrave? End the bullshit here."

I said nothing for a long time.

"It must be hard," I whispered. "Being the man who sees everything."

I cupped his cheek. Surprise flickered in his eyes.

"But everyone who hides something from you, isn't a threat, Cash. Some things"—I kissed him softly—"are just none of your damn business."

He growled.

"No," I shouted. "You don't get to be mad at me because you didn't see this, Cash. I was raped."

Cash reeled back. "By Angelo?"

"By men like him." The words choked in my throat. "Over and over again for *years*. Some of them couldn't take my screaming, so they beat me. Drugged me."

Tears stung my eyes. "I was a child, Killian. Trapped in my own body. Helpless. Praying someone would save me.

"So no, I don't expect you to see. To understand why on the day I'm tied up, beaten, and sexually assaulted on Angelo's orders, that after killing him I'd cry."

The anger was gone. Hard, unreadable Cash had slid into place, shuttering closed the brief glimpse inside. "I didn't know," he said. "I suspected but... didn't know."

"You couldn't begin to understand what I've been through," I cried.

"No, I couldn't."

"So don't tell me I'm not who I should be! I haven't been that person since I was ten years old." His anger was waning. Mine was not. I hated him for hearing my story. I hated myself for not knowing what else to tell him but the truth. I hated that my tears were real.

I grabbed him—shaking, punching, and pummeling his chest. "You're such a fucking asshole, Cash! What more do you want from me?" I raised a hand to smack him across the face. He didn't block the hit. Didn't react when it landed. "All I've done is love you idiots!"

So far.

"Why isn't that enough?"

Cash didn't answer.

"Ugh." I fell on his chest, burrowing in his jacket, and hugging him tight. "Dammit, Killian, hug me back."

"Why?" He sounded genuinely curious.

"Because I'm crying."

There was a pause, and arms wrapped around me. He secured my waist—firm and immovable, and on my head he laid his hand, stroking my hair with more tenderness than I knew he possessed.

I blubbered into his shirt—wracked by the feelings these men had forced out of me and shocked they still existed to be found.

Twelve feet from us, screams erupted from the club. Girls ran out in their eight-inch heels, signaling the impending arrival of the police.

"Why don't you trust me?" I asked softly.

"Because with you... I can't see."

I nodded. "Okay. Let's go." I took his hand, leading him to Raul's car.

"Go where?"

"We have to settle this tonight," I said. "This is the last time you stalk me, Killian Hunt. The last time I have to prove I'm devoted to the Merchants. Get in the car, and you'll find out everything you need to know about me."

Cash pulled me up short—turning over his decision in the middle of the street while the sirens got closer.

"Fine."

Chapter Three

C*ash*

I openly watched her from the passenger seat. Adeline gave no sign she noticed my observation. She glided in and out of the lanes, turning up the express for Waterford.

Adeline Redgrave. Weaknesses confirmed. History of abuse confirmed. Everything else...

There was nothing suspicious in her notepad. She was right to be angry at my questioning her sincerity after we were late rescuing her from Angelo's men. We should've been there. We should've prevented her suffering under the hands of another monster.

A lot of things should be that aren't. I should have this twenty-three-year-old chef figured out from her favorite food to her taste in men. But I didn't.

She made a new meal every day. Not going to repeats that would indicate a favorite. When we packed her old room, the walls were devoid of pictures of her childhood. Signs pointed to an organized personality but not much else. As for her taste in men, Sinjin pegged her as his soul mate within twelve minutes of meeting the woman, but as was becoming an annoying habit, I couldn't see what it was about her that made Adeline the girl for us.

"Why are you staring at me?"

"Why don't you trust the cops?"

"What?" She took her eyes off the road to frown at me. "Where did you get that from?"

"You didn't go to them after Sinjin killed Spencer and we tried to kidnap you. The first time. You employed your expert dangle game to get to Ivan instead of reporting him to the cops. Why?"

She sighed. "You know why I didn't go to the cops after Raiden Spencer, and I had no proof of who killed the Maldonados. Not until Ivan confessed to me. I have the same healthy suspicion of the cops as any girl who grew up in rough neighborhoods and watched dealers pay them to look the other way. No more, no less."

"That's no excuse for going into that club alone tonight. No backup. Recovering from a knife wound. The deadliest thing you were packing was a pen." I flicked to the red marks on her neck. My lips peeled back. "I put you down as a lot of things but not reckless or stupid."

"You're right, I'm neither of those things. So, I obviously know how to take care of myself. I faced the Merchants and lived, didn't I?"

"You don't do this shit again. Or the next time will be the same. I'll shoot first and ask questions later."

"More like shoot and fuck first." Adeline held my hand in her lap, blowing my irritation into a blaze. I was seconds away from jumping out of the car, hunting Ivan's body down in the morgue, and killing him again. While she was relaxed and rubbing her middle finger over my knuckle, tightening my balls in my pants.

"You keep saying, rather rudely, that I dangle my pussy to get what I want, but the only time I've done that was tonight, and it wasn't for you. Didn't stop you from taking it, Killian. What was the lesson supposed to be?" she asked. "That my pussy belongs to you? Because I didn't realize you were interested."

"I'm not."

"There's a thong abandoned on a bathroom floor that says otherwise."

The car slowed down, drifting to a stop in front of a nondescript apartment.

"The lesson was don't play games with me, Redgrave."

She hummed. "We're here. Let's go."

Adeline got out and waited for me on the street side. She linked her arm through mine as I fell in beside her, leading me across to a lone food truck in the silent neighborhood. A red and orange eyesore with pictures of food next to the serving window and "Kiwicha" written in bold yellow letters on the bottom.

"Addy, is that you?" The man climbed out of his truck to hug her.

"Hey, Vasco. It's been too long."

Vasco was a tall, portly man sporting a short beard covered by a hairnet. "Where have you been?"

"I took a new job. Got into a new relationship." Adeline rested her head on my arm, earning me a smile from Vasco. "But that's no excuse for not coming to see you sooner. This is Cash."

We shook hands.

"You must be the new guy. What can I get you?" he asked over my denial.

"Two number threes, please," Adeline replied.

"Coming right up."

He climbed back on his truck, and soon the air was full of sizzling meat.

"Why are we here?"

"Dinner."

"I'm not eating anything from that tin can. One in six people contract a foodborne illness every year."

She laughed. "You ate my food after locking me in a cage. You're clearly more adventurous than you let on. Trust me."

There was that word.

"This will be the best Peruvian food you've ever tasted. It'll be worth it even if we spend the night with our heads in a toilet."

"This is you selling it?"

She bumped my hip, giggling. "Vasco, a cup of ice too, please."

Twenty minutes later, Vasco handed us a takeout bag, a cup of ice, and a kiss for Addy. He was old enough to be her father, so I let it go on for half a second before pulling her back.

"Thank you." Adeline made to leave.

"How much?" I asked him.

He waved my bills away. "Adeline gets whatever she asks for on the house. Enjoy."

Adeline beckoned me from the sidewalk. "Don't fall behind, toy boy."

"My only acceptable nickname is Cash."

She laughed again—a light, flirty sound like raindrops sprinkling the window. Impossible to ignore. "You're so serious all the time. I'm seeing you at Christmas wearing a Santa hat and frowning it up Grinch-style while your nieces and nephews hang ornaments off your ears."

"Now who's stalking who?"

She gasped. "Killian Hunt, was that a joke?"

"Was it?"

Shaking her head, Adeline rounded a building and took off down the alley. A single door lay tucked behind a dumpster. Adeline reached for it but I was there first, opening it to allow her through. We stepped inside a dark, concrete stairwell.

"Why does that guy give you free food?"

"Vasco used to park his truck on my street. I warned him about staying open at night, but he said he'd be fine. He didn't keep much money on hand and there was little for anyone to steal. Vasco didn't understand that not much is still plenty to some people.

"One night, he was robbed at gunpoint. The guy took the money and then proceeded to kick his face in. I heard him screaming and came running. Hit the guy over the head with a sauté pan and pepper-sprayed the crap out of him. After, I told Vasco to come here. It looks chill right now, but this street is full of university students that don't know a spatula from their asshole. He's their got-to food truck with no competition. As you can tell, he's grateful."

"So, that's your thing," I said to her ass. Wasn't my fault it was eye level as I trailed her up the stairs. "You believe you're some caped crusader. Maybe you think the Merchants are too."

"That's not it," she replied, a faint trace of anger beneath her words. "I'm not on some crusade for justice. I don't step in because I don't believe the police can do their job. This is just who I am. If the nice man who gives me extra servings of steak strips is screaming for help, I don't keep walking.

"The homeless man outside of my apartment wants a homecooked meal, I give it to him. A drunk girl is fed drinks at a party, I help her to the bathroom. Make sure she's safe. I've only ever done what I thought was right, Cash. I've had five lifetimes' worth of people who do terrible things just because they can. Why is it strange that I do the right thing because I can?"

"Because people aren't that good, Adeline." The low reply resounded oddly in the close space. "Take it from the man who sees everything."

We fell silent, walking up the final five flights without sharing words or glances. Our trek ended at a door labeled "Roof Entrance."

"This is my favorite spot in the entire city," she said. "Sunsets at Mercy Park and rowing on the canal during the cherry blossom festival are contenders, but this remains the most beautiful sight in Cinco."

She swept open the door, and I nearly trod on the mouse scuddling to a hole in the plaster. I looked around at the slightly dirty, unimpressive space. Rainwater collected in little brown puddles scattered about the roof. An attempt was made to brighten the place with a row of potted plants. All were dying.

"Is this a joke? Because I suggest you're the one who's no good at them."

"Over here," she said, laughing.

Adeline ducked around the entrance to a raised deck. Two chairs and a small table sat on top.

I stepped up, and a low whistle slipped out unbidden.

All of Cinco City lay before us. Millions of flickering, still, and racing lights. The skyscrapers of Leighbridge. Trapp Tower. Ellington Conservatory. Cinco in a snapshot was right here—living and pulsing beneath us.

"You could almost believe we're like any other city. Beautiful, rich, and flawed."

I nodded.

"Sit," she said. "I'm starving."

I sat down, more contented to enjoy the view than I'd let her know.

She set out the food. Dumping out the ice, she wrapped it in the plastic and plopped down on my lap.

"What are you doing? Get off."

She gave me a look. "You just hate fucked me on a bathroom counter. You can handle me sitting on your lap. Give me your hand."

"Why?"

Adeline draped her legs over the arm of the chair and rested my hand on top of her knee. It was bruised and bleeding. I hadn't noticed my fight with the car window left us both battered.

She held the ice on my knuckles. "Put the food on my stomach. We'll have to feed each other."

"Get off."

"I refer you again to the hate fucking," she said, amused. "Stop being so grumpy. It doesn't work now that I know you want me."

Adeline wriggled on my lap reaching to get the food herself. My cock twitched a hello.

"You'll be extremely disappointed when you find out how untrue that is," I said in spite of the traitor.

"*Extremely* disappointed? Because you're a great catch?"

"Yes."

"Mmm. Then, I better try harder to melt the ice around your heart."

"You assume there is a heart inside."

"I know there is," she said. "I've seen it."

"What is this?" I asked, steering the conversation away.

"Lomo saltado. It's a stir-fry with beef, onions, rice, fries, and tomatoes." She stabbed a strip and pressed it to my lips. "If this is not the best thing you've ever eaten in your life, I will pay back every cent of my generous salary."

I wasn't a betting man like Sinjin, but not even I could turn down those terms. I accepted the bite, chewing the tender, marinated beef that exploded a different burst of flavor on its way down.

"It's pretty good," I said grudgingly.

"Knew you'd love it."

Slipping out from the ice, I took the tray from her.

"Cash, I don't mind."

"You can save that perching-on-a-chair-and-feeding-me-grapes crap for Sinjin. He'll love that shit. I can feed myself."

"At least let me hold it, so you can rest your hand."

"Feeling bad you made me break it?"

"No, I did nothing wrong." She let me be, taking her own food in hand. "You should feel bad for not trusting and accusing me of cheating." Adeline let her head fall back on the arm. "It's past time we did this. Me and you. Sitting down and getting to know each other. So, I'll make you a deal. Give and take. I'll tell you something about me as long as you reciprocate. If you stop sharing, so do I. Agreed?"

I inclined my head.

"Equal value or higher," she said. "Don't tell me about the day you lost Teddy at the fair after I share a traumatizing, soul-crushing secret."

"Losing Teddy was soul-crushing."

She laughed—eyes shining, round nose wrinkling, hair falling across her cheek. I decided I liked the sound, even if I wasn't sure about the girl it came from.

"Well, I'll go first. My name was supposed to be Madeline. The 'M' was forgotten in my mother's drugged stupor."

The fork paused halfway to my mouth.

"Imagine going your whole life with a name you shouldn't have, and knowing the reason why."

Adeline didn't sound angry. Though she lived with the knowledge long enough that she either accepted, or learned to mask it.

"Your turn, Cash. Equal or higher value."

I turned my response over, deciding between truth or lie.

"My name is Killian Hunt." I forced it out. "Killian Alfred Hunt."

"Alfred." Adeline grinned around her meat. "Really?"

"Like I'd lie about that."

"Why Alfred?"

"My mother is another woman who can't be understood."

She seemed to find that hilarious. "Why Killian?"

"My father grew up in Ireland. His childhood best friend was named Killian."

"That's sweet," she said. "Answer accepted. My turn. The weirdest place I've had sex was actually not a torture dungeon—"

"What the hell are you doing?"

The smile she flashed me could only be described as wicked. "Equal value, Cash. I get to hear about your sexual escapades after this."

"I knew I would regret this. Just didn't know it'd be this soon."

"Hey. You wanted a peek through the curtains. Get to know the real Adeline Redgrave. Buckle up, this is going to be a long night."

I gestured for her to go on.

"The weirdest place I've had sex was a porta potty at a music festival. Yes, it was as gross as you're imagining. Yes, I have regrets. I'd take the torture rack over that any day.

"Your turn."

"My first kill was Ruben 'Deathrow' Johnston. He took exception to Sinjin cleaning him out at the cards table and followed us into the alley. I regret nothing." I smirked into her eyes. "Higher value, Redgrave. Murder tops a go in a shit box."

"I knew you'd make this difficult. Just didn't know it'd be this soon."

I cracked a smile. It was gone as quickly as it appeared. But I knew she saw it, and suddenly I wanted her off my lap. Off this roof. And speeding off in my car with her in my rearview. Nothing good would come of this.

Adeline stroked my jaw. "Killian?"

Nothing.

"Don't do that," she whispered. "Stay with me."

I may not see the full picture of her, but I don't think she has that problem. With any of us. She never did.

"I don't know what you're talking about." My voice was flat. "Your turn."

Her next answer came slow. "I learned to cook... because I had no choice. Sometimes my mom disappeared. Days or weeks at a time. I had to learn to make the little left in the house, or starve," she rasped. "I try to see it as something good coming from the bad. Cooking gave me a future when I thought I had none."

"Is that why you're working at Salvatore's again?"

"Working at—? Oh." She shook her head. "I forgot you hitched a ride with me today. I'm not getting my old job back. I went to ask Ryan if he'd consider letting me work with him on catering jobs. He made me do a shift to prove I was still up to scratch."

"Why would you want to do that? Are we not paying you enough? Or do we need to give you more to do?"

A smile played at her lips. "Cash, I have a dad, mentor, male friends, and, at the rate we're going with the unprotected sex, I'll have a son. You have to learn to share me with other men."

My always working, running, calculating, planning mind ground to a halt.

"You're on the pill, right?"

"Ah. Now he asks," she teased. "How do you feel about Alfred Jr.? Little A.J."

I set my food down. Appetite gone.

Adeline seized the chance to rest my hand on her chest, cradling the melting ice on my bruises. I moved my hand down her stomach.

"I'm good with A.J.," I announced. "We'll need an heir to take over one day. Might as well start cooking the kid now."

Her lips parted. "Do you really—?"

I crooked a brow.

"Ah, Cash," she cried. "Stop messing with me."

I laughed out loud.

"You don't fool me. You'll be the one spending all night comparing crib safety ratings, and trading your gun holster for a baby carrier. If I can't tame you, little A.J. will."

The night carried on in the same strange vein of serious revelations glanced across the surface. Honesty with our eyes closed, backs up, and shields on. But honesty nonetheless.

Adeline told me of the day her father found her and she was rescued from her mother.

"I hadn't been able to speak a word of what was happening to me. To my teachers or my friends. Then one day, Dad was there. Standing outside my school like he used to. And I just knew that he would never let me go again."

I shared my life as the son of carnival ringmasters. Youngest of five siblings and a Sinjin.

"He was wild when we found him. Sounds like we picked up a feral cat, but it's not far off. He was put in a foster home after his father was killed, but something in him had already broken. His foster dad tried smacking him around, and Sinjin took a bat to him. Cracked his skull. Blinded him in one eye, and then took off running.

"He lived on the street for a few months till he ended up at the fairgrounds to pick our customers clean. The folks took him in and said I had to look after him. I wasn't that interested in Sinjin. He felt differently.

"Sinjin said, did, and took what he wanted without thought to consequences to himself or anyone else. My cool reservation sparked a challenge in him. It became his mission to crack my shell. Sinjin harassed, goaded, and messed me up every chance he got. One morning, he tripped me coming down the bleachers and busted my lip. I broke his nose and gave him a split lip to match. Our fight had to be broken up by four workers. Sinjin grinned through the blood and said, 'now we're brothers.'"

On and on we went until she was hoarse, and night bled into day. Adeline fell asleep on my chest, tucked in the coat she wrapped around herself, breathing softly on the spot she laid her cheek. And the sight to see became her.

I forgot about the view hours ago. For that must have been how long I traced the dips and curves of her face. Counted her lashes. Drifted to the tiny freckle hiding beneath her ear.

Adeline Redgrave. Beautiful. Smart. Determined. As bold and unpredictable as Sinjin. As strong and quietly burning as Brutal. Flirty and in command of her sexuality like Mercer.

Cold and calculating like me.

It was obvious to me now why she was made for all of us. She was our match. Our mirror. Our equal.

Our kryptonite.

Adeline was fashioned for our destruction, and if every statistical probability I ran wasn't turning up zero that she orchestrated our first meeting in that penthouse, I'd think she planned to find and destroy us from the start.

Everything about tonight was perfect. Taking me to a place that meant something to her. Constant skin contact. Caring for my wound. Making me laugh. Sharing stories and traumas from her childhood. Worse that I sensed what she told me was true. Worse that my responses were honest too.

If I was any other man, I'd have ended this night madly in love with her. The bleeding box carrying my still beating heart would be secure in her grasp.

I wouldn't have had another choice. That was how the con worked.

These were old cons. Among the most lethal. It was the single truth in the universe that once you had someone's love, you could get them to do anything. Steal, kill, give up everything they own.

Love was the con woman's greatest tool, and the methods our dear Adeline employed were designed to give her just that. I knew, because these were methods I had used myself.

I held her to me, gazing out at the rising sun.

Adeline Redgrave is dangerous, and I trust her even less than when I stepped on this roof.

My phone chimed in the folds of my coat.

Fishing it out, I was careful not to wake her.

Sinjin: Bodies found in the canal. The Kings know.

I shut off the cell.

It begins.

ADELINE

Cash and I stared at the empty space in silence.

"Well," I drew out. "You did leave an expensive car in front of a known club for a band of car thieves. Even had the busted window saying come on in. It was bound to get stolen."

His withering glare communicated how he felt about my logic. "I can't fucking believe this. These Blood Brothers have a knack for stealing from the wrong person that borders on a death wish."

"You're telling me," I mumbled.

He yanked out his phone, fingers flying across the screen.

"What are you doing?"

"Getting my car back. Give me your keys."

I handed them over, then grabbed his hand as he took off across the street. He didn't shake me off. On the contrary, he led me to the passenger side, put me in, and slammed my door shut. Cash slid in the other side and gunned the engine.

"How are you going to get it back?"

He showed me his phone. "GPS."

I narrowed on the flashing blue dot. "Can you track my car too?"

"Of course."

"Did you?"

"Whenever you left the house."

"It's you I can't believe, Cash. Just like I can't believe I'm not surprised. Promise me your stalking days are over."

"I promise."

"Are you lying?"

"Would I admit I was?"

"Maybe. If it would piss me off."

He chuckled. "I won't need to stalk you, Redgrave. Angelo's body has been fished out. Things are going to move very quickly from this point. Sinjin has ended your reprieve. You're coming back with me today."

They found Angelo's body. How long until the new leader of the Kings stakes their flag? Cash is right. Things will move quickly.

I itched to text Gianna. Ask her about the progress on acquiring funds. Tell her my own mission failed.

"You took the note from Ivan's body."

I caught his frown at my subject change. "No choice. It would've ended up in police lockup as prime evidence."

"Agreed. But this means the Blood Brothers don't know the real reason Ivan was killed. They can't carry on terrorizing Rockchapel like they have."

"The Merchants terrorize all of Cinco City. Why should we police other gangs when we're the worst of them all?"

"Even Sinjin has lines he doesn't cross. He enjoys killing but not for killing's sake. He wouldn't murder an old couple for a handful of trinkets."

"It's unwise to trick yourself into believing Sinjin has a sense of right and wrong. Don't turn us into men we're not, Redgrave." His tone was harsh. "You'll only be disappointed."

"I know the kind of men you are. So does Kaylee."

His knuckles whitened on the wheel.

"Look, I'm not saying you have to do this with me. I don't remember inviting you to in the first place. I'm just making it clear that if they don't stop, I will do something about it."

"Put the cape away, Super Chef. Ivan's dead. For all you know, the new regime will return to the old ways."

"They better." I let that be the end of it. "So, did we get that place in Waterford?"

He nodded. "The guys are setting it up now."

"It'll be nice to be back home. Nicer if I knew how extensive our lockdown will be. Are we lying low?"

"Yes. We can't move until we know who will become the new leader. Each potential candidate requires a different plan."

"Why?"

"They run different parts of the business. Have differing strengths, weaknesses, right hands, etc. One won't react the same as the others against a strike. Jace Parker is sixty percent more likely to kick off a full assault against the Merchants. Sending out men to hunt us down in the streets instead of Angelo's method of putting bounties on our heads. We'll need more weapons and more men if Jace takes over."

Yes, exactly right. I chose well aligning myself to the Merchants. Cash understands what needs to be done.

"We also need more men and more guns right now," I said. "You're driving us straight at that blue dot without all the things you got pissed at me about. That car is most likely in a chop shop surrounded by BBs."

We drove deeper into my old neighborhood, and Blood Brother territory.

"I don't need backup."

"You can't go in there alone. Which makes me your backup."

"No. I'll be in and out in ten minutes. Watching your ass will slow me down."

"I should think so."

He snagged the hand inching toward his lap and put it back on mine. "Flirting has little effect on me."

"So, it's only jealousy that works? That could get dangerous for both of us."

"Yes, it fucking would," he growled.

I cocked my head. "Is that why you're so grouchy about me, Sinjin, and Brutal? Saying I dangle and walking out when I'm with them?"

"Grouchy? What am I? A five-year-old throwing a tantrum because my cookie went down a grate? I had a problem with the guys getting close to you because there was something off about you."

"But now you trust me?"

"Yes."

"And you're willing to share me with the guys?" I asked, smile breaking out.

"We're not together."

"Not yet, but as a young Saint proved, you only shed the mask for those worthy of seeing beneath it. That's me."

"I'm willing to hate fuck you when the mood strikes me. Close enough?"

"Ugh." My treacherous lower belly heated at the thought. "You don't make it easy, do you?"

"What about last night gave you the impression I ever have?"

I rested my head on the window. I got many impressions of the stoic Killian Hunt last night. That he would make it easy to steal his heart was not one of them.

I was given his name and those of his siblings. Tales of his job caring for the animals of the circus. The places he's been. The reason why Cinco was best of them all.

But I wasn't given the story of how a promising young med student became a feared gang leader. He stood toe to toe with Sinjin since he entered his life. When and how did my wild love corrupt him? What does he stand to gain from getting his hands on that ledger?

"Did our game end when we stepped off the roof?"

The scenery was shifting. Red graffiti covered almost every building, sidewalk, dumpster, and sign.

"You want to ask me something," he said. "Ask."

"What's in this for you, Cash? Why do you want Kieran? The ledger?"

"We told you that already."

"You didn't tell me much of anything," I admitted. "Kieran is a shadow kingpin running the city, and no one can pretend to be the real power in Cinco while he has that ledger. I get that. I also understand why this is important to Saint, but not to you."

"Sinjin is my brother."

I relished him the same scrutiny he gave me the night before. "I doubt your motives are that simple."

"Ouch," he said mildly. "I am a cold bastard in your eyes."

"No. But you didn't veer your life off track to serve Saint's mission for vengeance. Even though you sympathized. Even if you agreed the person responsible should die. Sinjin's morality is whatever he decides it is, but I never got the impression you were the same. You hold standards of right and wrong, and your unbending sense of self wouldn't give in unless you had a reason. What is it, Cash? Does Kieran have something on you too?"

"Redgrave, I had an unexpectedly pleasant time with you last night, and after sampling a taste, I finally understand the lure of that pussy," he said, "but some things are just none of your damn business."

I bared my teeth, ripples of anger going up my spine. "You'll pay for that."

"I suspect so," he said with a chuckle.

"And I *will* find out what the rest of you are hiding from me," I snapped. "Once you find that ledger, I hope you're not imagining I won't take a look inside."

"Why are you imagining you'll be there when we find it?" Cash turned the corner at Lexington, narrowing in on the blue dot. "You've got an unbending sense of self and standards of right and wrong too." He looked me in the eye. "What's your reason for serving Saint's mission for vengeance?"

Walked right into that, didn't you, Adeline?

"I love Saint," I stated. "I can't be without Brutal. My feelings for Mercer are growing, and I want you. Most days. I tried walking away from you guys once, and I didn't get far. But you knew that was the answer. Stop fishing for some deep secret, Cash. You wouldn't have hired me if you hadn't picked through every inch of my life. You didn't find anything because there's nothing to find."

"You're right, I did pick through your life. A history of fighting to get the future you want and letting nothing, and no one, stand in your way. You never let a boyfriend knock you off course before, why now?" He blinked big eyes at me. "Or are we just *special*?"

"You'll pay for that too."

He barked a laugh.

"Maybe I like it, Cash." My glance drifted to the window. "Vengeance. Maybe Saint wasn't the only reason I was wet the night I beat that child-selling demon into a mass of vomit and tears. Maybe I like having power. Causing fear instead of knowing it. Never being helpless, or trapped, or used again." I met his gaze, and Bunny/Serenity/my other half looked through. "Did you ever think Sinjin chose me because he's known my secret from the beginning?"

Cash said nothing. I couldn't read his expression, but my own reflected in his eyes. He was first to look away.

"We're here." Rolling to a stop, Cash jerked his chin to a garage on the other side of the street. Men in greasy coveralls walked in and out of our sight—laughing back and forth with each other and bobbing their heads to the music blasting out of the shop.

Leviathan Auto Shop screamed its name on the sign, doors, and likely the patches on their clothes. They gave every appearance of regular guys on the job. If it wasn't for the red bandanas hanging off their hips, and Cash's car sitting plain in the middle of the garage.

"I thought they'd have taken it apart by now," I said. "One of the brothers must have taken a liking to it."

"Go back to Cross's place. I'll meet you there in an hour."

I caught the keys he tossed at me. "You can't go in there alone. You need help."

"No."

"You're going to get yourself shot to prove how macho you are!" I shouted as he climbed out.

I considered going in after him anyway. The only thing that stayed me was the fact Cash wasn't Sinjin. My blue-haired love would walk into certain death whistling and flipping a knife on his palm. Cash was the other side of his coin. Order versus chaos. Plans in place of unpredictability. He wouldn't walk in there unless he knew the odds of walking out were in his favor.

I climbed into the driver's seat, stalking his approach. *What the hell is he going to do? There are about a dozen guys in there.*

Cash strode directly into the shop. He wasn't noticed at first—covered by the noise and commotion. Then one guy lifted his head from beneath a hood.

He ran to Cash, putting a hand up to stop him. Cash sidestepped him and walked up to his car.

The scene pulled me from my seat, drawing me to the driver-side mirror.

Cash's new friend followed him, waving his hands. He pulled up short of his hood and paused to chat the man up. Killian pointed to his car a few times, and swept out his hand to encompass the whole garage.

Whatever he was saying had to be funny. The mechanic doubled over clutching his stomach. Straightening, he waved his bandana in Cash's face.

I inched for the glove box without looking away. Raul was bound to have some kind of weapon in there, and frustrating as Killian Hunt was, I would not watch him die.

The guy grabbed Killian's collar and two things happened at once. The music shut off, and Killian snatched up a wrench.

The banger's head snapped all the way around. Blood spurted from his ruined mouth clear from across the street. Shouts broke the brief silence.

One man rushed Killian, scrambling in his coveralls to pull a weapon. Killian flung the wrench and nailed him. He dropped on a tool cart. Both crashed to the floor.

That's when the shooting started.

Cash dove in his car. Bullets pinged off the door and hood. They ricocheted off tires and hydraulic beams to shower the garage in sparks.

His engine revved—headlights lamping the men in his path and more converging on him. Killian hit the gas, plowing them over, and through the chaos I saw him stick his hand out the window and an object go flying.

I could do nothing but sit, jaw hanging, as he rolled over three men, tore out of the garage, and sped off down Clark Street—roaring gangbangers spraying his tail and racing for their cars. They peeled after him, kicking off the high-speed chase.

Shaking my head, I stuck my key in the ignition and turned.

Boom!

My scream barely pierced the noise. Debris showered the hood, bits of car parts and those who didn't get clear in time.

Ears ringing, I stared in disbelief at the smoldering wreck of Leviathan Auto Shop.

As the girl with all the secrets, how did this man keep surprising me?

"WHAT HAPPENED TO YOU last night?" Gianna wiggled between me and the couch. She laid her cheek on my forehead. "You had me up all night worrying."

"Raul had you up all night."

"Yeah, him too."

I blew out a breath. "I got a surprise visit from Cash. He followed me, G. Been following me for days."

"What the fuck?" she cried. "What did he see?"

"Nothing I couldn't explain away. Except for me in the women's bathroom with Ivan between my legs, sucking on my throat."

"Shit."

"Summed it up exactly."

"What did he do?"

"Have you heard the expression 'fucked my brains out'?"

She snorted. "Think I know that one."

"Still doesn't come close," I said. "I was lucky, G. He didn't catch me dosing the guy with eye drops, or find out that I went there to kill him. I had to admit I was carrying out a vendetta though. I had to admit a lot of things."

"How bad is it? Should we be worried? Do we have to call it off?"

"Can't. Angelo's body was dredged up and my love has summoned me to his side. Cash is taking me back today."

"To their cage for all you know."

I shook my head. "We're past that now."

"Seriously, Adeline. Did he buy your explanation? He could follow me just as easily as he followed you. And he'd catch me doing a lot worse. I sent out the ransom demands yesterday."

"He says he trusts me now, but I've never known what that man is thinking." Blazing infernos flashed through my mind. "All I can say is last night was real. From the jealousy to his laughter and stories on the roof. I wouldn't have gotten so much as his favorite color if he didn't feel something for me. I've got to work with that until I crack his shell. In the meantime, I'll keep an eye on him."

A knock sounded on the door.

"Or he'll be keeping an eye on you."

There wasn't a reply for that. Mostly because the door swung open and Cash strolled inside.

"Oh, hello," Gianna mocked. "Come on in."

"The door was open."

"No, it wasn't."

"Check again." Cash slid to me. "Let's go, Redgrave."

Gianna's clock read 9:34 a.m. One hour he said he'd come for me. He beat it by two minutes.

"Shook off your tail," I remarked. "How did you lose them?"

He waited me out.

Heaving a sigh, I kissed Gianna's cheek and said goodbye. "Thanks for letting me stay. I'm going to visit Dad this weekend. I'll pop by with leftovers afterward."

"See ya, babe."

I sidled up to Cash, dropping my voice. "I can't believe you blew them up," I murmured. "Are you always packing bombs? Do you have one in your shorts?"

"You know what's in my shorts."

Surprise flicked on with the fire in my belly. *And he says he doesn't flirt.*

"I should check again. For everyone's safety."

Amusement lit his grin. "You were right about the Blood Brothers. Empty-headed morons. They only searched the usual places for a tracker, and didn't catch the spare bomb I keep under the passenger seat. We don't need fools like that running the streets. They give us all a bad name."

"We will mark this as a grand day in history. The day Killian Hunt agreed with me."

He grunted.

"Alright, toy boy." I tucked myself inside his jacket. "Take me home."

He spun me out and stalked off, leaving me laughing in his wake.

"I told you that doesn't work now that I know you want me." I skipped after him. Draping his arm around my shoulder, I cupped his hand over my breast. "You don't have to play this hard to get."

"In the car, Dangle."

"I like Sinjin's nickname for me better."

"Sinjin likes you better."

"You like me too. If only someone had been there to take a picture of the big, bad Cash holding me in his arms all night as I slept." I licked his jaw.

The world spun. Suddenly, my back was against a palm tree and my thighs clamped in his iron grip. Cash's lips skated over mine, trapping my breath in my lungs.

"I'd fuck you right here, Redgrave," he whispered. "Spread that pussy. Torture your clit till you scream loud enough to wake the neighborhood, and draw them all out of their homes to watch me pound you into the dirt."

"Promise?"

Chuckling, he nuzzled my nose, slipping away as I tried to capture his lips. "Dangle isn't a term of disrespect. Just the opposite. Never in our entire lives, has a woman turned Sinjin on his head. You had him dancing your tune, while the whole time, he thought you were dancing to his.

"Brutal's snapped necks for less than the shit you've put him through. And Mercer sees people as little more than toys. Sex toys. All exist to amuse or delight him. Those that don't might as well be shop mannequins for all the attention he pays them. But not you. He notices you, Adeline Redgrave.

"I have to admit a grudging admiration for the way you used your strengths against our weaknesses. Dangling not just sex, but everything we didn't expect to find in our future queen. Our equal."

"You say the sweetest things to me, Cash." I reared and finally got him, crashing our mouths together.

Killian plunged in unreservedly.

Glancing at him from the kitchen while Cash sat on the couch typing away, I'd wondered what his lips tasted like. If they were as smooth as they looked. Would I melt high on blackcurrants and bergamot?

Yes.

He was sweeter. His lips softer. My resolve to not fall harder than I had—was dust.

Our tongues tangled, battling raw, naked lust I hadn't let myself hope I'd get so soon again. I clamped my legs and arms around him. He wasn't going anywhere till I had my fill.

Cash scraped my lips between his teeth, drawing a moan out of me. I let my hands play free in his hair like at any minute they would get in trouble. Running the silky strands beneath my palms. Holding him close as I kissed his lips and then everywhere, peppering his cheeks, nose, forehead, and eyelids as he laughed.

"I respect you, Adeline," he said huskily. "Too much to let you play this game with me. My *heart* won't be in it."

I knew what he was saying to me. Killian would never love me.

Sex. Respect. Standing toe to toe with him as an equal. None of it would be enough.

"That's where you're wrong," I said against his lips. "You forget... I know your weaknesses too."

"I THINK I WILL TURN this into a little café." I hopped on the counter, kicking my feet between the old stools.

Far be it for me to give Cash a compliment when he's being a stubborn ass, but he nailed it with Merchant Base Number Two. The upstairs kitchen had a double oven and my dream bamboo countertops. My room was smaller, but next to Sinjin's and linked by a shared bathroom. The boys had moved my stuff in for me.

Cash and Brutal took the third floor. Mercer was on the second with us. The weapons were in their new basement home, and the first floor would be mine.

"It'll be cute with a little paint job," I said. "Clean off the dust. Replace the faded wallpaper. Get rid of these chairs. All in all, it won't be too big a job."

Mercer sat between my legs, leaning his head back on my lap. Brutal reclined in a booth across from Sinjin—whose legs were up on the table as he carved something into the wood with his knife.

I ran hands through Mercer's hair and then down his chest, massaging his pecs. "Bakery?" he suggested.

"Those sweet little cupcakes and muffins look simple to make, but I'd have to wake early every morning to prep and bake them fresh. I'm thinking soups and salads. Omelets in the morning, and roast beef sandwiches for lunch. We can do an eat-it-till-it's-sold-out type thing. Once I run out of stock, we close for the rest of the day."

"That's a nice dream you're spinning, Redgrave," Cash said. "But it's not happening."

"I'll wait until we can afford it."

"For there to be a 'we' concerning our money, you'd have to mask up and join the crew." He leaned on a booth, head tilted, brows raised. "Ready to pack heat and go full banger? Or is the little lady staying home while we steal the bacon?"

I stuck my tongue out at him.

"Mature."

"What if I say yes?"

"There's a bank I'm eyeing in Harlow. Those require a lot of shouting and waving guns in people's faces to get those vaults opened up quick. See you there?"

"No, thank you," I said—light and prim. "The little lady will stay home."

Sinjin crossed the room and popped my legs over Mercer's head. I yelped as I found myself flat on the countertop with Sinjin on top of me.

"We may need our bunny to set the trap again. Besides, despite my preference you remain unclothed at all times, you look damn good in our masks."

"Those were special circumstances."

Sinjin pressed his nose to my hair, inhaling me. He was like an animal getting reacquainted with his mate. Which meant the next step was me unclothed.

"I had to free those kids," I said. "But I'm still a cook, Sinjin. As much as I want to help you take down the Kings, I don't have your particular skill sets."

"Held your own just fine in Corbin's club and at the Castian." Cash's smooth voice broke in. "You picked up the education somewhere."

The skin around my eyes tightened. Cash would not let this go. Reason enough to keep him from getting another inside look into just how varied my skills were.

"Thought I was a wild card," I jabbed.

Sinjin was tugging my dress over my bare hips.

"Sometimes a wild is the only way to win."

"Why aren't you wearing underwear, Bunny?"

The soft question snatched my comeback. I thought fast. "Because I—"

"I screwed her in a bathroom next to the body of the man I found her making out with," Cash dropped without a lick of hesitation. "It got left behind."

Sinjin's voice was a low, dangerous hiss. "Run that by me again."

"I wasn't— Killian, tell him—" Cash strode upstairs. "Dammit, Cash!"

I was able to continue shouting threats at his back. Sinjin carried me up-stairs, slung over his shoulder. We split on the second-floor landing, and I tried telling him what really happened.

Saint brought me to his room, slamming the door on my explanations.

Two hours later, my ass was raw and stinging. Ragged breaths wracked my body, lifting and dropping Sinjin's head resting on my back. A nice little bump decorated my forehead. Where his pounding smashed my head against my cuffed hands.

"This changes things considerably, Bunny."

Sweat and various other body fluids soaked my skin. Sinjin drew lines in the cum on my backside.

"I didn't cheat on you. You believe me, don't you, baby?" I curled my legs, stroking him with my toes. Sinjin kissed them.

"Of course. You belong to me. You know that."

I did. Deep down in both halves of my soul. I was his. He was mine.

"But if you can go out and be the masked avenger for the Maldonados, you can do it for me too."

"What does that mean?" I asked, though I knew.

"You said you'd be my bride. Perch on my throne. So, that's where you'll be, next to us on every job. You'll wield your club on the next man to cross you. And the one after that. My bunny will stand at my side as we watch the Kings burn."

"We talked about this," I said. "There's a reason I was off to the side or behind you when we went after the Kings. I can barely fire a gun."

I bit my lip to hold in a laugh. Granted I wasn't the expert shot Gianna was, but if I missed, it was because I meant to.

"Anything you need to learn, your Saint will teach you." He rubbed his cheek on mine, snaking an arm around my neck. "How to shoot. How to stalk." The knife tip pressed to my throat. "How to kill."

I tipped my chin, gazing into those swirling gray pools. "What if I say no?" My lips barely moved.

"I'm hoping you will."

Laughing softly, I whispered, "Say it."

"I love you."

Bound to his bed. Knife to my throat. Subject to his mercy. And immeasurable satisfaction warmed the farthest corners of my being.

You'll never know just how perfect we are for each other. Well, you will, but by then it will be too late.

Letting Sinjin and the Merchants teach me how to kill could be good for us. You're supposed to indulge shared interests in a relationship. But then again, I was never the type to dumb myself down for a guy. How was I supposed to pretend to be bad at it?

The thought of that made me snort.

"What's funny?" Sinjin set the knife on the nightstand.

"I was just thinking that this isn't about my promises. It's foreplay." I bit his lip, then kissed it in apology. "You enjoy corrupting your sweet, innocent bunny."

"So very, very much."

I sobered. "I'm not going to shove guns in innocent people's faces. But taking down the Kings... yeah, I'll mask up for that."

Sinjin thought it over. "I accept your terms. It's better security cameras don't pick up we have a woman in our crew. We'll keep you our secret weapon."

"Subterfuge." *I'm good at that.*

Someone knocked.

"Come," Sinjin called.

Mercer walked inside to the full view of us naked on crumpled sheets and me cuffed to the bed.

"What?" Sinjin dropped kisses on the ridges of my spine.

"Jace Parker is dead."

My ears pricked up.

"How?"

"He made a move on Xavier Jameson. Less than twelve hours after they found Angelo," he said. "He and his guys broke into his office and tried to kill him. Jameson must've been expecting it because he had three times his normal security in the building. Jameson is in the hospital, and the others were taken out."

Wow. Cash said things would move quickly. Is that man ever wrong?

"How'd you find out?" Sinjin asked.

"I asked a few friends close to them to keep me informed."

"Three down. The others will know why Jace is dead." Sinjin spread my legs. "About now is the time they're asking themselves who to turn to get to the others, and who around them will be gotten to."

"Your money still on Enzo?"

I didn't see his nod, but I assumed he did. *Interesting that Sinjin assumes it will be Enzo too.*

Mercer smiled at me. "Hello, love."

"He— Ah." Sinjin's tongue swirled around my clit. "Hi."

"Would you like me to cover you? Protect your modesty?"

I cracked a smile. "Doesn't bother me if it doesn't bother you. And I'm betting nakedness doesn't bother you."

"Safe bet." Mercer openly feasted on my body. His tongue darted out, licking his lips like I imagined he wanted to lick mine. "Looks like you both settled this issue of the man in the bathroom."

"Misunderstanding," I gasped. Sinjin brought two fingers to the party. "Cash was being Cash."

"Good. Brutal wanted to know."

"Brutal? Tell you that, did he?"

"He has many ways of getting his point across. Beating the shit out of his training dummy being one."

"Did you want to know too?"

He shrugged. "Merely curious if we'd have to break in a new cook." Mercer backed out of the room. "Handcuffs, spankings, and an audience. That I did want to know. I'll remember this when our time comes."

"When will that be?" I called.

A soft click was his reply.

THE NEXT FEW DAYS I spent cooking, screwing, and covering my amusement as Saint taught me how to hold and handle his first love: knives.

Saturday morning, I finished off my bowl of baked apple oatmeal and returned to my scones. That was my boys' breakfast with a plate of corned beef hash.

I carefully cut and shaped the dough, transferring them to the baking sheet. I only baked for them when they were good—which they never were—but that day I was in a good mood, so they got a pass. I was finally going to see my dad.

While the scones baked, I checked on lunch for the fiftieth time, making sure I wasn't forgetting anything. Visits to Dad meant lunch for us, and extra bowls for flaring nostrils and licking lips that slinked into the dining room as I warmed up our food.

Mr. Finch would want a game of cards. Mrs. Mooney would try to sneak a cookie, so I'd have to bring the sugar free.

My phone rang.

"Hey, G," I answered. "Yes, I'm still coming over today. I'm bringing shrimp gumbo with rice."

"Damn, girl. I keep telling you we should give it a go."

I cracked up. "Why let sex complicate our relationship when I'll feed you either way?"

"Good point," she said. "When you do come over, I'll show you my new shoes. Amazon delivered them today."

"Great." We were back to code words, but this one wasn't too hard to figure out. "I can't wait to see them. How much were they?"

"Two hundred."

Two hundred with three zeros tacked on the end.

I couldn't resist a squeal. "You and I might give it a go because that's got to be the sexiest thing you ever said to me. Any more shoes on the way?"

"Two pairs scheduled for this week."

We talked a little longer, and then hung up to save the rest of the conversation for when we could speak freely.

I let the scones cool on the rack, and got to work on the hash. My mind spun with possibilities for that money. High on my list was taking a page out of Cash's book and setting up safe houses all over the city. Somewhere equipped if Gianna or my dad were ever threatened again.

We'll figure it out when the money's in and counted.

I filled a bowl with hash, popped a scone on a separate plate, and carried it to the third floor.

The new place was opposite the fire station in almost every way. A wide, open floor compared to this maze of rooms. White walls stretching high to the rafters. Dark wallpaper covering the top half and wooden paneling covering the bottom.

They managed to haul most of our furniture from the fire station. Familiarity struck me in Cash's favorite couch and the cross over Saint's bed.

I pushed into Brutal's room.

Everything about this space was familiar. He transplanted his room from one place to the next. Queen-size bed tucked into a corner. Sheets tucked tighter. His bookshelf was on the wall directly opposite. Rows of books from nearly every genre slipped between nonfiction reads. They were organized by alphabet and then by color.

I asked him once if his seemingly random taste was actually due to choosing his books by their colored spines. He laughed, picked me up, and put me out of his room. A fair response since I sneaked in.

Like I was doing then.

I set his food on the coffee table next to his armchair. I liked Baris's room. The books, landscape paintings, and television on the dresser. He filled his silent world with creations that spoke to him.

The shower was going on the other side of the door. I stuck my head inside and watched his fuzzy shape lather through the frosted glass.

"Baris?"

He slid the glass open, uncaring of exposing himself.

He should care. The man needs to come with a warning.

The spray beat his chest, sliding greedy droplets over the bumps and ridges of his fit body. I caught him in the middle of washing his hair. Slicked back, it was the same wet and dry, barring the suds clinging to his strands.

"Want some company?"

He nodded.

I stripped and hopped in, yelping on contact.

"Wow, that's hot. Protect me." I twisted us around, putting him between me and the showerhead. He leaned over—hands propped on the tile and shielding me as I needed. My protector.

I shimmied up and down his chest. "Now that I've rubbed my dirty body on you, do you have to shower again?"

Chuckling, Baris handed me the bodywash.

"My plan worked," I said.

I squirted the foaming bodywash on my hands, and went to work, gliding over his hard, unyielding form. You didn't have to tell me Brutal was a fighter. Every part of him was honed to peak physical condition. His ass rock hard. His calves sculpted perfection. He was human-made, but divinely formed, and I took my time.

"Baris." I wrote his name in the suds, then mine beneath it. "I love your name. So unique. Mercer believes the name you're given says nothing about you, but Baris was meant for you."

This was the part where people launched into their history. Why their parents chose their name. If they did or didn't like it. If they agreed with Mercer. What they watched on television the other night. What they're doing today.

Chatter. Chatter. Chatter.

We say so much we don't need to say, filling the air with noise to beat back the oppressive silence where our fears lived. The quiet place where our past came to haunt us. Where I looked deep inside of myself and wondered about the person I became, and who I could've been. Where I searched for regrets, and found none.

I couldn't say what lived in Brutal's silence. Did he play court to his demons because he was home among them, or was he their captive?

All I knew is it's where we met every day. In the secrets we shared. The jokes that were ours alone. The quick smiles and full-blown laughs. We said everything we needed to say to each other without speaking.

Brutal turned me around. He dripped shampoo on my hair, and curled my hand around his cock.

Yes, the man had no problem getting his point across.

We stayed in the shower for longer than I meant to. Getting each other off and cleaning the other up.

"Your breakfast is getting cold."

I formed his hair into a mohawk, earning me a swat on the backside. I hid my face in his neck giggling.

"I'm visiting my dad today," I told him. "Next time, I'll bring you to meet him. Do you want to?"

Cupping my chin, he nodded.

"My dad will like you. He'll probably only threaten three or four times to chop you up and dissolve your body in quicklime if you hurt me. Mercer will get it some more. Saint's going to be a straight-up hard sell."

Brutal laughed.

"He hasn't taken to a single one of my boyfriends. In the end, I didn't take to them too much either, so who can blame him. But you guys"—I rose and rubbed our noses—"I want him to meet you. Something tells me you'll eventually get the nod of approval."

He raised a brow.

"He won't care that there are three of you." I was still smarting over Cash landing me in the shit and walking off. "And he doesn't have to know what you do. Next time, okay?"

He delivered his agreement with kisses that made me even later getting out of the shower.

I padded out in my towel, passing Cash as he went into his office. The bigger digs had given him extra space and two rooms to make his own. My glimpse through the closing door was a wall covered with papers, clippings, names, and dates. The visual representation of his mind.

I wondered if there was a wall in his mind for me that looked like this, but that was almost a certainty.

Killian said he trusted me. Told me he would stop following me. However, he was still holding back. Saint put me at arm's length because he didn't know if he could love me. Cash flatly stated he wouldn't.

It's different with him. My unpredictability appeals to Saint, but Cash needs to know. What I'll do in a given situation. How I'll react. I present a problem to him that he can't solve, and my instinct says he won't let that go as easily as he claimed.

I inched the door open, watching him rub clean a whiteboard through the slit.

Cash was a threat to my plans. If he figured out what I was after before I got to it... that would be a problem.

My initial plan had been to kill the Merchants but it wasn't that simple anymore.

I could just kill Cash. I rested my head on the doorframe. *Do I still want him after the trouble he's caused me?*

A dry voice broke into my musing. "Do you want something?"

I pushed the crack wider. Cash turned, facing me.

"What—"

The towel pooled on the floor.

Surprise broke his mask.

I slowly padded toward him, drinking in his open stare, delighting in the quick swipe of his tongue across his mouth. Killian went to return the eraser and missed by a mile. It dropped on the floor—ignored as he closed the distance, gaze caressing my body to entice a shiver up my spine.

Saint once said I didn't spare the effort on makeup and fancy clothes because I knew I was the most beautiful woman in any room. That wasn't true.

It was when Killian looked at me. The naked desire he tried and failed to conceal behind his impenetrable wall of steel. That's when I knew.

He cupped the back of my neck, pressing his kiss to smiling lips.

I twirled out of his hold. The kiss over as quickly as it began.

"Yes, I do."

Killian blinked as if waking from a daze. "What?"

I do still want you. I said as much out loud.

"And you want me," I stated. "But you're bound and determined to make this difficult, and you know what, so am I."

I grinned. "I said I'd make you pay. From now on"—I cupped my breasts, pushing them together—"it's dropped towels, not-so-accidental brushes, and graphic details on all the things you will be getting once you apologize, Killian Hunt. Wait till you see my dangle game when I'm actually playing."

I tweaked my nipples, winning both a snarl and a tightening in his pants. "Want to surprise everyone and give in now?"

It's a strange mix. Blindingly furious and deeply aroused. Cash was giving off both in waves. I could've sworn he was asking himself the same question. Did he want me more than his desire to put his next bomb under my bed?

I blew him a kiss. "I have to go, baby, but I'll sext you when I get there."

Skipping out, I paused to bend over and pick up my towel, wiggling my ass. His roar sent me scurrying out the door just as the first object struck the wall. My laugh couldn't be heard over the rest.

Chapter Four

"Addy."

I quickly hit send on the detailed explanation of what I'd do to Cash's cock when I got home, adding a "have my apology on a platter, and you'll have me next," on the end.

Mrs. Rowe scooped me up in a hug tighter than the ones she gave her grandchildren. No joke. I witnessed the one-armed, side hugs myself. To be fair, I came to see her more than they ever did, and I brought snacks.

"How are you, dear?" She smiled that warm, pleasant smile that put me at ease the first day Dad and I set foot here. Her long, grayish hair wound in a beehive atop her head, and every day she came to work in colorful pantsuits. That day's pick was lime green.

"It's been so long. I was worried you and your father got into a fight."

Of course she thought something was wrong. I visited my father at least twice a week—rain or shine. Double shift or all-nighter. Dropping off the map for weeks, I wouldn't have been surprised if they called the morgue fearing the worst.

"No, nothing like that." *I was just kidnapped by a band of men who will inevitably further my plan of taking over the city. What do you think of Queenpin?*

"I got sick," I said. "Pretty bad. I couldn't risk Daddy and the other residents catching it. Then, I was out so many days at work, I got fired."

She clapped her hand over her mouth.

"Finding another job took up all my time," I finished. "But everything is good now. I'm working as a private chef, and I get every Sunday off to see Dad."

"Addy, dear, I had no idea," she breathed. "Oh, I feel so awful telling you that you couldn't send cash. If I'd known how you were struggling— Please, forgive me."

"There's nothing to forgive, Mrs. Rowe. It's all worked out."

"Thank goodness." Rowe tucked my arm in hers. "You must be anxious to see him. We booked a magician for a live performance in the ballroom."

Yes, ballroom. Waterford Retirement Home had the amenities to justify the eye-watering bill they sent me every month. Failing health and my father's penchant for disregarding it, brought us to the point that I either had to move in and look after him, or a staff of nurses would do it for me. He had a heart condition and high blood pressure that made taking it easy and monitoring the signs vital. Still, I'd come home to him smoking a cigar on the porch after his second glass of whiskey.

I chose moving in with him, and Dad chose the home. He refused to get in the way of my schooling and career, and nothing I said would change his mind. We settled on Waterford Home with its policy that families could visit whenever they wished, and the residents in his wing retained their independence.

The place was three floors of single bedrooms, full beds, attached bathrooms, downy comforters, and a menu that got my seal of approval.

Most of the residents were like Dad. Which gave them plenty to talk about on the nights they stayed up playing poker in the billiards room, or kicking their feet in the swimming pool while Mrs. Rowe and the staff grill up something special for another themed lunch.

My dad lived better than most people these days, but he earned it. Even if it meant lying about a pay raise from Salvatore's so he stopped fighting me on this place being too expensive. There's nothing I wouldn't do for him, and thanks to my new loves, I could keep Dad in comfort until I set us up in a grand penthouse overlooking our city.

"Here we are." Mrs. Rowe led us into the ballroom. "Would you like to stay and watch the show?"

Rows of blue leather chairs lined the floor, and nearly every one was taken. It was a packed house for the man on the stage. Dressed in a tight, black suit and exaggerated black eyeliner, Mysterio flourished an ornate hand mirror. As we watched, he held the mirror sideways and stuck his hand through the surface.

"Can you see my fingers wiggling?"

We couldn't. There was nothing to see.

"The trick, ladies and gentlemen"—he slid to the side—"is to make everyone look in the wrong place."

A mirror stood behind him. The disembodied hand waved and waggled its fingers at us.

The room burst into applause.

"He's pretty good," I said, "but I've got lunch cooling in the car. I'll set the table in Dad's room. It'll be ready when he's done."

"I'll help."

Mrs. Rowe and I made short work of setting the table and laying out my creations. The space Dad called his own mimicked Saint's in décor. As in, there were few personal touches. His clothes hung neat and pressed in the closet. His weekly borrow from the library rested on the side table by the armchair. On the windowsill was a spider plant dutifully tended.

Where they differed, were the photos of me on his dresser. Baby Adeline. Adeline at the animal sanctuary. Adeline's high school and college graduation.

I wonder what Saint would do if I snuck photos of myself on his mantle. Or if I moved my things into his room completely.

He'd tie you to the bed so you never thought of leaving again, another voice replied.

That was the correct answer.

"Addy."

I ran to hug my dad. Bad back and all, he spun me off my feet.

"There's my girl. Where have you been?"

"It's been crazy, Dad. I'll tell you all about it over gumbo."

"You spoil an old man."

I kissed his cheek. "Nothing old about you."

"I knew there was a reason you were my favorite."

"And your only."

Putting me on my feet, he shot me a wink. "That we know of. I could have dozens of bastards out there."

A throat cleared. "I'll let you two have family time," Rowe said. "Good-bye."

"I'll save some for you," I called.

"No, she won't," Dad called back. "There won't be a grain left when I'm through."

Laughing, I guided Dad to his chair, and then plopped into mine. I already felt ten times lighter than when I came in. There were so many walls I had to hide myself behind every minute of every day. But not from my father. With him, I could be myself.

How could I not be? I saw myself in the set to his chin and his wide smile. I was the result of his knowledge, teaching, and legacy. If only one heir could be fashioned in a father's image, that was me.

"What kept you away?" he asked.

"I didn't want to get into it on the phone," I began, "but you remember the Merchants?"

He inclined his head. "New gang. Unconventional. Flashy. Cocky. In my day, you didn't need masks. You walked into a room and people lowered their eyes out of respect."

"Or fear," I added.

"That too." Dad took my bowl and piled on more. I was the chef, but it was his mission to plump me up. "What about them?"

"I witnessed them kill Raiden Spencer, so they kidnapped me and gave me one of those job offers you can't say no to."

His face changed. Not by surprise. My father was too old and seasoned by experience to be shocked. He got up and flipped his mattress off the box spring. A gaping tear lay exposed for all to see.

"Daddy, you ripped another hole in the mattress? They make me pay to replace these things you know."

He pulled out a gun. "Where are they?"

"Relax." I eased him into the seat, hugging his shoulders, and rested my cheek on his brown and gray curls. "This is why I didn't tell you sooner. We were still ironing out the logistics and I didn't want you getting worked up and raising your blood pressure, when I could kill them just as easily."

"What did they do to you?" he demanded.

"Nothing. They didn't rape or force themselves on me. They didn't even draw blood," I said. "I made things pretty simple and took the job at an outrageous salary."

Dad was tense in my hold. "What job?"

"Cook and housemaid like I told you. That was true."

"Nothing else?"

"Nothing."

"Do they know who you are?" he pressed.

"No, Dad. They don't have a clue, and I'm not going to give any up. I'm dating one or more of them." I moved to my seat. "And my innocent act is a big draw."

Dad finally set the gun on the table. "If these boys are such gentlemen, you'll have no problem filling in the rest of what you left out."

I did—telling him about my short time with the leaders of the Merchants. Plus, the quirks and personalities of my new loves.

"When do I meet them?"

"Soon, I hope. I know you'll like them."

"Don't be so sure. They dragged you back into a life you worked hard to get out of." Dad gestured with the shrimp on the end of his fork. "Don't be sure of that at all."

"But you won't try to kill them, will you?"

He flashed me a stern look.

"Daddy, promise me."

"Depends." Dad bore into me. "Are these guys after the ledger?"

I held his gaze for a beat, then my eyes dropped.

"Adeline, you promised *me*."

"It's not like I told them to," I cried. "They've been after Kieran and the ledger long before I met them. What was I supposed to do?"

"Get out."

"I can't do that."

"Why?"

"I... love them." Not the only reason but that partial truth was enough to warm my cheeks. Especially as his eyes narrowed.

"Love them?" Dad waved that away. "You're twenty-three, Adeline. You'll love many men in your life. There's no reason you should risk it all for passing flames."

"It's not real love if you aren't willing to risk it all."

He observed me. "Never thought I'd hear my girl say something like that."

"What can I say?" I folded my arms—embarrassed for no good reason. "I've come around to majority opinion. Love isn't complete bullshit. Soul mates exist."

"Soul mates?" he snorted. "Don't be ridiculous."

My dad didn't intend to be harsh. Hell, a few months ago I would've been rolling my eyes along with him.

"Love is not a predetermined thing," he continued. "It's not fated or written in the stars. It's rarely felt even by those who promise they do. Love is action, Adeline. It's sacrificing all that matters because that person matters more. Can you say that about them?"

"Yes," I whispered.

His gaze didn't let me go. "Can they say that about you?"

I pressed my lips together, heart thumping audibly in my chest.

"Well?"

Clearing my throat, I said, "I wouldn't be here if they couldn't. Dad, I know what you said, and I know what I promised, but you have to tell me everything you know about Kieran and the ledger."

"Adeline!"

"They're going after him, and there's nothing I can do to stop them," I said. "It's personal, Dad. Sinjin's father was murdered before his eyes in the hunt for Kieran, and I can't begin to guess what Kieran has done to Brutal, Cash, and Mercer. They want that ledger, and they don't care that Cash predicts one or more of them will die in the attempt.

"I won't let that happen." And I meant that with every fiber of my being. "The Merchants have to get to it before the others discover they've joined the hunt. Before Kieran does. Tell me what you know, Dad."

"I have. I've told you countless times, Addy, and then I made you swear not to act. You made a promise to your father."

"And you made promises to me! You told me the city would be mine. That I was destined for greatness. Dad, you taught me everything you know. Molded me into the strongest version of myself, and then one day it was over. I was just supposed to disappear into a mediocre life with a blank future. How is that fair to me? What about what I want?"

"I was wrong to fill your head with that nonsense. Kieran. The ledger." He tossed his head roughly. "You were just a child, for fuck's sake."

"How can you say that? I wasn't just a child. I'm *your* child. This is my destiny—"

He smacked the table. "Dammit, Addy! Look at us! Look at what became of my foolish, arrogant quest for supposed greatness. You are my child, but where was I when you needed me? I let myself be consumed by Kieran and the ledger," he hissed. "Nothing mattered but finding it and keeping it, until you. By the time I realized that, it was too late."

"You weren't t-too late." My voice caught. "You found me. Saved me."

Shaking his head, he covered his face. "I should've taken you away from her the day you were born. I convinced myself you were safer with her. What was I going to do with a baby? Strap you in a carrier and take you on hits? My life was too dangerous. If my enemies knew about you, you'd be in danger. If Kieran got to you. Kieran. Kieran. Kieran. Excuse. Excuse. Excuse."

Dad laid his hand on mine. I squeezed it tight.

"After your mother disappeared with you, I finally woke up. I lost my home, my respect, the Lords, and Soren because of Kieran. I wouldn't lose you too." He tipped my chin up. "Be the woman you were meant to be, Addy. Be great. But do not become another casualty in this war. By the time you realize it's not worth it, it'll be too late."

I leaned into his touch, eyes filling. "You had no way of knowing how far Mom would sink. If you had, you would've protected me, and when you found out, that's exactly what you did. That's all that matters to me, Dad. You're there for me, and I'm there for you."

"Always, brown eyes."

Taking a deep breath, I let it out slow. "I don't want to get into the past. We both know what we lost. This is about now. Today," I said. "Today, the Merchants are getting into position to strike against Kieran, and they're not asking if I want to take part. I've already paid for it."

His tone sharpened. "What does that mean?"

"Sinjin brought me to a sit-down with Angelo Castillo." Dad's eyes flashed at the name. "I look more like you than either of us wants to admit," I said. "He took one look at me and knew who I was."

"What did you do?"

"Killed him, of course."

He nodded sharply. "That's my girl."

"Before I put an end to him, Angelo tried to take me. Three guesses why." I grabbed his hand as he reached for his fork. "I can't stay out of this fight, Dad. Sinjin would want a reason that I can't give him. If I'm going to be in the crosshairs, at least give me the edge."

"I've told you everything I know about Kieran."

"Yes, years ago. Then, you shut down all talk about him. Forgive me if I don't believe you gave up searching for him too. Tell me what you've learned since, Dad. If the Merchants get there soon, I can get out of this war before I'm dragged too deep into it."

More like, I can win this war before anyone realizes the woman with the whisk was the one to watch all along.

So, okay. I didn't tell my father everything. Not about this at least. There was a point in every father-daughter relationship when their need to protect their little girl got in the way of her interests. From the bad boy boyfriend with a rap sheet that she couldn't live without, to the citywide gang war she'd ignite by securing the ultimate prize and the enemies to go with it.

We had reached that point. But one day, when this was all over, my dad would see I was doing this to get back what was taken from us. Those sacrifices would no longer be meaningless.

"I don't know anything."

I gave him a long look. "You forget I play poker with you."

"You calling me a liar?" The old gangster in him roared up quick.

"Never, Daddy. I believe you don't know where Kieran or the ledger is. But anything you've discovered—even the smallest detail—could help me."

"Leave those boys," he stated. "They stirred this shit up again. This Sin-whoever put you in a room with Angelo. Break it off, go back to Salvatore's, and move on with your life."

"I told you I can't do that." My reply was calm. "They're mine now. Only child, Daddy. I never learned to share what's mine."

He kissed his teeth, glaring out the window.

I waited him out. His need to protect me was warring with his need to ensure I could protect myself. A parental battle I couldn't relate to. The least I could do was let him reconcile in peace.

I patiently ate my cooling food.

"I don't know, Adeline."

Slowly, I put down my fork.

"Years ago, I was on the trail of someone. There were whispers of a man that could be him, and I tried to get close. The trail ended four years ago at The Pleasure Center."

"The Pleasure Center?"

"The night that kid was murdered in the alley, the cops busted the place and TPC was dust. If Kieran was connected to the Center, it didn't matter after that. He went underground and no one heard a word from him since."

"In four years?"

"If Kieran was easy to find, he wouldn't be Kieran."

I grudgingly had to agree. There were no shortcuts. I had the same uphill battle tracking this guy down like everyone else.

"What will you do now?"

"Be thankful the Merchants have a thing for masks and hope I avoid another Angelo situation," I replied. "Most gangsters don't live to see retirement."

"Present company excluded."

"There are a few of the old boys kicking around, especially among the Kings. The Merchants are hunting them down to find out what they know of the early days of Kieran."

"Not a bad plan," he said. "Could actually get them somewhere if they found the right well to tap. At least these boys you chose have some brains among them."

I smiled. "You'll like them, Dad, I promise."

He grunted.

"Sinjin is *teaching me* how to kill, and you should see him. He favors a boning-style knife just like you. Thin blades. Close contact. Plenty of blood, but enough control that they die when he wants them to. One of his men put his hands on me, and he cut off his tongue and left him to die in an abandoned building." I grinned, high on two kinds of lust. "It was so sweet, Daddy."

"Hmm. Now, that's old school. Good to see there are still gangs out there that lead with action, and command respect. Not nowadays where bosses hole up in their safe houses, counting their money while they send cowards scurrying through the streets doing drive-bys instead of facing their rivals head-on. It's a disgrace."

Oh, boy. Get my dad going on the devolving state of modern gangs and crime families, and he'd go for hours.

"See, Dad? I know how to pick 'em."

Dad laughed. "I don't care about them, I care about you. Adeline, you admitted this is personal for Sinjin. Killing his father... He's not going to let that go, and I don't blame him. But let this gangster impart some wisdom my comrades rarely get old enough to acquire. Mix a vendetta with bloodlust and no fear of death, you get a man who will do anything—sacrifice anyone—to get what he wants."

"And if I win...?"

"The girl goes with you."

The words roared in my mind, coating my throat with bile.

"Sinjin loves me," I rasped. "He won't—"

"It's not just him. You admitted you don't know what Kieran has on the others. Why is that if they love you so much? There are secrets in that ledger worth killing to protect, Adeline. *You* are a secret worth killing to protect. What happens when you all have to make a choice? Love?

"Or the ledger?"

My father did not know everything about me, but then... he did.

"It's getting cold, Dad. Let's eat, watch a movie in the theater, and rob Kenny blind. It's been weeks. I just want to catch up with my dad."

"We can do that, brown eyes." He patted my hand. "And next time, you'll tell me what else you're hiding from me. You forget, I play poker with you too."

MY DAD WAS GOOD ABOUT easing up on the interrogation and allowing us to enjoy our day together. I left his room without the leftovers I promised Rowe, owing to him finishing the entire thing, but I did claim a kiss goodbye and orders to return the following Sunday in time for breakfast.

I was seeing it as an opportunity to get more information on the trail that led to Kieran, and not a grilling about the boys and what I was hiding. Either way, Brutal wasn't coming along on that visit.

"Bye, Mrs. Rowe."

"Bye, Addy. See you next week."

Waterford Retirement Home was a jewel in the middle of the city. The setting sun cast watercolors over the Victorian-style home nestled between a parking structure, and the alley that split the distance between a block of industrial office buildings.

I skirted the lawn's flower border, shooting another text to Cash.

Me: I can't wait to feel you inside of me again. I dreamed about you last night. You were an embezzling bank manager, and me the savvy assistant who caught on to your wrongdoing.

My phone beeped as I put it away.

Cash: And what did I do to ensure your silence?

I stopped dead. Was this happening? *Is he doing what I think he's doing?*

Me: Took me down to the vault and tied me to that big, spinning pirate wheel lock. You ripped my clothes off with a letter opener, and fisted your cock while you told me in no uncertain terms that you owned me now. It's around then I woke up.

Cash: No.

Me: No?

Cash: Let me correct that fantasy for you, Redgrave. Chains, cuffs, and cages are Sinjin's bag. Not mine. If I found the hot little assistant snooping, we'd fight. You'd pull my hair, rake your nails down my back, break me in half clamping your thighs around my waist. That I'd be fucking you on my desk for the whole bank to hear would make no difference.

My eyes were huge. Reading his reply once, three, five times.

Picking up the pace, I hurried through the gates and rounded for the parking lot. I don't know what the hell came over Cash, but I needed to get back home before he came to his senses. I'd have to see Gianna later that night.

Cash: I'd spread that pussy wide. Plunging—

"Hand it over!"

A force slammed into me. I careened into the wall, my skull bouncing off the brick. I didn't have time to recover. Hands were on me—snatching my phone. Tearing my purse off my shoulder.

"Give it up, bitch!" Fetid, hot breath invaded my nose. A scraggly, loose-skinned face got in mine. I reeled back as he swung.

"Get it, baby!"

I tripped over my feet, falling onto his companion. She shoved me off, and I hit the ground with him on top of me. He tried another punch. I snapped my head to the side, and his knuckles crunching on the pavement rang in my ears.

"Argh!"

"Hurry up," she screamed.

"Stop fucking standing there and hold her down!" He wrenched a Swiss blade from his pocket, brandishing it over my heart.

I smashed my knees in his balls. Howling, his hands flew to his groin and the knife sliced across my torso, tearing my shirt.

My next kick connected with his jaw. He flew off me.

I struggled to sit up, and was pushed back down. She dropped on my chest, crushing me on the concrete. Dazed, I weakly fought to shift her weight.

A tight, spangly tube top strained to contain her assets. The miniskirt didn't try at all. Bare, thong-covered ass pinned me. I made a swipe for her hair, yanking as hard as I could.

Shrieking, she slapped me across the face.

"Give me the knife."

"No," I croaked.

The blade glinted in the fading light.

They cut my purse free of its straps and took off, howling their victory.

It took me a while to collect myself—catch my breath and get to my feet. Two minutes to notice the wetness running down my cheek was blood. Ten to stumble to the parking lot and discover my car gone.

Mrs. Rowe dropped the five o'clock tray of juice and cookies at the sight of me.

"Oh, Addy," she cried. "Not again."

"ARE YOU SURE YOU'RE okay?"

"I'm fine. Thanks for fixing me up, G."

She stopped me reaching for the seat belt. "What will you do?" Her gaze drifted to the empty sandwich shop. "They're going to lose their minds when they see you."

Of course they were. Blood clumped my hair and dripped onto my top. The cuts and scrapes on my skin I could hide no better.

"I'll handle it," I said simply.

"Hey." She kissed my cheek. "It'll be okay."

I gave her what I hoped passed for a smile. "I'll call... when I get a new phone."

Climbing out, I paused on the sidewalk, still in the rush of people passing by. I wished it was just the mugging keeping me bound. I wished it could be top bill.

Love is action, Adeline. It's sacrificing all that matters because that person matters more.

"Here goes nothing."

I stepped inside, chiming the small bell over the doorway. The door to the second floor had no such bell. The boys did not hear me enter. Backs facing me, they watched the news with glasses of wine and whiskey in hand.

"Hey," I greeted. "I'm going to make something simple for dinner tonight. Quesadillas and black bean salad sound all right?"

Saint waved over his shoulder. "I'll take a blow job first if you're handing them out."

I almost cracked a smile. "Who says I am?"

"I—"

Brutal turned to me. The glass shattered on the floor.

"What the fuck?" Cash cried. "What's wrong with you?"

Brutal stalked up to me, drawing their eyes. Three glasses met the same end on our cherry hardwood.

"Who did this?"

"What happened?"

"I said it wasn't safe for her by herself," Sinjin roared.

"Guys—"

"Was it the Kings?" Cash asked.

"How'd they track you down?" Mercer practically carried me to the armchair. "Did they follow you to the home?"

"Who was it?!"

"Guys!" I screamed.

They hovered over me. Four walls of radiating, suffocating anger. But silent.

"It wasn't the Kings," I said softly. "Just a good old-fashioned mugging. And carjacking," I added.

"Describe them," Saint demanded.

"Man and woman," I replied. "Weedy, ratty-looking guy. I'm guessing her pimp."

"How did you get back?" Cash asked.

"Gianna came and got me."

"Why didn't you call us?" Saint and Cash asked at the same time.

Brutal hadn't spoken. His balled fists and flared nostrils said enough.

"Because I knew you'd freak out, and I'm fine."

Mercer walked off and returned with a towel and ice. He held it to the bump on my forehead.

"She didn't do much damage," I finished.

"She's going to fucking know damage," Saint growled. "Cash. Brutal, track the car. Take your time killing them—"

"No, you can't."

"Yes, we can," Saint snapped. "Go! Do it now."

The guys stalked off.

"Guys, wait." I knocked Mercer off jumping up. "You can't do this."

Cash ripped open the door, disappearing into the hallway.

"She's my mother!"

My shout halted the thundering footsteps.

Slowly. Deliberately. Brutal and Cash returned inside—even as I wished I could take the confession back.

"Your mother?" Mercer repeated.

"Yes, Mercer. My mother. Jocelyn Daniels." I returned to the seat, slapping his hand and the ice back on my forehead for good measure. "She's not dead or as absent from my life as I may have led you all to believe.

"Mommy Dearest likes to check in now and again, and relieve me of the cash or credit cards I have on hand. She often brings along whatever low-life piece of trash or pimp she's hooked up with to even the odds."

You could hear a fly buzz in the building opposite. It was deadly quiet in the room.

"I've been easy pickings since she found out where Dad lived. All she has to do is hang around the home. She knows nothing will stop me from seeing him."

Soft footfalls. Then Cash knelt before me. "How many times has she done this?"

My lips trembled. "Enough."

"Why?"

I didn't fault Mercer for the question. I hadn't shared my history with him as I had with Brutal and Cash. For this very reason. Men as ruthless and savage as them, did not know what to do when they faced a being more soulless than they could ever be. Of all the terrible things they had done, in the face of this, they asked, "Why?"

"After Dad saved me from her, she lost her best bartering chip for cash, drugs, and child support. She had nothing. Eventually, Jocelyn turned to selling herself. A crime she holds me responsible for. I owe her for not dumping my ass on the street and taking off. I'm an 'ungrateful bitch' because I don't take care of her the way I do Dad. She's only taking what she deserves."

"Brutal." Saint spoke in a tone I'd never heard. "Kill her."

I sighed, eyes falling shut. "You can't kill her, Saint."

"Why?" he demanded.

"She's still my mother."

"And?"

"Get the car back." I was tired. So very tired. "Kill the boyfriend/pimp/ whoever the hell he is for giving me this." I pointed to the shallow cut through my torn shirt. "She'll know why, and that's enough. Maybe she'll think twice next time."

"There won't be a next time." Brutal's soft voice reached inside and shook the dam holding back my tears.

Cash got to his feet. "We'll make the message clear. You're under the Merchants' protection. If she goes near you again, the pimp won't be the only one we kill. Everyone she's ever met will die until she truly knows what it is to have nothing."

They left. I grabbed Saint as he made to follow.

I couldn't trust him not to kill my mother if faced with her. He likely planned to do just that in spite of my wishes, believing he was doing me a favor.

Wouldn't he be?

I pushed the thought away. Jocelyn Daniels was my curse to bear. My demon to battle.

Weaving my fingers through Mercer's, I held their hands.

They let me.

CASH

I pushed into my room.

Adeline sat cross-legged on my bed. Her hair was damp from a shower and the baggy shirt was likely from Sinjin. The fresh hickey on her must also have been a gift from Sinjin. His attempt to comfort her the best he knew how. But her long, bare legs on my duvet. Soft and shapely and drawing my eye even now were all hers.

I flicked away—biting a rare flash of shame. This was not the time.

"She's alive," I stated. "Her boyfriend is not. Your car is out front where it should be."

She nodded, eyes down.

Crossing to my dresser, I unstrapped my holster, set it and my gun down. My belt was next. Rolled tight and put in its place in the second drawer from the top on the left side. Everything had its place.

I glanced at Adeline, slipping under my covers and curling on the pillow. *This is hers.*

"Thank you."

It was so soft, I almost didn't catch it.

"This is a rare moment," I said. "I'm going to do something I haven't done in five years, eight months, and two days."

She looked confused. "What?"

"Say that you were right, and I was wrong. Some things... are none of my damn business." My grip tightened on the gun handle. "All the same, thank you for letting me and Brutal handle this."

Fire burned my gut as the giver of Adeline's reddish-hair, light eyes, and the button nose that wrinkled as she promised to turn my world upside down, showered my face with spittle shouting and screaming abuse for her only child. I heard her shrieking. Felt the piercing nails and thrashing as I forced her to watch Brutal beat to death the bastard who attacked Adeline.

She pled for his well-being, but cursed Adeline to suffer every day as payment for imagined wrongs. We left her on the floor of their pig-slop apartment, swearing she'd never stop coming after Adeline. She'd get what was owed her.

"You've been through enough today," I finished.

"Mom was her usual winning self, I assume."

"Five minutes with her and I wanted to blow her brains out. Or mine. I wasn't fussed at that point."

She laughed softly.

I continued stripping, shedding my sweater, then the shirt. My pants joined them on the floor.

Adeline was correct about more than one thing. We'd had sex and spent an entire night opening up to each other. We could drop a few pretenses.

"I don't know how you survived all those years. Just a child. Living in her grip. But I do know, you're stronger than anyone can comprehend."

"I like you being sweet to me."

I slid in bed with her, expecting her to wiggle under my arm and letting it happen. She brushed her lips on my chin.

"Keep doing it."

"I knew something was up when you sent me this." I passed her my phone.

Adeline squinted at the screen. Scrolling. Scrolling.

Her eyes popped.

Our texts that day shone in stark black and white

Cash: Let me correct that fantasy for you, Redgrave. Chains, cuffs, and cages are Sinjin's bag. Not mine. If I found the hot little assistant snooping, we'd fight. You'd pull my hair, rake your nails down my back, break me in half clamping your thighs around my waist. That I'd be fucking you on my desk for the whole bank to hear would make no difference.

I'd spread that pussy wide. Plunging my fingers deep in that greedy cunt till you came screaming to crack the windows. You'll make your promises to keep that tasty mouth shut as you lick them clean. Got anything you want to add?

(Not) Adeline: Yes. I want to add a real man in this fantasy with a dick I don't need a map to find. I wouldn't let you near my cunt for all the money in Cinco City Bank. You're pathetic. A weak, sniveling virgin playing like the big man in Imagination Land because in reality, women want nothing to do with you. I want nothing to do with you. Cut that Skittle dick off and choke on it.

If you can.

Adeline gaped. "I swear, I didn't write a word of this."

"I know."

"Jocelyn is such a—! Skittle dick?!"

"Particularly cutting."

"Like I don't know from experience it's far from Skittle size. I was sore for days."

"Thank you."

She blew out a frustrated breath, burying her face in my neck. "Ever since she tracked me down my freshman year, she's made it her life's goal to ruin everything I touch," she said. "She slept with one of my boyfriends and took great pleasure in telling me the details. She hates that she can't use me anymore. That I won't put her up in the room next to Dad, and return her to a life of easy money and easy drugs. She hates me, Killian."

I wanted to say that wasn't true. But I saw the expression in those bulging eyes, and I found myself agreeing with Adeline for the third time that night. It was hard being the man who saw everything.

I held her close, fitting her body perfectly under mine. Adeline started shaking. Soft huffing noises slipped between our bodies.

"What are you doing?" I rose on my forearm and the muffled sound rang clear as day.

Her giggles lit her eyes, and that nose scrunched up. "What she did was awful but... I would've given every cent I had to see your face when you read Skittle dick."

"Shut up and go to sleep, Redgrave."

I flicked the lamp off to more giggling.

Adeline was there in an instant as I dropped my head on the pillow, draping my arm over her waist and tucking my hand between her legs. I played with her pussy to amuse myself, pleased when the giggles gave way to breathy moans.

"I hope this isn't the end of our sexting adventures," she said. "You're a mountain I intend to climb, Killian Hunt."

"I thought I was a mountain you intended to bring to heel."

"That too."

"You'll get neither." I pressed a kiss on the nape of her neck. "It's only fair to tell you. Fairer still to say this is a one-night-only pass."

"So, if I slip into your bed tomorrow night, you'll kick me out?"

"Yes."

She pushed my fingers deeper inside her. "I'd like to see you try."

ADELINE

The next night, I marched to Cash's room, pajamas on, and pillow under my arm. He was sitting on the end of his bed, fixed on the television. He didn't react when I climbed behind him and rested my chin on his shoulder.

"What are we watching?" I asked. Though I saw for myself. The news cameras panned on the inferno engulfing the building behind the reporter.

"Burning strip club."

"Morbid."

"That's Thiago Pais's strip club," he explained. "Finally."

"Finally? This is a good thing?"

"Yes. It's down to two and a half, and one of them struck in a big, obvious way that will bring attention they can't keep quiet. Everyone knows that club is a King club. They'll either think the Kings are still under attack and too weak to handle the problem. Or it's an internal dispute, and they're too weak to handle their own problems.

"Either way, the situation will escalate. In two days, Jameson will be dead, Thiago and his escorts will go on strike, and Enzo Bianchi will be the new leader of the Kings. Seventy-six percent probability."

Two days later, the guys and I stood in the living room. I absentmindedly whisked a bowl of eggs, sugar, and butter destined to become spice cookies.

"—body of Xavier Jameson found in his penthouse this morning," said Margot Rose, Channel Nine News. "Mr. Jameson was released from the hospital a few days ago, following a brutal attack at his law firm. Officers are unclear at this time if his death is connected to that assault."

"How do we know if it's Enzo?" I asked.

"You only have to ask, Bunny." Saint nodded to Mercer. "Or he does. Call those friends of yours."

Mercer did. Calling up three different people who told him the same rumor—which made it the truth.

In their time of upheaval, Lorenzo Bianchi was stepping up to claim the Kings' throne.

"What about Thiago?" I glanced at Cash. "Don't tell me you were right about that too. Are the escorts on strike?"

"We don't strike," Mercer said, amused. "But yeah, it was a safe bet to claim Thiago and his people wouldn't be thrilled about being burned alive. Thiago's going to demand negotiations for a new deal with his escorts and the Kings' cut. Enzo will trip over a few cash flow issues until that deal is made."

"Cash flow issues," Killian said. "Perfect choice of words."

With that, Cash disappeared upstairs to clear a whiteboard. The final pawn had fallen. One last King to contend with.

After putting my cookies in the oven, I went upstairs to his office. The door swung open as I reached for it. Mercer walked out.

"Give him a minute, love."

"I just wanted to—"

"I know what you want to do." He hooked an arm around my neck, carrying me off. "You want to know the strategy that won. Enzo is king of the Kings. Where will Cash move the first piece on the board?"

I blinked at him, surprised he used the same analogy.

We marched down the creaky steps, coming out on our floor.

"I can tell you that just as easily," Mercer said. "I'm the first piece, and his name is Dax Palmer."

"Dax Palmer?"

Mercer let me go and went into his room. I followed him.

"Who's Dax Palmer?"

Passing over the threshold was leaving old-class charm for modern allure. Triptych paintings and funky wall mirrors looked down on me. A king-size sleigh bed dominated the space, seducing all who entered to take the final step into its arms of black silk sheets and plush throws. He had two bedside tables. One with an erotic statuette, and the other bearing a lamp that stretched high and angled right over the bed.

"On the bed, gorgeous."

I obeyed, hopping on and getting comfortable. I listened to him shuffling around behind me. The current equation of him, plus me, plus bed wasn't lost on me. I had to wonder if he was thinking the same.

Mercer always called me love, lovely, beautiful, gorgeous. But for a man with such free ideas about sex, he hadn't so much as squeezed my boob. I've gotten more action from strangers on a crowded bus than this guy.

Hands squeezed my shoulders, shooting my brows up my forehead. I held frozen as his thumbs kneaded the base of my neck.

"It's not often I don't know what to say." Warm, experienced fingers skidded over my spine, finding a new spot to massage. A soft sigh escaped my lips. "These last few days, I've wanted to comfort you, Adeline. Say something that could make the last twenty-three years of... that woman... okay."

I closed my eyes.

"For the first time, I was at a loss for words." He pressed a soft kiss to my crown. "But you never are. You're a woman who knows what she wants.

What she feels. Tell me what to do to help. Whether it's to not mention it again, or renovate that sandwich shop overnight. I'll do it."

His hands didn't stop during. Kneading knots I didn't know I had. Pulling my shoulders back. Exposing my neck to his warm breath popping goose bumps on my skin. They spread webs of pleasure spiraling to my toes.

"Tell me," he whispered.

"I do know what I want," I began slowly, eyes opening. "And it isn't to talk about Jocelyn. It never will be. What I want is to talk about you, Mercer. To get to know you. Understand you."

"If there's something you want to know, ask me, lovely. I haven't told you that you shouldn't."

That much was true. Mercer didn't give direct answers, but I didn't ask direct questions.

He laid me flat on the bed, straddling me. My shirt was leisurely drawn up to my neck. Heat suffused my cheeks as my bra straps sprang apart.

Mercer tipped off and riffled in his bedside drawer. He came out holding a bottle of oil. It was cool on my back, but his diligent hands quickly warmed me up.

My eyes fought to close again—riding the waves of purring contentment.

"Keep that right next to the bed, do you?" I murmured.

"Wait till you see what else I've got in there."

"That's my first question, Mercer. Why are we doing this flirty, will-they, won't-they game? You could be balls deep in me right now."

A laugh ripped out of him. "Good to know. But let me ask a question first. What I do, does it bother you?"

"I don't judge you."

"I appreciate that, but it's not the answer I'm looking for, and you know it." He put his mouth to my ear. "Every night a different bed. A different body. A different woman begging for it"—he licked the shell of my ear—"balls deep."

I went rigid.

"Ah." His tone was light. Almost joking. "There's my answer."

"That's not your answer. This is," I said. "Yes. Yes, it would bother me if we were together, and you were sleeping with other people."

"You sleep with other people."

"That's different."

"How?"

"I'm in committed relationships with them."

"Cash has said more than once that he doesn't want a relationship with you."

"That stubborn ass will wake up soon enough."

"And when did you get declarations of commitment and exclusivity from Sinjin and Brutal?"

I snapped around, glaring. "They're mine. They belong to me. All of you do. You can wake the fuck up too." It was out of my mouth before I could stop it. Couldn't tell if it came from sweet cook Adeline, or her deadly alter ego. Both were pissed.

Chuckling, Mercer eased me down. "Yes, ma'am. Far be it for me to question my ownership, but this is what I do, Adeline. Where does that leave us?"

"You stop."

"If I don't want to?"

"*Do* you want to?" I asked. "Do you not?"

"I like what I do. Parties, wine, dancing, seduction, sex. Most people are desperate for a taste of the life I lead every day."

I hesitated. "Mercer, it doesn't seem like you take any of it seriously. Not even as enjoyment. Sometimes, I get the feeling you're not serious about much of anything. Sex. People. Death. It's all a game designed to amuse."

"Whew. We are getting real." He splayed his hands on the small of my back and dug deep as he moved to my neck. I imagined my skin rolling out like dough.

"Am I wrong?"

"What's to be serious about? It's only sex. Man or woman. They're all a collection of holes paying me to get off. Why shouldn't it amuse?" He knuckled a knot under my shoulder blade. "Why shouldn't I have my fun as they sneak me in beneath the security cameras? Dismiss their bodyguards for the night. Unlock their doors. Let me into their bedrooms. Set their phones on the stand to undress." He crept higher, rubbing a trail of circles. "Why not enjoy those hours before they fall asleep?

"I'm good at what I do, lovely, because what I do isn't who I am."

"Who are you?" I whispered.

"I'm with people at their most vulnerable. Walls down. Defenses offline. It's what makes me perfect."

"Perfect what?"

Mercer encircled my throat. "Assassin."

My throat bobbed against his fingers. "That's what you do as a leader of the Merchants. Kill your dates." It wasn't a question.

"Not all of them, of course." He laughed, resuming my massage. "Something like that would get around. What I do—what I will do with Dax Palmer—is collect information. You call Cash the man who knows everything, but he wouldn't know half as much without me. The intel. The plans. Getting in and out minus guns, bombs, fists, and wine bottles. That's where my *people skills* come in."

"It's you who does the recon," I said as it clicked into place. "Bryan Acker. If his flavor wasn't auburn-haired mommy clones, you would've gone in for the information."

"Absolutely," he said easily. "That's a play I've run on half a dozen marks, and I have no doubt there will be more. And there's your answer, love. I can't be a Merchant and be with you."

"You don't have to sleep with your marks," I tried.

"I'm effective because I sleep with them, Adeline. I've built a reputation that has the who's who of Leighbridge calling my number. They let me in where other strangers can't go because I drop my pants. Some like to joke escorts double as therapists, but if I actually tried charging for just a chat and a cuddle, my dates would lose my number.

"Picture how simple it is to pop their finger on their phone and laptop readers while they're snoring away. To crack safes when I have all night and them drugged and passed out in the other room. The best part, my tracks are covered for me. All trace of my presence is wiped. If ever questioned, they'd swear on their lives they didn't have sexual relations with that man. And for those I kill." He hummed. "There's almost no sport in it. It's just too easy."

Mercer lay on top of me, burrowing me into the mattress. "Have I shocked you?"

My head shook under him. "Were you looking for a reaction to rival the first bomb you dropped?"

"Possibly," he said, laughing.

"I'm not shocked, Mercer. I knew whatever you did as a Merchant, it wasn't party all night and pile up stacks of money. Saint said you were invaluable, and now I see why. He's the leader. Cash is the brains. Brutal is the muscle," I said. "And you're the shadow."

"Ooh. I was going with infiltrator, but I like your title much better."

I curled his arms under my neck, resting my chin on top. *Why would I be shocked? You, my love, are me.*

"So, how do we deal with this?"

"What do you mean?" he asked.

"You said you didn't question your ownership—which is good because it hasn't been revoked. You and I belong together." *More than you know.* "But as I explained recently to my father, I don't share. There has to be another way to do what you do minus the sex. Once we figure that out, you retire."

"Do I get a say in this?" He sounded amused.

"Yes."

Leaning back, he peered at me. "Really?"

"Of course." I caressed his arm with long, tapered fingers. "You can say you don't want me, Mercer."

He flicked to my hands, eyes glazing. "Who in their right mind would say that?"

"Shall we brainstorm?"

"Please, beautiful. Love to hear how an escort can make his living without *escorting*."

My internal clock went off, signaling my cookies were ready to be taken out. I got up and redressed. "There's something to be said for relying on your skills. But there are many ways to infiltrate the right place, and shadow the right people. You just have to think outside the box."

CASH

"I can't take the suspense." Adeline stood in my office doorway. "Enzo's taken over. What's the new plan?"

"Sit. I'll tell you."

I reclined in my desk chair, sweeping over the seemingly random scraps of information on my corkboards, whiteboards, and walls. It looked like unholy chaos. All I saw was order.

Adeline sat in my lap. I picked her up and dropped her laughing on the couch. I remained standing to prevent another attempt.

"Did Sinjin tell you the steps to destroying an empire?"

"Drain their funds, shake their followers' loyalty, cut off the head." She stretched out, hanging off the arm. "You cut off one head. Are you planning to kill Enzo now?"

"No. Angelo's death served many purposes. Enzo's would achieve little," I said. "The Kings are shaken. Trust is breaking down. Their get-out-of-jail-free lawyer is dead. They're losing money, and their reputation as untouchable is crumbling with every burning building on the news. Now is the time for the next step. Drain their funds."

"How will you do that?"

I circled a name on the board. "Richard La Roche."

"La Roche? That investment banker guy? What's he got to do with anything?"

Drifting to the photo beneath his name, I replied, "Richard La Roche is the best money-launderer, counterfeiter, art forger, and stolen antiquities dealer this city has ever seen. That any city has ever seen."

"He is?" She came over and jabbed the photo. "This guy right here?"

"That guy."

"How?" she cried. "I've never heard his name unless it was mentioned along with the other moneybags in Cinco."

"It's cute how you expect to know everything about the criminal underworld. When would talk of a master forger come up, Redgrave? While you and the prep chef were making canapes?"

She rolled her eyes. "This again? One doesn't get labeled the best by being unknown. There isn't a single whiff of crime connected to his public image. How did you find out otherwise?"

"Forgers are con men by nature. They shed aliases and identities as easily as they brush their teeth. Up, down, gargle, spit. They're someone else. No one knew who he was for years. He moved his phony bills through legitimate investments, and amassed a real art collection that gave credibility to the occasional fake that went up for auction. The up-close-and-personal con work he carried out overseas in Europe, Asia, and the Middle East. Then one day, he decided to do the criminal's version of retirement, and became a consultant."

"Consultant," she repeated. "As in he put his knowledge up for sale to budding thieves?"

"That's it in one, Redgrave.

"The contacts he formed, the active aliases, the money, and his reputation are invaluable. He's got teams of people working for him—which is impressive in and of itself. Con men prefer to work alone. In pairs if a double act will better get the job done. But in teams? No. Not until him.

"At any given time, someone in this city is running a scam that will make them, and La Roche, millions."

"But still, how did you find out?"

I went to the wet bar and poured a drink. Adeline shook her head at the offering.

"La Roche advertised."

"Advertised? You're saying the man put out a citywide memo that he was open for business and looking for employees?"

"That's exactly what I'm saying."

She gaped at his picture. "How?"

"Art gallery opening three years ago. La Roche donated pieces from his own collection, and within it was *La Libertad*."

"*La Libertad*," she said. "Freedom."

"The lost painting of Aurelio Molina."

Adeline pulled me next to her on the couch. "My goodness, we have the most interesting chats. Who's Aurelio Molina?"

I chuckled at her wide-eyed interest. "Aurelio Molina was a Spanish painter in the 1800s. He had modest success in his lifetime as a post-Impressionist. Before his death, he boasted about a new, inspired piece he painted that overshadowed his other works. A true masterpiece that he named *La Libertad*.

"He planned to unveil the painting at the party for his fiftieth birthday. He died a week before, and a search of his home and studio turned up nothing. The painting was lost."

I sipped my drink, indulging the pleasure of her full attention. Her hand gripping my thigh. Minty shampoo scenting the air. Breasts pushed together as she sat on her knees, leaning over me.

"Cash?"

I dragged myself to reality. "As tends to happen, Molina gained fame after his death," I continued. "His last painting to go up for auction sold for two million euro."

She whistled. "Not bad. So this lost painting must be worth a fortune."

"It would be," I said, "if it existed."

"What? But you said—"

"Molina was trying to drive up interest in his work. Create an air of mystery like a movie preview with a lot of sex and explosions that ultimately reveals nothing of what the movie is about. He tried to paint La Libertad and deliver his promise to the dozens of people expecting a masterpiece, but he set himself such a high standard, nothing he painted could hope to meet it. In a fit of artistic temperament, he burned his attempts to ash. Two days later, he died."

"Wow." She sat back, digesting what I said. "So, the painting in La Roche's collection. Where the hell did that come from?"

"Now you're asking the right question, Redgrave. After his death, Molina's widow didn't want the embarrassment of admitting her husband lied to everyone, and then burned their hopes in a fit of tantrum. Instead, she told the world Aurelio's final masterpiece was stolen by a thief in the night, and the shock of it killed him.

"Ever since, art forgers and collectors alike have been after that painting. Collectors bid outrageously for his surviving work. Experts studied his style in hope of matching it to the piece when it's finally found. La Libertad became the art world's hunt for the holy grail, and the family secret remained hidden until a particularly crafty grifter snuggled up to a great-great-great in Molina's family tree. She told him the truth over pillow talk."

"What did he do?" she breathed.

"What any good con man would do. There is no painting, Adeline. No one is going to pop up and say, 'I have the real one. I had it all along.' He hired a forger to paint him a canvas of bullshit and shouted to the world La Libertad was found. Experts eventually denounced it as a forgery, but he went to someone else. Got another painting, tried selling it under a different name. Again, it was revealed it couldn't have been painted during that time period. So, he got someone better, and he tried again.

"By then, word spread among a separate art community. La Libertad didn't exist, and collectors didn't know. It's the ultimate con up there with forging a Van Gogh. Everyone wants the score, but few have the skills. Until the night of the gallery, when the piece was unveiled as the jewel of La Roche's collection.

"Authenticated by three different experts who were there that night, people flew in from all over the world to gush over the piece. Ask him how he found it. Was it truly taken by a thief? Did the villain's descendants hide it, or did someone trip over it in an old storage shed? Dozens came for the story of his treasure hunt.

"But the other guests. The ones who knew that painting was as fake as any story that went with it, they didn't gush. And they only had one question for him."

"Who sold him the painting?" she whispered.

Smirking, I said, "Go on."

"That painting was colored with bullshit and signed with a lie. The real prize wasn't that it was found, it was that someone out there was so talented, they fooled the experts, the art community, and the world. A forger like that would be a legend. A legend any con man would want to be in bed with," she said. "And that legend is La Roche. He forged La Libertad. He put up a huge advertisement that brought con artists out of the shadows to find the person who was just that good. When they asked him the right question, he knew they were good enough too."

"I asked him the right question," I said. "I went to the gallery opening and saw La Libertad for myself. It wasn't Molina's masterpiece, but there is no denying it is one. I realized as we talked what La Roche was, and he did the same. When he invited me to his home for a chat a few days later, I didn't go. Many others did."

"You've known about him the whole time."

I nodded.

"What's the deal with him now? What does he have to do with the Kings or finding Kieran?"

"Since setting up his business, La Roche has formed multiple arrangements for him and his protégés. His most lucrative is an exclusive deal with the Kings."

"That makes sense," she said. "The Cinco elite go to the Kings for their escorts, blood sport, gambling, and all kinds of illegal fun. Why not add the finer things to the list?"

"I can't calculate how much funny money Angelo laundered for La Roche through his underground casinos. Suckers threw real cash on the table, and walked out with worthless paper. Gives new meaning to the phrase 'the house always wins.'"

"Oh my gosh." Adeline rocked back on her bum. "They're clearing millions at pure profit."

"As for the artwork, all the currently deceased Angelo had to do was keep an ear to the ground for his rich friends looking to add to their collection. They'd kill the original owner in a burglary gone wrong, sell it to the buyer, and then La Roche supplies him with a horde of fakes that he can sell for private bids—"

"—because no one will admit they bought a painting tied to a murder," she cried. "They get paid three, four, six times for more worthless paper. It's freaking genius."

I chuckled. "Even I have to admit it is. The Kings come by their reputation honest."

Adeline shot up, pacing the carpet. "So, if we're going to drain their funds. It has to be La Roche. We sever that business deal and the Kings are out more money than they can recover from." She spun on me. "Why'd you guys sit on this? You had the target. Knew who La Roche was. Why didn't you do this instead of putting me on an auction block?"

"Everything in its time, Redgrave. La Roche has worked with Angelo for three years. He knew him. Had a respect for him that was likely laced with fear. There was nothing anyone was going to say that would've made him break their deal. La Roche doesn't even have extended cousins to threaten. The Merchants had no leverage. Now, we do.

"A new leader has taken over. One who is all about the numbers, the cash, and the bottom line. I couldn't predict they'd burn his club down, but a man like Thiago reacts unfavorably to disrespect and disloyalty. If he survived an attack against him, he'd cut off the money drip from his escorts to the Kings. Eighty-eight percent probability. That would trigger other events."

She smiled at me. "I'd give anything to know what it's like in that head of yours, toy boy." I let the nickname slide. Along with her straddling my lap and hooking her fingers behind my head. "What else did you surmise?

"Enzo has big shoes to fill. He has to take over the casinos and manage without the clients the Merchants cost them through the Castian, fires, and bribes. On top of dealing with the loss of the escort money until he either makes it up to Thiago, or kills him. They're right on the edge of that financial blow they won't recover from, and for a dealmaker like Enzo, his most probable course is renegotiating the ones they have on the books for better terms."

"You think Enzo will demand La Roche cut the Kings in for more money?"

"In simple terms, yes."

"What's the Merchants' plan?"

"To approach La Roche with a deal of our own. It's the ideal opportunity. Some thug he barely knows or trusts, taking advantage to hit him up for more money. We convince him to work exclusively for us, and you can buy every sandwich shop in the city."

"Oooh." She pressed our foreheads together. "The little lady likes that," she said, getting a laugh out of me. "But how is that going to work? The Kings still hold the advantage. They have the strength, the numbers, and the resources. We can't funnel hundreds of thousands of dollars through our underground casinos. There's the little issue that we don't have any."

"Shit. I forgot all about that." I threw my hands up. "Guess we're out of luck."

Adeline whacked my arm. "Alright, asshole. I'm listening. Finish telling me the grand plan."

"It's true the Merchants can't offer everything the Kings do. Not yet," I said. "But there is something he wants that the Kings will never be able to get him."

"More than millions of dollars?"

"In addition to," I corrected. "The Merchants have built up contacts too. Who do you think hires us for jobs? We can run the same stolen painting scams. Sinjin, Brutal, and our men will launder the money through gambling and the underground fighting circuit. The terms of the deal are typed up and saved on my computer. But to get La Roche to make an enemy of the most feared gang in the city, he'd need more.

"We give him the ledger."

Adeline reeled away. "Excuse me? The fuck we are."

"Didn't realize it was up to you."

"What the hell are you talking about, Killian?" she cried. "We can't give him the ledger."

"We can't make the deal without it."

"We don't even have it!"

"We will," I said calmly. "Because now we go back to your earlier question. How does going after La Roche get us Kieran?"

"How does it?"

I slipped out from under her, drifting to the board.

"We told you that Kieran either is or was a King. Something is behind their rise to power, and forty years of ruling unchallenged. La Roche pulling out is a coup that could sink them. If Kieran is looking out for his old gang, he won't sit back while that happens.

"At some point in our talks with La Roche, someone will approach me and remind Killian Hunt of how much he has to lose by pissing off Kieran. They'll warn me to back off, and then Kieran's little assistant, if it's not Kieran himself, will enjoy a stay in our dungeon until we've extracted every bit of information he has on the location of the ledger."

A profound silence filled the room.

"You're putting yourself out there as bait," she said, voice soft.

"Essentially."

"Because Kieran does have something on you."

"Yes."

There was a pause. "Any point in asking what it is?"

"None."

"Okay, then let me ask this. Is it a secret against Killian Hunt the man, or Cash the Merchant?"

"Kieran can't possibly know I'm one of the leaders of the Merchants. Why do you think we wear masks?"

"So Kieran doesn't discover just how much of a hold he could have over you," she said mostly to herself. "We have to make a deal with La Roche. The deal hinges on goods we can't locate or deliver. And word has to get back to Kieran, where we hope he sends a messenger that gives up the final clue to the ledger under torture. Did I cover it all?"

"You missed the part where 'we' means you and me. Just you and me. All five of us can't be bait."

"What am I supposed to do?"

"We'll get to that, Redgrave. First things first. Dax Palmer is the assistant to La Roche's assistant. Mercer will get a line on him that'll get us La Roche's schedule. After, he'll get closer to Enzo. We have to find the right time to approach La Roche, and it must be after Enzo makes the demand for more money."

"This should be first," she said. Adeline turned me to face her. "I know I bitched you out for not letting me be your backup, but a couple of cocky Blood Brothers is nothing against Kieran himself, or this La Roche who's managed to fool the entire world into believing he's a boring banker. You don't throw wild cards in a game like this."

"I have every faith in you, Adeline." I held her chin between two fingers. Visions of the night I held her on the roof swam through my mind. Her laugh. Soft hair. Warm body. Steady stream of carefully chosen questions and answers designed to fool worse than La Roche's phony *La Libertad*. The days since then, the seduction techniques had been more effective than I wanted to admit.

I gently kissed her lips. "You're more than you seem."

ADELINE

I lay out on her floor snow angel-style, laughing as Gianna outlined me in stacks of hundreds.

"The first thing I'm buying is that gold headboard."

"Buy it for your new apartment. Anywhere in the city," I said. "Give this one to Captain. We'll get his couch moved here."

"So you know, I've started outing the pedophiles. I've contacted three different news outlets claiming to be a survivor of the Castian. I've asked to be kept anonymous, and told them the names and *preferences* that were in that guy's little black book. I gave them the details of that night so they know it's real. Those monsters won't get away with what they've done."

"Thank you."

"Happy talk now." She looped the trail around my feet. "How else will we make it rain? Can Momma G finally buy that new sniper she's been eyeing on the dark web?"

"She can buy two. As long as there's enough money left over to get information on a guy named Richard La Roche."

"La Roche? Why is that familiar?"

"Senior year. You and your troupe put on a private performance for alumni? La Roche was there. He came up to us to compliment you, and I remember thinking only the wealthy have names like Richard La Roche."

She nodded along. "Yeah. He was cute. Definitely silver fox vibes." Gianna reached the end of the outline. She continued on, encasing me in a wall of money. "What's the deal with him?"

"Apparently, he's the best white-collar criminal the world has never seen. He's set himself up with a stable of thieves and forgers that counterfeit, deal in stolen antiquities and forgery. He's also been the Kings' main bankroller for three years."

She stared at me.

"I'm serious, G. The silver fox is a sly fox."

"How do you know this?"

"Cash," I replied. "He finally told me the plan. Part of it anyway. The Merchants will offer La Roche a deal to break with the Kings."

"Ballpark bankroller for me."

I calculated the numbers. "Three years. Let's say about a quarter of a million changes hands every weekend in the casinos. Patrons dropping real bills, and Kings handing over phony cash. Minus the expenses of running a criminal enterprise. I'd guess their arrangement with La Roche nets seven point eight million a year. Even when you take out La Roche's cut, that's a great stinkin' hunk of money."

"Yeah, it is. Addy, if the Merchants pull this off, it'll be *the Kings who*? Money like that, they can buy everyone in this damn place and put a mask on them."

"I choose my men well."

"So, what's our angle? I'd love to snake this deal out from under them, but we have even less to offer La Roche."

I shook my head. "We're not messing with the deal. We can't. There is our lack of resources for one. And two, the double play in this plan is forcing Kieran to step in and stop the attacks on the Kings' business."

"Why would he?"

"The Merchants believe Kieran is connected to the Kings in some way, and their logic is sound. Dad traced Kieran to The Pleasure Center four years ago. Before the murder overhauled the business and Angelo tightened security.

"If Kieran or a messenger approaches Killian, I need to be there, and Kieran needs to believe this is nothing more than the Merchants trying to elevate their status. Killian's predictions haven't been wrong yet. I can't risk throwing this one off course."

"Just scoping La Roche out, then?"

"Yes. Whatever deal Killian makes with him will be my deal when I take over the Merchants. I want to know who I'm getting in bed with," I relayed. "So far, I know he's bold. Arrogantly so. He displayed a forged lost masterpiece for the entire world to see."

"You mean *La Libertad*?" I peeked over my money wall and saw her on her phone. "Searched his name and it was among the first articles to come up. You're telling me this is a forgery?"

"Yep, and a beacon to forgers worldwide—saying to all 'I'm better than you.'"

"He definitely sounds like my type," she mumbled.

Laughing, I nudged her shoulder. "Look into a guy named Dax Palmer. That's where Mercer is starting. He's an assistant."

"Got it. Scope out La Roche. Hang back. Let the Merchants bring Kieran to us."

My phone buzzed in my pocket.

"Exactly." Fishing it out, I answered, "Hello?"

"Hello, Miss Redgrave?"

"This is she."

"Hi, I apologize for disturbing your morning. I work at Waterford Retirement Home. I'm one of your father's caregivers. Ms. Duncan."

I sat up, knocking over a money stack. "Is something wrong?"

"Your father is well. He's currently enjoying a dip in the hot tub with Mrs. Arnold and Mrs. Peters."

That man lives the high life, doesn't he.

"But there is an issue," she continued. "We need to discuss the latest... incidents, and what we can do to address it moving forward. Destroying property, gambling, giving an eighty-four-year-old man with a bad hip a leg up over the wall—among other things."

I sighed. "Say no more. I'll be there in twenty minutes."

"Thank you, Miss Redgrave. See you soon."

I hung up. "I've got to go, G. Daddy Red is up to no good."

"Isn't he always?" She scooped up an armful of money and ran for her room. "Starting my apartment hunt. It'll have a fireplace and a sauna. Probably never use that bitch, but I want it anyway."

I left Gianna to her fun. Skipping downstairs, I climbed in my car and drove past the home for Salvatore's parking lot. The path from the home to the restaurant was bustling with people and had friends on either end. If Jocelyn was hanging about looking for revenge, I wouldn't make it easy for her.

The automatic doors released a blast of cool, lavender air. Mrs. Rowe jumped up at the sight of me.

"Adeline, I'm so happy to see you. How are you feeling, dear?"

"I'm fine." I sank into her hug. "It's becoming a familiar routine at this point. Cancel the cards. Never keep more than fifty dollars in cash on me. Order a new sushi wallet. Don't know what I'll do if they stop making them."

"Oh, Addy." She hugged me tighter, willing comfort into my bones. "You don't have to be strong for me."

No, I have to be strong for me. Jocelyn will never make me that helpless little girl again. My hand fisted on her shirt. *Never.*

"Miss Redgrave?"

Tara Duncan emerged from the double doors leading out of the lobby. She was a short, thin woman with ruddy cheeks and spots of adult acne. I didn't have many direct dealings with her. She was one of many caregivers looking after the residents.

"Right through here," she said.

"Is there a problem?" Rowe asked, echoing my question.

"Daddy has had—"

"No problem," Duncan cut in. "I just wanted to speak with Miss Redgrave on ways we can make Oscar's stay more comfortable."

"Of course." Rowe imparted one last hug.

I followed Ms. Duncan inside, trailing her down the hall to the game room. She pushed open the door and stepped aside for me to go in ahead.

The game room was a tiny corner of the home. Smaller than my bedroom. It boasted a small couch, two tables, four chairs, and a cabinet of board games. I took a seat at the table.

"Is it about the mattress?" I asked. "I'll pay to replace it."

"No, this isn't about the mattress."

"That old man didn't break something else going over that wall, did he? Jasmine said he was fine. Barely a scratch."

"He is fine," she replied, sitting across from me. "This is about Mrs. Watkins."

"Watkins? What about her?"

"Over the last several weeks, she and your father developed a friendship. At night, after lights out, they've taken to meeting in each other's rooms."

"Oooohkkayy," I drew out. "I'm afraid I haven't evolved to the point I can talk about my father's sex life. Whatever the old man's up to, if they're both willing, it's none of my business."

She put a hand out to stop me getting up. "They are both willing. The issue is Mrs. Watkins's children, and *Mr.* Watkins."

"Oh." I sat back down.

"Mr. Watkins lives here in the south wing."

The south wing was a locked wing. It was for residents who needed dedicated care and attention.

"He has dementia and doesn't recognize his wife most days. Even so, their children are very upset at the idea of their mother having a boyfriend. Usually, we don't intervene, but they've threatened to stop paying for her stay here if it doesn't end."

I massaged the bridge of my nose. "I understand. Do you want me to talk to him?"

"That won't be necessary. You see, the solution we came up with is baby monitors. We hid them in their rooms, so the night workers would hear if they met."

I stilled. "Excuse me?"

"The other day, Nancy forgot to turn off the monitor when she left. I took over the shift and overheard an interesting conversation while I was in the nurses' station."

Slowly, I raised my head. A smile played on that pimply face.

"Between you and your father," she spelled out, smirk widening.

"You put a listening device in his room without informing him?" I forced through gritted teeth. "That's a violation of his privacy. I could get you and Nancy fired."

"Right," she sang. "Because that's the issue here."

I sat up straight, back rigid. "What is the issue? I had lunch with my father. We talked about nonsense and joked around. Not a big deal."

"Yes, it did sound like a joke. You going on about witnessing the murder of Raiden Spencer. Kidnapped by his killers and then, plot twist! You fall in love with them." She howled, peeling my lips from my teeth. "But how could you not? You're a killer too. This Angelo Castillo guy didn't know what hit him."

Everything. She heard everything.

"By the time I realized it was real, you were halfway through your conversation. It's about then I turned on the recorder."

"Recorder?" I pulled my new notepad out of my purse. "What recorder?"

"The one I have safely tucked away. You'll never find it," she said. "But I will give it to you. For one hundred thousand dollars. I'll give you my phone and the recording on it. That'll be the last you hear of this."

"One hundred thousand dollars."

"It's not like you can't afford it." She swept out her hands. "No one that can afford this place can claim they're broke. Plus, I've seen that new car you're driving around these days."

"Have you," I said simply.

"Tell me, did you really witness the death of Raiden Spencer?"

Shaking my head, I scribbled something on my pad. "Nope. Didn't see a thing."

"Come on. It's just us." Duncan folded her arms, leaning back in her seat. "You clearly don't have a problem with gangsters or murder, but you couldn't have known then that all the Merchants— Did I use the right name? That all the Merchants wanted was a little pussy. I would've turned them in the second I got away. Told the cops that Sinjin, Cash, Brutal, and Mercer put a broken bottle in Raiden Spencer's neck."

"I have no idea what you're talking about, Ms. Duncan." I flipped the page. "I don't know anyone by those names." I laughed. "Are they names? Who calls their kid Brutal?"

"You going to play dumb about Angelo Castillo too?" Temper leaked into her voice. "That confession I did record, and I looked him up that night. A man matching his description was fished out of the water with another hole in his neck. Courtesy of the knife you plunged in it."

"Ms. Duncan, that's a load of poppycock."

She frowned. "Poppy... cock?"

"Big, fat load of it." I laughed. "Isn't poppycock a fun word to say? There are all sorts of fun words we never use. Like cattywampus."

I held up the notepad. Written in huge, uppercase letters were the words:

I will kill you.

Duncan froze, mouth open.

"Or balderdash," I cried. "Say that one with me. Balderdash. Balderdash." I flipped the page.

I'll slit your throat and drain the blood from those Pikachu cheeks.

"Balderdash."

I'll rip every hair from your head and stuff it down your throat.

Her cheeks weren't red anymore. Duncan paled dangerously in the fluorescent lights.

"And jabberwocky," I said. "Did you know it was a real word that means nonsense speech? I thought it was just a monster in a poem."

You'll die wishing all I did was stab you in the neck.

Duncan shot up, toppling the chair. "Threatening— You're threatening me!" she shrieked. "You just showed me a note saying I'll die wishing you stabbed me in the neck!"

"I did what?" Outrage kicked me up an octave. "What the hell are you talking about? Are you high?"

You'll regret this day, bitch.

"You wrote notes threatening to kill me! They said you'd rip out my hair and slit my throat."

And you just proved you're recording this conversation too.

"Ms. Duncan, I'm sitting here talking about funny words. I haven't harmed or threatened you in any way." I got up, and she lurched away, tripping over the fallen chair. "Is this some kind of psychotic break? Do I need to call a nurse?" I flipped to the last page.

And it's the last regret you'll ever have.

"Give me your phone," I said brightly. "I'll get someone for you."

"Get away from me!" She ripped it out and lobbed the phone at my head. It went wide, crashing into the wall. "I bought that this morning," Duncan hissed. "You want the right one, get me my money!"

My fingers twitched. It'd be all too easy to kill her right here. The chair legs she was wrestling with would dent her skull without a hitch.

But Mrs. Rowe saw me go in with her. As did the security cameras.

"I hope you get the help you need."

"You have two weeks," she flung at my back.

I walked out and went straight to Dad's room. He wasn't there, but he didn't need to be. I found the baby monitor under his bed quickly and set it on his nightstand. When he saw it, he'd take care of the rest.

"Bye, Adeline." Mrs. Rowe's cheery smile followed me out.

"Bye, Mrs. Rowe. See you soon."

I melded into the flow of pedestrian traffic, dialing Gianna.

"Hey, babe. How's Daddy Red?"

"I'm coming back to your place," I replied. "We have a problem."

Chapter Five

"**A**deline, where is the lobster crostini?"

"I brought it out, Chef."

"And the shrimp tartlets?"

"Waiting for your final approval."

"Excellent."

The praise was likely for him in congratulations for pulling off another successful event. I decided to take a little of it on. I did prep or cook most of the food.

Ryan kept me dangling till nearly the last minute. Two days before, he called me up and said I could work the Rothchild-Lysandro wedding. I jumped at the chance.

Gianna called our relationship ten times more dysfunctional than hers would ever be with Raul. She didn't understand that I needed to cook. This was how I did good.

I needed a double dose of good deeds. They'd make up for the bad ones to come.

Ten days since Duncan threatened me. Ten days to her deadline.

My mind wasn't made up on what to do. She called me again from the home to demand a ransom drop, and my distance of one hundred feet at all times. I also got a call from Mrs. Rowe apologizing left, right, and center for the baby monitor my father found in his room. The night nurse was fired, and my dad made the staff sweep every inch of the place daily while he watched.

Unfortunately, the night nurse didn't bring Duncan down with her. She was still there and holding our secret over my head.

I had the money to pay her. All the same, I knew without Saint's warning in my ear, that if I gave her the money, it would never stop. She had ammo in two murders, a robbery, a kidnapping, Kieran, the names of the Merchants, and that they were connected to Adeline Redgrave. Not to mention proof positive that the world forgot the Redgraves at their peril.

Whether or not the recording truly existed, Tara Duncan could not.

If she isn't stupid, she's got the recording and someone she trusts hanging on to it in case I come after her ass.

That thought stayed me for more than a week. Time was running out.

"Adeline, why are you standing there?" Ryan snapped me awake. "Put out the fruit skewers."

"Yes, Chef."

Picking up the tray, I left the kitchen of the Williamson Historical Home. A pocket of history in our industrial city. Williamson Home was a preserved Victorian-style house on the edge of Leighbridge. Beautiful and charming it was. Up to date it was not. The old-timey cookstove had two burners.

We cooked all of the food off-site, then drove them over with an army of heat lamps to keep them tasty as the wedding party shot two million photos outside.

I weaved through the staff and entered the ballroom. Saint was helping himself to a plate of marinated shrimp and stuffed mushrooms.

"Saint?" I hissed. "What are you doing here?"

"What are you doing here?" he returned. "You have a job, Bunny."

"One day, you guys will realize you don't have to pay your girlfriend to stick around."

"No shit?"

"When you do," I said with a laugh. "I'll have Ryan and Salvatore's to fall back on."

"When that happens, you'll have taken your place in the *organization*, and gotten the raise in pay that goes with it."

"Why are you here?" I arranged my skewers next to the summer berry martinis. "Better question. How did you get in? There are guards posted on every entrance."

"Easy. Bashed them over the heads and came in the back."

"Ha. Ha. I told you joking about maiming people isn't funny. Back to the original question."

He plucked a skewer off my plate, ignoring my squawking. "I'm here because we're going on a field trip. There's a party at La Roche's house tomorrow night. You need to be ready."

"Tomorrow night? Why is this the first I'm hearing about it?"

"Mercer secured the time, but Cash had to secure the invitation. It was a whole thing of him pretending to run into the guy by chance, striking up a conversation, and dropping the right hints. The invite was delivered today. He's got a plus-one. That's you, Bunny."

"Did you-know-who go to him to demand more?"

"He did. Pais's rage has loosened his tongue. He told Mercer his demand for an eighty-twenty split was rejected. Enzo said there was no need because they were negotiating other deals to cover the loss, and he could fuck off. Whores are a dime a dozen.

"Enzo went to La Roche and said they were dropping the sixty-forty deal in his favor for sixty-five/thirty-five in theirs. Pais didn't tell him what the response to that was, but I bet it wasn't civil."

I looked around. The serving staff checked the table arrangements for the final time. The band warmed up. No one was paying attention to us.

But this isn't the place to talk.

"Okay. Our job was to cook and deliver the food. Williamson staff do the serving. Let me finish this and I'll be ready." I turned to leave. Back to him, I said, "Put it back."

His chuckles followed me out.

I finished putting out the food, said my goodbyes, and met Saint in the hallway leading to the back entrance. He looked me up and down.

"You know, this uniform is working for me. We'll fuck in the car before we go."

"You say the most romantic things, baby." I linked our fingers, secretly thrilled we left the days of leading me around by my belt loop behind. "Careful. A girl could lose her head getting swept off her feet five times a day."

We walked out the back, bursting onto the two men lying unconscious half in the bushes.

"Dammit, Saint!"

"What?" He kept walking. "They left me no choice. I needed you. They were in my way."

"When they find them, they'll call the police and ruin this couple's reception. Salvatore's can't be connected with a brain-bashing maniac who happens to appear on every job I'm working!"

I ranted at his back the whole way to the car. Saint's response was to toss me inside, rip my chef's pants off, and use them to bind my arms behind my back. I came screaming into the driver's seat as he drilled me from behind.

"And I hope you learned your lesson." I peeled my coat off my sweaty body and tossed it in the back. Underneath, I wore a simple purple T-shirt and jean shorts.

Saint chuckled, turning on the car.

"Where are we going?" I asked.

"Elmshire Woods. We have a cabin out there."

"We do?" I lazily traced a tattoo on his neck. "When are you going to update me on the full list of marital assets? The hideaways. The finances."

"Cash handles the assets. He'll tell you what we own, and the bodies underneath them."

"Are there actual buried bodies?"

"Only three."

Again, I did not know if he was joking.

Sinjin drove us out of the city. An hour and a half to Elmshire Woods.

It was one of my favorite places on earth. I had to drive through the woods in Raul's borrowed car the days Ryan sent me out to the organic farm. Trees hung their branches over the road, defying the barrier that split their natural oasis. I remember long walks in the woods with my dad. Giggling as he swept me up over tree roots. Taught me to listen for the sounds of different animals. Engulfed my small hand on the knife hilt and showed me the right way to strike, slash, and skin.

Saint turned off onto a dirt road. We rumbled over the path for what seemed like miles, leaving the city's pulsing hum behind.

Through a break in the trees, I saw the beginnings of a wooden structure and a flash of red. The forest opened up, revealing a tiny pocket for four cars and a one-story cabin with a river stone chimney stack. Five steps led to a porch that wrapped around one side of the cabin. There was no furniture on the porch. No plants or a welcome home sign. An impersonal space that served a single purpose.

Mercer climbed out of his car as we parked. Our arrival signaled Brutal and Cash to come out of the cabin. Both carried guns.

"This is it," I said. "You've finally decided to kill me and dispose of my body. Can we make love one more time before I'm executed?"

"Yes," Saint agreed.

I hopped out, running up to Brutal and jumping in his arms. Our kiss curled my toes and pooled heat in my lower belly. I wanted that before I died too.

"Let me guess," I said. "We've moved on from knives, and now I'm being taught how to shoot."

He nodded.

"How does that get me ready for tomorrow night? Won't La Roche have security checking if people are packing?"

"It's not about tomorrow," Cash said. "In general, you need to be able to defend yourself."

"I *know* how to defend myself."

He looked me in the eye. "Angelo."

Jaw tightening, I replied, "I was outnumbered."

"We're outnumbered now and will be for the foreseeable future. At the hotel, you resisted taking a gun. That's over. No more hesitation."

"Brutal, Sinjin, and Mercer don't use guns."

"They're lethal with or without them."

"I'm—"

"You're what?" He cocked a brow. "Easily capable of killing men without a weapon? Since when?"

Pull back, Addy.

"I was going to say, I'm willing to learn how to shoot, but I don't see it being my weapon of choice. Or any weapon for that matter. Because as I explained, I'm just a cook. After you've secured La Roche and crippled the Kings, I'm done."

"Oh, I see. We have a misunderstanding." Killian swallowed the distance between us. "I assumed Sinjin made this clear. There is no done. There is no out. There is no sitting on the sidelines. Once I name you one of us, you do what we say. You take the jobs we give you."

Fire blazed in his glare to match the heat singeing my veins. "And if I say no?"

"You'll be relocated to a separate apartment where you can cook, and fuck Sinjin, Brutal, and no doubt Mercer to your heart's content. Since apparently, that's all you're interested in."

I climbed off Brutal, facing him head-on. "Are you saying I'll be your kept woman?"

"Good. Misunderstanding cleared up." His smirk was nasty. "We can't have someone in our business who isn't a part of it."

I tore away from him, sweeping over the other guys. Mercer shrugged with a grin like it couldn't be helped. Brutal's expression was impassive.

Sinjin kissed my forehead. "Them's the rules, Bunny. I still love you, though."

I took a deep breath and trapped it. *If it was me, I would do the same. Someone lurking in the background with as much information as I had was dangerous.*

You could only truly trust a person when they were facing the same life sentences as you.

I understood this. Knew this. Agreed with this.

Still, I ached to punch him in the face. For one sentence alone.

Once I name you one of us...

Which meant, he hadn't yet. Killian didn't trust me. The impossible part was, attempts to earn his trust may destroy it forever. Brought on jobs and my life on the line, I couldn't hold back. If he witnessed all I was capable of, Killian would know beyond all doubt I wasn't who I claimed to be.

You have to be there if Kieran approaches Cash. You must get to the ledger first. That doesn't happen if you're frittering away in another safe house.

He must've seen me make up my mind. Cash smacked the hilt on my palm. "Out back in five minutes."

Cash went inside. I beat back the temptation to give him that punch and stayed out, crossing the porch to the backyard.

Wooden posts were staked in the grass about a dozen yards from the porch steps. Five cans and glass bottles rested on top of them. I peeked more at my side.

Glancing over my shoulder, I confirmed the guys were inside. I lined up my shot and fired. The middle can flew into the depths of the woods. Quickly, I replaced it and was almost to the porch before the boys filed out.

"Did I hear a shot?" Killian drawled.

"I tried and missed. How close do I stand?"

"Right here." He pointed to the bottom step.

"That's too far."

"Believe in yourself."

I flipped him off, gun and all. The guy lived on making fun of me. *At least Saint's teasing comes with sex.* I went up to them and found myself in Killian's arms.

He turned me to the targets. Killian held me to his chest as he nudged my feet hip-width apart. I inhaled a heavy scent of pine, honey, and musk. It led me to the skin peeking through his unbuttoned shirt. I nuzzled my nose inside, body relaxing into him.

"Focus." He turned my chin—touch firm but gentle. "Get a good grip. Right hand on top. Left on the bottom. Take a breath, line up your shot, and pull. Don't rush it."

"Don't rush it. You have all the time you need." My father rang in my ears, recalling the days all those years ago when Gianna and I were learning how to shoot.

I took my deep breath, aimed my target dead center, and inched a micrometer to the right. The bullet flew past the can without a wobble.

If only Dad could see me now.

"Close," said Killian. "Try again."

I fired once. Twice. Eight times.

Miss.

Miss.

Miss.

The seventh time, I got cheeky and aimed for a tree two yards back. Nailed it bang on. The bottle not so much.

"Wow," Cash said. "You suck."

"I'm learning," I protested.

"How did you kill that King in the Castian? Sinjin, did you make that up?"

"Nah. It was all Bunny. But I see now I owe my life to divine intervention."

The four of them burst out laughing.

I flushed under a furious need to defend my honor. "Let's see you guys do better."

The challenge was hardly out of my mouth. Cash took the gun and the middle bottle blew apart. He passed it to Mercer who fired in quick succession, shooting both cans on the outside posts. Brutal's bottle was gone between blinks. Then, it was Sinjin.

He didn't bother with the gun. Claiming his knife from the holster, he sent the metal soaring through the air. It stabbed the can through the head of the German woman pictured. He got it and showed me.

Be still, my black heart.

I swayed, damp slicking my boy shorts. That was without a doubt the sexiest thing I'd ever witnessed men do. And the grins on their faces said they knew it.

"Don't seduce me when I'm pissed at you," I snapped.

The day continued in the same vein. The others drifted inside at some point, and it was just me and Cash. He made fun of me often and unashamedly. Even so, there was patience in his correcting my positioning, and calm as he repeated tips. He was content to be out there with me for hours.

Three times I gave in and made the shot. He'd smile at me and say, "Good." Practically forcing me to forget secrecy and blow them all out. Anything for that smile.

"You're not completely hopeless," he said, taking the gun from me. "You'll keep working on this. Brutal wants to teach you to box. I prefer you avoid close-contact fighting, and drop them with one shot."

"Do you worry about me?" I slipped under his arm on the way inside.

"You've proven I need to."

Brutal, Mercer, and Sinjin stretched out on the couch before an unlit fireplace. As I suspected, it was bare bones in here. A dining set, two couches, and a small kitchen were all the place had to say for itself. There were three doors I assumed led to two bedrooms and a bathroom. Otherwise, there wasn't a television, rug, or decorations.

"Are we staying here tonight?"

"No, we're going back to the city and sleeping at our place in Leigh-bridge." Killian kept me under his arm, continuing to the front door. "We'll pick some things up on the way."

"We? As in me and you?"

"Yes."

"Why?"

"La Roche has had a man tailing me since the day after I ran into him. I let him follow me around and shook him off at night. Yesterday, I let him see me going into the Leighbridge loft. La Roche will want to know where I live. As will Kieran, if he decides to tip his hand," he said.

Killian dropped this information like it was nothing.

"My new friend will be waiting near my supposed home for me to come back. That's what we're going to do, so they can begin digging into your history as well. By the party tomorrow night, we'll all know everything we need to know about each other."

"Well, that's not creepy at all," I mumbled. "Why is La Roche having you followed?"

"By law, con men don't believe in coincidences. He thinks something's up with our chance meeting."

I goggled at him. "How do we scam the man if he already knows he's being scammed?"

"You'll see."

CASH

A creak sounded in the space. My eyes drew open.

Soft footfalls. Then, a weight settled on my chest.

Adeline tucked herself between me and the couch, laying her head in the crook of my shoulder. I held still, waiting.

When she spoke, her whisper hardly reached me. "You wouldn't really put me up in some apartment, would you?"

"I would."

"But I work for you."

"We both know why Sinjin wanted you close. It wasn't to make his crepes."

"Those reasons haven't changed."

"They have." My tone was hard. It had to be. "You can't be half in and half out. If you don't want in our world, you'll get your wish."

"Why are you doing this, Killian?" Those big, brown eyes captured me in their shining pools. "Do you distrust me that much?"

"No." The confession surprised me. "I believe you won't reveal who we are, or betray us."

"Then why? Is it because you—"

"This isn't about me! Angelo attacked you. Let his men do what they did to you because we dragged you into this war. Why can't you see I'm giving you a way out? You want to be a chef at Salvatore's with friends, family, and a normal life. After we end the Kings, this is how you have it."

She was quiet for so long, I thought she fell asleep.

"Normal boyfriends too?"

"What?"

"If you're forcing me out of the Merchants to protect me, it'd be dangerous for us to have contact. Rivals could just as easily track me down alone in that apartment," she said. "I'd have to move on completely. Meet new men. Have their babies—"

"Careful," I leaked through clenched teeth.

"How can you be jealous?" Adeline laid her forehead over mine. "You said Sinjin, Mercer, and Brutal will come to see me. Not you."

My grip on her thighs would leave marks. Evidence of my eternal battle to bring her closer or push her away.

"Tell me you'll come to me, Killian," she whispered. "Hold me on your lap while you share how you see the world. Trace patterns on my skin when you think I'm sleeping. Keep me under the covers, promising everything will be okay as I put myself back together. Tell me you will."

I won't.

When you're gone, your smell will fade from my pillows. I'll stop drifting downstairs in the morning to listen to you hum over a steaming pot. I won't leave my office open a crack, waiting for you to peek inside. I won't need your taste on my tongue. Your body warm and willing in my hands.

When you're gone, I'll stop falling in love with you.

"I won't."

Adeline kissed me—light and soft and over too soon. "Then, I can't go. You need me, Killian. I won't leave you in pain."

"Go to bed, Adeline."

"Okay."

She padded across the room, her footsteps light where mine were heavy. I closed the door behind us.

Adeline reached for my boxers. I grasped her hands, leading her back to fall on the bed. She rested her feet on my chest—hands splayed above her head. The shirt she helped herself to, held together by one button.

The back of my fingers glided down her bare legs. Adeline was open and waiting for me. Trusting—though I gave her no reason to be. Relaxed—though our first time was a fight, and we had yet to declare a winner.

I slid beneath her lace panties, drawing them over her knees and flinging them somewhere behind me. Adeline's legs fell open, laying her bare before my eyes.

"You said I had to see your dangle game when you were playing," I said. "Show me."

For a moment, it seemed she didn't know what I meant. Then, she unbuttoned that final button, rising out of my shirt like a siren from the sea. I bent to meet her. Her lips were salty-sweet like she snuck a treat after lights out. I explored the depths of her mouth. Tangling with her tongue. Naming the candies I stopped eating at fourteen, and swearing she was sweeter than all combined.

Adeline fell back, grinning to proclaim her victory even as she spread her pussy for me.

She teased her clit with light, stroking fingers.

My boxers joined the rest on the floor. I stroked in time with her. Picking up the pace as she did. Slowing as she dipped inside, eyes fluttering shut.

Adeline spread herself as if to say, "*This will all be yours, when you get your head out of your ass.*"

I even heard it in her voice.

The urge to do just that welled in my chest, pushing to break through my ice calm. I lost control with her in the bathroom. I swore I'd never reduce to that state. A raging, possessive beast that wanted nothing, and no one, but her.

Adeline went faster—riding that wave that would bring her to climax. Full lips parted by feverish, staccato moans. Back tunneling over the sheets. Glazed whiskey eyes struggled to stay open. She wanted to watch me *watch* her come, and my cock jumped at the realization.

She smacked her pussy, and my resolve broke. I jumped on top of her—earning a delighted shriek.

"That was easy." She peppered my jaw, nose, lips, cheeks with kisses. "Will I get my apology that quickly too?"

"I apologize for all wrongs real and imagined. I don't apologize for this."

I took what was mine in one thrust. Adeline cried out, nails digging in my back.

"Never apologize for that," she gasped. "But do apologize for making me wait so long."

"It should make you feel better to know holding myself back has been a step below Chinese water torture."

"It helps," she said, grinning. "Fuck me, Alfred."

"I will pull the fuck out and leave now."

Adeline locked her legs behind my knees. "I'd like to see you try."

"You want me like this." I started pumping—fast and then faster still. "Crazed. Out of control."

I hitched her onto my lap, bouncing her to my thrusts. Adeline's screams would've woken the neighbors if we had any.

"Yes," she cried. "Just like this. D-don't hold back with me, Killian. I want... all of you."

Roaring, I flipped her, and gave Adeline her wish. I didn't hold back.

Clutching the headboard, I poured months of frustration, sexual tension, rage, and attraction into her soft, tight, willing body.

She spurred me on, yelling for more. Harder. Faster.

"Yes, Killian," she breathed. "I love you too."

And then I broke.

Hot ropes of cum burst from me, contorting me in a shape almost painful. A groan ripped out, trying to bring something else with it.

Adeline followed a second behind. She clung to me, writhing and bucking, the most beautiful thing I'd ever seen, and beautiful things were once my life.

"Damn, Dangle." I fell next to her. "Caught. Captured. Not giving it up."

"I'm very happy to hear you say that, toy boy." Adeline draped me over her, holding my arm to her chest. "You play hard to get at expert level."

I chuckled—till her confession sobered me. "Adeline, I have to say this. Sex is all I'm willing to give."

"Why?" She sounded genuinely curious.

"There can't be something more with Killian while Kieran is out there. And you deserve more than Cash."

There it was. The truth.

"If there's... you. I could be forced to make an impossible choice. Neither one of us should be in that situation, Adeline. We both can't come out the other side of it."

Adeline was quiet for a while.

"I understand," she whispered. "Thank you for being honest with me."

I nodded—nose buried in her hair.

I doubt my confession made her feel better. It hadn't for me.

This is how it has to be. Kieran's torn my life apart once before. He doesn't get to have you too. So neither do I.

"Say something sweet," Adeline asked.

"I could paint you every day for the rest of my life, and never come close to capturing the masterpiece that is you, Adeline Redgrave. I'd believe you were the inspiration for La Libertad, and the reason inadequacy drove Molina to madness, if time travel wasn't highly improbable."

Her laugh was a gentle, throaty purr. "I take it you're not a *Doctor Who* fan."

"Nah, that show is the shit. Seen every episode three times."

"Three times?" She twisted, facing me to nuzzle my jaw. "So, that's what Kieran has in his ledger. Killian Hunt is a huge geek."

"Massive," I said. "Your turn. Equal or higher value. The rules still apply."

"Okay. Here goes: I've watched *Doctor Who* four times."

The night continued on. Laughing, joking, messing around under the sheets.

We woke too late in the morning.

Adeline shopped my meager kitchen offerings, and turned them into scrambled eggs, yogurt with cut-up strawberries, and avocado toast. We ate in bed—Adeline secure under my arm—and talked about that night.

"Are you sure I should go in blind?"

"Yes," I replied. "La Roche will sniff a scam coming around the block. I'll sell it by wrapping every sentence in a kernel of truth. But it can't come off like we planned what to say."

"Why do you think La Roche got involved with Angelo?" she mused. Adeline fed me a strawberry. "He has money, respect, and everyone fooled. Why reveal yourself, risk La Libertad outing you as a criminal, and then get in bed with a bunch of criminals more ruthless than you? Were the millions in his account not enough?"

I dropped my head on the board. "I'd hazard a guess it wasn't about money. For years, he's been the best and no one knew. No recognition. No praise. No legacy. He has all of that now among the people who appreciate his talent. Plus, he wouldn't say no to more millions."

She rubbed my thigh. "What will we do when we're getting a cut of those millions?"

"New place. More men. Our own territory, and the money and weapons to defend it," I said. "La Roche will say yes. He doesn't know yet he has no choice."

"No more talk of sly old men." She hopped on her knees and kissed me. "I'm ready for my post-breakfast sex romp."

"Do you get tired?" I asked. "Are you capable?"

That wandering hand wandered farther. It struck gold.

"Do you?"

I pushed the tray off the bed. "Nope."

ADELINE

Killian leaned against the hood of the car. You had to be looking to catch the slight widening of his eyes, and I was.

"I do look good, don't I?" I teased.

One of our stops the day before was to get me a dress for the party. You'd think Cash could put his analytical mind away for the simple task of choosing clothes.

"Yellow is least liked by the majority of the population. Accurately, only five percent of people name it as their favorite color."

I tromped into the dressing room and discarded the canary yellow slip dress on the pile. My next pick was a blue strapless dress begging to take my curves out to dinner.

"Blue is the most-liked color. Thigh length and strapless is popular too."

I giggled. "I bet it is. But what's your favorite color, lover?"

Killian looked like he didn't want to say. "Red."

"Red it is."

There I stood in a ruby red off-the-shoulder maxi dress. My slit went all the way up the thigh, drawing Killian's eyes where I wanted them.

We climbed in and set off for the party. During the drive, I noticed Killian flicking to the rearview mirror.

"Something wrong?"

"See that black Mercedes two cars behind. That's our tail."

I checked, seeing the blinding glare of his headlights. "When will he stop?"

"When La Roche finds out what I want from him."

"Will I be with you when you two talk?"

"Of course."

I wasn't expecting an affirmative. "I am? What am I supposed to say? What are you going to say?"

"Just follow my lead. I can't have you sounding rehearsed in there, or like we're playing off each other. He'll see through that."

I let it be. Cash knew what he was doing. I trusted him.

The drive to La Roche's home wasn't long. We turned off Prescott Avenue, and ended up behind a long string of cars heading for the valet. I stuck my face to the windshield.

Four stories of pillars, balconies, white stone, and iron facades overtook Prescott and the few buildings that dared to share its space.

We rolled to a stop. Two valets sprang into action. One to take Killian's keys. The other to help me out with satin-gloved hands and a bow. "Good evening, ma'am. I hope you enjoy the party."

"Thank you."

He led me to the sidewalk. Killian wasn't there.

"Killian?"

"I'm here." The trunk slammed. Killian strode over carrying a gray case I hadn't seen him put into the car. He removed my hand from the valet and draped it over his arm.

I opened my mouth to ask him what was in the case, then my attention fell on a handsome couple brushing past us. She wore a gold, shimmering tulle gown. And a similar-sized satchel on her shoulder. The blue clashed horribly.

I should get used to this, I thought as we fell in behind them. *I'm not going to know what's going on all night.*

We stepped inside. The Waterford-Rockchapel girl in me let out a whistle she couldn't hold back. However Richard La Roche truly made his money, he made a whole heck of a lot of it, and he spent it well.

A grand staircase curved down the second floor and looped around to welcome us up. On the walls were masterpieces painted by renowned hands that I resigned to never lay eyes on in my lifetime. Gleaming marble floors reflected the well-dressed, diamond-encrusted, politely laughing crowd making their way down two paths. The double doors to our left where soft music floated out, and the hallway disappearing behind the stairs.

I took a step. A hulking mass of guard slid in my way.

"Good evening, sir. Ma'am. May I see your invitations?"

Inexplicably, Killian held out the case. "Here—"

"Killian Hunt." A deep, ringing baritone broke through the chatter.

Looking over the guard's head, it was his eyes I connected to first. Two almond-shaped robin's eggs that struck me the first time we met. Richard La Roche hadn't changed a whisker since that alumni party. His fitted gray suit and white scarf were on the right side of original. A trimmed mustache and beard encircled full, brown lips. That they were soft was answered by the peck on my knuckles.

"We haven't been introd— Hold on." He squinted at me. "Two years ago. Cinco University alumni dinner. I believe you were in the company of the charming young lady who provided that night's entertainment."

"Wow," I said. "I'm impressed." *Or I would be if I didn't know you had us followed and researched.*

"You barely looked at me," I continued. "As tends to happen when I'm in the company of that charming young lady."

La Roche grinned. "I very much doubt it's possible to miss your presence, Miss...?"

"Redgrave."

La Roche had the sweet talk and the silver fox looks to match. Salt sprinkled prominently in his beard and full head of wavy locks. He had a wide, pointed nose. Long face. And, of course, those eyes.

"Killian." La Roche hugged him warmly. "Good to see you, old friend. I'm pleased you could make it."

"As am I."

"What did you bring me?"

"You might kick me out when you see it."

The guard unstrapped Killian's case, flipping the top off. My eyes popped.

"Oh ho," La Roche laughed, clapping Killian on the back. "You devil!"

"I couldn't resist."

La Roche turned on Killian. "Don't think you're slipping away without me picking your brain. Until then, eat. Dance. Have a good time."

He moved on to foist a hug on another woman.

"Killian," I breathed. "Is that *The Lacemaker*? How did... you...?"

Killian's quirked brow silenced me. I looked from him to the Vermeer that should be hanging in the Louvre.

"Oh."

He took my hand to lead me away.

"Did you paint that?" I whispered.

We took the path away from the double doors. Inside, white-linen tables spread around the edges of a dance floor.

"Yes."

"You're a forger?"

"You don't have to whisper. Pretty much everyone here is."

I whipped around, seeing the well-dressed, diamond-encrusted, politely laughing crowd in a new light.

"Where the hell am I?"

He laughed. "Among the people who answered the advertisement."

"This is a party for grifters." My gaze drifted up to him. "And you're one too."

"Retired," he said. "That fact you should whisper. As far as La Roche is concerned, I've spent the last three years working in Canada."

The line turned down a hallway. Everyone seemed to know where they were going through these high-ceiling hallways, passing statues, antique tables carrying vases too exquisite to hold ordinary flowers, and the deeper we went, the more art whose originals could not be here.

"The paintings in the loft," I began. "Are they forgeries?"

"Some are. Some aren't. I practice to keep my skills sharp."

"Why?" There was more to the question but it stalled in my throat.

"I was the youngest of seven kids, Redgrave. My parents put all they had either into the circus, or keeping us alive. My brothers and sisters stayed on when they got older. I wanted to be a doctor," he explained. "Med school wasn't going to pay for itself."

"I'm not trying to sound judgmental." I linked my arms around his waist. "It just bowls me over sometimes how little I know about you. That's going to change, Killian Hunt." My finger snuck beneath his coat, rubbing small circles on that well-defined V leading to his length. "I will learn every sentence of your storied tale. If that sounds like a threat, it should."

"You're ridiculous," he said, humor lacing the reply.

"Why did La Roche wig out over *The Lacemaker*?"

"During our first conversation, we had an interesting, if veiled, talk about how none could match his talent. He mentioned that his only trouble was Vermeer and acquiring the right mixtures for seventeenth-century Dutch oil paint."

"Which of course, you have," I teased.

The line curved for the final time, leading past frosted glass doors. Killian and I stepped inside his home gallery. A crowd gathered at the far end of the room.

"What are we looking at?"

"The works of Aurelio Molina," he said, "and *La Libertad*."

Somehow, I didn't have to ask which one it was. My arms fell away from him. I crossed the space as if tugged by an invisible rope, tethering me to the rolling hills.

Seven paintings shared the wall. They could all be works of Molina. The paintings certainly seemed to be by the same hand. Bold colors and soft lines. Portraits of unsmiling people with heavy cheeks. There were secrets in every brushstroke. A colorful macaw hiding among the trees. Intricate patterns on the lady's skirt.

I saw the style that linked them. Then, I fell on the canvas in the middle of it all. A landscape where there were people, animals, and angels. Rolling Spanish hills came to life in a sea of greens and golds. Grass undulating in the wind seeking up to a cloudless sky, and there I was running through those hills.

The story of freedom was told in a way so different, naming it the jewel of his collection made sense.

That's why you're damn good, La Roche.

I had as much skill as a grifter as the average woman. We all learn how to smile, hedge, and manipulate to get what we wanted. While there were few I'd name better than me in any area, I mentally bowed a head to the talent that executed this con to perfection.

"Let's go." Killian's hand on my hip took me away.

We joined the party in the dining room. I spotted La Roche at a table nearest the terrace.

"Are we sitting with him?"

"A table close to him. We'll track him coming and going, and avoid conversation. We can't have him questioning you. You'll inevitably spill your life story."

"I will not," I protested.

Killian seated us at the neighboring table anyway. I gave him a look.

"If I'm not trusted to speak, I'll find other ways to amuse myself."

"Sounds like another threat."

"It is."

He grinned over the arm of the server setting out the first course.

"Moroccan carrot soup, madame. Please, enjoy."

"Thank you."

I tasted the creamy soup and moaned. Others joined our table, introducing themselves in a flurry of names, titles, and crimes.

"Trevor Le." A man sporting wire-framed glasses and an easy smile leaned over to shake our hands. "Forger. Documents."

"Killian Hunt. Forger. Art." He cupped my neck, trailing a line down my spine that sent a shiver through me. "Adeline. Lovely distraction."

"Ah. Lovely indeed." Trevor inclined his head to me. "What's your biggest score?"

"A Paul Gauguin sold to a private collector. The bastard still has it hanging on his wall!" Killian laughed uproariously, kicking off the whole table. It took me a second to laugh too.

"I should've sold him a Jean-Baptiste-Camille Corot."

Apparently, this was hysterical. Trevor teared up howling.

Who is this man?

Smacking the table, cracking jokes, greeting people like old friends. This was not the Cash I'd come to love and loathe in equal measure.

Suddenly, I saw him. The young, grinning con man using his natural skills to turn people around him into marks.

And that picture isn't any less sexy. I gripped his thigh under the table. *Do I know how to pick them, or what?*

My hand did something else under the table—fingers flying across my screen.

Me: I can still feel you pulsing inside of me. What I wouldn't give to take you into a closet right now, and swallow that cock to the hilt.

"It's all about patience," Killian said. He absentmindedly pulled out his phone. "Use a nail dryer to slowly age th-the paint."

Killian skipped a beat reading my message. The next one dropped a second behind.

Me: Have I told you how cute your ass looks in those pants? Fit and molded like you're not wearing underwear. I'm not either. If you were wondering.

"Tell me about the world of musical forgery, Malia." Killian threw the conversation to a short woman with long brown hair and golden roots. Her peach one-shoulder gown was held together by a sparkling diamond brooch.

"It's tricky. I don't have many colleagues in my field."

Me: You mentioned once spreading me and torturing my clit. Something about making me scream loud enough to wake a neighborhood. My reward was drawing an audience that would watch you pound me into the dirt.

Me: We've got soup and a room full of grifters. Does that count?

"—as a composer myself," Malia went on, "I'm able to effectively pass myself off."

I bent to type something else. A hand slipped through my dress slit. I had enough time for my eyes to widen before Killian flicked my clit.

The warning to not play games with him rang loud and clear. Killian called me out. In a room of people. With our mark sitting five feet away. And he didn't break his conversation.

"Fascinating," Killian said. He rolled his thumb over the helpless nub, zinging sparks through me that lit my face on fire. "Grady, I've heard whispers about your exploits with the superdollar. How did you replicate the color-shifting numerals?"

I scooted my chair over. Killian flashed out and gripped the underside, drawing me right back. He smiled into my eyes as two fingers pushed past my folds. "How's the soup, lover?"

"I-it's good," I rasped. "I've got to get the recip— Oh."

Killian picked up the pace—expertly fingering me and teasing my clit one-handed.

The tablecloth covered me at the waist. No one could see our activities, and yet I felt the spotlight on us. Each glance in my direction a question of when I'd come, how good was he, and could they get a taste?

Believe it or not, ruthless killer did not translate to adventurous sex life. Over the years, I've viewed my fellow man through a pane of glass. No one could understand me. The things I'd done would horrify them. My acts to come would send them screaming into the night.

The boyfriends I picked up over the years, were due to Adeline's human need for connection and a break from the monotony of life. The creature certainly did not need the string of forgettables I dated, and when they inevitably didn't satisfy mentally or sexually, she cut them loose.

But the Merchants were not those men. They blew up every wall I built to shield my true self. They took without asking. Destroyed without remorse. Screwed like it was their mission to kill me by mind-blowing orgasm. Neither Adeline nor her alter ego was ready for this.

"I dabbled in counterfeiting," Killian went on. Did anyone else notice the smugness lacing his words, or was it just me? "But came back to art in the end. So many rich bags willing to swear on their life, their piece isn't a fake. Anything to avoid looking the fool. Don't you agree, Adeline?"

I rocked on his hand, eyes fluttering as he hit that spot. "Uh... huh," I got out.

"Adeline, are you okay?" Malia asked. "You don't look well."

"Fine. Just a"—Killian spread my legs apart and inserted finger number three—"little queasy."

"Oh, I've got just the thing for that." Malia dug in her purse. "I get pretty bad motion sickness. Equilibrium of a drunk goose over here. So, I always have these on—"

The bottle slipped out of her hand.

"One second."

"No," I blurted.

Malia stuck her head under the cloth to rescue the runaway medicine.

I froze, mouth open in silent protest, and Killian kept on with what he was doing.

"There it..." Malia trailed off.

Slowly, she straightened in her seat. Her cheeks were tomato red.

"Did you find it?" Killian asked.

"No," she rushed. "It's gone."

I could've smacked him—if I wasn't on the edge of receiving one of the best orgasms of my life.

Killian crooked a finger, and I was gone. My climax took me so hard, it bucked me off the chair. I kneed the table, rattling the fine china and snapping every eye to me.

Bold as shit, Killian withdrew his fingers and licked them one by one.

"Excuse me." Malia ran from the table.

"My stomach," I croaked to the questioning looks. I clutched the table, breathing hard on lingering waves surging from my core. "I should... find a place to lie down."

"Allow me."

La Roche appeared at my side. "Forgive me, I overheard you weren't feeling well. Come with me. You can take a rest in my office."

"That's kind of you."

I flicked to Killian. He gave me an imperceptible nod.

"Thank you." I took his outstretched hand. "Sorry to put you out."

"Not at all, Miss Redgrave. The first rule of my parties is everyone leaves satisfied."

Together we left the dining room and ascended the swirling staircase. I kept a hand over my stomach to sell the bit.

La Roche brought me to the room opposite the landing. His office was the grand space I expected it to be. A sleek, black desk sat beneath a massive fish tank set in the wall. There were paintings here and there, but the jewel of this room was the bookshelves stretched to the loft, where there were even more books.

La Roche helped me to a leather couch next to a statue of an upright man bowing his head.

"If you're feeling up to it later, my chef will bring you a bowl of clear broth."

"Thanks again," I replied.

La Roche swept out, leaving me in the sanctum sanctorum.

This felt like a test if there ever was one. There was no reason to bring me to his office with his laptop, desktop, and a frame positioned perfectly to cover what could be a wall safe. I'd bet there were hidden cameras all over the place, and La Roche was interested in seeing what the date of his long-lost friend Killian, would do.

What she did was lie on the couch and didn't move a muscle except to shoot a few texts.

Not to Killian. I learned my delicious, exhibitionist lesson in a big way.

Me: Anything on our friend at the home?

Gianna replied in minutes.

Gianna: Single. No kids. Mountains of credit card debt.

Me: No one to use against her.

Gianna: No one to miss her when she's gone.

Gianna: Decided what you're going to do yet?

Me: Not yet. As Dad pointed out, people with nothing to lose play by different rules. Certainly better ones than people with everything to lose.

Gianna: She won't release that recording. It's not going to come to that. Whatever happens.

Me: No. She won't.

I dropped my phone in my purse, then stretched out, folding my arms behind my head. How long until I could reasonably make a full recovery?

Twenty minutes. Then I gave it another ten minutes. Then I decided to hang out and see if La Roche would come for me. I nearly dozed off.

"—in here."

The door swept open and Killian swept inside. My love was power and sex appeal personified in that suit. He came to me, fabric stretched over a different part of him to outline the hard line of his shoulder. The girth between his legs.

"How are you feeling?" he asked me.

"Much better." We shared a grin as he kissed my knuckles.

"Good. I'll take you back to the party."

"Don't rush off so soon." La Roche eased into his desk chair. "I finally have the opportunity to catch up with you, Killian. Please, sit."

Killian led me to the chairs placed before his desk.

"What have you been up to the last few years, Killian?"

"Like I mentioned, I moved to Canada where—"

He waved that away. "Enough of that. I know every major player and where they operate. I haven't heard word of anyone worth knowing about working in Canada for at least five years. You haven't been there. You haven't been anywhere by my reckoning. There hasn't been a whisper of your particular signature in play for years."

Killian reclined, crossing his ankle over his knee. "Getting right to the point, I see."

"I figure that would be best. I do have guests waiting."

"You're correct," Killian said. "I've made certain life changes since we last spoke. I'm out of the forgery racket. Currently, I work for a group that is interested in doing a deal with you."

"That group would be?"

"The Merchants."

If I expected shock, awe, or horror, I didn't get it. La Roche's expression remained the same.

"I've heard of them," he replied. "New gang making a name for themselves by selling their services to the highest bidder. Are you one of them?"

"No," Killian said easily. "I'm a go-between. If you've heard of them, you know they keep their identities secret. Someone has to meet and vet potential clients. That's what I do."

"You're the deal man."

Killian swept out his arms. "That's me."

"How much does this gig net you?"

"Twenty percent."

He hummed. "The diamonds they stole in their last hit were worth millions. I see why you left the uncertain world of grifting."

La Roche gestured to me.

"This young lady work for them as well?"

"This young lady can speak for herself," I said. "I don't work for them so much as I work with Killian-slash-sleep with him. I'm the girlfriend. Sometimes I tag along if my presence will smooth a prickly personality over."

La Roche chuckled. "Am I one such prickly personality?"

"I guess we'll find out."

He threw his head back laughing. "I like you already," he said. "Go on. What's this deal?"

"The Merchants know of the arrangement you have with the Kings." Leaning forward, Killian laid his crossed hands on the desk. "An arrangement that's served you and Angelo well for years, but has recently come into question with the promotion of Lorenzo Bianchi."

La Roche lost the amused twist to his lips. "Your bosses are well-informed."

"They are. You wanted to get to the point, so here it is. The Merchants are willing to offer you a sixty-five/thirty-five split in your favor, if you funnel your products exclusively through them."

"Exclusively," he repeated. "As in, sever ties with the most notorious gang in the city for a bunch of up-and-comers without the infrastructure to sell my products? I don't understand, Killian. Why didn't you tell those fools not to waste my and your time with this?"

Killian showed no reaction. "I explained the odds were unlikely. The Merchants maintain they have an offer worth your while."

"The Merchants," he scoffed. "They knocked over a jewelry store that was a Kings' front—whether they knew it at the time or not. Suddenly, warehouses are burning down, the Kings are child sex peddlers, and Angelo is telling me a small annoyance has grown into a big one. Next thing I know, he's dead and Thug Junior tells me he refuses to honor the original contract. Are the Merchants responsible for this?"

"If you're asking if the Merchants killed Angelo, I don't know. They don't share those details with me."

La Roche hummed, observing him steadily. "If you had to guess..."

"I'd say no. Killing Angelo would serve no purpose. The Kings are still going strong."

"That is true," he said, inclining his head. "Though men like that tend to act first, think later."

"They're not the men you think they are. They're smarter than that, Richard. The fact they have me on the payroll proves it," he said. "They can recoup the losses you'd incur breaking with the Kings. I'll tell you how if you're open to alternatives. If not, let's part as friends."

La Roche looked from Killian to me and back to Killian. "I'll hear you out," he finally said. "Then, I'll decide if I'm open to alternatives."

Killian outlined the terms by which Cinco casinos and underground fighting rings would become their vehicle for passing off counterfeit cash. In terms of moving the forgeries, Killian's own experience in that area should assure him they'd be able to continue on without issue.

"This is all well and good," La Roche said when he was finished. "But what you're essentially asking is for me to provide the start-up capital to get these operations off the ground. I'm sure they will be profitable once they do, but until then, I *will* incur losses as well as make an enemy of the Kings.

"Enzo is an upstart shit, but I can survive on thirty-five percent of seven million. How long until the Merchants reach that bracket?"

"Certainly not this tax year," Killian replied.

I sat there silently. Killian insisted I not know the script beforehand. I was to jump in at the right opportunities, naturally sensing when my two cents were needed. So far, I wasn't seeing an opening in this volley.

La Roche clapped. "Well, if that's all, there's a party downstairs." He rose from his seat.

"In the event you said no," Killian spoke up, "I've been authorized to sweeten the pot."

"Forget it, Killian. There's nothing they've got that can make up for over two million—"

"Kieran's ledger."

The phrase dropped like a missile through a blimp, blowing the pretense to shreds.

"It's yours."

La Roche returned to his seat. "Excuse me?"

"In exchange for your business, the Merchants will sell their services to your highest bid. They'll get you the ledger, Richard. The one thing that's eluded you for half your career."

"Give it to me?" He frowned. "Do they have it?"

"No."

Fervor drew him over the desk, mimicking Killian's position. "Do they know where it is? Who has it?"

"They will."

"Will?" he repeated the word like he didn't understand it. "What do you mean will?"

"The Merchants are searching for the ledger. Once they have it, they will give it to you as a signing bonus," Killian said. "My job is to make sure both parties get what they want. This is what you want, Richard. Take it."

"Take what?" he cried. "They don't even have it. You can't just pick the ledger up in aisle six next to the toilet paper. I've spent twenty years of my life searching for it. I'm supposed to wait another twenty on the promise they come through? All the while they're profiting off my business." He barked a laugh. "Is your job comedian too?"

Killian took the derision in stride. "It won't take twenty years. We all know Kieran isn't the checkout boy scanning that toilet paper. He's someone with money and influence, and if the respectable world doesn't know his name, then the criminal world certainly does. There's a limited pool of people he could be. Those jobs the Merchants took weren't just for the money. They've narrowed that pool down considerably. I project they'll have Kieran and his ledger in two months."

"Two months, huh? So, what do they need me for? Do they even know what that ledger is?"

"They know," was the calm reply.

"And they're just going to give it to me? Why? What's to stop them using the ledger against me instead?"

"Against you? How could they do that?" Killian raised a brow. "Is there a page in that ledger with your name on it?"

"Of course not!" La Roche tore off the scarf and threw it in a crumpled heap on his desk.

Irrational anger and swift denial seemed to be the standard response when that question was asked.

"You know what I meant," he said. "They could hold it over my head instead. Say I can't have the ledger unless I work for them with whatever terms they like."

Killian shook his head. "They aren't interested in fostering a negative business relationship, or I wouldn't be here. A break with the Kings is dangerous for you, and them. This is what we call hazard pay, Richard. Take the deal."

"No, no." La Roche tossed his head. The sly, friendly con man routine was coming apart at the seams. "This is nonsense. You approaching so soon after Angelo died and Lorenzo is forced to take desperate steps. It reeks of a plot, and I don't like it, Killian. I'm not impressed at all."

Gotta give it to the man. He didn't get where he was by being a sucker.

"I don't know these men. These— These *Merchants*," he spat. "Bring them here. Let me speak to them myself."

"I'm afraid that's impossible."

He threw out his hands. "Then it's impossible for me to do business with them. I know a fake when I see one, Killian, and I will look them in the eye while they spin me this fairy tale of gifting me the prize not even I could get my hands on. It'll be fun to watch them try to keep a straight face."

"You know what. You're right." Killian stood, pacing behind me. "How can you trust them? Fuck knows if I got my hands on the ledger, I wouldn't give it up."

I wheeled around, goggling at him. *What are you saying?!*

"Exactly," said La Roche. "It's dangling the carrot for the horse. A well-chosen carrot certainly, but there are no guarantees it'll be mine at the end of the road."

"Okay. What if I sold them on another deal?" Killian gripped the back of the chair. "They're not going to meet you, Richard. There's no way. But the Merchants can still prove themselves to you."

"No, they can't. I will not be conned, Killian."

"I get your hesitation, but they're not us. Grifters are in it for what they can get. Merchants are about what they can trade. If you heard about them, then you know all of their customers got what they paid for. No scams. No tricks."

La Roche lifted his chin—jaw ticing, but no protest followed.

"Give them a job," Killian stated. "Something you've wanted that you can't get yourself. They'll do it, Richard. They'll prove their skill and gain your trust in one move."

"What I want is that ledger."

"And you'll have it," he returned in an instant. "In two months. But by then, I'll be out of a job. They expect me to make this deal, and I believe we can do that. Something else. Anything else. When they deliver it to you, the Merchants become your new partners."

"Something I can't get myself? Look around. There's nothing I'm unable to acquire through means or money alone."

"Is that true? Every con you've run has succeeded? All your marks delivered as promised?"

A tell flickered across La Roche's face—gone as quickly as it came. I saw it. I knew Killian had too.

"There's nothing you want?" Killian pressed.

La Roche turned to me. "You've been quiet, Miss Redgrave. Nothing to add? I thought your purpose was to close?"

I smiled. "That's only for clients who can't see they're getting a good deal. You know you are despite all this blustering."

"I beg your pardon?"

"Come on." I crossed my legs, flicking my hair over my shoulder. "You're not afraid of the Kings or Lorenzo Bianchi. Why should you be? *He* needs *you*, not the other way around. That's why the first thing he did when he took over his shaky empire was go running to you. The Kings expanded their reach on the millions you made them, and if you take it away, it all comes crumbling down.

"I mean, seriously. What is Enzo going to do? Kill you?" I asked. "Your business dies with you and then what does he have?"

La Roche stroked his silvery beard, listening.

"You set the terms, Mr. La Roche, and if you go with the side giving you a better offer, that's your right. Sounds like the upstart could use a lesson in humility either way." I motioned to Killian. "Make the deal... with a few provisions. The Merchants rise to your challenge and deliver the second thing the great Richard La Roche can't acquire on his own. If they do, you end your contract with the Kings and provide that seed money to the Merchants.

"In two months' time, if the ledger isn't in your hands, cut off the tap. Go back to the Kings, or open bidding to the gangs and crime families of Cinco. They all want what you have to offer. They'll pay for it."

"So, your upsell is that I win either way," he said.

"Do you disagree?"

La Roche held my gaze steady. My smile held. As did my eye contact. He wouldn't find a crack on my end.

Without looking away, La Roche asked Killian, "Why do they want this deal? The truth."

"Harlow." Killian dropped in the seat. "The Merchants can't move in on that borough, and the opportunities it provides, unless the Kings are moved out."

He nodded, taking that in. "And they can get their hands on anything?"

"I wouldn't hold out hope on borrowing that book from the Vatican secret archives," Killian said. "But yeah. Their retrieval rate is a hundred percent so far."

"I've visited the secret archives. You could practically take school groups through there for its security. No, what I want takes a lot more skill."

"Name it," I said.

"Name him," La Roche corrected. "Sebastian Vega."

"Vega. The philanthropist?"

He nodded. "Sebastian inherited his family's import-export business. He took those billions and funneled them into charities, causes, and committees for some sad case or another. His single vice is ancient, beautiful things. Who can blame him?"

"What ancient beautiful thing does he have that you want?"

"Several. I was a tad roguish in my younger days," he said. "I had brief affairs with his wife and his sister. At the same time."

A tad roguish?

"Since the dissolution of his marriage, Sebastian has seen fit to take what *I* love most. He has outbid me in nearly every legitimate auction for the last decade. Paintings, antiques, Persian rugs. He's gone so far as to bribe auction houses to reveal my silent bids with the promise whatever I pay, he will double. His pockets are as bottomless as his grudge."

I guess when you've got nothing but time and money, why not make a cocky bastard eat it?

"All the pieces he took from me are displayed proudly in his East Leighbridge home." There was a hard twist to his mouth. "That's what your Merchants will get me. One of the most expensive pieces in his collection. The nine-hundred-year-old Biyu vase dating to the Northern Song Dynasty. The Medici necklace. Agnes of France's tiara."

"Why haven't you been able to get your hands on them?" I asked.

La Roche turned away. "Obviously, there is no disguise or alias I could use that would fool him. I've tried the straightforward approach—offers to mend fences or bribing his household staff. Neither worked. Associates of mine have taken up the challenge as well.

"Sebastian has avoided serious relationships since his divorce. He has custody of their daughter, and rather than bring dates home, they're wined, dined, and bedded in hotel rooms. Hotels are also his designated location for parties and events. No chance to slip in amongst a crowd. I've sent in people disguised as delivery men, potential employees, city workers, etcetera. All have failed."

"The Merchants won't," Killian said.

He held out his hand.

"They bring you the most expensive item in his collection, and you sign on for an exclusive deal with the Merchants for the stated split. Yes?"

"On a two-month probationary period," La Roche amended. "At the end of which, I have the ledger in hand."

"Agreed."

La Roche shook. "Agreed."

Chapter Six

"I wish you had been there, G. He twisted La Roche up expertly. One minute the guy thinks we're not worth his time, and then the next he's signing up believing he has us coming and going."

"Think it will get back to Kieran?"

Gianna and I sat on a bench in Mercy Park, munching on stolen ice cream cones. She stole them, not me. Distracted the couple that snatched our parking spot, grabbed the cones from their hands, and took off running. My side still hurt from laughing so hard.

Yes, we've evolved from petty crime. Didn't make it less fun.

"It will when we get that vase, and La Roche drops the Kings."

"Why the vase and not the tiara? I'd look good in a tiara," she mused.

"You would," I agreed. "But I don't get to pick. Cash, Sinjin, and the guys have been holed up in Cash's office planning the heist for the last four days. It's not that they don't let me in, but I go in there and it's all Barron safes, exit and entry points, and combinations. My extensive education did not include safecracking. Daddy's method would've been to hold a gun to the guy's head until he opened the damn thing."

"Not an option?"

The park was paradise that morning. Sunlight filtered through the trees, dotting us with sunbeams. Owners chased their dogs across the grass. Children shrieked on the playground nearby. Gardenias and lilacs sprouted in the flower garden at our backs. They spread a sweet scent that tricked you into believing a cloudless sky, perfumed air, and ice cream cones with your best friend were the makings of a perfect day.

"No," I replied. "Sebastian Vega's daughter is twelve years old. If Dad's home, she'll be home, and we can't count on a well-timed sleepover. We're not trying to traumatize the girl. Or Vega for that matter. I actually feel bad for him. La Roche destroyed his marriage, and it looks like Mom hasn't been around since. Snaking a few antiques from La Roche's grasp was the most harmless retribution."

"Need me on standby?" she asked.

"Can't hurt."

"Look." Gianna handed me her phone. "Pics of the apartments I'm looking at. These are close to the hotel and you."

"Is Raul moving with you?"

She flashed me a knowing look. "He is my boyfriend."

"Yeah, but how much do we like him?"

She laughed. "Both our feelings combined? Doesn't look good for him. Just me? He's wicked good in bed. Plus, he's super sweet when no one's looking."

"That a yes?"

Gianna swatted me, nearly knocking my cone. We spent the rest of the time poring over apartment photos, and planning the décor. She offered to do my room up in blues and silvers for when the Merchants discovered my plans for citywide domination and kicked me out. That earned her the swat.

"Hey." She held up her watch. "Almost nine. Get going."

"Right."

I picked up the backpack at my feet.

The morning was perfect. Pups zipped past me as I crossed the lawn. Mothers pushed their strollers at my side, the group of us heading toward Mercy Tunnel where they broke off down one path and I continued on.

I came out of the dim for a less populated part of the park. This tunnel led to two miles of curving running and biking trails. The trees closed in, providing cool and privacy for the joggers.

And blackmailers.

I put the bag in a trash can by the second water fountain as instructed. Then, I retreated into the trees to wait.

Five.

Ten.

Fifteen minutes.

A jogger came down the path from the opposite way. I recognized Duncan instantly. The green running outfit and matching cap pulled low over her eyes didn't fool me.

She stopped at the water fountain. Stretched. Rolled her neck. Bent to take a sip. While she drank, Duncan reached into the trash and pulled out the bag.

She made to run off, then skidded to a stop. She ripped the bag open.

"Oops."

Duncan snapped her head up.

"Did I forget something?"

From where I was standing, I saw her flush neon red.

"Where is the—?!" She cut herself off, glancing around. "Where is it?"

"It's all there," I replied, closing the distance. "All you're going to get from me. Hope you like the backpack. I thought pink would suit you."

Duncan threw the empty pack on the ground. "I'm not bluffing," she said through gritted teeth. "I'll hand that recording to the police and wave as they march you and Granddaddy Felon off in cuffs."

"All because I gave you the pink backpack? Ugh. Fine," I moaned. "I'll get you the blue."

"What is wrong with you?" She got in my face. "Are you capable of comprehending that you'll never get that recording back if I don't—"

"No, Duncan, it's you who doesn't understand. I don't want the recording back. I want you to keep it. In fact, I insist on it."

She stepped back. "But—"

"You see, I'm crazy busy right now. Planning a heist, fooling a con man, taking over the city. All the while, lying to my men about my true motives. This takes up a lot of time which leaves me none to spare on killing you, getting rid of your body, and fabricating a fake story where you fuck off to Peru and get lost in the jungle."

"You can't—"

"Oh, but I can," I sang, "and I will, two seconds after that recording hits cyberspace or ends up in the hands of the police. The knowledge you have that phone hidden away somewhere has stayed me. Once it's out, you don't really matter anymore, do you?

"It's your leverage. The single thing keeping you alive and my attention elsewhere. Ask yourself if you want that to change?" I leaned in till our noses bonked. "Do you want my full attention?" I whispered.

"I want my money." Her voice shook.

"I'm not giving you any money, sweetie. So run on home," I said. "I'm certain you feel motivated now to put that phone under lock and key. Guard it like your life depends on it because, of course, it does."

I sidestepped her, jogging off. "Ta!"

Gianna waited for me on the bench. "Scared the bitch good?"

"She was standing in a puddle, babe." I reclined on the bench, basking in what had turned out to be a perfect day. "It hasn't rained."

BRUTAL TURNED MY WRIST out. He folded my fingers down one by one in a tight fist.

It was interesting being taught to box by a teacher that didn't speak to you. His method of correction was to catch a flying punch, and fix me to do it right.

"I know how to fight," I put out there. "I took down Felix in Corbin's club."

Brutal squared my hips.

"Bashed Bryan Acker over the head. Don't forget the bullies and potential muggers I've defeated over the years. Maybe you should be taking lessons from me."

His laugh banished the last traces of Tara Duncan from my mind. Who could think of that sad, manipulative woman when Baris Alexander stood shirtless before them?

It had been three days since I left her standing in the park. Not a peep from her in that time. I assumed she got the message, but like I said, I wasn't thinking of her then.

"When do you hit Vega's place?" I asked. "Did Cash decide on the night?"

Brutal moved to his calendar. He pointed to the coming Friday, then moved down one. Then two.

"Three weeks? Why so long?"

He tilted his head. *Cash will explain.*

My interpretations of his gestures were all guesses. Despite that, when I asked if I got it right, he nodded yes. I understood him. He understood me.

"Is this right?" I dropped the tease for more touching, and struck the dummy in the solar plexus. A hit like that would've left him doubled over and wheezing for air. It got me picked up and set on Baris's bed. "Are you going to have your way with me now?"

He tugged my shirt off. *Yes.*

I wiggled his shorts over his bare ass, giggling into the kiss.

"Gorgeous." Mercer knocked. "Your phone's been going off for the last twenty minutes. Someone desperately wants to speak to you."

My flirty smile faded. "Baris, I'll be right back."

Outside my room, the chime cut off as the call ended. I went in and it started back up.

"Hello?"

"Addy, it's me, Mrs. Rowe," she said. "I've been trying to get ahold of you."

"What's going on?"

"It's your father. We had to call an ambulance. He was having trouble breathing, and collapsed when staff tried to help him up. His heart rate gave us cause for concern..."

Mrs. Rowe grew small. The phone fell on the mattress, forgotten as I rushed to dress and grab my keys.

"Addy? Addy, are you there?"

I snatched up my cell. "What hospital?!"

"Cinco General. I'm here now, Addy. I won't leave until you arrive."

I hurried out and ran into Mercer. He set me on my feet. "Whatever it is, I'll drive."

There wasn't time to argue. We got into his convertible, and drove the twenty minutes to Cinco General Hospital.

"Hello," I said to the woman behind the desk. "I'm here for Oscar Redgrave. What room is he in?"

"Addy." Mrs. Rowe waved from the elevators. "This way."

"I'll stay here," said Mercer. "Call if you need me."

Mrs. Rowe repeated what she said on the phone on the way up. It was *wah wah wah* for all I understood.

Dad collapsed. How could that happen? He was fine last I saw him. Happy. Joking.

I pressed on the elevator doors, willing them open. They released me much too slowly.

"Room 311, dear."

Running down the hall, a nurse called for me to slow down. I picked up the pace with Dad's room in sight. Bursting in, I startled the doctor checking his pulse.

"What's going on? How is he?" I fell on Dad. He appeared almost peaceful lying on the bed. He didn't wake as I cradled his head, though my shaking limbs should've jostled him from sleep.

"Good afternoon." He placed Dad's hand on the blanket. "You must be his daughter."

"How is he?" I repeated.

"Stable."

His doctor was a large man with hands that dwarfed mine, leading me to the side.

"I'm Dr. Weber. I'll be looking after your dad. Your father has suffered an overdose of beta blockers," he explained. "I understand he took these for his heart condition."

I tossed my head, fighting to keep up. "An overdose? Why? How? He's been on these meds for years."

"Mr. Redgrave is in his sixties. It's not uncommon for elderly patients to become confused. They forget they've already taken their daily dose, and they take it again. Then again, causing an overdose through no intention of their own—"

"No," I cried. "My dad doesn't have dementia or any issues with his memory. He's sharper than both of us put together! And he doesn't dole his meds out himself. They give it to him—"

I cut myself off, lancing the sentence right through the middle. A deep, abiding frost spread through my veins, pulling my being back from blind panic and forcing logic down its throat.

"Yes?" Weber prompted.

"The residents aren't in charge of their meds." The words sounded like they came from someone else. "The nurses arrange the doses... and caregivers give them out."

"I see. That's a different matter." Faint click of his pen, then light scratching as he wrote in my father's chart. "We are doing everything we can. He's on a solution of saline to combat the toxicity. We're monitoring his heart as well. As for the circumstances that brought him here, if you suspect negligence, there are steps you can take. I'm more than willing to put you in contact with people who will explain your options."

He grasped my shoulders. "We have every reason to believe he'll recover. Do not worry, Miss Redgrave. Your father is in good hands."

A part of me might have appreciated his warmth. His contact. Speaking to me like a grieving daughter instead of a line on a checklist before he got to his break. That part of me would've liked Dr. Weber.

But Adeline Redgrave wasn't here.

It was hard for even me to explain the way I saw myself. Growing up, my father taught me to do things other little girls did not. I understood these things to be wrong by society's standards, and right by his.

Yes, I knew right from wrong. My world was more black and white than many would think. It was wrong to kill if not in self-defense or the defense of others. It was wrong to steal. Lie. Trick. Or cheat. It was wrong for mothers to abuse their daughters, and grown men to assault them.

I knew what was wrong, so the person I became when I stepped out the door did what was right. She showed up for work on time. Did not talk back to her boss. Waited at the crosswalk for the signal to go. Paid her bills. Held the door open for the elderly and parents with strollers.

Adeline Redgrave did good in public, and no one questioned what she did in private. They didn't wonder if behind their backs she was an entirely different person—who knew what was wrong, and did it anyway.

Without remorse.

Without guilt.

And often with a laugh on the tip of her lips.

I was who I was made to be by a man who taught me, defended me, killed for me, and gave up his entire world... for me. For him to lie here now—weak and helpless. Hanging on to life by a dripping bag. This was an injustice that would be righted by the girl he named "avenging angel."

That side of me would no longer be private.

From this day, everyone would know her wrath.

"I'LL BE BACK TONIGHT, Daddy."

I kissed his papery cheek.

"Hmm." Dad squeezed my hand, mumbling something. He was still groggy from the effects.

"I know, Dad," I said, mindful of Mercer in the room. "I'll take care of everything. You focus on getting better."

He loosened his hold. Dad's eyes fluttered shut, and he eased into sleep. He could relax. Dad knew that *I* knew. Everything would be fine.

"Goes without saying that you have time off to look after him," Mercer said.

His hand was warm on the small of my back. Uppercase in its comforting. Lowercase in possession. That hand let those looking know that he was there for me, because I was his.

"Seriously, Adeline. The cooking, cleaning, La Roche, and the rest. We've got it. This is where you need to be."

"Thank you. But my dad will be okay. He's not allowed to leave me. He knows that."

Chuckling, Mercer brushed a barely-there kiss over my temple. "That's what I like about you, gorgeous."

A chime sounded in my pocket.

"Give me a minute?" I asked.

"I'll pull up the car."

Only when the elevator closed on him, did I take it out.

Waterford Retirement Home

"Hello, Duncan." I didn't need to ask. I knew who it was.

"Hello, Miss Redgrave. How is your father? We're all worried sick about him."

"I'm sure." My voice was calm. Even.

"Nurse Leila is beside herself thinking she gave him the wrong pills."

"Tell her not to beat herself up," I said. "It's not her fault."

"To be fair, it's no one's fault but yours. If you'd done what I asked, your father would be making eyes at Mrs. Watkins right now." The sweet, syrupy tone dug into my skin and ignited me to blow.

I pushed the feeling down.

"Yes," I agreed. "This is my fault."

"I'm glad you understand now." There was a noise. Voices on the other end. Then a thump. "You think if you act like a psycho, I'll turn tail and run. It's not going to happen, Redgrave. You don't scare me. You're a silly little girl, and your father another useless old man going senile. You're both nothing, and that is why you have *nothing*."

I blinked slow—still in the bustle around me.

"Nothing but each other," Duncan said. "I don't know what you are, Adeline Redgrave, but I know you care about losing him. Just as much as he cares about losing you. *Daddy* swallowed the pills without a fight when I played him that recording."

My eyes flared. "You did what?"

"Like you said, this phone is leverage. If not against you, then against someone else. Fathers really will do anything for their daughters, won't they?"

"But not yours, I suspect." The anger broke through. Sizzling and charging the air like desert heat. "What did he do? Drink himself to death all day, and beat you all night? And where was your mother? If you knew the woman at all.

"I'm truly sorry for the circumstances that led to you becoming this person, Tara Duncan. Trust me, I know something about that. It's a bitch that makes bitches out of all of us." I stepped to the side, leaning on the wall. "In recognition and respect to a fellow psycho, I'll stop fighting you.

"Tell me what you want," I spat.

"Simple. The price is two hundred grand now. Leave it in the same place," she said. "If it's all there, I'll drop the phone in the trash and you can do what you want with it."

"No."

"No?" she hissed. "You just said—"

"I need some guarantees. How do I know the only copy of the recording is on that phone?"

"I swear it is."

"You swear?" I snorted. "And I swear Santa Claus does exist."

"You'll just have to take my word for it, won't you?"

"Your phone, computer, and your damn Apple watch. Hand it all over. You'll certainly have enough money to buy more after we're through."

"That's true." She laughed. "Fine. I'll give you my laptop too. One week. A backpack for your backpack. Oh, and this time, I want the blue."

Click.

"WHAT ARE YOU GOING to do?"

"I know exactly what I'm going to do."

"We have to get rid of her, Addy," said Gianna. "She brought your dad into this. We end this, or he'll try to."

"I said I know what to do," I replied. "How much money do we have left over that isn't marked for something else?"

She hesitated. "Not two hundred grand," she admitted. "Not even close. But, I haven't signed the leases yet. Captain's been paid, but the girl I have in La Roche's office hasn't. All of that will have to wait. This is more important."

"No, G. We can't turn back now. We did too much to get that money for it to end up in the hands of another vile predator," I said. "I have an idea. Just pack up the leftover money, put it in a case, and I'll be by to get it tonight."

"Alright. Love you, babe."

"Love you."

I hung up, and returned to examine the collection.

Our new weapons dungeon was an upgrade on the old one. Twice as big, and bearing a small wooden door that led to the tunnel beneath the city streets.

I chose a small pistol that fit in my palm like a baby bird. I don't know that the guys used half the stuff down here. I did know they rarely checked the inventory.

I have a fucking idea all right. I stuffed the gun in my pocket and rescued the bullets from the ammo trunk next to the rack. *Tara Duncan will get exactly what's coming to her.*

I went upstairs to my room. Someone was waiting for me.

"Killian."

He stood in the middle of the room. Standing there. He didn't move at my greeting.

"Everything okay?"

Cash looked at me. An odd expression crossed his face. I gave him a crazy one in return.

"You gearing up to fight me or something?"

Killian scoffed. "Ridiculous."

That sounded more like him.

"No, Redgrave. I'm not here to fight you." He raised that prominent jaw. "I noticed the other day you making a fucking mess with the muffin batter. Brutal was all over you cleaning it up. From now on, use this."

Killian stepped to the side.

A purple box sat on my bed. I picked it up, squinting at the label.

"Pancake and cupcake batter dispenser," I read. "Durable and easy to use, it's the number one gift for your favorite baker." I turned my grin on him. "Killian Alfred Hunt."

"Fuck you."

"Did you get me a present?"

"No," he said too quickly. "It's a practical item that you can put to some use. If you don't want it—"

I shot away. "Don't you dare take my gift. I love it. It's exactly what I was thinking I needed when I was making those muffins, and Brutal was making me regret it. Why didn't I know this existed?" I hugged it to my chest. "Thank you, baby. This is so sweet."

His jaw ticced a rhythm I could dance to. He looked like he wanted to be anywhere but here.

Eyes fixed on my print of Cinco City, he held out his hand. I curled mine in his.

If I wasn't already in love with him, I would've been a puddle of goo to be poured in the dispenser.

"I've got a present for you too."

"Yeah?"

I pushed him down on my bed. "Yes."

Getting on my knees, one hand unzipped him, and the other slid the gun and bullets under my bed.

Killian sprung free in all his glory. He was half hard and pointed at the ceiling to rocket to the moon. The image made me smile.

"Something funny?"

"I was just thinking how many orgasms I was going to wring out of you to get you to admit you love me." I licked the tip. "Pretty sure one will do it."

"I'm not a betting man, Redgrave. But I'm willing to let you keep at it till you get your result."

I was laughing as I swallowed him, sending vibrations down his shaft that drew a hiss from his lips. That was one of my favorite sounds in the world. Killian losing control.

I palmed him, stroking till I got another hiss, then swallowed to the back of my throat. Killian instantly grasped my head, giving me more.

A man like him did not cede control easily. A fact which suddenly reminded me there were handcuffs in the dungeon, and Killian had a metal headboard.

I bet I get my I love you when you're bucking under my mercy.

Picking up the pace, I bobbed in time with his thrusts, heat pooling in my middle on the heady high of cum, musk, cologne, and Killian.

His thighs tightened on me, and I knew what was coming. I relaxed. Killian spilled all he had to offer inside me.

I climbed on top of him, stealing a kiss. "Did that do it?"

"You should try going for a few more."

I checked my desk clock. I wasn't going anywhere until after dinner. The guys would be shut away in Killian's office, going over every detail. I wouldn't be missed.

Which means I've got plenty of time for a few more.

Killian broke my zipper ripping it down.

CASH

"Is this all your guys could get?" Mercer gestured at both of my whiteboards. "There is a Barron security system, but he doesn't know what type. There are guards on the premises, but he doesn't know how many patrol a shift. A break-in could send an instant alert to the police, but it might not. We're going in blind, Cash."

"We're not," I said. I pointed to the picture of our targets. "There's one hundred and twenty-eight million dollars' worth of antiques in that home. Minimum. Sebastian Vega is a reasonably intelligent man and he has a young daughter. I don't need to do the calculations on the effort he'd put into security. If he's got a Barron, it'll be the best one on the market."

"Seguro Twenty-Five," Mercer echoed. "A worthy opponent."

"You can get in." It wasn't a question. We didn't have time for those anymore.

He nodded. "It'll take me at least an hour. At least." Mercer heaved a sigh. "Normally, I have all night to make a lock purr while that night's playmate sleeps soundly. This job is starting to get stressful."

I moved on. "Security. I anticipate two on each entrance, and two sweeping the home when Vega is inside. He'll take those two with him when he leaves."

"Four guards are manageable," Sinjin said. "We'll opt for overkill just the same."

I agreed. "The alarm to the police is also a given. Anyone with his net worth will have the panic button tied around his neck like he'll break a hip falling down the stairs. Disabling it without him knowing will take some doing," I said. "Diego has three weeks. That will be enough time."

Mercer waved his hands. "All this sounds good, but has anyone considered the reasonably intelligent man with a young daughter, wised up and stored the eight-figure valuables in a safe-deposit box? La Roche hasn't been on the property since he was caught in bed with the wife. He hasn't seen the necklace or tiara after he lost them at auction. How do we know they're there?"

"They're there," Sinjin stated. He was draped on the couch, sipping a glass of scotch in the same position I was with Adeline not long ago.

Adeline.

An impish smile and auburn waves crashed over me.

I tossed my head. I did that a lot lately. Adeline had worked her way into my mind like an illness.

There wasn't a better way to describe it.

All-consuming. Eroding will and self-control. Impossible to cure.

Lethal.

If that wasn't a disease, what was?

"Vega needs them close," Sinjin continued, dragging me back. "La Roche fucked his wife and sister, and he was too weak to do anything. Too weak to satisfy. Too weak to stop it. Too weak to keep her.

"What he should've done was thrash the smug, arrogant shit within an inch of his life, but he was too weak to do that too. For the last ten years, the only measure of revenge he could get was through his money—taking away La Roche's toys," he said. "He won't be separated from those antiques. By now, they're more his manhood than his dick."

"Which of his dicks are we after?"

"We only need one for La Roche," I said.

"So, we take the others for fun," Sinjin threw in. "Bunny in a crown is a sex dream of mine."

The image jumped in my head. Diamonds twisting through her hair. Sweat dripping between her breasts as she flung her jeweled head back—riding me to the tune of her filthy desires pouring from her lips.

I shook my head again.

Damn.

ADELINE

Gianna handed me a lime-green and yellow polka-dot carry-on.

"I didn't have time to buy something else," she said to my look. "The money's all there. Want me to come with you?"

"It'll be hard enough to get in on my own." We kissed cheeks over her threshold. Sticking my head in afforded me a look at the packing boxes scattered throughout the living room. "I'll text you when I get there, and when

I leave. If that last text doesn't come through by midnight. Please, come in shooting."

"That was the plan."

We said goodbye, and I hopped in Raul's car. I could've asked the guys to take the tracker out of mine. I decided against that after Jocelyn. I handled my business without a car for years. It wasn't an inconvenience to leave it behind, and when I did drive it, it was nice to know this was one thing no one could take from me.

Strange thoughts like that plagued me throughout the drive. What the guys had done for me. What I'd done for them. They'd become so embedded in my life, it was difficult to recall a time I wasn't bantering with Sinjin. Flirting with Mercer. Teasing Brutal, or seducing Cash.

I let them track me for heaven's sake. The last boyfriend who tried sneaking a tracking app on my phone didn't survive to distrust the next girl.

No, I didn't kill him. Just a figure of speech.

My Waterford borough dropped away for streets paved with gold. Or that was the impression Leighbridge gave. Suited men and ball-gowned women spilled out of a hotel into waiting limos. The lampposts in Leighbridge were modeled in Victorian style. It sent me back to grand parties, lace parasols, and an age before crime families ruled the day.

I turned the final corner and his home came into sight. It looked rather lonely without the line of cars outside.

I parked, checked the gun was safely tucked in my purse, grabbed the bag of money, and marched up to the door. The guard who let me and Killian in the other night opened the door.

"Evening. Tell Mr. La Roche Adeline Redgrave is here to see him."

"Is he expecting you?"

"No, but I think he'd like to talk to me. Tell him I'm here."

"Jackson? Who is it?"

I glanced around his bulk.

"Hello, Mr. La Roche. Can I come in? This won't take a minute."

There was a pause where the eye I could see observed me. "You have it so soon? This is quite mortifying. Took less than a week to do what I couldn't in years."

"That's not why I'm here. This isn't about what we discussed the other night at all. I'd love to tell you about it when I'm not out on the front porch."

He chuckled. "Forgive me. I forgot my manners in the excitement. Come in, Miss Redgrave. Jackson, step aside."

Jackson snapped to the left, letting me pass. La Roche eyed my bag.

"What have you brought me?"

"This isn't for you," I replied. "I came for a number. I have the name. Grady Shelton."

"I'm sorry, but everyone who enters my home must have something for me." A smile stretched his lips. "You saw as much the other night."

I frowned. "The painting? Killian said that was his invitation into the party."

"That was his invitation onto the premises." La Roche came closer. He had on a silk, gray suit that could've been his pajamas for all I knew—he seemed the type to wear a suit to bed. "My home is sacred. As Killian has no doubt told you, I've opened it and myself to my colleagues worldwide, but for my own paranoia, I insist everyone who gets close to me provides means."

"Means to what?"

The smile widened. "Bury them."

"Excuse me?"

Sighing, La Roche circled me. "That masterful forgery of The Lacemaker your boyfriend handed me, could one day be discovered in a black-market auction, with his fingerprints all over it. He knows I have that option. It's what nudges him to the right decision if he ever considered revealing the truth about me to the public. I was curious about you, so you received one free pass. There isn't a second."

I stiffened. "I don't have a copy of a priceless masterpiece. I just came for a number. One of the men seated at my table the other night. I need to speak with him, and Killian does not need to know I was here."

He gave me his back. "Jackson, show her out."

Rolling my eyes, I said, "Left leg. Above the knee."

"What—"

Bang!

Jackson dropped, howling. He clutched his knee—rolling on the floor.

"What have you done?!" La Roche roared.

"You asked, I gave," I replied. "I made that shot with barely a glance, smack where I said the wound would be. You have the bullet, the victim, yourself as a witness, and proof my skills extend far beyond closer and girlfriend. Is that enough to bury me, La Roche?"

Fury poured from his eyes.

"Can we stop playing games now?"

Jackson wailed on the floor.

"Be quiet," I snapped. "It's a flesh wound. Put a Band-Aid on it."

Thunderous footsteps echoed down the hall.

"Well?" I asked La Roche. The gun disappeared into my bag as two guards appeared on the scene, guns pointed and sweeping for threats.

"Sir," one cried. "What happened?"

La Roche didn't look away from me. "What happened is I would be dead by now if there'd been an actual threat. Jackson had an accident. Get him cleaned up. Remember the contracts you signed."

"Sir?"

"Go," he ordered.

They helped Jackson up and left, leaving the two of us alone.

"Come to my office."

There wasn't a reason not to follow him. La Roche led me up a familiar path to the grand room where we made a precarious deal. Fitting it should be home to another one.

He slammed inside, making straight for the wet bar.

"Grady Shelton," he said. "What do you want with him?"

"I have a situation. I need a large amount of money fast. Doesn't need to be real."

La Roche paused with the whiskey halfway to his lips. "He mentioned his work with the superdollar."

"He did," I confirmed. "I believe we can make a trade in his favor. Naturally, typing 'Grady Shelton, Counterfeiter' gets me nothing on Google. How do I get in contact with him?"

"You're under a mistaken impression of how my organization works," he said. "People don't just show up on my doorstep, shoot my staff, and walk out with the name and contact of my associates. They expect me to protect them as diligently as I protect myself."

"Meaning?"

La Roche claimed his seat. "Meaning, you tell me exactly what you want from him and why, and I'll consider passing the message on. That was a party. This is business. Business goes through me."

I sensed the shift of the balance of power tilting his way.

Silently, I opened my bag and tipped forty thousand dollars on his desk. He didn't blink.

"I need two hundred grand to pay a ransom," I said bluntly. "I have it, but paying would wipe me out, and we all know blackmailers can't resist coming back for more. This is how much I can spare. I need to make it stretch."

"You want two hundred thousand dollars for forty?"

"I want two hundred thousand pieces of worthless paper for forty thousand American smackaroos. I could give him ten dollars and he'd have the better deal. You know it, La Roche. Grady will be very interested in talking to me. Give me the number."

Nodding, he peeled a bill off the pack, holding it to the light. "Who is blackmailing you?"

"That's not important."

"It's important enough that you're coming to me instead of Killian, or the men you work for. I'm certain there's a reason. I'd like to hear it."

"Whatever it is you're trying to hint at, you're wrong. It's not that I don't trust Killian or the Merchants." I cleared my throat. "I was... indiscrete in my past. There's a tape of me saying and doing things with an old boyfriend. It was made without my knowledge or permission."

Wrap every lie in a kernel of truth.

"The wrong person got their hands on it, and they're threatening to release it if I don't give them the money. I don't want this getting bigger than it is," I said. "I don't want Killian to know. I'm looking to end this quickly and quietly, Mr. La Roche. Will you give me the number?"

He drew out the silence to almost dramatic effect.

"No," he said.

"Why not?"

"Because you don't need Grady. I keep a healthy stash of his product on hand—as I mentioned, everyone must give me means," he said. "You can have your two hundred grand in the time it takes me to fill a duffel bag."

"You're helping me," I said slowly. "Why?"

"Believe it or not, I don't approve of young women being taken advantage of in this way. My business of separating fools from their money is an art form. It takes skill, ingenuity, patience, and timing. It's your intelligence outwitting someone who should know better.

"These types of situations are none of the above. Even the lowest form of trash can bed a woman, and hide his camera phone in the bookcase. As you've proven yourself up to the task of turning the con on them, it's only right of me to assist." He held out his hands. "That's why I'm here. To help the smart and patient get what they're after."

I said nothing.

"Come with me."

La Roche and I left the room. I was on his heels down the stairs and through the hall the men took Jackson. Voices sounded on the other side of the door at the end of the corridor.

"—not that bad. How'd you fucking shoot yourself?"

We turned a corner, and I realized where we were going.

La Roche stepped inside his gallery, heading for *La Libertad* and his wall of Aurelio Molina. I stopped in the archway. Curiosity stayed me, not fear. If La Roche did something foolish, my gun was in reach.

What are we doing in here?

The aging con artist reached behind a portrait of a curly-haired woman in a poofy dress.

"Do you keep a safe back there?"

"I do."

A soft hiss hit my ears.

La Roche stepped out of the way as *La Libertad* came off the wall, hanging on the door that appeared.

"Safe room," I said.

"Safe room. Vault. Keeper of the items my associates entrust to me." La Roche stepped inside. "You may come in."

I did so—walking inside the opposite of my imaginings.

La Roche's safe room was a cozy den complete with a sunken area for the leather couch and coffee table. Decorative wall lamps provided a light brown hue over the room. He had a big-screen television, desk, and computer. None of those were the sight to see.

Paintings covered the walls. Hanging proudly above a bust of a stern man was Killian's *The Lacemaker.* There were many display stands, all holding items that looked priceless—though that may have been just to the person whose life would be ruined if La Roche made use of his leverage.

La Roche moved a painting and revealed an actual wall safe. My tension loosened at the stacks of money he counted out on the coffee table.

"Here you are, my dear." La Roche put them in a bag and handed it to me. "I truly hope you resolve this indiscretion. If they don't return your tape or ask for more, feel free to come back. I'm certain I can consult on methods to end this threat for good."

"I appreciate that," I said. "I'd also appreciate—"

"Me keeping our little meeting to myself," he finished. "You have my word."

I was tempted to ask if his word meant anything, but there was no use in antagonizing the man after he handed me a bag full of all my problems solved.

"Thank you."

He waved me on.

I walked out of La Roche's Leighbridge mansion with a bag of worthless paper that was worth everything to me. Duncan would not harm my father again.

It was time to take her leverage away.

Chapter Seven

"**I** can't do that."

"You have to."

"I can't," I repeated. "I don't have a say in these things."

"Get one."

I scowled. "Have you noted your habit of telling me what to do instead of asking?"

"It's a quirky trait of mine."

"Quirky wasn't the word I was going to use."

Sinjin lay sprawled across my lap, preventing me from doing something about Cash's smirk.

We were in his office—because where else would we be. Going over the plan for Vega—because what else would we be doing. The guys were so close to finding Kieran, they could smell his aftershave. All they had to do was go through La Roche to get him. Nothing would stop them.

"Mercer convinced Emily Chandler that she really wanted the great Ryan Sinclair to cater her charity event," Cash said. "She dumped the old one with two weeks to go. If Sinclair doesn't say yes, she'll be forced to hire someone else, and *you* won't have an excuse to be there."

I folded my arms. "Wouldn't it be easier to get me on the guest list? I can keep an eye on Vega just as easily. Actually, it'll be easier."

Mercer shook his head. "Tickets are twenty grand a pop."

"Twenty?" I cried.

He chuckled. "It's all for charity, right? Either way, Emily would only spare two, and she's sending them to Vega for free because she knows he's not stingy about supporting a worthy cause. It's one for him and his daughter, beautiful. She wouldn't spring for a third."

"No, I get it," I sighed. "The best way to get me in the party is for me to work it. And as luck would have it, I'm the sous chef to a caterer. It's a good plan, but it doesn't take into account that the mere act of asking him last minute would enrage Ryan into saying no."

"You make him say yes," Killian repeated.

"I cannot make that man do anything. It's a ton of work pulling these things together at the last minute. He already runs a full kitchen. Why would he take on this job just because I ask him to?"

"We could always trade assignments," Sinjin put forth. "You break into the heavily secured mansion, and I'll convince the cook to do this job. I'm willing, Bunny, but I've got a feeling Sinclair won't like my method of persuasion."

I gritted my teeth. Sinjin didn't go for subtlety.

Two weeks until the heist. One hour until I had to be in Mercy Park, dropping off a bag of money. He was right. We all had our jobs to do.

"I'll talk to him," I got out. "Today. I'm meeting up with Gianna anyway. Ryan will get a visit, and I'll convince him to work the party."

"Good," said Cash. "It's a straight hit on this one. Break in while he's out of the house and take the vase. Based on the projected resistance and security measures, I calculate four hours to do the job."

"Who leaves a party in less than four hours?" I asked. "My part will be simple. I'll keep an eye on him, and text you when he leaves." I lifted Saint's head from my lap. "No time like the present. It's best to talk to Ryan before the lunch rush. Bye."

I popped a kiss on Sinjin's lips, then did the same to Brutal and Killian. Mercer was meant to receive one too. I bent to kiss him, and spider fingers crawled up my bare thigh.

"Mercer!" I danced away, giggling. "Stop. I told you I'm ticklish."

I tried again. He skated up the other one.

I nipped his nose in retribution.

Leaving the office, I grabbed my things from my bedroom, and went out back where we kept our cars. I chanced a glance to the third floor.

The blinds were closed. No reason they should look and see me. Nothing out of place if they do.

Just a normal woman checking the trunk to ensure the bag of counterfeit hundreds she got from a crafty con man is where it should be.

It was.

The blue backpack sat innocently next to my spare tire.

I closed the trunk, got in, and made the short drive to Salvatore's.

Ryan was in his office when I arrived. He mumbled to himself as he organized next week's menu. Frowning. Stabbing the keys. Shaking his head. Then nodding at the final choice. I knew for this was a state I found him in many times.

"Chef?"

Raising his head, he squinted at me over his glasses. "Adeline. Come in."

"Sorry to bother you, Chef." I closed us in the small space.

A tiny, tucked-away corner of the kitchen, the office didn't have much to say for itself besides a desk, computer, file cabinet, and a small wine cooler. I pulled a chair next to him.

"What is it?" he asked.

"I heard about the breast cancer charity dinner in two weeks," I began. "A friend of mine said Salvatore's was called to cater."

"Ah. I see where you're going with this. I would've asked you to join us, but I turned down that event."

"My friend told me that too. I know how busy you are, Chef, and that this cause means a lot to you."

Ryan's mother passed a few years ago in a battle with breast cancer. It was something he didn't speak much about. It came out in the early hours of the morning over glasses of wine and plates of our latest test recipes.

"I was thinking this was another chance for me to help. I could plan the menu, give it to you for final approval, and handle the prep myself."

His brows scrunched. "You plan the menu? People book Ryan Sinclair for Ryan Sinclair's food. Not Adeline Redgrave's."

A straight shot through the heart. Accurate all the same.

"I don't mean to overstep."

"You are," he stated. "I've turned down that event. That's the end of it. If there's nothing else, go."

"I'll convince the cook to do this job. I've got a feeling Sinclair won't like my method of persuasion."

I sighed. *I like you, Ryan. I'm trying to save you a stay in our dungeon. Work with me.*

I checked the time. *Work with me quickly.*

"Sorry, Chef. I guess I got too excited at the mention of Mateo Rivas. Having a legend like him eat my food is a dream of mine. Even if my name isn't on it." I got to my feet. "I'll leave you to it—"

"Hold on." Ryan stopped me with my hand on the knob. "Did you say Mateo Rivas?"

"Yes. The chef and critic. Do you know him?"

Ryan reddened. "Of course I know him."

"I have every cookbook he's published. He's amazing." The red was shifting to a purple hue. "I messed up every attempt to make béarnaise sauce until I used his recipe. He is—"

"Did you say he was attending the event?" Ryan sliced in. "How do you know? Who told you that?"

"The friend I told you about. She said how great it was we were catering because I might meet Rivas."

"Rivas," he hissed.

I bit back a smile.

The ride that brought the great Ryan Sinclair, Leighbridge's up-and-coming jewel, down to a family restaurant in Waterford, was the kind of crash you looked away from. He'd always been haughty and difficult to work with. In those days, he was even worse. Everything he cooked was perfection, and he wouldn't hear otherwise.

One night, the critic Mateo Rivas ate at his restaurant, Sinclair's. He ordered penne alla vodka with a roasted pepper salad, and a bottle of prosecco. He wrote the next day how glad he was the sommelier recommended an excellent bottle of wine. It drowned his taste buds and then his sorrows after forcing himself to swallow that "bland, uninspired, could-order-off-a-drive-thru-menu meal."

Ryan's explosion at the review kicked off a chain of events that landed him here. If people had archenemies outside of comic books, Mateo Rivas would be his.

"Maybe Rivas's company will cater the dinner," I mused. "He'll be attending, but there's little time left, and they could spin it as an opportunity for publicity. I'll tell her to give that spin a try if they can't find anyone—"

"No," Ryan barked. "We'll do the event. Adeline, make yourself available tomorrow and every day for the next two weeks. We begin menu-planning tomorrow."

"Are you sure? I thought you were too busy."

"That was before I realized what a bind they were in. To bend to serving Rivas's slop is less than they deserve." I'd never seen his lip curl like that. "This is a good cause. The least we can do is lend our time."

"Of course, Chef." I didn't grin. That would be wrong. "I'll be here tomorrow."

"Eight a.m."

I waved bye over my shoulder. In the alleyway, I dialed Mercer.

"Lovely."

"Mercer," I greeted. "I need you to call your friend, Emily, and get her to put Mateo Rivas on the guest list. He's—"

"The critic," he said. "We've met."

I couldn't read in his tone what kind of meeting they had. I chose not to ask.

"He's Ryan's nemesis, and the sole reason he changed his mind on catering the party. Ryan's going to make him eat his food and like it. As such, I need the organizer to back me up when he calls to confirm he'll be there."

"A nemesis? I thought my life was interesting. Even I don't have one of those."

I made my way to the parking lot. "Really? You're a cup of sugar and honey in the life of everyone you've met?" I teased.

"Of those still living, yes."

I laughed. "Don't sound so disappointed. You could drive someone into a pit of deep, abiding, petty hatred too."

"Put that on my bucket list," he said. "I'll talk Emily into sending the invitation. It won't be free though. I'll have to work on Mateo to get him to accept."

Again, I swallowed the urge to ask for more details.

"Never fear, lovely, this is what I do. Mateo will be there."

My heart panged at the thought I sent Mercer into someone else's bed.

"Adeline?"

I was quiet.

"I'm not going to sleep with him, love." How he always knew what I was thinking was his secret power. "I'll invite him out for drinks, talk up the event, and sweeten the deal with a number for one of my more influential friends. No sex needed for this one. And if there was, credit me with enough tact not to brag to you about it."

"Thanks," I whispered.

"See you at three?"

"Yes." I visited my father every day at three. Mercer went with me.

"Bye, gorgeous."

"Bye."

I strode through the alley, passing the spot the Merchants cornered me for the second time. My feelings that day came roaring back. Curious about these men who were once nothing more than masked faces on security tapes. Baffled that fate dropped them in my lap. Equally frightened and furious that circumstances had forced me into the arms of men who might beat and abuse me.

Of course I fought them in the beginning. I didn't know what they do. Now, I asked myself why I didn't stand in this alley and know they were mine.

I walked to my car, got the bag out of the trunk, and went to the silver ride idling in the back. Gianna honked me out of my boots.

"Whoo," she hooted. "What do you think? Like it."

"Love it." I slid into her new car, getting comfortable on the leather. "Although, I was expecting gold."

She winked. "I'm getting the next one in that color."

I flicked to the dashboard clock.

"Seriously," Gianna went on. "I didn't go crazy. I got this for a good price. Figured it was time we stopped relying on Raul and public transportation to take care of business. If there's an emergency, we need to go and get quickly." She squeezed my hand. "Like today. You ready?"

"I'm ready."

Gianna cracked a smile. "Why am I acting like you need emotional support?"

"There is something I need," I said over the hum of the starting engine.

"It'll take me a while. Few weeks. Will that be a problem?"

"I'll just have to figure something out." I nudged her arm. "Hey, did this thing come with busted speakers? Blast the music."

"Now that I can do."

We played old songs through the whole ride—singing them aloud to make a mumble or skipped word obvious.

We arrived at the park with ten minutes to spare. Found a parking space minus an incident or a need to result to petty crime.

"Wait in the car," I told her.

She nodded.

This was no Mercy Park on a perfect day. Dark clouds promised rain, and plenty of it. Damp in the air blanketed the flowers. The playground didn't hold shrieking children. I was alone on the path to the tunnel—missing the babies in their strollers.

Duncan had chosen the right date for this. It wasn't a good day.

I should've taken her seriously that day in the game room. I definitely should've remembered the easy access she had to Dad. I guess I keep expecting goodness from those who get to be.

I had no choice but to become this creature. Duncan did.

Years of good service and a spotless criminal record. She turned to this knowing there was another way. Chose to become like me, and I was outsmarted.

Time to pay the price.

The garbage can loomed before me. I had to assume she was here somewhere watching me, like I did to her.

I dropped the bag in the can. Doubling back, I disappeared into the shadows of the tunnel.

Minutes passed.

At ten o'clock on the dot, a figure came jogging around the curve. She wore a green backpack.

Duncan went through the routine again. Looking around. Stretching. Taking a sip of water.

She set her bag down, and reached inside for mine. Duncan opened it in full view. Two hundred thousand fake bucks for the taking.

She let out a whoop.

Dropping her bag in the trash, Duncan set off the way she came, backpack slung over her shoulder.

I pulled the detonator from my pocket. The small red button gave way to a featherlight touch.

Boom!

I flew off my feet, smacking into the wall, and dropping down.

Witnessing the power of Killian's explosives still hadn't prepared me for the heat on my face. Spots dancing in my eyes. The ringing in my ears disorienting me.

Scorched bills floated through the air—the final legacy of the smoldering pile of ash that was Tara Duncan.

Pushing myself up, I ran to the garbage, claimed her bag, and took off the way I came.

Yes, Duncan outsmarted me. For all of a day.

That was how long it took me to recall Killian kept a spare bomb under the passenger seat.

"You think if you act like a psycho, I'll turn tail and run."

Her mistake was thinking I was acting.

Gianna was dancing and bobbing her head to music as I climbed inside. "So?"

I ripped open the bag. "Laptop, tablet, phone"—I played a snippet of the recorded conversation—"evidence."

"How accommodating."

"Leave a fake trail, will you, G? Make it obvious she was blackmailing a dangerous person, and got it in the ass. Pick someone off the pedophile list."

"No problem."

Gianna put the car in gear as the sirens rang out. "Damn, we're good."

"That's what I keep saying."

"REMEMBER WHAT TO DO?"

Cash adjusted my grip on the gun, erection digging into my butt cheek as he did so. He lifted my arms to line the shot. But that wasn't what he was talking about.

"Gee. I don't know. My role is soooo hard, and you know what trouble us little ladies have with keeping two thoughts in our—"

Cash bit my ear.

"Ow," I cried, giggling.

"Just won't let that little lady thing go, will you?"

"Could be persuaded to get over it." I tapped my lips. "Right here."

Cash kissed me—slow and lethal. I broke away dizzy.

"You know, you said I suck at this, but it seems you like me with a gun just fine."

"You're every man's fantasy, Adeline Redgrave."

"But your reality."

I turned for more of the activities that ate half our day, and left me standing naked in his room wearing only his shirt and our cooling sweat on my body.

Cash turned me back. "Hit the target three times."

I heaved a sigh. "Fine. And yes, I remember what to do. Keep an eye on Vega. Warn you when he leaves. Definitely warn you if he suddenly springs out of his seat and runs for the exit."

"This won't be simple. Mercer tapped two of Vega's friends for as much information as he could get. It's not so much a safe as it is a safe room."

Vega and La Roche have more in common than they think.

"Insurance won't pay out if he doesn't take every measure to keep them safe, so the stashed coffee tin in the kitchen won't cut it," said Cash. "Especially for a man who needs to flaunt his revenge. The most expensive items are placed in the room under display cases. Every now and then, he allows people inside to view the pieces."

"Getting into that room won't be easy," I confirmed.

"No, but once again Mercer's information-gathering is invaluable. If he regularly lets people inside, the room can't be rigged to send an automatic alert to the police. One less thing to worry about. On to the rest.

"Mercer needs at least an hour to get in. Then there's taking out the guards and household staff, disabling additional security measures, and clearing the scene. Four hours. Vega cannot leave before then. If he shows up, nothing changes. We still pull the job."

"But then Kendall Vega enters the equation," I finished.

"Parents do out-of-character things when they believe their children are in danger."

"One-hundred-percent probability," I said, thinking of my dad.

I adopted the proper stance, aiming for the silhouette taped to the door. "Neither of us wants you guys forced into restraining and traumatizing a little girl. Or her witnessing a shoot-out if their guards pull their weapons. I will make sure they don't leave the party early. Four hours. I can do it."

In the two weeks since Tara Duncan decorated Mercy Park with her parts, the Merchants and I had been busy. Their men were hand-selected and readied for the strike against Vega. I spent every day from early in the morning to late at night, prepping for the charity dinner.

Emily Chandler requested a five-course meal to be served prompt, and cleared away at designated times during the evening. A good chunk we prepared ahead of time. For the remaining to be cooked on site, Ryan had checked, double-checked, and triple-checked the ingredients were fresh and top quality. I was back to driving out of the city to buy organic farm-to-table produce—in between ducking into the walk-in freezer to check the news.

The trending story for the last two weeks was the death of Tara Duncan. Mercy Park closed. Crime scene techs swarmed the area. The residents and staff of the home were questioned.

Reporters suggested ransom almost immediately. How could they not when the wind carried burned bits of money as far as Ninth Street, and the cops had to restrain park stragglers who stomped over the crime scene, snatching up the bills.

The only question was if Tara was delivering a ransom or picking one up. No one had flashed my picture under a wanted label, so whoever they were searching for in connection with her death, it wasn't me. The final loose end to tie up was replacing the bomb under Killian's seat.

Just my luck that was the only thing not stashed in the torture room.

Gianna was in the process of finding me a replacement with the same look and style. All I could do was wait and keep Killian occupied.

Which he was. Sebastian Vega accepted the invitation for him and his daughter. Mercer convinced Rivas a charity dinner for cancer was exactly what he wanted to do on a Saturday night. The Merchants were ready to go.

I glanced at the clock.

In one hour.

"All right," Killian said. "Fire."

Taking a deep breath, I pulled the trigger.

The door flew open.

Mercer jerked—struck dead-on. Red stained his shirt, spreading to soak his chest in wet crimson.

"Bit of a harsh reaction for not knocking."

I smothered a laugh. "Sorry. Did that sting?"

"Like a bitch." Mercer shrugged off the shirt now covered with paint. "Your phone is going off again. You should make sure everything's all right."

"Excuse me." I slipped out of Killian's hold and hurried downstairs.

My father was released from the hospital a week ago. Currently, he was back at the home under the tender care of Mrs. Watkins and his many girlfriends. Didn't stop the kick start of panic through my heart every time my phone rang off the desk. I prayed Tara Duncan enjoyed a long stay in hell for that crime alone.

I picked my phone off the bed, glancing at the screen.

"Hello, Chef."

"Adeline, where are you? I'm at the venue, and you're nowhere to be found."

I double-checked the time. "I'm still at home. You said to be half an hour early."

"I told *everyone else* to be half an hour early. You needed to be here five minutes ago."

"Yes, Chef," I said simply. "Heading out now."

He hung up on me.

Quickly, I dressed, said a rushed goodbye and good luck to the guys, and ran out the door.

It was time. Sooner than I planned. But it was time.

This was the first true domino to fall in the search for Kieran. Let him walk into my trap. Let my twisted love coax me into torturing him, egging me on to drain every drop of info on the ledger. And then let me get there first—claiming the ledger and my mantle as shadow ruler of this city.

Now that I think of it, I'm glad I've been summoned earlier. The fun starts even sooner.

CASH

Sinjin and I ducked into the shadows, peering at number 11. The biggest home on Midsomer Street. Our masks were tight over our noses and mouths. Sinjin's addition was the knit cap pulled low over his blue hair.

"Diego?" I asked.

"Hacked the cameras. They're showing what we want them to see."

"Good. Three minutes."

"No blood."

I nodded.

In a flash, we were out of the alley and running across the street.

This was a quiet, wealthy neighborhood. Residents were either out spending their money, or faced away from the window and at the television—sipping a glass of port in between basking in the lack of worries only millions could bring. No one would observe our activities.

I knocked on the front door.

"Hello?" The voice came through the intercom.

"Yeah, hi." I adopted a deep, booming voice. "This is Terry Molletto from number 13. The keypad lock isn't working, and I left my phone inside. Is Sebastian home? I just need to use the phone to call my wife."

"Mr. Vega isn't here right now," he returned. "I'm not authorized to let you inside. But if you wait there, sir, I'll bring the phone for you to make your call."

"Very good."

I checked my watch. One minute and fifty-two seconds remaining.

Fifty-one.

Fifty.

Forty-nine.

Forty-eight.

Forty-seven.

The door opened.

"Wha—?"

Sinjin grabbed his outstretched hand, yanking him out onto the porch. He flew into my punch, and sounded a groan that signaled eight masked men to emerge from their holes.

Sinjin and I carried the struggling guard inside. We dropped him on the welcome mat. Brutal took over.

Backpack slung on his shoulders, he wrenched the gun the guard tried to pull from his grip. It went flying as he buried a gloved fist in his gut.

We wouldn't spill blood. Didn't mean we were going easy on them. The guards had to go down, and stay down. Everyone made it out alive that way.

"Kitchen. Living room. Back door. Ten minutes," I ordered. "Brutal."

Brutal knocked him out. The man slumped limp on the floor.

"Stash him in that closet," I said.

A slim figure in a tailor-made suit and a silk mask stepped inside over the body. A bag of his own was hooked around his neck.

"You and Mercer. Eight minutes, fifteen seconds."

Mercer and Brutal went one way to look for the safe room. Sinjin and I trailed the men hunting for more guards and the household staff. Breaking ahead, I walked the most likely path to the kitchen.

Stepping through that house, it was clear La Roche downplayed Vega's obsession with ancient, beautiful things.

The entire estate was an antique, for all that the home was built in 1920. We passed by a French Louis XVI-style sofa with curved gold legs. It rested next to an old, gleaming cabinet that looked too delicate to breathe on. Even the wallpaper was the type favored in the old days. A garish burgundy and gold damask designs.

"—ooh, yes."

Voices poured out of the entrance up ahead.

"Take it, slut."

"Right there!"

I rounded the corner.

A naked woman lay spread-eagle on the dining room table, screeching her orgasm for the rutting hunk of tattoos and cheap suit between her legs.

The half-kneaded dough beside them gave a clue to what she was in the middle of before he interrupted.

I let the man finish. I wasn't a complete bastard.

"Ahem." Sinjin cleared his throat.

The guy whipped around, condom flying off.

"I believe this is the part where I say stick 'em up."

She opened her mouth to scream.

"Don't," I said. I pulled my gun. "Or I'll shoot you. Simple as that."

She snapped her mouth shut.

"Get dressed. These nice men will assist in gagging and tying you up."

Pistol, Cain, Lucky, Frankie, and Ted streamed around us. They stuffed gags first down their throats, muffling the shouts as they were put on the ground and tied up. They moved them into the pantry while I checked the time.

"Six minutes. Find the rest."

ADELINE

Gazpacho. Crostini with smoked salmon and honey cream cheese. Sicilian pasta salad. Roasted pork loin with baked apple slices. Baked brie and blueberry compote. And finally, dessert, cherries jubilee with lavender coconut macarons.

Ryan outdid himself with this menu and three guesses why.

Not to say the man slacked off in general. Everything he put out was delicious. But the arrival of his nemesis kicked him into a new stratosphere. At one point, I thought he was inventing his own flavors.

Emily asked for a light, fruity meal boasting lots of colors, flavors, and tastes. Ryan delivered—to the detriment of my health and sleep.

But all that matters is you're right where you should be.

I stood just outside the kitchen doors, watching Sebastian Vega. I knew what he looked like, of course. I'd seen his face pinned on Killian's whiteboard enough times.

His beard was just as neatly trimmed. His suit similarly expensive and re‑fined. A pronounced nose hung over thin lips—that he dabbed with a nap‑kin after every three bites. Seated next to him was his daughter, Kendall.

I assumed Kendall took after her mother. Kendall's mouth was full. Her nose snubbed. And long black hair swept down her back while Sebastian's was a lighter brown.

The two of them chatted quietly as the event went on around them. Emi‑ly organized the evening for the auction to start after the main course. Every‑one would be sufficiently full, happy, and ready to open their wallets.

Two hours.

Two hours since Vega arrived. Two more hours he had to stay to give my boys plenty of time to rob him blind. I should—

"Adeline!"

I jumped out of my skin.

"What are you doing out here?" Ryan hissed. "You're supposed to be pureeing the blueberries."

"It's done," I told him. "I just popped out to see how Rivas is enjoying the food. He's cleaned every plate, Chef."

"Has he?" Self-satisfaction rolled off him in waves. "Of course, he has. In‑side. Now."

I did as ordered.

Sebastian Vega was settled in and enjoying himself. He wasn't going any‑where anytime soon.

CASH

Lucky tossed the final guard in the wine cellar with the others. The man tripped over his feet, and went down at the shoes of the hastily dressed cook.

His lack of gentleness I put down to the wet stain on his mask. The guard clocked him good when we surprised him near the back door. It was to be expected. We weren't going to catch them all with their pants down.

Sinjin slammed the cellar shut and broke the lock.

I checked the time. "One hour forty-five minutes," I said. "Pistol. Cain, you stay on this door. The rest of you, watch the streets."

Ted, Frankie, and Lucky headed upstairs. Sinjin and I followed a beat behind, splitting on the first-floor landing, and continuing up.

Mercer's texts led us to the second-floor library. We didn't need the texts though. We heard him from down the hall.

Mercer knelt in front of a metal door once hidden behind a fake bookshelf panel. The portable plasma cutter sparked white heat that reflected in his protective goggles. Two hours in, he scored an unfinished semicircle around the lock.

"This is taking longer than I thought," he shouted. "Another twenty minutes. Maybe thirty. Leaves us an hour and a half max to get at what's inside."

"Just get it done," I said.

"Bunny will keep Vega there." Sinjin reclined in the man's armchair. "If not, she'll warn us when he leaves, and we'll still get what we're after."

Beside him was a small, rectangular box. Sinjin flipped the top and unearthed two cigars. He tossed one to me.

"Relax, C. Our retrieval rate is a hundred percent for a reason. No one gets in the way of what we came for."

ADELINE

I waved out the servers carrying the brie and blueberry compote. Peeking around the swinging door, I sought Sebastian Vega.

Oh no.

"—with us, ladies and gentlemen. This is an important cause, and we're grateful you came out tonight to support us."

Emily Chandler was resplendent in a glittery gold gown, shining like a disco ball on the stage. She was the sight to see. The focus of attention for all in the room—except for Vega.

He spoke in low tones to his daughter. Hands up and placating.

Kendall flung herself back in the seat. She gave her father a miserable, furious look I knew well. Everyone who had been a kid for more than ten seconds knew that look.

She was bored, and she wanted to leave *now*.

I hugged the wall, slinking around the back to Vega's table at the right corner of the room, near the stage.

"Daddy, I feel sick. The pork was bad."

"It wasn't bad, sweetie. Daddy had some and—"

"Yes, it was!"

The high-pitched whine drew the attention of half the table. Vega apologized to them.

"I want to go home."

"One more hour, Kendall. Give me a chance to bid on one of the items. Miss Chandler was so nice to invite us." The poor man sounded like he was asking her permission.

"No, my stomach hurts."

Dammit, Vega, don't give in. The guys need another hour and a half.

But I knew that look too. The average woman is a natural grifter. We learn how to manipulate to get what we want, and we start with our dads. My father couldn't say no to my misery—real or faked—and neither could Vega.

He was going to break.

Vega sighed. "All right, Kendall. Get your—"

I sprang off the wall. "Oh, poor thing."

Kendall blinked at my sudden appearance.

"Are you not feeling well?" I knelt beside her. "We have ginger candies in the kitchen. They're magic for an upset stomach."

She latched on one word. "Candy?"

"Yep. Why don't you come with me? I'm setting things on fire back there," I said, grinning. "You can watch."

"Cool." Kendall hopped off the chair. She grabbed my hand and led me away. "Bye, Daddy."

"Wha— Wait," he cried.

"It's okay, Mr.— sir. We'll be right in the kitchen."

Vega chased after us. He had to at the speed Kendall was tugging me along. "The kitchen? Is it safe? Is she allowed?"

"Perfectly safe," I replied, "and she's allowed as long as she's with me."

"But, Kendall, this nice lady must be very busy—"

"She said it was okay, Daddy, gawwwdd."

I stifled a laugh.

"Come get me when the party's over." We pushed in the kitchen, letting the door swing shut on him. "Bye."

Vega didn't follow.

"You will do great things one day, Kendall."

She beamed—though I suspect she only heard the compliment and didn't connect it to the reason. "Thanks."

"But there are some rules." I drew her to the side by the sheet pan cart. "You stick with me at all times. No running. No cooking unless you've got one of these."

I tapped my chef's coat and she laughed.

"You can hang out with me at my station."

"Will you really set the food on fire?"

"Really, really."

"And candy?"

"You can have as much as you want." I stuck out my hand. "Deal?"

She shook. "Deal."

I took Kendall to the sink to wash her hands, and then to the back where the venue kept a candy stash. She grabbed a handful, popping them in her mouth as I brought her to my station.

The entire time I managed to steer clear of or shield her from Ryan's eye. The man was in the final stretch of culinary revenge against Rivas. He was preoccupied.

Kendall spied the ingredients taking up my table.

"What are you making?"

"Cherries jubilee. Ever had that before?"

She shook her head.

"It's pretty tasty, and easy to make." I got the kitchen stool from the corner for her. She hopped up, leaning on the table to watch. "You can't help me with this, but every venue my boss works, he leaves food for the cleanup staff. We can cook that together if you want to."

"Yeah!"

Truth was, I liked kids. They were chaos, recklessness, and unbound energy all rolled in one. They said and did what they felt without the bullshit. The only time in a terrible person's life when they weren't vile is when they were a child.

Jocelyn was once sweet and innocent. There had to be a time Angelo Castillo wasn't a violent psychopath. Somewhere along the way, we grow either into the best or worst version of ourselves. Sometimes a mix of both.

If you ask me, the only time it's worth knowing a person is when they're a child. Once they reach adulthood, they're iffy.

Kendall watched me rapt.

I arranged my plating, got my stovetop going, and melted creamy butter in a pan. Our dessert chef came by a few times to add the lavender coconut macarons to my plates. She, and others, gave us curious looks, but I was the sous chef. They weren't about to question me.

"Ready?" I asked. "Watch this."

I poured brandy over my vanilla-cherry concoction. It burst into blue flames.

"Ah!" Kendall clapped, shrieking delight. "That was so cool. Will you give me the recipe, so I can make it with my dad?"

"Sure thing—"

"Adeline." Ryan stopped at my station. The spoon in his hand revealed his intent to taste-test my jubilee. "What's this?"

"Hi." Kendall waved.

Ryan looked at her like he'd never seen a miniature human before. "What are you doing here?"

"I told her she could watch me make dessert."

"No, she cannot. A kitchen is no place for a child."

"Chef," Stevie broke in. "Table thirty-five is requesting a different dessert. He doesn't eat cherries or coconut."

"Rivas."

It was a mystery why Ryan assumed it was Rivas. There were nine other people at that table.

"He said to serve him chocolate mousse with raspberries. We should be able to handle that."

Okay, that was Rivas.

"I'll take care of this." Ryan blew past her, marching out the door.

Turning to Kendall, I swiped imaginary sweat off my brow, winking at her.

Her giggles ran in my ear as I checked the clock.

CASH

"Done."

After cutting through the reinforced metal door, the locks put up as much of a fight as melted butter. Two hours and forty-five minutes in, the safe door swung open.

The four of us fanned inside.

Yellow marble tile covered from door to wall. Vega's safe room was circular. You swept the length of the space three-sixty and everywhere were cabinets, weapons, hanging rugs, tapestries, and furniture that'd feed your family for a lifetime.

In the middle of it all, stood three museum pedestals and the items inside their display cases. Glittering rubies, emeralds, and sapphires set in gold. A crystal-blue vase with fine designs etched in the surface. A rather ugly headpiece lined with jewels.

"The vase, the necklace, and the tiara," said Sinjin. "Nice of him to put it out in the open for us."

"Anyone else thinking this is a test within our test?"

Mercer's question hung in the air.

"We're running out of time," I said.

I walked the length of the room, taking in everything.

"The rest of the antiques here are too heavy or bulky to be easily removed from this room," Mercer said. "These three could be slipped into a purse or briefcase." He pressed his nose almost to the glass. "Vega wouldn't make it that easy for them."

"What do you see?" I asked. I paused in front of a cabinet.

"Sin, look at this," he said.

Sinjin adopted his position, peering up close and personal to the vase. "I see it."

I turned away. "What?"

"There are small, round lights in the perimeter of the case," Mercer said. "Sensors. If we move it, something will go off."

"Diego took care of the alarms," Sinjin said.

"We better fucking hope he did. That door may not be wired to the police, but this sure as hell will be. We set this off and they'll be here in three minutes. The shortened response time that comes with a Leighbridge zip code."

"How long will it take you to get in the case?" I asked.

"Longer than three minutes."

"Do it," Sinjin ordered. "We've got our guys watching the streets. If the cops show up, we take the whole damn thing and get out."

"Do it," I confirmed, turning back to the cabinet. "Three minutes is enough time to go out the back and escape over the fence in the neighbor's yard. Mr. and Mrs. Rumsfield aren't home. I checked."

"Brutal?" Mercer prompted.

He nodded. We were agreed.

"All right. Have the boys on standby."

Mercer secured his safety goggles, bent before the vase's case, and pressed the cutter to the plastic. He flipped it on.

Beep! Beep! Beep!

A piercing, ear-shattering alarm ripped through the room.

"Fuck!"

ADELINE

"Drizzle that bad boy on just like this." I poured the cherry sauce over bowls of homemade vanilla ice cream. "Voila."

Kendall clapped, hopping on her little stool.

I should've gotten a hype man in the kitchen years ago.

"Okay, now—"

"Excuse me?"

I turned toward the door. Sebastian Vega stuck his head in the kitchen. He lit upon us.

"There you are." He ducked around Stevie carrying my finished desserts out. "It was very nice of you to entertain her, but we should get going."

"You're leaving?"

"Yes." He put his arms around Kendall. "Let's go, honey."

"But, Daddy," she whined. "Miss Addy was going to show me how to make strawberry fans and roses out of tomatoes."

"It's almost your bedtime."

I flicked to the clock. *One hour. The boys haven't texted me that they got it. He can't leave.*

What are you supposed to say to stop him? Kendall can't go to bed because she has to play with scraps of fruit?

I have one job. I have to keep him here.

"I understand," I spoke up. "Do you mind waiting while I write up some recipes for Kendall? She was really excited to make them with you."

"Yeah, Daddy."

"Oh." He set Kendall on her feet. "Of course. Thank you."

"One sec." I ducked in the back to grab paper and a pen. I returned to find someone else at my station.

"—can't be in here," said Ryan.

Kendall lifted her chin. "Miss Addy is giving us the recipes."

"Here." Ryan plucked a menu off the table. "Take this. You can look up the inferior versions of my creations at home."

Yes, he said that.

"Have a good evening."

"But—"

"He's right, Kendall. Time to—"

His phone went off. Vega fished it out and checked the screen. His eyes widened, and hardened in the same breath.

"Time to go. Now, Kendall." This wasn't the same man who broke under her whining. "Anymore complaining and it's no television for a week."

Vega marched her out the door. I might've tried again to stop him if I didn't share the same sense as Kendall. Dad was not to be argued with.

I trailed them out, stopping short just outside the door to watch him snatch up their things, and leave the hall.

Me: Something's wrong. Vega's leaving. Get out now.

CASH

"Frankie and Lucky are on both ends of the street," said Sinjin. "No sirens. Diego cut the signal for this alarm too. Don't stop, Mercer."

"Didn't come this far to stop," he shouted over the noise.

"Cain can hear the fucking thing downstairs."

Sinjin closed us in. Better we lose our hearing than the neighbors call the cops.

"Cash, what the hell are you looking at?"

This.

I circled the cabinet, peering around the back. Antiques weren't my specialty. My early days were in art. Still, I brushed up on different topics to fool the moneybags I was trying to fleece. To the casual eye, this cabinet was no different from the other priceless pieces in this room. I was certain it was expensive—

But it's not an antique.

The molding. Stain. Design. And finish. It couldn't be more than fifty years old.

Why lock this away when the cabinet in your sitting room is twice as old and three times the cost?

I threw open the doors. Feeling around, I ran my hands over the wood, pressed the back wall, lifted the shelf.

I felt something give away. Releasing the wood, I stepped away as the back of the cabinet swung open, revealing another room. I ducked under the shelf and went inside.

I was not a man easily surprised. A point of contention for my nieces and nephews, who took great delight in jumping off and popping out from behind things to scare me.

None of them earned the look that came over me as I stood inside that room within a room.

My lips parted—eyes widening at the metals, helmets, daggers, statuettes, busts, flags, and carvings. Resting on a small pillow, the centerpiece of the table's collection, was an ugly, gold ring. It couldn't be more than a few thousand dollars. Maybe tens of thousands to the right person.

I snapped pictures of the room. A message popped up midway on the screen.

Adeline: Something's wrong. Vega's leaving. Get out now.

I moved faster. On my way out, I pocketed the ring.

Crouching down, I ducked out.

Mercer turned off the cutter. Carefully, he reached inside the hole and removed the vase. He passed it to Sinjin who grinned like a man looking down at his newborn.

My phone in hand, I felt the second buzz.

Lucky: Cops.

"Time to go," I barked. "Sinjin, drop the vase."

He did. Opening his hands, he let the priceless artifact slip through his fingers, smashing to pieces on the floor.

Mercer gaped at the mess. "What the fuck, Cash?"

"No time. Cops are on the way."

That cut off the argument at its knees.

Mercer snatched up his shit, and we bolted, leaving the remains of our prize behind. We ran into Cain and Pistol on the first floor.

"Out the back!" Sinjin ordered.

We heard the safe room alarm blaring away upstairs. The only sound louder was the oncoming police sirens.

Running through the halls, we burst out the back doors and didn't stop. Past the pool and hot tub. Trampling the garden. Climbing the deck chair to vault over the fence.

As blue, red, and purple lit the sky, the Merchants ran through the Rumsfields' yard, and were gone.

"HELP ME UNDERSTAND this," Adeline carried on.

She paced the length of the carpet. Her chef's jacket had been abandoned for the tank top underneath, leaving just the baggy checkered pants to go.

Sinjin must have felt the same because he was making an effort to snag them as she went past.

"You broke into the safe room."

"Yes," I confirmed.

"You had the vase in your hands."

"Yes."

"And you dropped it?!"

"Correct," Sinjin added.

"Why?"

He shrugged. "I don't know. Why, C?"

"You didn't even ask?!"

Sinjin finally got her. He gave one firm tug, yanking her yelping on his lap.

"Relax, Redgrave," I said. "When I was in there, I realized what Richard La Roche truly wanted and it wasn't a vase or tiara."

I held up the ring. She squinted at the gaudy little thing.

"What is that?"

"Gold ring."

"How much is it worth?"

"A couple hundred dollars."

She blinked at me. "Cash, I don't think you know what La Roche wanted."

I chuckled. "We'll find out, won't we?"

"The hard way—like always with you."

Getting to my feet, I said, "If I'm so difficult, you won't be sneaking into my bed tonight, burning me with that furnace you call a body."

"The fuck I won't," she snapped. "This is the kind of thing I'm talking about."

"Then I'll see you tomorrow night too. We're paying La Roche a visit. By this time tomorrow, he'll be working for the Merchants."

ADELINE

Sinjin's arm slung over my waist. Possessive waking and sleeping, he kept me close by.

Inch by inch, I wriggled out from under him, sliding off the edge of the mattress. My feet were soundless padding across the floor to the multiple places Saint flung my clothes. I gathered them up and dressed out in the hall.

My phone lit up again.

"I'm coming, G," I whispered. "Meet me at the front door."

Our two-story abode was silent, and my slipping out and traveling downstairs didn't disturb the peace.

A shadowed figure moved on the other side of the frosted glass. Gianna stuck her head through the door crack to kiss me.

"Hey. We still good?"

"We're good," I confirmed. I came out, following Gianna to her car parked at the end of the block. "Killian doesn't know we used his plan B to take care of a quick problem. Is it the same size and look?"

"The guy did his best." We climbed inside. Gianna popped open the glove box. "What do you think?"

I handled it carefully, examining the small block of C4 and its accompaniments. "Perfect. Exact down to the colored wires."

"Put that under the seat, and he'll never know it was missing. This Tara Duncan shit is finally over."

I released a breath I'd been holding for weeks.

"Finally."

THAT NEXT NIGHT, I met Cash in his room. He filled up a mirror with each sexy inch of him, fixing his reflection's tie.

"I'm ready," I said.

I wore a long, red drape dress whose hem flirted with the straps of my heels. La Roche's home required a dress code, as did our parts as gentleman and lady criminal consultants.

Cash swept a slow, lingering look over me that shivered my bones. "Nice," he said simply, though his eyes said something else.

"Thank you."

I came up behind him, slipping my arms around his waist. "Five minutes in these heels and they're already killing me. Keys, please. I'll wait for you in the car."

Killian handed them to me without question. I brushed my lips over his ear. "Love you," I whispered.

I headed downstairs to the car—the bomb tucked in my purse. We were parked on the side street. I got in, crouched down, and felt for the little pouch sewn to the underside that housed the stolen bomb. I slid the replacement inside.

I was seated and fussing with my hair in the mirror when Cash arrived.

"You going to tell me the reason you smashed our only chance now?"

He didn't answer. Cash started the car and pulled into traffic.

"Come on, Cash. You can't play the 'we'll sound rehearsed' card on me. La Roche will expect me to know."

"Fine. Here it is."

Cash explained the secret room behind the cabinet, what he found, why he took the ring, and why he reigned supreme as a leader of the Merchants.

The last part he didn't say, but he didn't have to. The truth of it settled in my bones as I sank in the seat—stunned. Cash knew what he was doing. He did choose the item La Roche must have truly wanted.

Which makes me wonder if he knew that secret room was in there?

I shook my head. If he did, he'd tell the Merchants straight out to go in the room and get it. He had no reason to play coy. He didn't know—which made me fortunate to be there for his reaction.

Killian arrived at La Roche's mansion thirty minutes later.

We were ushered in by two guards. The two who carried their bleeding friend away from me.

They patted us down, turned out Killian's pockets, checked my purse, and patted me down again.

I smiled into their narrowed-eyed looks, cool and calm.

"Forgive the added security." La Roche came down the stairs. "A friend pointed out there were a few holes I needed to plug."

"No problem," said Killian.

"Do you have it?"

"We do." Killian picked up the ring box security put on the table. "Shall we go upstairs?"

La Roche swept his hands in an "after you" gesture. He grinned at me on the way up.

"Hello again, Miss Adeline. Always a pleasure."

"Nice to see you too."

"I trust life is treating you well?"

"It is."

"Glad to hear it."

We ended the conversation, continuing to his office in silence.

La Roche motioned for us to sit. "So, which one did they get? Am I to assume it's on its way?"

"No, it's here."

Killian set the ring box on the desk. He used one finger to slide it over.

La Roche watched its approach, face crumpling in a frown. "I don't understand. What is this?"

"Open it."

Opening the box, he tipped the contents out. The frown solidified.

"Is this a joke?" The jovial, devil-may-care tone vanished. "How dare you."

"This is not a joke, Richard," Killian said. "Or an insult. You asked the Merchants to bring you one of the most expensive items in Vega's collection, and that's what they did."

"This can't be worth more than two hundred dollars," he growled. "The break-in is on the news. Vega will have tripled security by now. They won't get another chance to get my vase *or* make this deal!"

Killian weathered the explosion in silence. "Richard, you didn't seem to have heard me. The Merchants stole that from *Vega's collection*," he repeated. "That would be the collection of flags, medals, books, statues, and other Nazi memorabilia he kept hidden in a secret room within his safe."

"He..."

I was right La Roche's face was worth seeing in person. The red leeched with his rage, leaving true shock. "Nazi memorabilia?"

"I had the same expression when I saw the pictures." Killian handed over his phone. "They went in there for the vase. Sinjin tells me they had it in hand. Then one of their guys noticed something odd about a cabinet and stumbled on a secret entrance.

"Sinjin had a theory—and if he's wrong, he'll return for that tiara, security or no—that this war of antiques you're both in is more than bids at an auction. Vega is determined to prove that despite your looks, money, and influence, you can't get everything you want. And the point of sending the Merchants after him, was to say yes you can."

Disbelief etched into his face, swiping through the photos. Disgust was my emotion of choice.

"It's a good, old-fashioned dick-measuring contest that wouldn't end with the theft of a single vase." Killian tapped the ring bearing a swastika. "Sebastian Vega is quite a collector. Without a doubt, we can say he's more than a collector, he's an admirer. A fact he's taken great pains for no one to know."

"Now you know, Richard. You have the photos. You have the ring. You can end this war between the two of you once and for all. Demand he hand over all the pieces he snaked from you. Warn him to behave himself from now on, or the world finds out the truth about the great philanthropist, Sebastian Vega.

"Secrets, Richard. Those have always been worth infinitely more than furniture or jewelry." He pointed. "The Merchants delivered the most expensive item in that home, but you tell me, would you rather have Vega's dick in hand, or his balls in a vise?"

La Roche stared at the ring and phone.

He burst out laughing.

"Good. Very good," he boomed. "Balls in a vise, indeed." La Roche squeezed the ring in his fist—a look of such wicked glee overtook him, I leaned back in my seat. "I have that duplicitous, sneaking worm now. For years I combed through that perfect façade and came up with nothing. No dirt. No affairs. No double-dealing. He even pays his taxes on time. Finally, I have him."

What La Roche planned to do with him, I no longer cared. Vega's daughter was a gem, but one look at those pictures, and my twinge of sympathy for the innocent man vanished. There was no good reason behind that room, or the worship laid in their pedestals and arrangement. La Roche could do whatever he wanted to the Nazi-lover.

"Turned out all you needed was a Merchant," Killian said.

"Yes." La Roche replaced the ring and put the box in his top drawer. The lock slid into place with a soft click. "You can tell them I accept this substitute. This Sinjin was right. The ring is a far more valuable prize."

"May I make a suggestion?" I asked. "Vega has a big insurance check coming for that broken vase. If it was me, I'd kindly request he donate it to a charity for survivors of the Holocaust and their families."

"Excellent suggestion, Miss Adeline."

"Richard," Killian cut in. "Can I tell them the good news? Do we have a deal?"

"Killian, Killian." He shook his head. "Not so fast. I haven't had a chance to act on this information yet. Once I do, and ensure his 'balls are in a vise,' you and I can discuss terms. A conversation that wasn't worth having until the Merchants proved themselves." He patted the desk drawer. "I don't deny that they have. If Vega falls in line, we can move on to the next part of negotiations."

I opened my mouth. Killian's hand on my knee stayed me.

"I understand," he said simply. "I'm just pleased we're moving in the right direction. I look forward to that call, Richard."

"Good evening."

We left. I spoke up as the door closed behind us.

"Give me the keys."

"I'm driving."

"Killian." I ran out in front of him, blocking the driver's side. "I'm driving. You're taking me on a date."

His brows crowded together. "What?"

"Every time we go out, you're either stalking me or bringing me along for cover. Tonight, we go out like a real couple."

"No." He picked me up to put me aside. I wrapped my arms and legs around him, holding tight.

"Yes," I said. "Give me those keys, Killian Hunt. Since it's short notice, I'll pick the place, and you'll supply the romance and sweet talk."

"No."

"Why not?"

Killian was warm and solid in my hold. He dressed up to visit La Roche. A painted-on black suit clung to the bumps and ridges under my wandering hands. Moonlight did wild things to Killian's eyes. In the glare of sun, they were defiant pools of molten gold. At night, they darkened to almost black. Dual sides of light and dark.

"You know why not, Adeline. We're not a real couple," he said. "We can't be while Kieran is out there with that ledger."

I pressed a kiss to his eyelid. Then the other. "Kieran is the invisible hand behind Killian Hunt's trigger. If he were to find out he could put me in his sight, it'd be dangerous for both of us. I understand that, Killian, I really do." I smiled. "That's why Cash is taking me out."

"Excuse me?"

"Put on a mask, baby. You're gonna need it."

CASH DID NOT LET ME drive. I was directed to the passenger seat where I gave him directions.

"Turn here," I said, looking up from my phone. "It'll be at the end of the street. Picturesque Theaters."

"We're seeing a movie?"

"Nope." I was having too much fun. How could I not? There was an eighty-nine point nine percent chance Killian said no and drove us home. He was here with me. I was enjoying every last second of this till the clock struck midnight on this pumpkin.

Killian parallel parked in front of the theater. He took one look at the crowd going in and said, "No."

I laughed. "There's my favorite grouch. Come on, Killian, you know this is the perfect date for us. We'll be in masks. It'll be fun."

Couples, friends, and singles strolled inside the theater wearing capes and deep red gowns. The most important feature of their outfits were the masks of all sizes, shapes, and designs.

"It's a Phantom of the Opera party."

"Redgrave," he said clearly, "I am not going into that building."

"Can I ply you with sexual favors?"

He halted reaching for the ignition. "I'm listening."

"Wake up by blow job every morning for two weeks."

"Tempting."

"I'll wear that naughty maid costume I didn't quite throw away."

He groaned, eyes falling shut. "Dirty pool."

"I'll pose as your model in a few original works—after you've ravished me within an inch of my sanity, of course."

Killian took out the key. "Let's go."

"Here." I pulled two gold, half-face masks from my purse. "Mask up, lover."

"You planned this."

"Yep. I heard about it from Gianna. They have these pop-up parties all over the city. A different night, a different theme, a different location. A group of people rent the venue, and send out word to anyone who wants to crash. Gianna's been to a bunch with her acting group friends."

Killian came around and helped me out. We walked arm in arm across the street, Killian a strong, imposing presence that drew passing eyes even in his mask. I loved being on his arm. Loved his hands swallowing my waist as I rode him. Loved the smell of him lingering on my pillow, and the ice chipping away bit by bit every day.

Killian had been the one to worry about. The Merchant poised to uncover more than he should.

But not anymore.

Kieran or no Kieran, I had him.

A theater didn't seem the best place for a party. You'd have thought the rows and rows of plush red chairs would make dancing, flirting, and drinking awkward.

And you would be right.

There was barely room to move. Down the center aisle was a long table packed with food and beer. On the outer aisles, people bunched up in packs to chat while others pushed through them to the stage.

Pulsing strobe lights shone on the dancers. They swirled around the stage. Capes swishing. Hems flaring. It was a haunting scene from a dream that faded as you woke up. And in that scene, awkward became perfect.

I laid my head on his arm. "Will you dance with me?"

"Yes." The soft agreement carried to my ears. "But not down there." He grabbed my hand. "Come with me."

We ran back the way we came, meeting a winding staircase that carried us to the top. He led me down a red-carpeted hallway, shushing my giggles like we'd get in trouble.

"Where are we going?"

He chose a door midway down the hall. "Here."

I stepped inside, breath catching.

The magnificence of the theater laid out before me. The dancers. The revelers. The subtle magic of the dim lights encasing us in a long-forgotten world. It was just us in the red and black opera house box, high above the party. La Roche. The Kings. Kieran.

Killian moved the chairs aside. He reached for my hand as I reached for his.

Curling into him, I laid my head on his chest—safe in the hands around my waist and cupping my neck.

"This is a hard song to slow dance to," I murmured.

Pop-y punk rock floated to the rafters.

"You asked."

I laughed softly. "Touché."

We swayed slow circles in the small space. Killian spun me, bringing me to rest my back against him, and hold me close in our linked arms. He kissed the sensitive spot under my ear.

"There's that sweetness, Erik."

"And there's yours. Now I'm the disfigured obsessive lurking in the bowels of a theater."

I giggled. "That's one way to interpret the story. The Phantom was alone, never knowing kindness or compassion, so he gave it in the limited way he knew how. Once he truly understands what it is to love, he sacrificed everything for it. The Phantom of the Opera is a fairy tale, not a tragedy, Killian. It's the hope that there's someone out there who sees beneath the mask—beneath the monster the world deemed unworthy of love—and only sees you."

Killian turned me, taking my chin between his fingers. "Whose fairy tale is this, Christine? Mine or yours?"

"Ours." It was the truest thing I said to him.

"No. You don't hide or wear a mask because we're the monsters in this story. I do so because Kieran is mine. You do... because I'm yours," he said. "And that story is a tragedy—for what both of us have made of you."

I shook my head, smiling. "You're wrong, but in every good story, you won't see it until the end. I can wait, Killian."

"You shouldn't—"

Rising up, I captured his lips in a fierce kiss. Killian swept across my lower lip, demanding its surrender to his dominance. I defied him, breaking away shaking.

"I want to, Erik. I'm your someone."

His mouth crashed on mine. This kiss I would not escape.

Killian pressed me to the wall—my legs tight in his grip. Our masks bumping together as he sought my lace boy shorts and tugged them down.

Christine and Erik. Killian and Adeline.

That ours was a tragedy didn't make it less of a love story.

Killian carried me to the ledge, draping me over the three-story fall. I put my arms out, laughing at the upside-down red, gold, and black swirls. My legs around his waist and the hands around mine separated me from certain death. A thought that lazily made its way through my mind, and vanished on a single thrust.

My moan tried to pierce the music. "Erik never did this with Christine."

The glittering gold mask did nothing to conceal the wicked curve of his lips. "I'm an entirely different kind of monster."

Killian started pumping—fast at first, and then slow. He took his time, driving me over the literal edge to the curious eyes of the crowd below. To them, we were nothing more than shadowed figures in a game of pretend.

I ached to reach between us. Tease my clit the way Killian did when he wasn't trying to keep me alive.

"Killian," I gasped.

He dropped to his knees, bringing us in. Killian grabbed the chair and me the ledge, using the leverage to meet thrust for thrust. Our bodies rolling and connecting in rippling explosions that went off in every nerve ending.

Sweat beaded under my dress. Our cries were louder than the music now, pushing it to the background. We were all that existed.

"Killian, I—"

"I love you."

The confession stole mine off my tongue. Round eyes met his as a feeling spread through my body. Killian struck that spot, and it overwhelmed me, shrouding my soul in the unique love I could feel for him and only him.

I fell on top of him, clutching his jacket and hearing his heart rocket in his chest in time to his orgasm.

Killian tucked my head under his chin. "How many orgasms are we up to?" he asked, slightly out of breath.

"I lost count," I said with a laugh.

"That's about how many."

I wriggled up and kissed him. "I fully expected to work for it. But you're worth the wait."

Chapter Eight

Cash

Adeline smirked at me throughout the drive home. She was Sylvester with Tweety hanging out of her mouth. The satisfaction permeated the car better than the air conditioner.

Any woman I fell for deserved to walk around smug as shit. She accomplished the impossible.

"Say it again." Redgrave was cheesing so hard, her face threatened to crack in half. "You know you want to."

I blew out a gusty sigh.

"I made the great Killian Hunt put his heart on the line, and now it's mine. Say it."

"It's yours."

She kissed my cheek. "See? Isn't that better?"

Our building came into sight. "I hope you realize what this teasing means for your ability to walk in the morning."

Adeline visibly shivered. "I was counting on it."

I parked the car, and shot out. Adeline ran squealing up the steps—fast, but not fast enough. I trapped her between me and the door.

"I believe you mentioned something about a maid costume?"

She nipped my nose. "And an early morning blow job. We can move up the timeline on that one." She glanced over my shoulder. "Oh. I forgot my purse."

"I've got it. Upstairs. Change. Now."

Adeline stole one more kiss, then went inside. I doubled back to the car. Her purse wasn't on the seat. I glanced in the back. On the floor. Nothing.

Crouching, I felt under the passenger seat, hoping I wouldn't have to go back to the theater for it. My hand fell on the leather clutch. Drawing it out, I brushed my under-seat pouch with the back of my hand.

I halted.

I dropped the purse, probing the bag properly.

The bomb is where it should be, but...

Jaw tightening, the beginnings of my grin vanished. I traveled up to the lit window of Adeline's bedroom, seeing her shadowed figure flit about.

Christine, what did you do?

ADELINE

I stretched beneath the sheets, working out the kinks and tightness courtesy of Killian. He was like an animal the night before. Pounced on me coming through the door, strings of my costume half tied, and he didn't pull back the throttle till we both collapsed in an exhausted sleep.

Grinning, I flipped over, feeling for him.

My hand landed on pillow.

"Killian?"

No one. His half of the bed was empty.

Sitting up, I called for him again. "Killian?"

He was a card-stamped early bird, but that morning a special wake-up call was due. No way he'd miss that.

"Killian?"

I wrapped the sheets around me, and padded out of the room, searching for him. If he was doing something sweet like making me breakfast, I'd ride him right there on the kitchen floor. I had more than half of my men right where I wanted them—Mercer and his work was an ongoing process—that was reason to celebrate.

I stuck my head in the kitchen, found it empty, and continued to his favorite place. Killian glanced up from his desk when I walked in. He pushed his drawer in.

"Hey, baby." I rounded the desk and kissed him. "Did you forget our deal? I owe you a present this morning." I pushed his chair to give him just that.

Killian closed over my arms. "I didn't forget, and trust me, I want you to deliver. Something happened."

"What's wrong?"

"I got an alert from one of our accounts that a large amount was withdrawn. None of us authorized it."

"What? You mean someone stole from you?"

"Looks that way," he said, turning those hardening pools on the screen. "It could be a bank glitch, but it's serious either way. Money's short. Lucky, Pistol, and the guys are expecting their cut of the Vega robbery. The timing of this is so terrible, it borders on purposeful."

"How much did they take?"

"About thirty grand."

"Holy shit. That can't be a glitch."

Cash rubbed my arms. "I've got to take care of this right now. You understand, right?"

"Of course. What will you do? How will you get the money back?"

"I've got to work it out with the bank first. Then, I'll track down where it went."

"Okay." We kissed. "I'll make your favorite breakfast, toy boy. Keep you fueled up for hunting down thieves."

"Thanks." He smiled. "Love you."

"Love you too."

CASH

I dropped the smile on the click of the lock. Shifting, I reopened the drawer, gazing at the bomb.

It looked exact. I could almost believe it was one of mine.

I shut it, moving to my computer. The fake bank sites were closed, and the news tab opened. As rough a place as Cinco City was, bombings were not a common occurrence.

I'd been lax in recent weeks. My daily news scanning was downgraded to background noise while I planned the Vega robbery, or Redgrave was doing her best to twist my mind around her finger.

I hit search. A million hits returned in half a second.

Top headline: **Explosion at Leviathan Auto Shop kills—**

Next.

I scrolled down, clicking on the second.

Woman killed in Mercy Park explosion identified as Tara Duncan.

Tara Duncan?

I read every line of the article twice, sticking on two points. Charred bits of money at the scene, and the mourning of her fellow coworkers at Waterford Retirement Home.

Oscar Redgrave's retirement home.

I don't know how long I sat there, hunched over the screen, but I only looked up once at Adeline's return. She placed the food next to me, and followed it with a kiss.

The next arrival broke my trance.

"You didn't eat your breakfast?" Adeline was dressed and beautiful in a simple white top and skirt. She carried a second tray.

I glanced at the clock. Four hours had passed.

"Lost track of time," I admitted. "It's certain now. We were robbed. Betrayed by someone close to us."

"Do you know who?"

I tracked her approach. "I have a pretty good idea."

"Well then, you definitely need to eat. Can't plan revenge on an empty stomach." She traded my cold steak and eggs for a bowl of noodles. "Sesame garlic noodles. I felt like crossing borders today."

"Looks good."

She waited. Picking up the hint, I took a couple of bites.

Satisfied, she left.

I fished my phone out of my pocket.

Me: Get up here. I need to talk to you.

I knew for a fact he was just downstairs, yet it was an hour before my door flew open again.

"What do you want?"

"We really are as close as brothers can be."

"I should think so." Sinjin sprawled on my couch, hanging a leg over the arm. "We run a business. We haven't killed each other. Can't ask for more than that."

"I can ask for something." Getting up, I closed and locked the door.

"I'm afraid I have to refuse. Hooking up with my foster brother goes beyond my eclectic tastes."

"Shut the fuck up."

I dropped a chair in front of him. Leaning in, I began, "Do you—"

I stopped. If Redgrave listening at doors was a concern, so was her bugging my office.

Would she?

"Play Count Basie," I ordered. My music flicked on, filling the room with jazz. "Do you ever wonder about Redgrave? That there's something off about her."

Sinjin straightened, dropping the grin. "Off? What the hell are you talking about?"

"Sin, think about it. From the first time we met her, there's been something not quite right about Adeline Redgrave. You said it yourself. She's in the hands of four men she just saw commit murder, and she didn't crack even to plead for her life."

"And?"

"And," I ground out. "That's not normal. Neither is the fact she never tried to escape. Anyone else would've left your ass bleeding on the concrete, taken your truck, and gotten out of the city. She didn't try running for the door when we opened it. She didn't smash the windows for a prison break. She has always been exactly where she wanted to be. Why?"

"She hasn't been where she wanted, she's been with who she wanted," Sinjin stated. "Redgrave belongs with me. She's known that from the start, and wisely stopped fighting it shortly after."

I tossed my head roughly. "Sinjin, think about Angelo. Her version of events never quite added up—"

"That's enough."

"Dammit! Listen," I bellowed. "Stop thinking with your dick for once in your life. She's been lying to us!"

Sinjin flashed out.

I blocked the strike at my neck, twisting his arm, and shoving him down on the couch. I breathed hard against the knife tip digging in my side.

"You make some good points, brother." That I was in a position to snap his arm, and him to perforate my liver, didn't leech his calm. "But I know exactly who Adeline Redgrave is. Whatever trust issues you've got, work them out yourself."

"It's been you and me long before it was you and her. It's me you should trust."

He laughed. "It's not my trust you're questioning. By work it out, I mean both of you settle your shit. I haven't done this girlfriend thing in over a decade. I'm not the one to be your couples counselor."

"Fuck off." I threw him off, rocking back in my seat. "Remember this, Sinjin," I said as he walked out. "Remember I fucking warned you."

He spun, saluted me, and disappeared down the hall.

It was just as well he told me to handle it myself. I didn't need him getting in the way.

ADELINE

Brutal and I lounged on his bed. He rested his head on my lap, reading a book from the green section of the shelves. I fought the urge to run my fingers through his hair. He would not thank me for it. But the memory of his soft strands teased me, recalling sudsy shower memories.

I finger-walked across my thighs, sinking in the minty fields of silk.

Brutal caught my hand and laid it over his chest, covering it in a move both warm and ensuring it behaved.

Cash stepped inside. "Adeline, I need to talk to you."

"Okay. What's up?"

"Outside."

With reluctance, I untangled myself from Baris and met Cash out in the living room.

"Everything okay?" I asked. "Did you hear from La Roche?"

It had been three days since the Merchants handed him Sebastian Vega on a platter. Was planning blackmail as tricky to arrange as a wedding? Did it need this much lead time?

"No, actually," Cash said. "Not a word. I'm not surprised though. Richard isn't one to act hastily. If I know him, he'll put his considerable resources toward confirming what the ring and pictures told him. Guarantee he has Vega backward and forward."

"Fair enough." I slinked my arms around him. "Then, what were you hoping to get out of me?"

Cash cracked a smile. "What you said the other night—how we don't go out together unless it's business. It's not true. That night on the roof wasn't business."

"True," I said, dropping my chin on his chest.

"Tonight won't be either."

Cash cupped the back of my neck the way I loved.

"No games. No masks. I'm taking you on a real date, Redgrave, with dinner and flowers and shit."

"Are you serious?" My smile split my face. "But what about Kieran?"

"La Roche hasn't made the deal yet. He hasn't had reason to put me back on his radar. Just in case, we'll avoid the usual places. Dinner at a restaurant in Leighbridge, booked under another name. A movie, then we'll spend the night in a hotel."

"Sounds perfect, baby. I can't wait."

He kissed me.

"I'm swinging by Gianna's place today to feed her, and help with the packing. Mind picking me up there?"

"Don't mind at all. Seven o'clock."

"Seven."

We kissed again—thorough and mind-scrambling till I tugged on his belt. Cash scooped me laughing in his arms, carrying me to bed.

"SO, YOU'RE JUST WAITING?" Gianna attacked the box with a tape gun. "Three days and not a word from him?"

"Nothing."

I was in the kitchen, packing away her meager kitchen supplies. I was the cook in this family.

"Doesn't that concern you? La Roche got what he wanted twice over. His enemy in his pocket, and the Kings on his hook. He doesn't need the Merchants, they need him. He might've remembered that."

"It's possible," I admitted. "If three days turns into three months, then yes, screw you is likely our answer. But Killian knows La Roche better than all of us. He doesn't seem worried."

"Not if he's taking you out for a night of fun." She waved the tape gun at me. "Never thought I'd be jealous of your sex life."

"Because it was practically nonexistent before I met the Merchants."

"Enough about guys." Enough with packing too since she threw down the tape. "Time for girl talk. We've got the money. We're in the process of upgrading the digs and equipment. It's time for the crew. I've approached the victims of the Dock Slasher—don't know what else to call him—and made an offer. A dozen said yes. The others are thinking about it."

"Gianna, you're amazing." I hugged her. "Who else?"

"You know Josephine," she said. "The owner of From Scratch who you had suspicions about. I figured she'd be a warm lead since you two are tight. I had her followed to a club in Leighbridge. She's a promotor for the underground fights, Addy. And she's got bodies in the ring. She covers their losses if they lose, and takes a cut of the win. Plus, they're trained for free in her husband's gym. It's a sweet deal that nearly every fighter who isn't managed by the Kings has taken her up on. That's how she affords to serve caviar soup at five dollars a bowl."

I whistled. "And Daddy mourns the state of modern criminals. If you ask me, they're more ingenious than ever. Did you work out a deal with her?"

Shaking her head, Gianna took over packing away the pans. "She remembers me from the times we ate at the restaurant together, but it's you she knows. She wants you to make the approach, and then she'll consider what we have to say."

"I respect her caution," I replied. "I'll swing by the restaurant tomorrow. Anything else?"

"We don't have much money left over, but there's another issue we've been going back and forth on. One that Tara Duncan made real in a big way."

"I know," I cut in. "That one is on me. Actually, I've already started on it. It won't be a problem by the end of the week."

"Good. Now we can finally move on."

"Finally," I agreed.

I glanced at her clock. "I've got to start getting ready in an hour. Tell me what else you need packed up."

"Suitcases are on the bed. Strip the hangers, please. Please, please, please." She chased me to her room.

"All right," I cried, laughing. "My labor is at your disposal."

"Love you."

We finished up as much as we could together. An hour in, I broke off for the shower, freshening up, doing my hair, and changing into a pink chiffon wrap dress. Killian said we were eating at a restaurant in Leighbridge. I anticipated swanky.

I put on a pair of gold drop earrings and paired them with a slim, gold watch I borrowed from Gianna. The pink peep-toe stilettos were all mine.

"Addy," Gianna called. "He's here."

One last twirl in the mirror and I was ready. I went out to Killian standing on the threshold, holding a bouquet of red roses and snapdragons.

"Wow," he breathed.

"Hello to you too." I cradled the flowers to my chest. "Killian, they're beautiful. I can't believe you really got me roses."

"Your surprise is evidence of my shortcomings in the romance department."

"You made up for it in other departments." I rose as he bent, indulging a lingering kiss.

Someone cleared their throat. "Let me put those flowers in water, Addy," Gianna said, taking them off me. "You kids have fun."

"Thanks, G. I'll be back to help you with the rest of this tomorrow."

She waved that away. "Nah. The boyfriend takes over from here. He rented us a van. We'll have it all moved in the next couple of days."

"Can't wait to see it." Killian put his arm around me, leading me out. "Bye."

He pulled ahead of me on the sidewalk, sweeping open my door like a proper gentleman. "Why thank you." He rounded to his side. "Where are we going?"

"The Purple Door."

I gasped.

"Guess you've heard of it." Amusement laced his tone.

"Have I heard of it? It was named Cinco's top restaurant three years in a row. Chef Carlotta Bauer is a genius. Not even Ryan can get a reservation at that place."

"Glad I chose well."

"The menu changes every week. Her wealthier patrons reserve a standing table for the entire year, so they don't let a single creation of hers slip by without making it into their stomachs. How did you get a reservation?"

"Can't reveal all my tricks."

"Fine. Be all mysteriously sexy."

He chuckled.

"Can I get some hints about after dinner? A movie still in our plans?"

"Yes," he replied. "We're having dessert there. Feature Theaters is an upgrade on every cinema you've gone to. We lounge on adjustable beds, and ring for attendants during the movie. They'll bring us what we want off the dessert menu."

"Killian, I'm trying to think of a better date and coming up with nada. You've nailed it for yourself and all men to come."

"Beats Sinjin taking you on a job and cutting a man's tongue for you?"

"Was that a date?"

"He thinks it was."

I hummed. "Then, tied."

"Yeah, I'm not feeling as great about your compliment now."

We cracked up. I waited so long for Killian to be like this with me. The night could've ended on the doorstep with a handful of flowers, and I would've named it amazing.

We talked about this and that on the drive. His work to track down the stolen money. La Roche. His latest call with his parents and how Kaylee was doing. The conversation continued to Peach Street, Leighbridge's home for the culinary connoisseurs.

Killian got stuck behind a line of cars each waiting their turn for a different valet stand. It was impossible to go around for our restaurant due to the cars street-parked on both sides.

"Are we going to be late?"

"We have plenty of time. Reservation is for eight-thirty." Killian closed over my hand. His thumb traced circles on my palm, bringing heat to my cheeks. "Tonight will be perfect, Adeline."

It was eight twenty-eight when we pulled up to the valet at The Purple Door. Killian came around to help me out, turning me for my first full look at the restaurant.

"What do you think?"

"Incredible."

The Purple Door wasn't a coy name.

I was ushered down a palm-lined walkway. The fronds tickled my shoulders, inviting me to the velvet purple door looming ahead.

"I don't want to say this," I whispered, "because this is all so amazing. But I'd be perfectly happy dining at a hole-in-the-wall, and munching on popcorn at the drive-in. I know money is even tighter right now."

Killian pulled me up short, drawing me to him. "It's not so tight I can't treat you the way you deserve. This night is for you, Adeline. You're going to get what's long overdue."

Happiness filled me like bubbles—bursting and spreading beneath my skin.

"I love you," I said.

"I love you too."

THE PURPLE DOOR WAS class with a big C. Fresh, expertly prepared seafood was Chef Carlotta's specialty. Paintings of the ocean guided us through the intimate space. Two long booths took up the side walls, and individual tables covered in laundered linen and crystal dinnerware broke up the seating. Most of the tables were filled, spreading the soft hum of conversation drifting to the high terraces.

Looking out to the terrace, I saw the same pleasing atmosphere was replicated within a cover of plants and palm trees decked by fairy lights. The hostess continued walking till we arrived on the terrace. She placed our menus on the table as Killian held out my chair.

"Your server and sommelier will be by shortly."

"Thank you," I murmured.

Killian unfurled his napkin, placed it in half across his lap, and then spaced his utensils a certain distance apart. I noticed he did this every meal. I wonder if he did.

"How's your father?" he spoke up. "I should've asked sooner."

"It's okay. He's doing much better now. Full recovery."

"What happened exactly?"

I replied with eyes on the menu. "Overdose of his heart medication."

"I didn't realize he had issues with his memory."

"He doesn't," I said automatically. "My dad's sharper than Sinjin's knifepoints."

Cash's smile sought me across the table. "My mistake. I assumed he overdosed because he took too many on accident. How did it happen? Nurse error? Was there a mix-up of his dosage?"

"It happened because he took too many on purpose."

His smile dimmed. "Ah. I didn't know... I shouldn't have pushed."

"It's okay." I held his hand. "All that matters is he's doing better now. But if it's all the same, I would like to talk about something else."

"Of course."

We shifted the conversation to talk of school, the places Killian's previous life took him, and the places we wanted life to take us.

"I've had this very clear picture in my mind of my father sitting in a big armchair," I said. "It's Christmas Eve, and the tree is lit up with so many lights, we don't need to turn ours on. A little girl in sleighbell pajamas runs up to him and jumps in his lap. Dad reads to her till she falls asleep in his arms like I used to do.

"So, I guess that's my answer. Whenever I ask myself if I want kids, that picture pops in my head. More destiny than prophecy."

"What's the difference?" he asked.

"Prophecies are vague and often misinterpreted. Destiny is known in the deepest part of you."

He hummed. "Can't say I know what it's like to experience either."

"Never had a vision of your future you were determined to make real?"

"We have no control over our futures, Redgrave. Attempts to steer what will be, down another path will result in disappointment. One-hundred-percent probability."

Grinning a half smile, I propped my elbow on the table and rested my chin in my hand. "Guess I have to do the steering for both of us."

"Will you?"

"Yep," I said with a pop. "'Cause I've got a picture, and you just happen to be in it. I don't know if you accepted this yet, but I always get what I want. One hundred percent."

His laugh rang throughout the courtyard. "Then, I leave my future in your capable hands."

We toasted our outrageously expensive glasses of sauvignon blanc.

Our meal was served in three courses. First was a plate of oysters we shared, feeding each other over the flickering candle. For the main course, Killian chose ceviche-style salmon, while I scarfed down black truffle pasta. Last was dessert. Freshly made vanilla ice cream covered with delicate chocolate wafers.

"That was the best meal I've ever had."

We stumbled out together, me tucked under his arm.

"I used to think I was a good cook," I commented. "Carlotta Bauer rid me of that delusion. Let's thank her for teaching me I need to up my game."

"She's no better than you," he said. "Actually, having eaten both of your cooking, I can fairly say your Cajun butter steak is better than anything she put on our plates."

"It's talk like this that gets you laid, Killian Hunt."

At the end of the walkway, we veered left instead of right.

"The movie theater is a couple of blocks away," he explained. "Mind if we walk?"

"I don't mind at all."

We passed the sea of lights, horns, and cars—all desperate for their night of pampered luxury.

Killian and I slipped between The Purple Door and a two-story, warehouse-type restaurant called Brick Lane.

"Do you see it?" Killian pointed in the distance. "Feature Theaters."

There it was.

Blue neon letters stuck to the side of a building rising higher than its neighbors.

"Not too far a walk," I confirmed. "What movie are we seeing?"

"There are a few playing within the hour. We'll watch whatever you pick."

We passed by The Purple Door's outdoor seating, catching the muted sounds of an argument. It faded as we turned a corner, venturing deeper into the alley.

There wasn't much back here but two dumpsters for the restaurants, and a chain-link fence we'd skirt to take the shortcut to Feature Theaters.

Killian's hand moved up my arm, gripping my shoulder.

"Do you think this is far enough?" he asked.

"For what?"

"For me to have my way with you with no one seeing?"

I grinned. "Oh, yeah," I said, spinning around. "This is definitely..."

My reply died in my throat, throttled by the barrel leveled between my eyes.

CASH

"Killian? What are you doing?"

Adeline's nose wrinkled with a frown I once thought endearing. She swiped at my arm, missing as I smoothly stepped out of reach.

"Who are you?"

"Who am I? If this is a joke, it's not funny. Get that out of my face."

"Who are you?" I repeated. "Or if that's too difficult a question for you, who is Tara Duncan?"

"Tara Duncan?" I had to give it to her. Adeline gave off nothing but confusion. "The name sounds familiar. What does she have to do with anything— Or why you're pointing a gun at me!"

Smart. She didn't pretend right off that she never heard of the name.

"Tara Duncan was a caregiver at the Waterford Retirement Home. She retired herself a short while ago."

"Okay. And?"

"You're still pretending you don't know who I'm talking about."

Adeline threw her hands up. "If she was a caregiver at the home, that's obviously where I heard her name. The place has three stories, two wings, and over a hundred employees. What does that one have to do with anything?"

"You blew her up in Mercy Park. That's what she has to do with this."

A profound silence fell over us—unbroken by traffic or city unrest.

"That is crazy," she hissed. "Once again I have to ask, are you having a psychotic break?"

I went on like she hadn't spoken. "I'm going to make a few assumptions here. Blink twice if I'm right. Tara Duncan was blackmailing *you*, not some pedophile as the news insinuates."

Adeline didn't twitch.

"I'm taking that as a yes," I said. "Second, you were short on time, so you stole the bomb I mentioned I always had tucked under the seat."

"Killian, I don't know—"

"Third," I sliced in. "You didn't notice when you removed it, that I positioned the bomb faceup, and wires in, so I don't pull or jostle anything important when I take it out." A smile stretched across my lips. "I'm all about the little details, Redgrave. If you had been too, I never would've noticed something was off. I wouldn't have examined it to discover an almost exact replica. We wouldn't be here right now.

"The little details are everything. But I suspect you know that—barring this one mistake. You left a clever trail in the wake of Duncan's death, all leading to one of the Castian's regulars." I snapped my fingers. "Got him right off the list I handed you. Impressive. Not good enough, but skillful all the same."

She said nothing, hanging on to that wide-eyed, shocked look.

"Well?" I pressed. "Anything you vaint to say for yourself?"

"What? Is this supposed to be the part where I defend against these wild accusations? Why should I, Cash? You know the answer to your question. You *know* me. I didn't do this."

"I'm getting tired of your lies, Redgrave."

She reached for me. "Cash—"

I cocked the hammer. Adeline flung herself away from me.

"Cash!"

"The next thing out of your mouth will be the truth."

"Or what?" she shrieked.

"I shoot you. Thought that was obvious."

"You're not going to shoot me, you paranoid, delusional idiot! You love me."

I shrugged. "Got over that fast when I realized nothing about you is real. So, give it up. Who are you really? An assassin? A banger?" I asked. "No matter how I look at it, you couldn't have arranged that meeting in the bathroom, but it doesn't mean it didn't work in your favor."

"Work in my favor? You ripped me from my life. I was forced to relive my worst trauma because of you, but I made my peace because I love you. All of you. That's real, Killian." Her eyes filled with tears. "And that's why you're destroying it."

"Don't turn this on me." My hand shook. "I never trusted you. Every instinct said to put you back where we fucking found you, and forget we ever heard your name. I ignored them. I let you spin me in your web. No. More." I punctuated with a thrust of my gun. "Tell me the truth. Who are you? What did Tara Duncan know that she had to die for?"

"Killian—"

"Tell me!"

"Killian! Look out!"

She lunged at me, shoving me to the side. A shot pierced the silent alleyway.

And it wasn't mine.

Crashing to the ground, I landed hard on my shoulder.

Pop! Pop, pop!

A thud shook the ground.

Dazed, I landed on Adeline sprawled on the ground. Unmoving.

"Adeline!"

Screams filled the air.

I scrambled toward her, reaching—

Pop!

Pain exploded in my arm. "Argh!"

Twisting, I fired wild shots at the darkened figure standing out of lamplight. They ran behind the dumpster, taking cover.

"You've been a naughty boy, Killian." The chilling, deep voice slithered down the alley. "You didn't think Kieran would find out, did you? Tsk, tsk, tsk."

My muscles went rigid.

"You were told to stay straight, and make your payments on time. Now he's hearing about you negotiating deals out from under the Kings. Very bad."

Stiffly, I gathered Adeline in my arms. The pretty pink dress soaked with blood. So much, I couldn't make out the wounds in the dim light. All I saw was the color I once thought my favorite.

I fired again, keeping him pinned. Brick Lane's dumpster was on the other side of the alley. I'd have to run in the open for cover. But at least we'd have it.

"Kieran doesn't give second chances. You—"

I bolted, racing for the dumpster.

Pop! Pop! Pop!

Bullets struck the ground at my feet. Adeline didn't stir.

Placing her down, I searched for the wound.

There.

A small hole in the fabric over her abdomen.

Quickly, I peered around the obstruction. I didn't know this man. Didn't recognize the voice. Couldn't make out anything but the knit cap poking out as he looked for me.

This is what we wanted. Kieran found out. He sent the man who'd answer all of our questions—whether he wanted to or not. But...

Adeline's head lolled, dropping on the metal.

But not this.

"What do you want?" I barked.

"You know what he wants."

The further away his voice, the more time I had. Setting aside decades of honed survival instinct, I dropped my gun. Moving fast, I unbuttoned and shrugged off my shirt.

"Wake up," I said to her. "Open your eyes."

"You were supposed to learn a lesson. One Mommy and Daddy never taught you, so Kieran graciously took up the responsibility.

"There are consequences to your actions."

"Talk to me." I encircled Adeline, tying my shirt around her stomach, applying pressure. "Come on."

Louder, I called, "It was just a job! I was hired to approach him. I didn't know—"

"Stay away from Richard La Roche and the Kings." He laughed. "No clue why I'm telling you this. You won't get a chance to pass on the message. But they'll get the hint when I dump your and your bitch's mangled corpses off the dock, and you end up the evening news."

I palmed my gun in one hand. The other felt desperately for her pulse.

"So, it's true," I spat. "The Kings have Kieran on speed dial. Whining and crying to him when they can't clean up their own mess."

"This is your mess, Killian."

I snapped up. That voice was close. Too close.

"And I do the cleanup."

Whipping around, I squeezed off a shot as he burst from behind our dumpster.

"Argh!" My bullet winged him—snapping him around. His gun went flying.

Turning tail, the briefest glimpse of a sallow-faced, white-haired man raced down the alley.

"Stop!" He couldn't get away. The only chance I'd get to end Kieran and his stranglehold on my life would go with him. "Stop!"

I fired again. The man slid on the slick concrete, going down on his last good leg. Forcing himself up, he limped to the green barrier of The Purple Door, and the crowd that would swallow him fifteen feet away.

I gave chase—uncaring of screams or approaching sirens. Kieran would fucking pay for this. For my mother. My father. Ophelia.

Adeline.

Skidding to a halt, I turned back to the woman I couldn't see. Still and silent as she lay dying.

"Fuck!"

I ran to her, holding Adeline in my arms, I raced to the car. The sirens. After him—I didn't know.

Rounding the corner, a street full of fleeing people met my eyes.

Kieran's man was gone.

Chapter Nine

The gears groaned.

Screeching. Screaming. Crying.

They pleaded for relief age and wear promised them.

I climbed on board the rusting carousel, revolving so slowly, it carried me away at half my leisurely gait.

"I'm betting on tires and butterflies..."

"What?" Glancing around, I searched for the owner of the voice.

"...tires and butterflies..."

"I don't understand," I called. "Where are you?"

"Butterflies. Tired of your lies."

A chill crept into my bones.

"I'm getting tired of your lies!"

Spinning around, the once-mechanical horse reared. He brought his hooves down, exiling me to a world of black.

My eyes snapped open, throwing off the dream.

Or did it? Was I still sleeping?

Blurred vision cleared on a silver picture frame housing the photo of a single rose. I swept the space. I was in a plain white bedroom.

I tried moving, felt a sharp burst of pain, and stopped. I was also lying on a queen-size bed beneath white sheets.

White dresser. Television. White egg chair.

I turned my head.

Killian.

He fiddled with an IV bag. Tall. Handsome. Imposing. A bandage wrapped around his arm.

"Killian," I croaked.

"Redgrave." He could've been an actual doctor speaking to a faceless patient. "Don't try to sit up."

"What... happened?"

"You were shot." Killian let the bag be. Cradling my wrist, he used his watch to check my pulse. "I let them take you to the hospital, booked under Jane Doe. When I was sure you were out of the woods, I brought you here. The rest I can do myself."

"I don't remember."

"You wouldn't," he said. "You lost a lot of blood. Unconscious for three days."

"How bad is it?"

"For a minute there, it was very bad. The doctors got the bullet out and sewed you up. Some time in bed and proper wound care, you'll make it out with just a scar."

"Who shot me?"

"He was shooting at me. You pushed me out of the way." Killian rested my hand on the comforter. "Saved my life."

"Who?" I repeated.

"Kieran's messenger." Those words settled like an anvil on my chest.

An agent of Kieran's found us. Tried to kill us.

"Your arm."

"It was a graze. I'm fine."

"Where is he?"

"Got away."

I squeezed my eyes shut. "Why?" I whispered. "Why did he do this? You never said he'd kill you for going to La Roche."

"I didn't know he would," Killian admitted. "A threat. A painful lesson. All expected. Trying to kill me and almost killing you was not."

"So he got away," I sighed.

"Yes. And running into him, or any more of Kieran's men, again is not ideal unless I control the situation. They're shooting to kill."

My wits were slowly returning. I latched on to something he said. "Where is here?"

"An apartment in Harlow."

"Why are we here instead of home? Where's Saint, Mercer, and Brutal?"

"How much of that night do you remember, Adeline?"

"I'm getting sick of your lies!"

The shout ripped through my head, bringing all that came with it.

"Ah," he said, observing my expression. "There it is."

"Why are we here?" I repeated.

"Where else would I take you? This is your apartment."

"What?"

"You bought it with the money you stole from our account."

My mouth opened, but nothing came out.

"Set yourself up nice too," he mused. "Seventy-five-inch television in the living room. Leather couches. Chef's kitchen. Thirty thousand dollars gets you far."

"Killian," I breathed.

"The guys are raging. Mercer took off yesterday and we haven't seen him since. Brutal beat his dummy till his knuckles bled, and hasn't stopped. As for Sinjin... Don't think there's anything left in the house he hasn't taken his knife to."

My eyes grew with every horrible sentence.

"I've been out looking for you, of course. I won't stop till I bring you back."

"What did you do?" I rasped.

"Nothing I can't undo. Tell me the truth, and I'll go back to the guys and admit I lied. I'll take the beating I've got coming, and if they want you back, they'll be told where you are."

"Sinjin and Brutal think I left them. Mercer—"

"Focus."

Killian held my chin the way that used to be sweet. Anger flared hot and choking. I slapped him away.

"How could you?!" I bit down on my side's aching pain. "This is between you and me—!"

"Funny you should say that because Sinjin told me the same thing." Killian held out his hands. "This is us. Working it out one on one. How long this takes is up to you."

"All right, then take me home now. I've told you everything, Killian. More than I've shared with most people."

"Why did you kill Tara Duncan?"

"I didn't," I gritted out.

"What do you want from us? The Merchants. You chose to stay with us before *love* got involved."

"There was no choice before love got involved."

"Not exactly. You could've taken off when Sinjin took you back to your old apartment. Anyone else would've."

"This is ridiculous." I tossed my head, the only thing I could move with minimal pain. "Where's my phone? I'm calling Saint."

"Your phone is safe with me. Tell me why you killed Tara Duncan."

"I didn't kill anyone. I barely knew that woman."

"Why was she blackmailing you?" Cash plowed on.

I wondered if I was still dreaming. Could he even hear me? Was this real? How had I gone from the best night of my life to lying helpless in a white room while my love interrogated me?

With that icy, granite look I'd thought I'd never see again.

"What did she know that earned her a death sentence?"

I dropped my head on the pillow, eyes falling shut. This was a dream. And like all dreams, it would fade.

"It's alright, Adeline." Cold lips brushed my forehead. "Sleep. You and I have all the time we need."

The door clicked shut behind him.

I was alone.

THE NEXT DAY—I THINK it was the next day—Killian arrived carrying a tray.

I hadn't truly been alone. He seemed to appear every time I winced. He carried me to the bathroom. Changed my dressing. Fed me in between my demands to be let out of here. The whole time, he was a silent blank wall. Saying nothing. Refusing to acknowledge my existence beyond caring for me.

Cash set the food on my lap. Pillows were propped under me to raise my head.

"Where's my phone?" I asked.

"Where did you get the money that burned up in that park?"

"I want my phone, Cash."

"Were you the one blackmailing pedophiles?" He pressed the oatmeal-covered spoon to my unsmiling lips.

I gripped his wrist. "You decided what happened all on your own. Why go through the charade if you refuse to believe anything I say?"

"Someone replaced that bomb, Redgrave. Any version of events where you play innocent and continue treating me like a fool, will be rejected," he said. "It's important you know that. Your hope of leaving this apartment depends on it."

"You can't keep me here."

"Why not? This is what we agreed. If you can't be with us, I'd set you up in your own place—"

"—and you guys would come to me! We'd still be together."

Cash removed my hand. He pressed the spoon to my lips again. I opened, not knowing what else to do. He was gentle feeding me and withdrawing for more.

"Did you lie to me?" I whispered. "Did you not love me at all?"

He paused slightly dipping the spoon in the bowl, then recovered like nothing happened.

"I've suspected something was off for a while," he continued. "I *knew* it was that night on the roof."

"The roof? Why?"

"Grifter tactics," he stated. "You used advanced con man techniques to initiate warm feelings toward you. I used to follow the same script."

I shook my head, staring at him in disbelief. "Grifter tactics? Are you hearing yourself, Cash? That wasn't a con, ice man! It's called opening up. Being vulnerable."

"I believe that of anyone else. But that wasn't a normal night, and you aren't a normal person. Tell me who you really are, Adeline."

A frustrated noise burst out of me. "Killian, this is doing serious damage to our sex life. Expect long, difficult weeks of celibacy."

He laughed. "It's not looking too good for yours either. You just dumped all of your boyfriends and took off with their money."

"When I get out of here, I'll tell them the truth, and the beating you'll have coming will be from me."

The smile still hung on his lips. "Should I take it this is our breakup?"

My throat squeezed around the reply. "If you don't take me home now... Yes."

"Eat up." Killian rose from the bed. "I'll be back in a few hours."

The door closed shut on him.

I waited, ears pricked up. Thudding footfalls, then a door slamming.

Gathering every ounce of my strength, I set the tray aside and slid out of bed. I bit hard on my lip righting myself. The bullet I took for that bastard missed any vital organs. It was shock and heavy blood loss that almost did me in. He forgot to mention the pain would come back to finish me off.

I breathed slow, channeling calm the way Dad taught me to. Pain was a construct. It was signals and impulses in your mind, warning you to stop, slow down, fix your broken parts.

I had all the warning I needed. Time for the pain to go away.

Bit by bit, it faded to a dull ache. My breathing evened out. I held on to that steady rhythm as I wheeled my IV along for the ride, stepping out into the living room.

Killian hadn't had much time to set up his charade. It explained the bare bones décor of the place. A huge television hung on the wall as promised. It was the only thing on the walls. No pictures. No paintings. No prints.

He gifted me a leather couch set without carpet or end tables. Moving to the windows, I peered down, down, and down. This Harlow high-rise apartment would've set him back quite an amount. Though it came with the added bonus of being too high for me to signal the moving dots below for help.

Slowly, I went to the kitchen. A chef's paradise indeed. The stainless-steel appliances came with the apartment. The fully stocked fridge was courtesy of Cash. My final stop was the welcome mat.

My feet sank in the scratchy material. The feel of it surprised me more than the lock's refusal to give. I twisted—yanking as much as my weakened state would allow.

No use. Killian outfitted this place for a long stay.
Mine.

Food, bed, toilet, entertainment, and a view. Maybe I should thank him. This cage was a lot nicer than the one Saint put me in.

I returned to my bed, easing my aching body beneath the sheets. I thought I was through underestimating Killian Hunt. He was not Sinjin's wild impulsivity or Mercer's shadowed evasiveness. He was cool and calm as a stream eroding the riverbed. He would wait as long as it took to hear my story. And that wait would be long.

I shut my eyes, letting sleep take me.

The dance begins, Erik.

CASH

"Well?" Sinjin was on me when I came through the door. "Did you find her?"

"No."

"Where the fuck are you looking?! You said you could track the money down and it would lead to her."

"I can, and it will," I said calmly. "But I also told you Adeline Redgrave was not what she seemed. She covered her tracks better than expected."

It had been a week since Adeline woke up in her new home. It was better to say I covered my tracks well. They didn't know a thing about that night except that I took Adeline out to dinner, and found her gone when I returned from the bathroom. I even left out my run-in with Kieran's errand boy, lest they make the assumption he did something to her instead of her running off.

"What about the friend?"

His noise brought Brutal out of his room. His interrogation was silent, but no less effective. He shoved me against the wall, holding me in place. I took it in stride.

"Cross was in the process of moving," I replied. "Did it by the time Adeline took off. She didn't leave a forwarding."

"Fuck!" Saint seized a chair and flung it at the television. It died in a shower of glass and sparks. Our living room was a mess of feathers, gutted couch cushions, broken glass, and plaster.

Fuck is right. I can add that to the items I have to replace. Redgrave is cost-ing a lot more than thirty thousand.

"Her father's gone too."

I frowned. "What?"

"Went to the home today. They said he moved out. That Rowe woman refused to say where. I'm going to pay her another visit."

"No, you're not." He advanced on me, eyes blazing. "I am," I finished. "You're not thinking straight, Sin. Leaving a trail of bodies in her wake isn't going to draw her out. I'll find her. Trust me."

My phone vibrated in my pocket.

"Then, what the fuck are you doing here? Go back out there and look."

"I got a message from the bank. I came back to call and see what they can tell me."

He jerked a nod. "Good. I'm going to her old neighborhood to find out what her roommates and her homeless best friend knows. Brutal's tracking down Jocelyn Daniels."

My lips curled at the name. "That woman is the last person Adeline would go to."

"Yes, but from the few details Bunny gave, I got the impression her moth-er has made a job out of stalking her. She will tell me where Adeline likes to go."

The tone brokered no argument. He wouldn't get one from me anyway. The more time they spent spinning their wheels, the easier for me.

"Good idea." I pried Brutal's fist from my coat. "I'll let you know what the bank rep has for me. Where's Mercer?"

"Gone."

Sinjin blew out the door—end of conversation.

Brutal returned to his room, emerged carrying his backpack, and fol-lowed Sinjin out.

My phone went off again.

"Hello."

"We need to meet."

"Richard."

"Are you alone?" An odd quality tinged his voice. "Come now. Corner of Belmont and Grand. Black convertible."

Is that... fear?

Grimace deepening, I said, "I don't think I should, Richard. I'm in a spot of trouble these days, and I think you know something about it."

"Why else would I be calling?" he snapped. "Belmont and Grand. Now."

"No." I slammed into my office. "Tell me who you spoke to. Now."

"This isn't my fault!"

Yelling? Richard La Roche never yelled when oozing smug would do just as well. This was serious.

"I didn't ask for you to blow into my life with your double-faced deals. You and your bloody Merchants! Last chance. Be there in twenty min—"

"No, you be at Randolph and Wells in thirty minutes. No guards. Take a taxi. If you do not follow these instructions, I'll disappear and leave you in whatever mess you created."

"I cannot leave the house without Samuel. It's not safe."

"Then, you've made your choice."

I hung up.

Richard called back immediately.

Then again.

Then three more times.

I took the ringer's eventual silence to mean he got the hint.

Twenty minutes later, I was at the corner of Randolph and Wells. Parked in the lot for Mercy Park.

A black taxi rolled to a stop at the sign. La Roche climbed out, leaned in to pay the man, and cast a squinting glance around him.

I watched him walk up and down for a few minutes.

He didn't recognize the car I drove to his home among the half a dozen in the lot. I borrowed Adeline's car. It wasn't like she was using it.

I lowered the window. "Richard," I called.

He spun at my voice.

"Over here."

Head bent, Richard quick-walked across the parking lot and slammed inside.

"Drive," he ordered. "Keep— Whoa!"

My gun jammed between his ribs. "Turn out your pockets. Slow."

"I don't have a weapon, Killian. Don't be ridiculous."

"Then, we'll get through this part quick and painless."

Teeth bared, La Roche did as I ordered. Fixed as I was on him, I noted the bags under his eyes and the attempt to conceal them with makeup. There was a small tear in his collar that a fastidious man like him should've caught, and the darting eyes were telling enough.

Richard La Roche. Investment banker. One of the best forgers in the country. Leader of the biggest fraud operation in this city.

Afraid for his life.

"There," he said, flinging his jacket off. "May we go?"

Without a word, I holstered my gun and started driving.

He broke the silence. "I know what you're thinking."

"I doubt it."

"You and Enzo came to me with offers. You should've known I'd pit one against the other."

Yes, I should've known you were a double-dealing bastard. It's the nature of con men.

"I told Enzo the Merchants approached me with better terms and a generous signing bonus—to the tune of half of Vega's insurance payout. Said if he reverted to our original agreement, and did not dare to renegotiate again, I wouldn't take my business elsewhere."

"Let me guess, the murderous crime boss didn't appreciate an ultimatum." I tsked. "You've been living in the world of gentlemen thieves for far too long, Richard. Out here, they don't settle their differences by clever tricks."

"Do not patronize me," he spat. "I couldn't know what that puffed-up thug in a knock-off Brioni suit was capable of. I didn't have dealings with the man to know what he'd unleash."

"Kieran."

I saw his jerky nod out of the corner of my eye.

"The day after our meeting, I received a phone call. I did not recognize the voice."

"Deep. Guttural. Mocking."

He gripped my shoulder. "He called you as well?"

"No, Richard. He opted to meet me in person," I said, "while I was out with Adeline. The bullets did most of the talking."

"Was Miss Redgrave harmed?" Damned if he didn't sound genuinely concerned.

"Yes."

A heavy pause blanketed the car.

"Did she survive?"

I hesitated. "Yes."

He released me. "Thank goodness. I would've truly regretted if she died as an indirect cause of my actions."

"Would you?" I pressed.

"Yes. She is a lovely young creature. Smart. Unique. The world is a more interesting place with women like her in it."

My hands tightened on the wheel. I turned down a side street, considering my words carefully.

"You'd know from the private, quality time you've had with her."

"She told you," La Roche stated.

"Yes," I forced out. "Adeline told me everything."

"I could not help but sympathize. Like her, I have a few *indiscretions* in my past. I wasn't as wise in my youth. I was learning—sharpening my skills. And there were mistakes along the way. Kieran dug up all of them. One page in his ledger holds the power to destroy my life and send me to prison. When whoever that was called demanding I tell him everything I knew about the Merchants, I had no choice but to give him your name."

"You had a choice." I slammed the brakes, flinging him at the dashboard. The red light taunted us both. "The name George Flanders would have done just as well."

"Risk everything I've built to protect you?" he asked, lips curling. "Why should I? I figured a Merchant can take care of himself."

"I'm not—"

He slashed his hand through the air. "Please, Killian, let us dispense with that foolishness. I knew the second you put that ring on my desk. How easily you forgot I know you. Know your style. Anyone else would've handed over the damn vase, but you got inside Vega's head. Picked apart his weaknesses and exposed them bare. That job was a Killian Hunt masterpiece signed with a flourish."

"I'm losing my patience with you, Richard. You drag me out in the open after blatantly admitting you gave me and my girlfriend up to die to save your own skin. Tell me what you want now, or I'll drop you in the worst part of Rockchapel and we'll see how far you get in that two-thousand-dollar suit and platinum watch."

He gave me a flat look. "We have left the world of gentlemen thieves behind."

"We did that when Adeline almost died jumping in front of a bullet meant for me." Anger bled into the reply. Real. Corrosive. Consuming.

Rage that anyone would dare hurt her. Fury that after everything, when the time came, I couldn't choose Kieran over her.

But she unapologetically chooses her hidden alliances over me.

I was a fucking fool. Worse than Sinjin ever was for dragging the woman into our lives in the first place. At least he didn't know she couldn't be trusted. I did, and I went back.

La Roche had the decency to look away. "I called you because I accept. You delivered your end of the bargain. The deal is made."

"What are you talking about?"

"You said you would deliver Kieran, and you have. He and the ledger are within reach. Get it for me, and this is all over."

"Kieran is within reach? Do you know more about your anonymous caller than you mentioned?"

"He isn't important," he replied, a touch impatient. "Don't you see? Enzo, Killian. Lorenzo Bianchi is Kieran."

I abruptly drove out of traffic and parked in front of a bistro. "Impossible. Lorenzo is no more than five years older than me. A seventeen-year-old did not take over the city, and throw it on its head."

"Of course not! It wasn't Lorenzo who retired his fixing days, and turned to blackmail. It was Angelo Castillo."

I made to speak, and closed my mouth.

"Angelo was Kieran the whole time. After he was dredged up like flotsam, the battle between Kings went down not because they never heard of a democratic election, but because their race was to find the ledger first. Once Enzo did, his last standing opponent backed down. Or do you not think it strange Thiago Pais hasn't taken revenge?"

I was quiet. Very, very quiet.

"It's the only explanation that makes sense, Killian." His voice echoed strangely in my ear. "Kieran's reaction after I demanded Enzo keep our original terms was a bit uneven, wouldn't you say? He threatened to destroy me, and tried to kill you. Neither of which would've gotten Enzo what he wanted.

"Killing one Merchant wouldn't prevent me from making a deal with the survivors, or from taking my products elsewhere. Putting me in prison doesn't grant him my business. This retaliation isn't the mark of the intelligent man who stayed ahead of everyone for decades. This is—"

"The act of a bold, young man suddenly flush with power. We had him," I said to myself. "We had Kieran in our grip and we lost him."

"If you Merchants can kill one Kieran, you can kill another."

I raised my head.

"This is what we agreed. Get rid of Enzo, bring me the ledger, and you'll be bigger than the Kings ever were." He held out his hand. "Can I trust you? Gentleman to gentleman."

I shook.

ADELINE WAS SITTING up in bed when I returned. Wary eyes trailed me placing her sandwich, chips, and juice on her lap.

"Something interesting happened today." My tone was light. Conversational.

I dragged the chair beside her bed, waiting.

"What?" she asked.

"I spoke to La Roche. He told me you went to him for help with an indiscretion."

No reaction.

"Somewhere in the middle of our conversation, the sum of two hundred thousand counterfeit bills was brought up."

"And you believe he gave that money to me, and I gave it to Tara Duncan the day I blew her up in a park like a raving psychopath." She made a harsh noise. "Tell me, Killian, why kill her if I had access to a counterfeit stash to keep her occupied. Seems an awfully big risk."

"I'm sure you had your reasons."

Her gaze hardened. "I didn't do this. What will it take for you to believe me?"

I leaned in, peering deep into those swirling, enigmatic eyes. "Answer this next question honestly."

"Kill—"

"Do you love me?"

She froze—mouth open as if the question surprised her.

"Yes," she whispered. "You know I do."

Enzo. Kieran. And that twisted, sallow face burned in my mind.

"Then, play a game with me," I said. "Equal or higher value."

She stared at me for a while. "Okay. You first."

"Fine," I said. "When I was five, I was diagnosed with leukemia."

That brought a reaction. Surprise flickered in her eyes, breaking the mask of innocence.

"My parents were desperate. They had the circus to run, kids fostered and theirs to raise, and no health insurance. I don't need to say it was a bad situation. No story with this beginning has a good ending."

"But... you beat it. You're here."

"I am," I said. "My folks brought Merriman back to Cinco. We stayed here for two years while I got the best treatment money could buy."

"How did they afford it?"

"Loan shark."

She winced.

See? I said this wasn't a happy story.

"All treatments covered in exchange for repayments at thirty percent interest, but believe it or not, the loan shark wasn't the trouble. Maybe he had a soft spot for bald, puking kids, because he agreed to a reasonable payment plan. Two years in, he died and the business passed on to his son—who decided his future was meant for better things. All the outstanding loans were sold."

"Sold?"

I nodded. "Passed off to other loan sharks willing to pay the remaining balance. They'd take over collections from there, using whatever methods they chose."

"Your parents' loan ended up in the hands of someone unreasonable."

"My parents' loan ended up in the hands of Kieran."

Adeline clapped her hand over her mouth. I can't say why I sensed she wasn't faking, but deep down I did. Her horror was genuine.

"Kieran didn't want money. What he needed was a couple hauling big vans and tons of equipment across state lines legitimately. In the space of time it took to buy a loan, he had his couple."

"What did he want moved?"

"Guns."

She nodded, as if that was the only thing it could've been.

"They were forced to run Kieran's guns for ten years. That's how long it took for him to finally call the debt paid." The words were bitter on my tongue. "But they weren't free. Afterward, it was whatever product he needed moved on a whim, and the price was not turning them over to the police."

"When did you find out? You were a child when all of this started."

"My parents hid it from us. There were caravans we weren't allowed to go inside. Locked crates we couldn't go near. That the secret survived Sinjin's many attempts to break in was a miracle in and of itself," I said. "I didn't know a thing, until Kieran called and told me."

"Wha—" Adeline sat up and regretted it instantly. Grimacing, she eased back down. "He called you?"

"I still remember the day that mechanical voice poured in my ear. I was sitting in the quad, eating a quick lunch before class. I dropped my sandwich, staining my pants with mustard at the word 'gunrunners.'

"He blackmailed me with my parents' past, squeezing every ounce of guilt that they were forced into that life to save mine."

"What did he want from you?" she cried. "Why come out of nowhere?"

"He doesn't give explanations or a line to call for complaints." I forced out the rest. "But in this, I believe the fault was mine. I was grifting to pay my way through school. Conning marks with pretty creations I whipped up in my downtown apartment. I must've conned the wrong person. Someone tied to Kieran.

"He tracked me down, found out who I was, and—as luck would have it—there was another pair of Hunts in his little black book. It's the only explanation for why his demands were that I leave the forgery business and repay him ten grand a month."

"A month? Every month?" she repeated. "How long have you been paying him?"

"Years. After two months, I dropped out of med school. Shortly after, Sinjin and I formed a team, that eventually became a group, that grew into a gang called the Merchants. I had to make money someway."

"I'm so sorry, Killian."

The sympathy brushed off me.

"After all of that, you don't know who he is?"

"No contact is required to make a monthly bank transfer. Though, I once thought I could force one by... skipping payments." The sheets fisted in my grip.

I made up my mind to do this. Get it out.

"I tried once to force him into contacting me. Figured if I missed a few, he'd have no choice, and this time, I'd know what to do. I'd track him down."

"Did he call?" she asked when my silence stretched past comfortable.

"No, Adeline. What Kieran did was send a bunch of guys to beat the shit out of me on a basketball court while my girlfriend watched, screaming for them to stop. They didn't hurt her, but they tied us both up and locked us in the trunk of my car."

The night came back in sharp focus. A curse of my above-average memory. Their blows breaking bones, shattering cartilage, spurting blood. Ophelia's screams. My shoes scraping the ground as I was dragged to the car. Her desperate, panicked breaths.

"Kieran couldn't have known Ophelia had asthma. Or the stress of my beating and the trunk would trigger an attack.

"She died right next to me. Close enough to touch, but unable to help. I haven't missed a payment since."

"Killian," she breathed, closing her eyes. "I'm sorry. I wish I could do more than... say I'm sorry. I see now why you kept me at arm's length."

"I want you to know, I didn't get you involved in this thinking something like the other night could happen. Ophelia was a tragic accident. The Kieran I thought I was dealing with, wouldn't have involved you."

"Why did you get me involved? I wonder now how much I helped you."

"You were there for La Roche, not me. You were my means."

Her brows shot up. "Means?"

"An old painting by a forger years out of the game was never going to get me in with him. He needed to know he could take something I care about if I ever betrayed him. I thought I was smart having the woman I didn't give a shit for pose as my weakness. My bases were covered since I had no intention of betraying him."

"What the hell does that mean? Take something you care about? I'm not a fucking piece of canvas and paint, Cash."

There's that fire. There was just no dousing it.

"La Roche is a different class of criminal," I said. "*Taking you from me* would be old-fashioned seduction, and piles of money to dump me and sprinkle my secrets in his ear. If you were just another grifter like us—the role you played to perfection—you would have taken him up on it.

"Again, I did not predict in any scenario that this would happen."

"Would it have mattered if you did?" she returned.

"Yes." The truth burned my tongue. "I had him, Adeline. I had to make a choice, chase down Kieran's man, or save you. And in the end, it wasn't a choice. I couldn't leave you there."

My hand inched across the sheets, reaching for hers as she reached for mine. Our fingers laced.

"I love you," I stated. "I don't trust you. I don't believe a single fucking syllable that comes out of your mouth. But I still love you."

Tears spilled, soaking her cheeks. "Killian…"

"Your turn, Christine."

She looked at me—lips trembling. Hand shaking. And for the first time, I knew exactly what was going on in her mind. I watched the battle, felt the strain, wrenched in the struggle, and witnessed the final result.

"Killian, I wish there was more for me to give you," she whispered. A tear caught and painted her lips. "You'll never know how much. But I've told you everything."

I broke free of her grip, pulling away from a hand trying to hold on to me.

"My mother. My abuse. That is my truth. They're the events that shaped the woman you can't trust. There's nothing else I could tell you that could be of higher value."

"Tara Duncan," was all I could manage.

"Please, Killian."

And again, I knew what she was saying.

Please, Killian. Don't make me lie to you anymore.

"So," I began.

The walls slid into place.

"This is your answer."

"This... was always my answer."

The line rubbed away. The mask settled where it belonged.

"You understand that this is the end of us."

More tears filled her eyes. "I do."

The disease was purged from my mind.

"Then, you should know what happens next." Cash spoke, not Killian. "Today is the last day I come here. Starting tomorrow, one of my men, Lucky, will be looking after you until you're on your feet. The apartment will remain locked till we have the funds to move. I suspect your true skills are formidable and you'll put them toward finding us, but I intend to bury our names and location so deep, even I'll need a reminder of who we are."

She choked on a sob.

"Goodbye, Adeline."

"K-Killian, please." She stopped me at the door. "I love you."

"I love you too."

I shut it behind, leaving those feelings inside the room with her. Cold, hard Cash—the man who made real the nickname—walked out.

ADELINE

I cried all day and into the night, then I fell asleep to strange, twisted dreams.

I dreamed every night I slept in my new home. Odd for someone who rarely dreamed at all. I assumed it had to do with the painkillers Killian had me on.

Killian.

My eyes filled.

I had no choice but to lie to him. The truth wouldn't have saved us.

I didn't try to run from my captors because I planned to learn everything about your gang structure, slit your throats, and run it myself. I changed my mind after falling for you, and accepting I could achieve the same result by letting you find the ledger for me.

Oh— And about the ledger. It's mine. Cinco City is mine. And love you as much as I do, I don't plan to share my crown.

What was Killian going to say to that?

"Thanks for being honest, baby. Let's go home now."

Whatever picture he holds of me, it's not of a woman who plans to betray him. She still has his love if not his trust. The woman I truly am.

She would have neither.

I heard a noise in the apartment.

Pushing myself up, I listened close to the door swinging shut. Then a thud of something hitting the counter.

My heart thumped in my ear.

"Cash?" I called.

"How long do I heat this shit up for?"

That was not Cash.

The door flew open. A man in a plaid shirt and light jeans stood in my entrance. Long brown hair fell to his shoulders, framing a young, pleasant face. Brown eyes and full lips.

"Hey, mama," he greeted.

"I've got instructions to give you this soup." He shook the container at me. "How long in the microwave?"

Red-rimmed, swimming eyes beheld him. "Who are you?"

"Jaden," he said. "Everyone calls me Lucky. How long?"

"Three... minutes."

"Cool. Want crackers too?"

"Cash sent you to take care of me." The heart-splintering conversation I tried to block out came back. "You're a Merchant."

"Yes and yes."

"Why are you letting me see your face?"

"You're the boss's girl. You're good."

The reply struck my stomach, doubling me over like a physical blow. I was anything but the boss's girl. Not Cash's. Not Saint's. Not Mercer's or Brutal's. One night and one red-faced scheming employee, I lost all of them.

"Whoa," Lucky said. "Are you in pain?"

"Yes! Why the fuck do people bother with love? It's got to be the stupidest, illogical lie spread on a wave of mass hysteria. Who puts themselves through this on purpose!"

Lucky backed out of the room. "Three minutes," he muttered. "Got it."

I sunk in the sheets, staining the white with tears.

I made the right choice. I made the right choice. I made the only choice.

Gianna and my father would confirm the decision.

Gianna and I had come too far and risked too much to make enemies out of the Merchants. That people looked at us and saw a chef and a hotel employee were our masks. As for my father, telling him I gave up the men I loved in the hunt for Kieran wouldn't garner an ounce of sympathy. He warned me of this. Made me promise I'd give up the fight and live for myself. An "I told you so" from Dad would just about finish me off.

So, what now?

My best lead to Kieran shot me in an alleyway, and the bullet wasn't signed with his name or address. Killian dumped and locked me in a Harlow high-rise. Saint and the guys will look for me unaware one of their own is erasing the tracks. I couldn't call my father or best friend for help. I couldn't call anyone.

I let Killian walk out the door to conceal my secrets.

What did it get me?

The horrid question echoed through my mind. Whispering wetness down my cheeks. Stoking flames of misery into depression.

What did it get you, Adeline?

Nothing. And no one.

Chapter Ten

C*ash*

    "Are you at the club?"

"I'm looking at it," I confirmed.

"The Kings are short of casino venues due to the fires," said La Roche. "Enzo put together that the ones spared were attached to populated clubs or restaurants. His plan now is to invest in both, so the Kings can make use of their underground facilities. The arsonist won't get a chance to try again."

I observed the two-story mass of brick, paint, and neon lights. Infinity Nightclub rose from a renovated warehouse removed from Harlow's party street. I passed by it twice the night before—driving through the borough unable to return to the place she was, or the bed lingering with her scent.

"A simplistic plan," I said. "Buildings can be evacuated before they're blown up."

"Touché. Although, I do not suggest that approach. Lorenzo must tell you where the ledger is first."

"I will do my part, Richard. You do yours."

"My part is the easiest of the arrangement. Enzo insists we invest jointly in the venture. I told him I'd need to tour the club and speak to the previous owners. It's simply a matter of telling him the date and time that meeting will take place, and sending him to the club to meet you and the Merchants instead."

"I'm not a Merchant." My standard, unwavering reply. I would not give confirmation to his hunch. "Though, it flatters that you associate their ingenious quick thinking to me."

"I've no time for this. Just tell me the Merchants will be ready," he said. "This Saturday. Noon."

"They will."

"And, Killian." La Roche's voice dropped several degrees. "Do not think of betraying me. That ledger is mine. If the thought crosses to keep it and use the information within to bend me to your services, it's you I will come for. The Merchants will find themselves short a leader or a servant. May not matter to them which, but it will to you. I hope that provides incentive to ensure the ledger makes its way into my hands."

The threat passed through my ear, stirred no emotion, and went out.

"Saturday. Noon," I said. "Goodbye, Richard."

I hung up.

Starting the car, I drove out of the lot and turned right for the expressway.

It wasn't deliberate I passed by her building. It wasn't intended to slow, look up the glaring glint of windows, and seek out the one as hers.

Blaring horns mocked me. *"Move the fuck on, Killian. She's not looking for you."*

I heeded them, stomping on the pedal.

Out of Harlow I drove, getting on the express and taking it to Rockchapel. The sun was beginning to set by the time I arrived at the club.

I parked curbside to wait some more—the clock ticking down the hours it'd been since I'd eaten or slept.

It was a weeknight. Half the usual crowd wasn't out tonight, but this half was who I needed. No early morning alarms, shits to give, or affiliations you'd share with mother.

A pack of guys bypassed the line. The bandanas on their hips serving as identification.

I took off, driving my car away from temptation. I walked back and was waved in by the guards. Red bandanas were easy to find.

The mass of bodies was thinner tonight. I pushed through them, forging a path. I kept going till the velvet rope held me back.

"Hey!"

A few of the Blood Brothers looked up, pulling faces at the random guy daring to speak to them.

"What the fuck do you want?" asked the man seated at the end of the booth. He had a piercing through his bottom lip and dagger tattoos where eyebrows should be.

I slid a glance toward the bathroom. "I'm surprised they opened this place up so soon after that shit stain Ivan was smeared on the bathroom floor."

He jumped up. "What did you say?!"

"I said," I shouted louder. "I'm surprised they reopened this place after that bitch Ivan got what was coming to him! Did you hear me that time?"

Half were on their feet now. The others were dropping their grins and drinks, picking up on the mood shift.

Dagger Brows lifted his shirt, revealing the knife poking out of his hip. Nothing.

No fear. No panic. My heart pumped evenly in my chest. I pressed my palm to it to feel a reaction—satisfy I was still capable of them.

He got in my face.

"You don't seem to know who you're talking to, homie. Turn around and walk out of here while you can make it to the door."

"What are you going to do? Stab yourself trying to fight me? Get yourself blown up?" I barked a laugh. "The Blood Brothers are weak! You've been getting your asses handed—"

His punch smashed my jaw, snapping my head around. I had time to stop it, and made no move to. He unsheathed his knife. The next strike aimed for my gut.

I grabbed his wrist, wrenching it behind his back till his scream confirmed the break.

"Ahh!" The knife slipped through limp fingers. I kicked him at his incoming friends.

He took three down. They dropped on the table, tipping it over, and showered the platform with alcohol and glass. The last five standing jumped me.

I didn't register the hit that broke my nose. The knee strike that felled me elicited screams from dancers running from the fight. It didn't bat my eye. Disappearing under their boots, I felt nothing. What Adeline Redgrave awakened, hadn't been put back under ice. It had been rubbed out completely.

And then I felt something.

Relief.

The last remnants of Killian Hunt were gone. Cash would not make this mistake again.

He wouldn't love. He could not give what didn't exist.

"That's enough," I said through bleeding lips.

"The fuck it is!" The banger hefted his foot, poised to stomp my face. "You—"

I wrenched out my gun and blew through his boot.

Screams ripped through the club. The music cut off, giving sound to the stampede of clubbers, and the howling banger they trampled to get out the door.

I mixed in with the chaos, ducked into the street, and was gone.

SINJIN LOOKED OUT FROM the ruins of his room. He hunched on the edge of his bed, shuffling and reshuffling his deck.

"What happened to you?" he drawled.

"Kieran."

The cards showered the floor. "What?"

"It worked." I motioned to my busted nose and lip. "Kieran sent a message in the form of eight guys beating my face in."

"How do you know it was Kieran?"

"They reminded me of our agreement that I stay straight. Kieran knows we went to La Roche. Either I get the Merchants to back off, or the next time they put a bullet through my skull."

"Kieran knew about a deal we haven't fucking made yet?"

"La Roche helped him with that." I slid down the frame, letting it prop me up as I dropped to the floor. "He leveraged our interest for better terms with Enzo. Didn't feel an ounce of guilt for it when I called him up either."

Sinjin rose, eyes shadowed. "That's fine. We would've killed him eventually."

"Eventually," I agreed. "But today he's done us a favor.

"We found Kieran, Sinjin. It's Lorenzo Bianchi."

A slow smile curled into his cheeks. "Even better."

ADELINE

"Can't."

I peeled puffy eyes open, landing on the table loaded down with trays, bowls, and cups. What Lucky lacked in caution... he also lacked in cleanliness.

"Got a job from the boss. He'll kill me if I cut out early."

Rising up, I set my feet on the floor. An ache pounded my side as I stood. But if it hurt less than the day before. Or the day before that, I hadn't let on.

"It's an easy gig. Heat up food. Dump pills next to the bowl. Replace bandages. Nah. Yes. Shit, yeah, I want to come over."

I cracked open the door. Lucky leaned on the kitchen counter, watching the microwave countdown while he talked on his cell.

"What time you going out?" Pause. "Give me an hour, baby. I'll get it in her fast, then I'll be in you."

I cringed. *Does my kind really fall for lines like that?*

Lucky lit on me entering the kitchen.

"Gotta go." He shoved the phone in his back pocket. "What are you doing out of bed? Do you need something?"

I stopped in front of him, and smashed the tray on his temple. Lucky dropped like a sack. Raising the tray high, I bashed him again to be sure.

Lucky wouldn't see Baby in an hour. He was in for a good, long nap.

I patted his pockets, removing two sets of keys, the phone, and his wallet.

"Hello? Who is this?"

"Gianna."

"Addy!" The shout pierced my eardrum. "Where the hell have you been?"

"I got shot. My boyfriend locked me in a penthouse prison, and then he dumped me." I took Lucky's cash and credit cards. The empty wallet I dropped on his chest. "I'm somewhere in Harlow. Can you pick me up?"

"Addy, I was out the fucking door at 'penthouse prison.' Are you okay?"

"I will be." I tried both keys in the lock. "I've made a decision."

"To do what exactly?"

"Something I'll regret."

CASH

"You what?"

"She came out of nowhere, boss," Lucky moaned. "Next thing I fucking knew, I was lying on the floor with a bleeding head."

"I told you *not* to bring a phone inside!"

My voice went up in pitch. As did my pulse.

Anger. Irritation. All feelings I closed in that apartment with Adeline.

Looks like they broke the fuck out too.

"How was I supposed to know she'd bash my head in for it? You didn't say those were anti-psychotic meds," he growled.

"Who the fuck do you think you're talking to?"

"Sorry, boss," Lucky said quickly, and in a more suitable tone. "I'll find her. She couldn't have gotten far."

"You've done enough."

I hung up.

My hand fisted on the cell. With enough strength, I'd break it. And I wouldn't have to make the call.

It was Friday evening. Tomorrow, we stormed Infinity and picked up the ledger's new owner. For years I waited. For longer Sinjin waited. For decades my parents waited. Kieran was my focus now. Forgetting that a second time would be disastrous.

One hundred percent.

I dialed Lucky's number. It picked up on the second ring.

"Hello, toy boy."

Crack.

"Redgrave."

"I was wondering how long it'd take you to call," she mused. "It's been eight hours. Those love taps knocked Lucky out cold."

"Where are you?" I crossed the room, locking my door. "I'm surprised you didn't come back. Tell Sinjin what I did."

"I figured we should talk first."

"There's nothing left for us to talk about."

"We can do this at your place or mine. The choice is yours."

Silence stretched between us.

"Where are you?" I repeated.

"You know where I am, Erik."

DARKNESS CREPT IN, rushing to fill the corners my flashlight invaded. A glow slipped under the door partway through the hall.

I paused grabbing the knob.

This could be a trap.

I gripped my hilt. I didn't know this woman, or what she was capable of. Why should I expect what she's never given me?

"Killian? Is that you?"

Crack.

My hand fell to my side. The door swung open, revealing no one.

"Ade—" *No. There she is.*

A crown of auburn waves rose over the seat. She didn't shift at my arrival.

"I'm here," I announced for no reason. "Say what you have to say."

"I killed Tara Duncan."

I felt that crack. My armor buckled in the strike of her confession, forcing a flash of true shock that was gone before she turned to look at me.

She frowned. "What happened to you?"

"I can't possibly think of anything less fucking important."

Adeline smiled, laughing softly, and the second blow was struck. "No, I guess not. This is the part where I explain."

I moved closer—stopping short of the ledge I draped her over.

"Why?" I asked.

She dropped her gaze in the dim glow of the sconces. She was quiet for so long, I assumed she changed her mind.

"When I was ten, my mother figured out I was her best bargaining chip for an easy score—"

"Adeline, you don't have to go through this again."

"I do," she said. "Please, just let me get this out."

I nodded.

"There were six men in total... who raped me on a regular basis," she said. "My life was an endless carousel of pain until my dad rescued me."

She gestured for me to sit. I did.

"When he found out what those strung-out pieces of garbage did to me, he couldn't let it go, and going to the police wasn't an option." She stopped and took a breath. "Time for another truth. I'm more comfortable with gangsters than I admitted. I've loved one my whole life."

"Your father."

"Yes," she whispered. "He used to be an enforcer for a gang called the Lords. You've probably never heard of them."

I shook my head.

"The history doesn't really matter. I'm only telling you this, so you understand why my father would accept only one type of vengeance."

"He killed them."

"No, Killian," she said. "I killed them."

"You? But..." I trailed off. Adeline was right. This wasn't a story I should interrupt.

"I was thirteen. I had nightmares every night. I slept in a room with half a dozen locks, and wet my bed rather than leave to use the bathroom. And the whole time, Daddy was working to help me. To give me my power back. 'You may not be able to stop people from hurting you, but you can ensure they never do it again.'

"He said that to me as we stood over the bound and gagged man who took my virginity." She lifted her palms. "I still remember his hands so big over mine, hiding the tiny fist he wrapped around the hilt."

A tear splashed on her palm. I wiped it away, lacing through her cold fingers.

"That day I went to see my dad, we talked as we always did. And we were open as we always were—unaware we were secretly recorded by Tara Duncan.

"She threatened me, Killian. One hundred grand or she'd tell the world my father and I were killers. You can't understand the fear that crippled me at the thought of people finding out what was done to me." Her voice was barely above a rasp. "Somehow so much worse than them knowing what I'd done in return. I couldn't stomach it... but still, I refused."

She peered in my eyes. "I said *no*. I wouldn't pay her a fucking cent, and she couldn't bluff me into changing my mind."

"She proved she was serious."

"Duncan f-forced my father to swallow those pills. She almost killed him!" Wetness dripped furiously down her cheeks. "I went to see him—frail and broken in that hospital bed—and again he told me what to do."

"Why didn't you come to us?" I couldn't resist asking. "Did you think we wouldn't help? I chased down a fucking car thief pimp for a cut on your forehead. A blackmailing attempted murderer wouldn't have gotten off with a lighter sentence."

She made a noise in her throat. "Is that how it works? I give you a name and you rush off to kill them. You wouldn't have asked me why?"

My silence spoke volumes.

"Exactly," she said. "No one knows what I did to those men. Not even Gianna. It's a secret I buried deep to give me any chance of having a normal life. I didn't want Tara Duncan to happen. I didn't want you to see me as you do now.

"A monster."

I was quiet, taking it in. "I understand why you didn't come to us. I also understand why your father would tell you killing her was the only option. What I don't comprehend is the lengths you went through to carry out her murder. Going to Richard, blowing her up, replacing the bomb, planting a trail to frame someone else. Does one pick those skills up in the course of having a normal life?"

"You tell me, Killian. From carnival son to con man to med student to gangster. Did your normal life go off course with the need to survive?"

"You think I'm judging you—"

"You are."

"I'm trying to trust you!" *Crack.* "I want to believe you're telling me the truth!"

She stroked my cheek. "I've told you so many lies, I don't expect you to trust me. Not for a while. But this is me taking the first step to earning it. There is a side of me. A dark side that is capable of just about anything if it protects the people I love.

"That side lets me love you for all that you are, Killian. Carnie. Con man. Med Student. Gangster. It lets me understand Saint. Connect with Brutal. Challenge Mercer. And it's that side that makes it impossible for me to betray you," she said, "because I know there is no one else who could hear my story, and hold my hand as they say they understood.

"The Merchants aren't a gang, love. We're a band of misfit toys the world doesn't know what to do with, coming together to set things right." She glided along my jaw, tracing my lips. "But you're the man who sees everything. Tell me, Killian. Am I lying?"

I studied every inch of her perfect face. "Did you know Angelo Castillo was Kieran?"

Her brows blew up her forehead. "What? Angelo? Are you sure—"

I drew her in, swallowing her cry of surprise.

Adeline didn't respond at first, then she jumped on me, knocking us both off the seat. We fell to the last crack in the ice, raining everything I tried so hard not to feel for her.

We made love twice on the opera box floor. Lights flooding the auditorium interrupted the third time. We grabbed our clothes and ran out of there, Adeline letting me drive her to our Leighbridge loft.

I tangled in her hair. "Nice of you to allow the postponement of my beating."

Giggles got in the way of her kissing a trail down my chest. "Looks like you've been punched in the face enough this week. What happened?"

"I covered up Kieran's first attack. The second had to be faked."

"Angelo Castillo," she murmured. "Are you sure it's him?"

Adeline burrowed into my side, draping me over her. I lifted the cover over our heads.

"We assumed a lot of things. That Kieran was connected to the Kings. That he was staying out of the public eye. That no one knew his true identity and he stepped in when it suited him. But probability and likelihood isn't fact.

"We never considered that Kieran *led* the Kings. That he was out there for everyone to fucking see, and his lieutenants knew exactly who he was. They were just waiting for him to fall off the twig."

"Unbelievable," she breathed. "He forced your parents into gunrunning. Blackmailed you. Caused Saint's father's death in the never-ending search for him. And now Enzo holds all that power in his hands. We've already seen what Angelo's done with it. Lord knows what the cold, efficient moneyman with another forty years on his life expectancy will do."

"Closer to forty hours," I said. "We know who he is, and we know where he'll be tomorrow at noon."

"You do?"

I spilled everything on the meeting at the club. Did I trust her completely? No. But what I needed was her to tell me something real. The surprise over Angelo was genuine. The tears on her cheeks not forced. But for the first time since she walked into our fire station, I sensed I was speaking to both sides of her.

"How many guys are going with you?" she asked. "Enzo's tried to kill you once already." She placed my hand over her bandage. "Almost succeeded."

"I'm very much looking forward to making him apologize."

She kissed my jaw. "After you've bagged your man, will you bring me home?"

"Yes," I said against her lips. "You should know, Sinjin broke, stabbed, or destroyed... everything."

"Did he spare the kitchen?"

"Everything means everything."

Adeline groaned. "I'm feeling less sorry for you and this beating now."

"I'll take my punishment." I flipped her squealing onto my lap, gripping her hips. "Tomorrow."

"What would you like now?"

"I trade you equal or higher. Blow job for blow job. Orgasm for orgasm."

"This is my favorite game."

THE NEXT MORNING, I left Adeline sleeping in a twisted tangle of sheets.

I drove to Harlow, meeting Sinjin and Brutal an hour before Enzo's meeting. I parked between their cars in the lot, rolling down the window.

"Where's Mercer?"

"Says he'll be here," Sinjin replied. "He wants that ledger as much as the rest of us."

"It's a simple in and out. La Roche, Bianchi, his guards, and the owner. Pistol, Cain, Ted, Ming, Ryder, and Frankie are on the exits. Once we have him, we'll put him in the trunk and take him to the cabin."

Sinjin inclined his head. "What are you planning to do about your friend La Roche?"

"Too much time hanging out with Angelo had a bad influence on him. It tricked him into thinking he has the authority to dole out orders and threats. The original plan was to forge a copy of the ledger and let him play around with it. Now, I'm going to kill him. Like you said, we would've eventually."

I fixed on the deserted club. "Also, I believe I've tracked down Redgrave."

"Believe?" His tone sharpened. "Have you or haven't you?"

"I have. I'll pick her up after we're done here."

Brutal punched his dash.

"*We* will pick her up," Sinjin translated.

"Fine with me."

We didn't speak for the next hour—rousing twice for the arrival of our men, and then the arrival of Bianchi and his guys. Ten minutes to twelve, La Roche's town car turned off the road and parked in the back. Just one man missing.

With three minutes to go, Mercer pulled into the parking lot. He rolled out of the car—mask on and suit pressed—but the bags under his eyes were jumbo jet luggage, and the stench of morning-after tequila wafted out the door. I said nothing other than what he wanted to hear.

"I found Adeline."

Mercer's head snapped up.

"She comes home today."

"Where is she? Did she really steal that money?"

Climbing out, I secured my mask in place. "We don't have time to get into it. We're here for the ledger."

Cloudy eyes cleared. "The ledger," he confirmed. "Afterward, I'm bringing her home."

It was risky surveilling the club, or attempting to go inside and check it out beforehand. Enzo had to walk inside with minimal security thinking he was heading into a regular meeting. Still, I did my homework. La Roche sent his bodyguard in, taking pictures of every exit, entrance, corner, and bathroom.

Infinity Nightclub had the main entrance, back doors, and a staircase that led to the second-floor exits. Our guys posted on each—guns ready.

Lorenzo's new station afforded him a second, Damien Chance, and their two six-foot-tall guards. Enzo brought the three of them to business deals. A deal that would take place in the manager's office behind the bar. The respectable businessmen they were all pretending to be, they'd be shaking hands over the desk right then as they sat down to talk terms.

"Let's go," said Sinjin.

Pistol and Cain pulled open the front doors, running in on our heels as we stormed inside the cavernous space.

Years after Ophelia's death, finally the reign of Kieran would end. And ours would begin.

ADELINE

"*It's this one.*"

"*That one.*"

"*This one.*"

I spun in a white corridor, panic rising. Half a dozen purple velvet doors on each side. Which was the way out? Who was speaking? Why wouldn't they stop talking at once?

I ran to the second door on the left. I grabbed the knob.

"*Not that one!*"

"*Yes, that one.*"

"*It's the one behind you.*"

Spinning, I raced through the opposite door. It shut behind me, and I can't say why I knew I couldn't return to the hallway of purple.

The entrance to the alley stretched out before me—narrowing till it shrouded in darkness. Wealthy couples and cars streamed past. They laughed and giggled unaware that tonight was a tragedy. There was nothing to smile about.

A hard shove from behind propelled me into the dark.

I shot awake, adrenaline kicking my heart into my mouth.

My chest heaved. Beads of sweat dotted my skin and soaked the sheets. As the remnants of the dream tried to fade, I latched onto one escaping fragment.

"It can't be," I whispered. "Were you really there that night?"

I cast my memory to our almost perfect date, flipping through the drive, dinner, toasting over expensive wine, sharing dessert, strolling arm in arm down the sidewalk. Fighting in the alley. A figure briefly illuminated in the light from the restaurant.

I smacked the bedside table, snatching up Lucky's phone.

12:10 p.m.

"Shit!"

I never slept this late. The pain meds coupled with sleeping pills Killian gave me when I said there was no chance of me going to bed after hours of fun, but gentle, sex. He placed the pills on my tongue saying I still needed rest.

"Doctor's orders."

I'd gotten fucking plenty of that!

It was already past noon. Killian timed an attack down to the millisecond. They were inside and the odds were slim he'd answer while in the club.

I called him anyway.

Again.

And again.

And five times as I dressed and stumbled to the door.

Killian didn't answer.

Frantic fingers dialed Gianna.

"Hello? Please. Please, answer!"

"Hey, this is Gianna. I can't come to the phone right now—"

I hung up and tried again.

"Hey, this is Gianna. I can't come to the—"

"Ahh!" I screamed.

"—right now, but leave a message and I'll get back to you. If I feel like it. Or maybe just text me, weirdo."

The beep sounded in my ear.

"Gianna, call me the second you get this. It's an emergency. The guys are walking into a trap."

CASH

Trash littered the dance floor, awaiting the cleanup crew to rid it of broken plastic cups, earrings missing their pair, and one or two used condoms. Nightclubs were useless, sad places during the day.

Our boots squelched on the sticky floor. I gritted my teeth, moving slower to the bar. Tipped-over beer bottles littered the counter. Sinjin picked one up.

I motioned to the door. La Roche's photos indicated the one on the left was the one we wanted. The right door led to a room full of kegs.

I eased it open.

Eeeeeee.

The squeaky hinges about trumpeted our entry. But there was no one in the darkened hallway to hear.

At the end of the stretch, light poured from under a door, followed by voices as we drew closer.

Sinjin and I posted up on either side, nodding at Brutal. He raised a polished shoe to kick the door in.

My phone vibrated. I held up a hand, checking to see if it was our men on the doors.

Adeline.

Stuffing it away, I made to tell him to go.

My phone went off again. Then twice. Then three times.

Adeline knew how important this day was. She wouldn't be calling—

—*unless it couldn't wait.*

"Stop," I hissed as my cell buzzed again. "Something's wrong. Let's go."

The guys retreated without a fight, backing toward the door.

"What about Enzo?" Mercer asked. "The ledger?"

My voice was barely above a whisper. "We'll pick him up in the open, coming out of the building. Something about this is too—"

We pushed in the squeaking door.

"—convenient," Sinjin finished.

The men were still filing out of the keg room, forming an armed line between us and the exit—six, seven, eight men long. I drifted to the second floor, and the four with guns propped on the railing, aimed at us.

One answered his phone. "They're here, boss," he said clearly. "We've got them."

A door opened behind us.

"Leaving so soon, gentlemen?" A low, honeyed baritone bounced off the walls. "Good thing we caught you before you missed the party."

I faced Lorenzo Bianchi.

Photos didn't do the man justice. In person, he was taller, thicker, and the curve to his smirk held twice the contempt.

Waves of raven hair swept back from his forehead, and gelled into submission in stereotypical mobster style. He wore a black suit tailored to slim the paunch around his middle, and his shoes shined brighter than Brutal's.

"Where is La Roche?" I demanded.

Enzo smiled. "He won't be joining us."

Lorenzo Bianchi. Fanatical about appearance both physically and in standing with the Kings. Smart. Patient. Analytical. Holds stronger sway over Richard La Roche than I knew. Bested me.

"The Merchants," he drawled. "I've been waiting to meet you for some time. There's the question of how you discovered the operations at the Castian, not to mention the location of our casinos. Have you turned one or two of my Kings to feeding you information and, of course, how exactly did Angelo end up floating in the harbor?"

He moved around us, joining his line of men. "All of those questions will be answered—and I do hope you choose the hard way. But first, proper introductions." The conversational tone vanished. "Take the masks off. Now."

We weren't given a chance to do it ourselves. Six guys advanced on us—guns and hands out.

He hooked stinking fingers through the fabric.

Bang!

The King dropped, hand slipping free to smack my raised gun on the way down. Fucking fools should've taken that off us before the pieces of cloth.

His death set off a chain of events.

Sinjin smashed the bottle over his guy's head, following with a swift knife to the throat.

"Kill them!" Enzo roared.

The Kings opened fire. Sinjin's kill stumbled in front of me, clutching his throat. His body jerked as he was riddled with bullets.

Jumping over the bar top, I landed hard on the rubber mat, pain zinging up the same arm shot and sore from Kieran's first volley. The guys crowded in next to me, taking cover to return fire.

Either Richard set us up at Kieran/Enzo's behest, or his corpse was lying in the back room. Whatever the case, it was done and dusted. What I had to focus on was getting us out of here.

Fifteen Kings. Exits blocked. Poor cover. Unable to leave position. Unable to get backup here in under ten minutes. Chances of survival:

Three percent probability.

ADELINE

I flipped through the wallet of a guy I lifted off the street. Five crisp tens, more than enough for the taxi to rumble its way to Harlow.

I went through Lucky's phone, feet jiggling on the carpeted floor. *Why wouldn't this man drive faster?!*

"Hello?"

"Hey, is this Lucky's girlfriend?" A question I asked to five different women.

"Yes." An answer I received from three of them. "What are you doing with his phone?"

"Is he with you?"

"Yes."

I sat up straight. "He is? I need to talk to him right now."

"Whatever," she muttered. "Hey, Lucky. It's some chick calling from your phone."

There was a shuffle, then a male voice spoke.

"You owe me a cellphone and three hundred dollars, bitch!"

"I understand tempers are hot after being bashed over the head, but we don't have time for your problems," I snapped. "You Merchants aren't supposed to know each other. I want to hear that you break the rules, Lucky."

"What?"

"Your bosses are pulling a job at the Infinity club in Harlow. It's a trap," I said. "How ever many men they brought with them, I bet it's not enough. You need to round up all the Merchants you aren't supposed to know and get there now."

"How do you know this?" Lucky turned serious in a blink. "What's the situation?"

"Lorenzo Bianchi. They thought their informant was betraying Bianchi, but Enzo flipped him. They're going into what's supposed to be an empty club to kidnap him. He has the full force of the Kings at his disposal. If it's a trap, the situation is bad."

He cursed. "I know four guys personally. The guy who brought me in, and the real Diego, Colt, and Titan. That's not nearly fucking enough. Even if they called who they know. We'd need everyone on this."

"Just get everyone and every weapon you can, and meet me at the club. I'll take over from there."

"You?"

"I'll remember that tone of surprise."

I hung up.

"Sir, I will give you all the cash in this wallet if you go faster."

"Yes, ma'am." He stomped the gas, flinging me back in my seat.

Again, I tried Gianna. Again, I tried Killian. Then, I called Mercer, Brutal, and Sinjin one after the other.

No one picked up.

I couldn't think about what that meant. I just couldn't. The boys were okay. I didn't spin my way back into Cash's good graces to lose them all over again. I did it for the precise reason I couldn't.

"Love is action, Adeline. It's sacrificing all that matters because that person matters more."

My father was right like he was in all things. For Killian, I bent. I unveiled the only secret that made the others worth keeping and laid it bare for his judgment. It wasn't that I didn't believe Killian, Sinjin, Mercer, or Brutal could love the creature. It was that she wasn't the one they chose. For once, it was regular old Adeline Redgrave, who was second place to drugs for her mother. Second to Kieran for her father. Second in the kitchen. Second in life.

First to the Merchants.

They saw something special in Adeline, and for the first time, I loved being her. She was no longer the person I was supposed to be, but finally, the person I was. Kind. Fierce. Moral. Happy. I wished to be her for a little while longer.

But the vacation's over now. I poked between the seats, invading the driver's personal space as we got off the express into Harlow. *The real Addy's back, and it's been so long since she's made a grown man scream.*

Sinjin's a given. Hopefully the rest of my boys still love me covered in blood.

CASH

"We've gotta get the fuck out of here!" Mercer bellowed.

A bottle exploded, showering us in vodka and glass.

"Any suggestions!" I returned. "If I got behind the VIP couches, I could pick off the men on the door, but our friends upstairs would put a bullet in my head first!"

The four up top were our main problem. They couldn't get an angle to shoot us outright. Their main method of shooting wild at the bottles and shelves above our heads was still an effective second-best option. Trying to lift up more than a few inches to fire was a death sentence. We were trapped, and our bullets were running out.

"Where's Enzo?" Sinjin peered over the tub of mini umbrellas. "He doesn't get away! Whatever happens, you track him down and get that ledger." Sinjin faced us, the look in his eyes pinning us to the floor. "Find the bastard who had my father killed, and you tell him why. You tell him St. John Bellisario claims his death in the name of Father Paul Bellisario. Swear it!"

A mission for the survivor. If there was one.

Faces grim, we nodded.

"Tear out my parents' page and burn it," I said. "Free them."

Brutal said two words. The only two he needed to say.

"My sister."

I clapped his shoulder, looking to Mercer.

"Don't look at me," he said. "I'm not saying my last words, or passing off what I've fucking stayed alive all this time to see through. And neither are you! Pull yourselves together. We're getting out of this."

"I called Pistol and Cain," Sinjin said. "Nothing. They're dead."

"I've got an idea," Mercer said. "If it works, we'll have seconds to move behind the couches. Be ready."

Mercer snatched one of the few remaining intact bottles off the counter. Glass crunched under his feet as he crawled to the sink. He grabbed a washcloth. I realized what he was doing immediately.

"You're setting fire to the building with us inside!"

"Needs must." He whipped out his lighter, lit the end, and hefted the bottle over our heads.

"Hey!" someone shouted.

Mercer let it fly.

I didn't watch its flight, but I knew when it struck. A flash of brilliance lit the club brighter than the dark hole had ever been.

Cries sounded, and then the slam of the doors flying open and shut.

Did Enzo get away?

"Come on," Mercer hissed. "Come on!"

The ceiling opened up.

Wetness showered us, soaking us through in seconds.

"Now!"

Vaulting over the bar top, we sprinted to the leather couches arranged in a circle for the VIP area. Brutal wasn't with us. A gun nestled somewhere in his backpack, and it wouldn't be used unless it was a last resort. He had his own plan for putting his skills to use.

"Shoot them!"

There was no mistaking that voice. Enzo. He hadn't cut and run like a coward.

Which meant this fight wasn't over.

Sinjin hollered, neck snapping to the side. He fell hard behind the couch, sprawling flat on the floor.

He didn't get up.

"Sinjin!"

I dropped behind cover, hauling my brother up. Blood and water soaked his face—flowing free from the vicious gash in his temple.

"Wake up, man," I patted his cheeks. "Wake up!"

"There's no way out, Merchants," Enzo called from the depths of the club. "I could lock you inside with the fire, or pick you off running out. Drop the guns! Surrender to me. You'll survive."

"Grandpa Angelo gave us the same speech," Mercer replied.

Looking out, I watched a banger run out from behind a column. He bore down on Brutal's hiding place, racing through the bar entrance.

"Argh!" He flung back, legs flying up in the air. The landing shook the floor, and his cries and grunts soon followed.

"Damien? Damien!" Enzo yelled.

Through the water, flames, and smoke, I sought Enzo. Moving masses ducked behind columns, platforms, and the DJ booth. I flicked up, catching a glimpse in sudden light to the sniper aimed at my head.

I squeezed off a shot. The gun crashed to the floor. Its owner fell over the side with it.

Another second-floor shooter abruptly spun—winged by a bullet that crumpled him on his ass.

Tight jeans and a shirt saying "Who's Your Mac & Cheese Daddy?" stepped over him.

ADELINE

I pried the gun free of the dead Merchant's hands.

"Lucky, I can't wait for you," I said. "When you get here, I want two men on each door where ours were supposed to be. There are no windows in this place. Coming in will flood the club with light, announcing your presence. Come in here when you're ready to fight."

"Understood."

"Do you all know what Lorenzo Bianchi looks like?"

"Of course."

"Do not under any circumstances kill him. Do *not*. If you can't follow that order under the haze of bullets, stay the fuck outside and knock them off running out the door. Do you understand?"

"Yes, ma'am."

I shoved a spare gun in my waistband. "You better be here in the next six minutes."

"Working on it."

A chime beeped in my ear.

"Six minutes," I warned.

I hung up and answered Gianna.

"Addy? What's going on? Are you okay?"

"I'm at Infinity Nightclub in Harlow," I rushed out. "The boys walked into a trap. I'm listening to alarms and gunshots right outside the door. Get here as fast as you can. We need backup."

"On my way."

I tapped *end*, shoving it in my pocket. Grabbing the knob, I flung inside—gun aloft.

The horrible scene unfolded before me in an instant. Over a dozen men spraying the VIP lounge with bullets. A hissing, resilient fire fought to spread from the dance floor—held back by rushing jets of water simultaneously saving my boys lives and killing them.

Once their ammo ran out, the fire alone would hold the Kings back. When that was out, they were dead.

Sunlight rushed in with me, illuminating the nuisances in my way. One suddenly fell over the balcony. I got a line on the other and killed him.

I stepped over the body as the final two came for me.

"Adeline?" Killian cried.

"Hi, baby. Sorry I'm late."

Bang! Bang!

They dropped one on top of the other. Dead.

The tide turned.

Killian and Mercer stood and began evening the odds of the shoot-out. One King cried out. Another splashed face-first in a pool of red.

The wall exploded above my head. I spun, killed the thug lining up another shot, and bolted—charging for the staircase. From above, I counted six men aimed at Mercer and Killian, shooting through the wall of fire.

Where's Sinjin? Brutal?

A seventh man broke from cover of a column. He fired at me running past, dropping me on my ass. My foot slipped. I skidded down the staircase, my back scraping painfully on the steps.

I fell in a heap at the bottom. My attacker leaned over the bar, firing wildly into the space like a lunatic.

What the hell is he—?

Brutal jumped up. Seizing his gun arm, he yanked him over the counter and the two disappeared.

Six left. We have a chance.

Using the rail, I pulled myself up. I zeroed in on a blond head.

Mercer flew off his feet. He slammed into the wall and sunk down, smearing a trail of blood.

"No! Mercer!"

The scream turned half of Enzo's men on me. They fired without prejudice, sending me running behind the bar. I rounded the counter, and slipped.

"Ahh!" Strong arms caught me before I hit the floor.

My Brutal was brains and brawn. He spread out his plastic—slick with water and wine—and laid the trap I fell into.

"Thank you," I said, cradled to his chest. "And I will explain everything. Right now, you just need to know I didn't leave you. I never would."

A soft kiss brushed my forehead, spreading warmth to my chilled body.

"There are six men left," I said.

He shook his head. Putting me down, he held up seven fingers.

"Enzo."

Brutal nodded.

"Mercer's hurt. I think Sinjin's down. We have to end this."

He looked down at the gun in my hand.

"I can explain this too." I got to my feet. "Later."

The advancing six edged around the flames, narrowing on Killian. The fire was beginning to die down. Four guys fired while the two scooped water on it, aiding the sprinklers too efficiently in their job.

Breathing deep, I steadied my pulse, sensing the calming pace of beats.

Thump.

Bang! Bang!

Thump.

Two kissed the floor with matching holes in their skulls.

I laughed. "Whoo! I thought you guys would put up more of a fight than—"

The next thing I knew, they were on me. Abandoning Killian, they jumped me, hauling me over the bar. An arm was around my throat and a gun to my temple in the time it took Brutal and Killian to shout.

"Enough!" The final man emerged from a hallway. "Toss the gun, or Nicco splatters her brains on the bar. Do it now!"

The doors burst open.

Men in masks poured in, led by a figure in plaid.

One.

Three.

Five.

Seven.

I dropped my weight. My slippery body escaped his hold, robbing him of a hostage.

The Merchants let loose.

One of my would-be captors fell to be stomped by the others running for the back door.

And Lorenzo "Enzo" Bianchi.

Leader of the Kings.

Holder of the ledger.

He turned tail and fled upstairs.

I plucked the gun off the body. My shot clipped his leg, giving him the same unwelcome raking down the stairs I took.

He bellowed his pain.

Rising up, I strode over to him. His cries choked on the shoe to his throat. He scrambled to aim his gun.

I took it off him, and cracked the hilt over his head. Enzo went limp—head lolling.

"Hush, please," I told him. "I'm about to get in a tiff with my boyfriends."

I tipped my head to the fire sprinklers. The fire was out. Enough with the rain.

"Lucky, shut that off."

"Yes, ma'am." He ran off to do as ordered.

"Ma'am?"

I faced Killian. He stood up, ripping off his mask. An unsteady Sinjin hung off his shoulder, his face a mask of gore. Coming slow behind him, Mercer clutched his bleeding arm. The four of them faced me—masks gone, allowing the full force of their blank, surprised, or furious looks.

The sprinklers abruptly shut off.

I heaved a sigh. "Alright with the look, Killian. I admit it. I left some stuff out. But can you blame me? Sometimes the truth is better in bite-size amounts."

"What... stuff?" Sinjin rasped.

"I didn't steal your money and run away," I admitted. "Killian said that so he could lock me up and find out my true motives after he discovered I blew up a scheming bitch."

Dumbfounded was the correct term for the expressions on their faces as they looked from me to Killian.

"And it was a waste of time. Everything you said last night was bullshit," Killian replied. "You—"

"No," I broke in. "When I was thirteen years old, my father and I did hunt down every man who dare put their hands on me. I just left out the part that I was hardly *scarred for life*." I laughed. "That was the first time I felt true power. The warmth of blood on my hands. Weighing a life on the balance of my scales and delivering justice. There's nothing quite like it."

I winked at Sinjin. "You understand."

"Ignore my semi, Bunny. I'm leaning toward being angry with you."

"Why?"

"For keeping this incredibly delicious side of you to yourself."

"Sinjin!" Killian barked.

"I doubt your reasons were pure," Saint continued. "Why have you been lying to us?"

"I love you," I said. "That is true. It's the purest thing I've ever felt, and I never lied about it. I knew it'd be a mistake to come back to you." I slid to Killian. "But I couldn't take another minute being a weepy, soaking-my-pillow, living-on-ice-cream mess for missing you guys. Even though I knew you'd discover the truth about me sooner rather than later, and I might lose you anyway. One more night was worth it."

Killian's jaw ticced. I watched his struggle to not let my words reach him.

"Again," Killian said. "Why did you lie if you love us so much?"

"Ah. See, this is where it gets tricky, and again I'd like to remind you, I didn't technically lie. My father was a gangster for a gang called the Lords, and while their forgotten history doesn't matter to anyone else, it's defined me. It's the reason all of this started.

"And the reason why when it came time to choose between love and the ledger. I chose both." I shrugged. "Why shouldn't I? A real queen doesn't choose between the crown and that naughty, smirking courtesan. I won't either."

"The ledger?"

"Courtesan?" Saint muttered.

"I've always known about the ledger." I met their eyes in turn. "It's mine. My birthright. There was never going to be any outcome of events where you guys got your hands on it, and I didn't take it from you."

Killian's lips peeled from his teeth. To be fair, the others weren't looking too pleased either.

"So, that's what this is about," Mercer said.

I ignored Enzo slapping at my calf.

"You used us to get to the ledger."

"*We* used each other," I corrected. "Or have you conveniently forgotten about a certain auction, pervert billionaire, and a charity event where you made me stalk a middle-aged man and his kid. You were happy enough to use me when it suited you."

"That's different," Killian snapped.

"How?"

"We weren't planning on stabbing you in the fucking back!"

"Neither was I. We'd all get what we want from this," I said. "Sinjin, we'll find the person who had your father killed and serve his punishment together. Killian, I'd free you and your parents permanently. Mercer. Brutal, whatever it is you're after, I'll give it to you."

I held up a finger. "As long as you understand, the ledger is mine. Cinco City is mine. You, my loves, will help me rule it."

"How can you say you love us?" Killian asked. "You only came here to get to Bianchi first."

"I came here to save your lives," I cried. "I remembered what was off about the night Killian and I went on our date. There was a car parked on the street. The same car that Killian said had been following him when we drove to La Roche's house.

"Today, it came back to me. La Roche's man shot at us, and all the crap he fed Killian was just that. La Roche is still under Kieran's, or I should say Enzo's thumb."

I waved my gun at the slack-jawed man under my shoe.

"He was gift-wrapping you on a platter for Enzo and, you're welcome, by the way. I lost my mind trying to... get to... you..."

I drifted off. Five pairs of eyes glanced down.

Enzo was shaking. Bucking. Convulsing. Smacking his hand on the floor.

He laughed so hard, his trouble with breathing wasn't due to me.

"La— La Roche told you... I was Kieran?" he wheezed.

His uproarious howls echoed in the club.

"What's so funny?" Sinjin asked.

"Me? Kieran? Do you have shit between your ears? How could I be Kieran?"

"You grave-robbed Angelo after he turned up a bloated corpse," I said. "It secured your position as leader of the— Stop laughing!"

Enzo wiped a tear from his eyes. "*I* secured my position the old-fashioned way, sweetheart. I had Jameson killed. Then, I tracked down one or three of Pais's illegitimate bastards and threatened to run them over on the playground if he didn't fall in line.

"I'm not Kieran, and I don't have the ledger. Neither did Angelo." He shook his head, glaring at us like we were the fools while he was flat out on his back. "Don't you get it? Richard La Roche is Kieran."

I stumbled back, falling off his neck. Enzo pushed up and dusted himself off. He smoothed down his damp, wrinkled suit.

"Where was I?" he continued with a grin. "Oh, yes. I was explaining how we both got played. La Roche wanted this. For both groups of us to come here and blow each other away. I should've seen it coming. He was apoplectic when I discovered he was Kieran, and told him if he didn't cut the casino split in our favor, I'd tell the whole of Cinco underground who he was. He wouldn't survive a day."

"How?" I croaked. I couldn't get more out.

"In one part, you were right. I kept track of Angelo's finances. I knew the apartments, warehouses, and dependents left off the tax return. I ransacked them looking for something I could use to take over. I found his notes on Kieran.

"He had six possibilities on the list. Richard La Roche was number three," he said. "La Roche approached him with information he shouldn't have, and pressured Angelo into making the deal that eventually made us all rich. Angelo never got a chance to learn if La Roche was a run-of-the-mill blackmailer and con artist, or if he was the legend himself. La Roche held all the cards either way.

"But I didn't have that problem. There's nothing about me in that ledger. I went to every man on the list and bluffed them. Threatened to hit send on an email to Channel Five News. La Roche flew over his desk to stop me."

I looked to Killian—speechless.

Visions of that night in his office swam in my mind. Every moment with that man came back to me.

Means. Everyone gives him means to destroy them.

To note in his little black book.

We sat down before Kieran himself and bragged that we'd reveal him and steal his ledger in two months. So soon after Enzo's discovery, he couldn't know if we were playing some kind of game, or bluffing him.

I bet he decided right there and then to take us out.

I skipped the obvious conclusion and assumed La Roche's man tried to kill us for Enzo, instead of under Richard Fucking La Roche's orders.

And he still almost got what he wanted. The guy nearly killed me—the woman dubbed Killian's weakness—and La Roche used his rage and guilt to twist Cash's mind on the wrong man and send him into this club with only days to prepare and even less time to consider the truth.

"The trick, ladies and gentlemen, is to make everyone look in the wrong place."

"Oh my gosh," I breathed.

"Look at that, she's got it." Enzo's taunts burned my ears. "You're not just a pair of tits."

"Richard La Roche has the ledger." As I said it, I felt its truth in my bones. "Thank you for that information, Mr. Bianchi."

The grin twitched. "Whoa. Wait—"

I shot him between the eyes.

"Hey!"

I took off, boots splashing in the water, and rapid footfalls on their trail.

"Adeline!" Killian shouted. "Stop!"

"Sorry, baby. I can't let you get to him first." I threw open the door. "I still love you!"

Slamming it behind me, I focused on the Merchants whose guns were aimed at my head.

"It's okay. The bosses. I'm their girl, Adeline," I rushed out.

A hard body hit the metal, nearly popping me off my feet.

"Help me!"

"Oh, sorry." They sprang into place, straining to keep their own boss in.

"The Merchants are doing cleanup," I said, backing away. "Don't let anyone out unless they do the 'Shave and a Haircut' knock."

"Yes, ma'am."

Thump!

"Also, I need twenty dollars."

A confused banger handed me the bill. I hurried across the street, concealing the gun at my side. The boys were so nice to line their cars in a row, making it easy for me.

"Still love you," I said.

I shot out their tires.

The Merchants rushed out the upstairs door as I flagged the taxi—Killian and Brutal faster than their injured counterparts.

"Bye," I called. I hopped inside. "Leighbridge. Prescott Avenue."

My driver sped off, leaving the guys as shouting, shrinking figures in our wake.

I was on the literal edge of my seat the entire ride. Head between the driver and passenger seat, I willed him to drive faster.

After years of searching. After all my father and I lost because of and for Kieran. The ledger was twenty minutes away from me. It would be in my hands, and I'd set things right for everyone I loved. I'd return my world to its natural course with Sinjin, Mercer, Brutal, and Cash by my side.

Once they cooled down.

I called Gianna on the way.

"Addy, where are you?! I'm at the club. I see a bunch of bodies but no you."

"I'm fine," I said. "I had to run out of there, G. The ledger. We found it."

"Wait, what?"

I told her everything, collecting strange glances from the driver the whole time.

"Meet me here. The Merchants are behind me and it's better I drive off in your car tonight than there's."

"I'll get there as fast as I can."

"Here we are," the driver said as we turned on Prescott. "Where should I—"

I tossed the twenty at him. "Keep the change."

Car still moving, I got out and ran down the sidewalk to his mansion. Rushing through the gate, I skidded to a halt and tripped on the front steps.

My blood ran cold.

Richard La Roche's door was open, held ajar by the foot jammed in the entrance.

Stiffly, I righted myself and climbed the stairs. I pushed on the wood, knowing even before it swung open on their bodies who I would see.

La Roche's bodyguards.

Their unseeing eyes followed me as I stepped lightly up the stairs, gun tight in my grip.

Halfway up, I stopped.

I turned and went downstairs.

Where did La Roche keep his treasures? It wasn't in his office.

I was soundless through the gilded path of priceless paintings, antiques, and furniture. Kieran fashioned himself a life of endless luxury on the backs of people coming to him for help.

Most of that illegal or vile help, but still.

La Roche didn't deserve the power of the ledger. At least I wouldn't squander my time blackmailing gangsters into making me richer, and playing around with thieves and forgers. I had real plans for this city.

The gallery entrance loomed ahead.

Plans to reform it from the lawless pit stain on the fabric of America to a shining city.

I paused on the threshold.

Plans to succeed where you failed.

La Roche slumped on the floor.

Blood painted the hills of *La Libertad*, dripping from the ruin of his head. It looked like his attacker beat him with it. Smashing the frame over and over on his skull till finally making him wear it. His head stuck through the hole in the forged masterpiece.

Beside him, the safe room invited me in.

I went inside.

The place was a disaster. Pieces of the shattered busts littered the carpet. Paintings slashed. The television tipped over. The only thing still intact was a portrait of a young woman, resting harmlessly on the couch now that her secret was revealed.

The vault within La Roche's vault was empty. I picked up all that remained in the safe. The torn edge of a piece of paper.

The ledger was gone.

Time to go. I can't be found here with three corpses.

I stepped out of the vault...

...and into the hands of Sinjin.

"Urgh!"

Sinjin wrestled my arms to the side, holding me captive as Mercer gagged me with his tie. I bucked in his grip.

"Easy, Bunny." Saint licked my ear. "It seems a little couples counseling is in order. The five of us are going to have a long fucking talk. Don't worry, I kept your cage clean and polished for you."

If you'd like to read the next book in the series, Brutal, click here.[1]

---

1. *http://mybook.to/BrutalBookThree*

Keep In Touch

Join Ruby's mailing list for news, teasers, and more: https://www.sub-scribepage.com/rubyvincentpage
Join Ruby's Facebook Reader Group:
https://bit.ly/3bNuCOq

ABOUT THE AUTHOR

Ruby Vincent is a published author with many novels under her belt but after taking a fun foray into contemporary romance, she found her love of saucy heroines, bold alpha males, and weaving a tale where both get their happy ever after.

VERY DARK THOUGHTS

Kyle Harrison